Also by Kate Thompson

The Little Wartime Library

The WARTIME BOOK CLUB

KATE THOMPSON

FOREVER

New York   Boston

Forever
Hachette Book Group
1290 Avenue of the Americas, New York, NY 10104
read-forever.com
@readforeverpub

Originally published in Great Britain in 2024 by Hodder & Stoughton,
a Hachette UK company
First US edition: April 2024

Forever is an imprint of Grand Central Publishing. The Forever name and logo are registered trademarks of Hachette Book Group, Inc.

The publisher is not responsible for websites (or their content) that are not owned by the publisher.

Forever books may be purchased in bulk for business, educational, or promotional use. For information, please contact your local bookseller or the Hachette Book Group Special Markets Department at special.markets@hbgusa.com.

Library of Congress Control Number: 2023948817

ISBNs: 9781538757017 (trade paperback), 9781538757031 (ebook)

Printed in the United States of America

LSC-C

Printing 1, 2024

This book is dedicated to the Channel Islanders who did not return from Nazi concentration camps, prisons and internment camps after the war.

I would also like to dedicate it to my fearless friend Beatrice Orwell, otherwise known as "Beatty," who took a stand against the Blackshirts at the Battle of Cable Street in 1936. Beatty, like the character she inspired in this book, also worked as a wartime postwoman and was never afraid to fight fascism, persecution or discrimination of any kind. She died two weeks shy of her 106th birthday. I shall miss her big laugh and her even bigger heart.

When we ban books we are declaring certain people to be un-acceptable. When we ban books we shut down conversations. When we ban books we let the bullies win.

—Elana K. Arnold

PROLOGUE

Grace
28 June 1940

Late June brings Jersey its most perfect and heaven-sent days. The sky is a cloudless blue and the midsummer sunshine casts a warm syrupy glow over Havre des Pas.

Grace La Mottée floats on her back in the saltwater lido after work and listens to the splash of swimmers. High above her, birds perform swooping ellipses. She breathes in, drawing the cool sea air deep into her belly. Salt and vraic. The familiar smells and sounds of her island home. Grace needs the familiar, the routine right now.

It has been one week since the majority of the evacuees left the island. Over 6,500 of them. Over the course of several days they poured out of the harbor in a chaotic tidal wave of human traffic. The dull throb of the coal boat engines belching smoke over the sound of sobbing. And in their wake, an eerie silence has descended over the library. It's not every librarian who can lose half their patrons almost overnight.

Grace and Arscott, St. Helier's Chief Librarian, have done what they can to retrieve the books still out on loan and keep their remaining patrons happy.

"People will need books now more than ever," Arscott, or "Ash" as she calls him, keeps saying. He's right. People have

already been gravitating toward the library, as if the graceful pink-granite building in the Royal Square could wrap
her comforting arms around them and throw them the lifeline of books. And so the grand matriarch has remained—
for Grace is sure the library is a she—dignified and graceful, with all her treasures locked safe inside.

Now Grace exists in a dreamlike space. Watching.
Waiting. For what no one is quite sure. She adjusts her
bathing-suit strap and waves away a fly.

A muffled thud shudders the water and reluctantly she
lifts her head. Above the horseshoe-shaped wall of the lido,
the sea and sky shimmer. A blur of black scratches the eggshell blue.

The fly buzzes closer, too fast, too dark. The fly has a
black cross on the underside of its wing.

"It's Heinkels," yells a voice. "They're bombing the
harbor."

Grace treads water, her mind reeling. Sticks of bombs
begin to fall from the undercarriage of the plane, sailing
down gracefully, until they hit land and then plumes of
thick gray smoke spiral up into the blue. She watches
motionless as the swimmers run slithering and tripping
from the lido, grabbing bathing towels and children's
hands. She sees their mouths, black empty maws, spilling
words, but she can't seem to hear. Then the noise rushes
in, screams, blood hissing in her ears.

Safety. She must get to safety. Grace swims to the edge
of the pool and leaps out dripping. She can't find her towel.
There's no time. The German aircraft are turning, machine-
gunning the streets. She begins to run barefoot, past

shattered buildings and splintered flesh. The basketworks are on fire. Billowing smoke surrounds the Pomme d'Or Hotel. A woman runs from the ash cloud, the severed remains of her arm twitching. Grace slips on something fleshy. But she doesn't dare to stop or breathe until she arrives at the library.

"Grace—"

"Ash—"

They speak as one.

She glances down, incongruously she is still wearing her bathing costume and yellow daisy swimming cap on the library steps. Her knee is bleeding. She doesn't remember falling.

"Go home, get changed, then come back," Ash orders. "We have work to do. They are coming."

Her teeth are chattering from the shock. "W-what must we do?"

He is unlocking the library door now, his fingers trembling as he stabs the lock.

"They'll come for the books whose authors they don't approve of. We must hide them."

It has never occurred to Grace that there would be books the Germans didn't approve of. Later, much later, her naivety and innocence in this moment would be almost laughable, were it not for the horrors that were to unravel.

"Hurry, Grace. There's no time to waste. The invasion has begun."

Bea
Two days later

Two streets away from the library, counter clerk Bea Gold stands rigid at the taped-over windows of Broad Street post office, along with the rest of the counter staff. Behind them, bundled into every available space, are mountains of brown paper packages, left behind by the evacuees, attempting to forward their possessions on to England before the occupation. It is, Bea realizes, perhaps too late now.

They hear them before they see them. The perfectly synchronized thud of jackboots on cobbles, echoing up the narrow streets of St. Helier. Panic seizes her in an icy grip.

"You're the fastest. Go upstairs. Tell them they've arrived," urges Winnie. "Hurry."

Bea turns, takes the stairs up to the phonograph room on the top floor two at a time.

Vera Le Dain, the telegraph girl, is waiting, eyes as round as pebbles.

"Quick, V. Let London know."

Vera turns without a word and begins to punch out a message to the Central Telegraph Office in London. Bea stands behind and reads over her shoulder: *They're entering the building; I'll have to close down now; Hope to be back on circuit after the war, God help us all; God save the King; Bye for now.*

I

Bea
8 September 1943. Three years later.

BANNED BOOK

The Artificial Silk Girl, published in 1932 by German novelist Irmgard Keun, tells the story of a young Berlin woman who resorts to prostitution in her quest to become a cabaret star. The Nazis deplored its "vulgar depiction of German womanhood." Irmgard's own life reads like a novel. Following her blacklisting and unsuccessful attempt to sue the Gestapo for loss of earnings, she fled Germany, faking her own death in 1940 in order to visit her parents with false papers.

Beatrice Gold burned through life like a wildfire. Not a beauty in the traditional sense. Each individual feature was too much for her face. Lips a great wide dollop of strawberry jam, wild dark curls and a glint in her eye that spelt mischief. And right now, in about as much trouble as it was possible to be.

Naked, she lay crushed beneath a man's hot body, his salt-brined skin burning next to hers, the sand dunes prickling the flesh on her back.

"Jimmy, you sod! Why did you have to distract me? I'll have missed the last bus into town."

He grinned and ran his hands down her arms, pinning them down into the sand.

"*Distract* you? How's that for romantic!"

"You know what I mean."

"Listen, you might as well stay. Don't want you getting caught out after curfew."

She smiled sweetly. "Oh please, the blockhead Boche won't catch me. Most of them couldn't find their own arsehole with both hands."

He trailed kisses down her neck. "You're so beautiful, Bea. Even if you do have a mouth like a sailor."

"Behave," she snorted. "Look at the state of me. I haven't seen lipstick in three years and a coat hanger's got more curves than me."

Her thoughts instantly strayed to some of the Jerrybags in town walking round freshly rouged and scented. Some of the girls in Jersey would do anything for a handful of dirty Reichsmarks.

Jimmy leaned down to kiss her, but a well-placed knee in the groin soon had her free as she groped for her frock and pulled it over her head, before jamming her feet into an ugly pair of Summerland wooden clogs.

"I'll get a proper tongue-lashing if I'm late," she muttered, fastening up the buttons on her cardigan. "You know my mum...the only woman who can go on holiday and come back with a sunburnt tongue."

Jimmy laughed, his cheeks creasing into dimples. The early evening sun brought out the deep muddy green of his eyes.

"Holidays." He sighed, reluctantly getting to his feet. "Remember those?"

He pulled her close, trailed sandy kisses up her neck. "One day, Bea, we'll travel all round Europe, no curfews, no barbed wire. Just empty beaches and cold beers."

Jimmy La Mottée, a farmer's son from St. Ouen's. If she didn't love him so much she would never have stuck it out. The cycle ride to his home on the west of the island from St. Helier was quite a feat on a bike with hosepipes for wheels. Bea's physical health was at its lowest ebb. Before the war it had been a cinch, but now after each trip her lungs felt like they could split open.

The moment of purgatory began at 6 p.m. when the post office on Broad Street closed. Bea stared down at her skinny legs. The hunger was an actual gnawing pain in her tummy. It felt wrong to grumble—everyone was in the same boat after all—but three years of occupation had taken its toll. Even her soul felt emaciated.

Bea realized with a pang what she had actually missed even more than a good meal. Going to the library where Jimmy's sister, her best friend Grace, worked and getting out any book she wanted. Losing herself in the glamour of a Hollywood motion picture. Skinny-dipping under the stars. The iron grip over the most petty details of their lives had tightened, the tentacles of Nazification slowly spreading.

Bea was still brooding when she realized Jimmy had asked her something.

"Huh? Did you say something?"

"That's a charming response to my marriage proposal."

He stared at her with a wry smile, grains of sand speckling his dirty blond hair.

"Don't be so daft! Wait...you're not serious, are you?"

"Please, Bea, just listen. It's important."

Jimmy pulled her back down into the sand dunes, hidden from view.

"I want to marry you."

"You're up to something. What is it?"

He laughed and rubbed his hands through his hair shaking loose the sand.

"Very well. I'm going to get off the island." A nerve was jumping beneath his jawline.

"When?" she demanded.

"Tomorrow, if the tides are right. But listen, Bea, you have to believe me. When I make it to England, I'll wait there for you. Then when the war is over you can come and join me and we can get married there. Maybe even move to London. You can't stay working at the post office all your life."

"B-but this is madness, Jimmy. You're a farmer, not a fisherman. What do you know of the seas? The tidal currents around Jersey are lethal."

"There are three of us, plus a French fisherman on the east of the island who has petrol."

"But you can't possibly escape from the east coast. It'd be suicide."

"We aren't. We're going from the west."

"But that's even more dangerous! You'll have to catch exactly the right current. If you don't get blown up by a mine, you'll be dashed against a rocky outcrop."

"Denis Vibert managed to escape to England and in an

eight-foot rowing boat," he said, defensively, scooping up sand and letting it trickle between his fingers.

"Besides," he continued slyly, "I have insurance."

He opened his coat a fraction and she spotted the tip of a gun.

"Walther P38 pistol," he said as proudly as if he were showing her a fatted calf.

"German?" she gasped. "Did you steal that?"

"Come on, Bea, it's not considered stealing if it's from Jerry."

Panic slammed through her.

"And...and what about Dennis Audrain last year, and Peter Hassall and Maurice Gould? Dennis drowned. Peter and Maurice are in prison God knows where on the continent. No. It's too dangerous, especially if you have that thing."

The final grain of sand slipped from his hand and he turned to her.

"The point is, Bea, for every ten men that failed there's one who didn't, proving it can be done. I may end up in the Gloucester Street Mansion, but so what, at least I'll have a story to tell the grandkids."

A story to tell the grandkids?

There were no fables or heroic endings to be found in this occupation, just uncertainty, hunger and survival. Bea stared out through the dunes at the long sweep of St. Ouen's Bay, its golden sands now smothered in an ugly scrawl of barbed wire and felt something calcify inside her. This island, once so beautiful, was now an anchored fortress. She felt hermetically sealed behind hundreds of thousands of cubic yards of concrete and all the other detritus of war. Day and night the engines smoked and machines pounded, to turn these ancient green islands into part of Hitler's mighty, impregnable Atlantic wall.

She closed her eyes against the image of war and felt the cool ocean breeze combing her hair. Jimmy sighed into the wind. Being dissuaded by his parents from joining the British forces had been a bitter blow to Jimmy's ego. He'd watched most of his friends virtually run onto the evacuee boats, champing at the bit to join the fight, leaving him behind to help on the farm as a reserved occupation. His parents had dressed his farming exemption up as a noble and heroic contribution to the war effort, but milking cows was never going to be enough for a man as patriotic as Jimmy.

"Bea…" He nudged her with his shoulder. "I'm not asking your permission," he said. "I'm going." He took her hand and his voice softened. "But I'd like to go knowing that you've agreed to be my wife. Please believe me. If I stay here, I think my mind'll snap."

"Oh, thanks very much!"

"No, you misunderstand, Bea. Try to see it through my eyes. My brothers are fighting alongside the British and what am I doing? Growing wheat for the Germans' bread. Only today I had one of their agricultural commandos breathing down my neck. They don't seem to understand that Mother Nature doesn't abide by the orders of Feldkommandantur 515. I found one of the buggers in the yard the other day checking my cows' teats and demanding stats on yields to see whether I'm selling on the black market."

He broke off, wiped a hand across the stubble on his chin.

Jimmy's anger was palpable. He bristled with it, like iron filings under a magnet. "I feel like a caged animal, Bea. Don't you see? This island is a prison without walls."

Bea ran her hand down his neck, feeling the tension of his corded muscles.

"Very well. You've made up your mind, but for the record, I think you're barmy."

"Are you barmy enough to be my wife?"

She laughed because if she didn't she would cry.

"Certifiable."

"Is that a yes?"

She nodded and dashed back her tears. She would never let him see her cry. Even when her father died, she hadn't shown her frailty to anyone.

"Oh, Bea, I can't tell you how happy you've made me," Jimmy said, crushing his lips against hers with a scalding relief. But she tasted the fear seeping through his kisses and felt the cold hard weight of his stolen gun pressing into her chest.

He pulled something from his pocket.

"Oh, Jimmy…" She turned the battered tin ring over with her fingers.

"I engraved it with our initials. See."

JLM. BG.

"It's only temporary, until I can get something better," he went on, scanning her face for her reaction. And in that moment she saw the whole of the occupation and its tedium and privation wash over his face.

She slipped it on her finger.

"This *is* something better." Bea kissed him softly. "I love you so much, Jimmy La Mottée."

She smelled them before she saw them, and fear rose inside her. Jimmy realized it too and pulled back, instinctively pushing her back down among the dunes.

Through the rushes, they spotted an Organisation Todt patrol, leading a group of Russian and Polish slave workers up the beach. There was a quarry not far from where they were sitting, and the prisoners were being marched back to their labor camp. Bea moaned softly at the sight of them dressed in nothing but rags, covered in mud and cement from a day's labor, crawling with lice and disease.

Since the slaves' and forced-laborers' arrival on the island last August it felt like the trickle had turned to a flood and now, one year on, the place was filled with the wretched souls. She had seen their camps dotted round the island: long low wooden huts surrounded by barbed wire, full of people hollowed out with hunger and pain. There were no more sweet-smelling freesias and carnations, delicious tomatoes or new potatoes to be found in Jersey's fields any longer. Just walking skeletons.

Their rigid, melancholy silhouettes grew closer and Bea found herself transfixed by their faces, eyes haunted under their peaked caps. Bea forced herself to look closely at one, trying to humanize a life that to the Germans was *Untermensch*—sub-human.

"He's nothing but a boy," she murmured in horror.

"Ssh. If they're on their way back it must be past curfew.

We're in the military zone, don't forget. They'll shoot us on the spot if they see us here."

The boy was 14…15 at most. She winced as he trudged closer. She was thin, but he was nothing but bones draped in skin.

Before she could stop herself, she reached into her satchel and pulled out an old turnip she had found by the roadside. With all her might she flung it over the top of the dune and watched it bounce and roll up the beach, coming to rest at the boy's foot.

Jimmy whipped round, horrified, his eyes so wide she could see all the whites.

"*Halt!*" screamed a guard, his harsh accent carrying on the wind.

The slaves fell on the turnip, but the boy, smaller and nimbler, grabbed it and devoured it, foam and mud bubbling from his mouth.

"What have you done, Bea?" Jimmy whispered.

The khaki-clad OT guard, hair gleaming like patent leather, face like a knife, strode up to the boy and as calmly as if he were stroking a cat, took his rifle and slammed it into the boy's face. Bea heard the cracking of bone, as he crumpled to the sand.

"*Nehmen Sie Ihren Hut ab!*" Remove your hat. The boy lifted his head, blood streaming from a gash on his forehead, and yanked off his cap.

"Why is your hat off? Put it back on!" he ordered, winking at his fellow guards.

No sooner had the boy replaced it, the guard brought his rifle butt crashing down on his head. This time the cap flew off backward from the force of the blow. Laughing, another guard replaced the cap and gestured to his colleague. Two of the guards pinned the boy between them, his blood-soaked legs dangling off the ground.

The awful truth dawned on Bea. It was nothing but a sick game to these scum to see how many times they could knock his cap off before he died.

"I- I can't watch this," she whispered. Tears blurred her vision as she turned and crawled back along the dunes to where they had left their bikes, hidden in a thicket of trees by the coast road.

She leaned over the frame of her bike, consumed with guilt at the stupidity of her actions. The scorching pain of her anger dislodged other, darker memories that streamed over her uninvited. *The dull thud of bombs. Blood seeping over the white planks of her father's fishing boat.* The fields of Jersey had run red with blood and tomatoes that summer's day in 1940. Bea had been working late at the post office when the bombers had come. The night her father had bled to death in his fishing boat. And in their fear, confusion and grief, they had all wondered what would happen next.

Three years on, this was what.

"I hate them," she seethed, feeling a sense of loathing sneak into every nook and cranny of her soul. "I hate the bastards!" Jimmy pulled her into his arms and moved his mouth to her ear.

"You see, Bea? You see now why I *have* to escape? People have to hear of this. The Nazis are telling England this is a model occupation. They have to know what is really happening here."

She nodded, surprised to find herself agreeing, but more astonished to realize that, for the first time since her father had been ripped apart by a German bomb, she was finally crying.

The wind whipped through the long dune grass, spinning whirlpools of sand into their faces.

"I'm so sorry, Bea," Jimmy said, struggling to hold back his tears. "Stay with me tonight, please."

She nodded and lifted her sharp little chin. "I will. Because I've decided—I'm coming with you. I'm getting off this island too."

2

Grace

BANNED BOOK

John Steinbeck, The Grapes of Wrath. *Banned in occupied countries by Nazi Germany by order of the Propaganda Administration.*

Grace La Mottée considered herself very lucky to be the acting Chief Librarian of St. Helier Public Library, or as it was known to most, the "Bibliothèque Publique." One of the oldest libraries in the British Isles, established in 1736, as she was very proud to tell anyone who would listen (and those that wouldn't).

It was her very own book-lined palace of dreams. Perhaps in the current climate, *palace* was overstating it. These days everything was subject to rationing and even their book stock had been severely depleted by the Germans' idea of what constituted an affront to the Third Reich.

Shortly after the invasion, they had received a directive from the Feldkommandantur informing them the library would soon be visited for a full evaluation of stock and that all banned books must be turned over. She and Ash had weeded out most of the *verboten*—forbidden—books, hiding them in a secure place, leaving some behind as collateral damage so the Germans hadn't suspected.

They had come back of course, three months after the invasion and again last year, little gray men with rat-like faces, and stripped yet more. More authors uncongenial to the Nazi regime had vanished from the stacks. The expurgation didn't end there. Montagu Burton's, the Jewish tailors on the corner of King Street, had also received a visit. It didn't sell suits any longer, but was now a German bookshop. *Mein Kampf* and *Famine in England* were advertised in the window display under swastikas. It was so offensive that each time Grace walked past, she instinctively turned the other cheek.

Grace flicked her duster over the stacks and sighed. Not that they were faring much better! Her poor bookshelves looked like a smile with missing teeth. Jack London, H. G. Wells, John Steinbeck, Sigmund Freud and Ernest Hemingway all gone. Anyone considered by the Germans to be a "dangerous, disruptive influence."

"But you're still here, my old friends," she said, smiling as she ran her finger down the spine of *Pride and Prejudice* and the very last Agatha Christie which had been delivered to the island on the mail boat before the Germans arrived: *Cards on the Table.*

Agatha looked down at her knowingly. Eight hundred new books, the lifeblood of a library were delivered yearly, but no more. This last book from England had had more loans than any other over the past three years. When the war was over, Grace was tempted to write to Agatha

Christie, to tell her how her books had escaped a Nazi cull. Unlike so many others.

Grace slid her finger into her skirt pocket and felt the cold nub of the steel key with her finger, checking it was still there. This key was the last thing Ash had handed her before the Nazis had shipped him to a German internment camp, along with most of the other English-born nationals, the previous September. He had pressed it into her hand with a request. *Keep these books safe. And secret.*

In a locked cupboard behind a bookshelf in the Reading Room were "the others."

"One day, you'll all be back together on the same shelf," she remarked. "Until then, Mrs. Christie, enjoy your shelf space."

She spotted Jane Austen, chiding her gently from the shelf above.

"Come on, Grace, pull yourself together," she muttered. "All this self-pity is most self-indulgent."

"Do you always talk to your books, Grace, my love?"

Grace jumped. Five minutes before closing on a Saturday afternoon and the library was usually empty.

"Mrs. Moisan. Lovely to see you. Not usually," she lied. "How can I help?"

She pushed down a flutter of anxiety as she glanced at the clock over her desk. He'd be waiting for her.

"Oh, you're soaked," Grace said, noticing the water pooling round the country woman's wooden sabot clogs. "Is it raining?"

"Never rain, only liquid sunshine."

Mrs. Moisan was an eternal optimist and with good reason. Everyone knew Mr. Moisan was handy with his fists and now that he was away fighting in North Africa, she had been spared the annual confinement.

Grace had no idea how she did it. Mrs. Moisan had once confided in her that she'd had 19 pregnancies and 11 children had survived. She was as tough as old boots, but with the occupation, for Mrs. M at least, had come a curious liberation now she was no longer under the thumb and fist of her husband.

"How's Dolly?"

Mrs. Moisan's cheerful demeanor faltered at the mention of her youngest daughter.

"Not good is the truth of it, Grace, my love. That's why I'm here. Thought a book might cheer her up."

A diphtheria epidemic had been sweeping the island for weeks now.

"Mrs. Rishon came round today, gave her some of her potions, so I'm sure that'll work." Grace wasn't convinced the country women's old folklore herbal remedies of crushed-up snails would do much to help little Dolly, but in the absence of medicine, it would have to do.

"Well, I know just the thing," Grace said, heading to the children's section.

She pulled out *Milly, Molly, Mandy.* Six-year-old Dolly gobbled up books and Grace had a feeling that the adventures of another little girl in a pink-and-white-striped dress would be medicine in its own way.

"And what about something for you, Mrs. M?"

Mrs. Moisan had a fondness for novels that featured heroines who clung to the chest of a dashing scoundrel, before finally succumbing to his affections in a hayloft.

"Shorts and Merries" as some of the fustier members of the committee dubbed their stock of romances. They could never hope to understand what these books might mean to women like Mrs. Moisan. What might seem like sentimental trash to them was pure escapism from the grind for the island's women.

"How about an Ethel M. Dell? Can I tempt you with *Juice of the Pomegranate*?"

"Ooh, I should say. That'll help me escape..."

"If only for a chapter," Grace finished, stamping Mrs. Moisan's library card.

Mrs. M left a slice of stale cake and an egg on the library counter.

"Really, there's no need," Grace protested.

"Hush now," the bluff country woman ordered, gripping her hand with surprising strength. "It's only this place keeping us going, my love."

She knocked four times on the library counter. Three soft, one brisk. The "V Knock." Then she stomped from the library. Churchill's "V for Victory" had become a rallying emblem for those unfortunate enough to be living under occupation, but lately islanders had turned it into something even more subversive and ephemeral. The sound seemed to quiver through the stacks, almost reducing Grace to tears. Women like Mrs. M were why she did this. Reading was the only true form of joy and solace, the only intellectual freedom they still possessed and they cherished it like life itself.

Grace glanced up at the clock. Oh Lord. Now she really was late.

Outside the library the rain had died off and the light was softening. The streets glistened as she worked hard to get her rusty old bone-shaker bicycle to turn on its hose-pipe wheels.

The library was in the Royal Square, which contained the offices of the States of Jersey, the seat of legislation in the island. She stared back at the rain-slicked windows, imagined all those Nazis beavering away. It was an affront to all that the library stood for to have to work next door to such a snakepit.

Shivering, she bumped her way through St. Helier, past the scoured faces of the mothers queuing at the Central Market for the last specks, shabby and downtrodden in their patched-up coats. The air was a stew of smells. Horse shit, asphalt, salt and the stench of something darker—desperation.

It wasn't until she had made her way toward the coast road that the knot in her tummy unwound and she finally felt she could breathe in the fresh scent of pine. At the top of Jubilee Hill she paused to take in the breathtaking view of the glittering blue-green sea and the tip of Corbière Lighthouse in the distance.

A cuckoo called from a nearby tree and she listened, entranced.

The patrol was on her before she even realized. "*Halt!*" ordered the German. "Papers, Fraulein." The branches rustled as the cuckoo's wings took flight.

She pulled out her identification card.

"What are you doing?"

"I'm the librarian. I'm delivering books."

He stared at her for what felt like an eternity, as if he couldn't quite believe the notion of anyone using up precious energy to deliver books.

He lifted his hand and Grace thought he was waving her on, but instead he pointed at her satchel. "Open it."

Grace's heart picked up speed.

"Open it?" she managed.

"That's what I said. Are you dumb?" He turned to the other German and laughed as if he'd told the funniest joke imaginable.

Slowly, as if in a dream, she pulled open the satchel, and felt as exposed as if the German had peeled off all her clothes.

She closed her eyes as he thrust his hand into her bag. Her heart was banging so loudly she was surprised they couldn't hear it.

The German guard shrank back, a look of disgust on his face.

"*Was ist das?*" His fingers were coated in something sticky. Grace recognized the eggshell and started to laugh, more out of hysteria.

"It's my egg. It broke."

The German looked at her as if she was simple, and tutting, waved her on, wiping his hands on a handkerchief in disgust.

Twenty minutes later Grace pulled up at Louisa Gould's, the widow who ran Millais Stores, still trembling.

The door opened with a soft tinkle of the bell and when Louisa saw her, she turned the sign to CLOSED and pulled down the blackout blind.

"*Bouônjour!*"

"I don't speak Jèrriais, Lou."

"You should learn then. It might be an archaic language to you youngsters but it has its uses in wartime."

Grace said nothing.

"What's wrong?" the older woman asked.

"I nearly got caught."

"What? Where?"

"A new checkpoint they've set up, about a mile from here."

Louisa shrugged.

"What's the worst that'll happen?"

"The worst that will happen? I think you know where we could all end up."

Louisa sighed and slid her arm around Grace. "It's all right. Those krauts are too slow and stupid to catch a cold. They want to get home as much as we want them to leave. They know the war's finished for them." She waved her hand dismissively.

"Maybe the ones round here, but not the ones in town," Grace replied. "Do you know how many people have been marched to see the Secret Field Police for questioning? They're so paranoid, they even threw a schoolgirl in jail last week."

"Relax. I can deal with it."

Grace sensed movement from behind the door at the back of the store.

"That's my nephew. He's over from France, helping me out," Louisa said unconvincingly.

"I have something for you." She pulled out the Russian–English dictionary and slid it over the counter.

"Thank you, Grace. This will be very helpful with my… *houseguest.*"

Grace nodded. She had so many questions. How much longer would the escaped Russian slave everyone knew simply as "Bill" be staying? He had already been hiding in plain sight at the store, masquerading as Lou's nephew for too many months. He should have been moved on to another safehouse by now. Louisa was taking unnecessary risks and in doing so, risking the lives of all those around her. Guilt sneaked in at the edges. *Wasn't Grace doing exactly the same thing?*

"What can I do?" Louisa said. "He's another mother's son. I've already lost one of my boys in this war and the other is away fighting. He's a comfort to me."

At this there was nothing Grace could say. She wasn't a mother, she couldn't hope to understand. Mrs. Gould was, and a grieving one at that. Her son Edward, an anti-aircraft officer, had been killed in action in 1941, fighting with the Royal Naval Volunteer Reserve.

"Our island is being stained with the blood of innocent men and women, Grace. To turn the other cheek is to be complicit."

"You're right, Lou," she sighed. "But now I must go."

At the door Mrs. Gould called her back. "You're a brave woman, Grace."

Grace smiled weakly. She didn't want to be a brave woman. She wanted simply to be a good librarian and live quietly. But then she thought of the hidden box of books in the library. *The others,* where that dictionary had come from. Grace knew that to be a good librarian in wartime, it was impossible not to face terrible choices in the quest for freedom.

Back at home, her family farmhouse slumbered in the creamy moonlight. In relief she pushed open the door. Something to eat then she would at last go and see *him*.

"Surprise," Bea yelled. The room was filled with blazing light, and people and music.

"What are you doing here?"

"Aren't you pleased to see me?" Bea asked, throwing her arms around Grace.

"Yes, of course but what about curfew, Bea? You'll never get back in time."

"Your mum said I can stay over tonight. We've something to celebrate."

And then she was waving her fingers in Grace's face. It took a moment for Grace's clogged thoughts to register the ring.

"Hello, sis," said her brother, Jimmy. "She's promised to make an honest man of me."

"We're getting married, Grace," Bea said. "Isn't it wonderful news?"

Grace tried hard to assemble her thoughts into an appropriate reaction. It wasn't that she wasn't pleased for the two most important people in her life. They'd always knocked about, she, Bea and her big brother. Bea had always been the tomboy, daring her and Jimmy to launch homemade rafts, pinching cigarettes from the back of Mr. Staite's delivery van. Somewhere along the way, Bea and Jimmy had become a couple. She may have lost the bashed-up shins and developed into a woman, but to

Grace, Bea was still an impulsive 13-year-old on the look-out for trouble. *Not a wife.*

"I'm happy for you both, but what about your dreams of London? Art college?"

"I'm not a Nazi," Jimmy laughed, lighting a roll-up. "Just because she'll be my wife doesn't mean I don't want her to pursue her dreams."

"Besides, we'll make it to London, won't we, Bea?" A secret look passed between them as he offered Bea his smoke. In that moment, her dark hair shimmering in the candlelight, her eyes shining, Bea looked as if she was lit from within.

She shot Grace a look that said, "Please be happy for me." And how could Grace not be. This was the happiest she had seen her friend since her father's death.

"Congratulations." She hugged Bea tightly.

"You'll still be my best friend first," she said, whispering in Bea's ear.

"Hey, let me in on this," Jimmy said, throwing his arms around the pair of them. "You are happy for us, aren't you, Racy Gracey?" he teased. Her irritating big brother felt there was some humor to be had in the nickname. Unfortunately he subscribed to the clumsy (mainly male) stereotype that underneath their cardigans, all librarians were seething with unrequited passion.

She punched him on the arm. "Librarian's stamp."

"Ouch!"

"Course I'm happy for you, but you do realize, Jimmy, that marriage entails growing up?" she laughed.

"Stop it, you two," said her mother, bustling over. "My nerves aren't up to this."

Poor Mary La Mottée. She'd had a nervous constitution even before the war. Now every time Grace was even so much as five minutes late, she faced a firing squad.

"Sorry I'm late, Mum. I just dropped a book in to Lou Gould."

"Stop your fretting, woman," called their father teasingly from his easychair by the fire.

They joined their father as he filled their glasses with his homebrew apple brandy.

"To Bea and Jimmy. *B'vons eune fais à la santé d's engages.* Let's drink to the happy couple."

His eyes rested on Jimmy and, for a fleeting moment, Grace felt sorry for her brother. She had always been free to a certain degree to pursue her own ambitions, but as the eldest son of their centuries-old Jersey farm, Jimmy's life was already carved in stone. The trouble was, Bea was not a natural farmer's wife. She had her own rhythm that didn't tally with the seasons of farming. Pinning her down to that kind of life would be like nailing a butterfly to the wall.

Grace pushed aside her worries and drank to the happy couple. She choked on the amber liquid. "Good grief, Dad, that's like carbolic. I think I'll stick to water."

"Tsk. Only horses drink water."

"It's the perfect heart-starter, Mr. La Mottée." Bea winked, chucking it down in one without so much as a shudder.

"I knew there was a reason I liked you," Mr. La Mottée laughed. "Welcome to the family."

"To be honest with you, Mr. La Mottée, I'm pleased to be joining your family. My own aren't exactly covering the Gold name in glory."

"How so?" asked Mrs. La Mottée, ears pricking up at the thought of some juicy town gossip.

"Well, I found out today, my younger sister Nancy—"

"The one who works at Boots?"

"Yes, she's got herself a new boyfriend. One of our uninvited guests. A Luftwaffe pilot, would you believe."

Grace and Jimmy's mother tutted. "Your poor mother."

"I'm ashamed of her too to be honest with you, Mrs. La Mottée."

"Go easy on her, Bea," Grace cautioned. "She's only seventeen. She's lonely."

"Lonely!" Bea scoffed. "She's only doing it for silk stockings and extra rations." She held her glass out for Grace's father to refill. "The only extra ration she'll get is bratwurst. He'll have a hand up her jumper before you can say *Heil Hitler*."

"Bea!" Grace scolded. She did love Bea, but there were times when her volubility went too far.

The rest of the evening passed in a blur of apple brandy, with Grace sneaking ever desperate glances at the clock every twenty minutes. *He'd think she'd forgotten him!* She was about to make her escape when a neighbor came in with an accordion and a tin of fruit from before the war. Another delay. Then as the clock struck 10 p.m. they got out the hidden wireless, heard the BBC news telling them the incredible news that Italy had surrendered unconditionally.

Jimmy swooped Bea off her feet. "It's happening. The Allies are winning."

Her mother clasped her tightly. "Oh, Grace," she shuddered. "It can't be long now, can it?"

From outside came the sound of shouts and heavy boots.

"Get rid of the wireless," Jimmy hissed.

They all froze as Mr. La Mottée silently replaced it and smoothed down the rag rug.

Her mother peeked behind the blackout. "It's a German patrol. We were making too much noise."

The group fell into silence and the thundering of jackboots grew louder on the narrow country road.

"They're chasing someone," her mother hissed, quickly securing the blackout blinds.

"Probably a runaway from Lager Mölders camp," her father said.

"Hush!"

They stood in silence as the heavy tread of boots thundered past the farmhouse door. She saw her brother's hands curl into fists. "Bastards. Hope he gets away."

Her mother raised her finger to her lips, then jumped as a terrific explosion sounded.

It was unmistakably a gunshot. The sound reverberated out over the dark fields and straight into Grace's soul.

Mary made the sign of the cross over her heart. "Poor wretch. There's another who'll never make it home." Tears shone in her eyes. "What diabolical world is this?"

There was no answer to that. After that, no one had the heart to continue the party. The neighbor packed up his accordion and went home.

"I'm going to turn in. I have to be at the library early tomorrow," Grace said.

"Jimmy, give Bea your bed and make up a bed on the sofa," their father ordered.

Grace and Bea went upstairs, the darkness lit by a flickering candle, the old sloping floorboards creaking under foot. They paused outside Grace's room.

"Grace, are you all right?" Bea asked. "You've been watching that clock all evening."

"I'm sorry, Bea. I'm so tired is all. This occupation is…"

She tailed off and thought of little sick Dolly and poor grieving Mrs. Gould. Of all the darkness and blood seeping over their beautiful island. And let's be honest here, Grace… *and him, waiting out there in the darkness. For you.*

"I know," Bea soothed, reaching out and gently touching her cheek with the palm of her hand. Grace felt the cold of her brother's ring on her best friend's finger.

"Is marriage what you really want, Bea?"

"Yes," she replied.

"But why now?"

"Do you trust me, Grace?"

"Against my better judgment," she joked feebly.

"Do you love me?"

She smiled. "Always."

"And I love you too, Gracie."

"You haven't used that nickname in forever."

"I'm feeling nostalgic I guess. I…I…"

"What is it, Bea?"

"Nothing. Night night. Don't let the bed bugs bite."

Grace shut the door and waited, heart thudding. That patrol was too close for comfort. She waited until she heard Bea shut the bedroom door before grabbing a book from her satchel and tiptoeing back down the stairs and out into the garden.

Her breath pooled like smoke as she walked silently through the wet grass. Shadows spread through the garden like blots of black ink bleeding over paper.

"Red," she whispered, pulling open the door of the shed and peering into the gloom. "Are you there? Did you hear that shot?"

A deep American voice rumbled through the darkness. "I could hardly have missed it, Miss La Mottée."

His smile lit up the musty old shed and Grace felt her tummy fold.

"I'm sorry I'm late. There was an unexpected celebration."

"I thought you'd forgotten me. It's lonelier than a Siberian salt mine in this shed." Even in the darkness she could hear the hint of laughter in his voice. He lit a roll-up. The sudden halo of light from the match illuminated his face.

He was what Bea would describe as "a dish," the sort of man who graced the covers of Mrs. Moisan's favorite novels. Well-defined cheekbones and the whitest teeth Grace had ever seen gave him a look of rude health. But it wasn't his overt physicality that struck Grace, but his confidence. His intense green eyes were trained on her and suddenly, Grace didn't know where to put herself.

"I brought you a book," she blurted. "Thought it might help while away the time."

"Say, *Huckleberry Finn*," he exclaimed. "This was my favorite growing up. How did you know?"

"Lucky guess."

"No luck about it. Brains as well as beauty."

Grace flushed.

"Well, I really ought…"

"Please don't go," he begged. "Stay a while."

"Are you all right?" she asked, concern overriding her shyness.

"It's the gunshot." He rubbed the spine of the book. "Rattled me, I guess."

"Of course, I wasn't thinking. Sorry."

First Lieutenant Daniel Patrick O'Sullivan, or "Red" as he insisted on her calling him, had been piloting his C-47 transport plane over Jersey when he'd been fired on by a German Flak battery. He'd crash-landed in the sea off Bouley Bay over a month ago and Grace had got the shock of her life when she'd come to the shed to find a trowel and found a shivering American instead. She'd been shocked, of course, but she'd done what any right-minded islander would. She'd fed him, given him sanctuary and alerted the Jersey Resistance. She hated keeping Red a secret from her family, but the less they knew, the safer it made them all. Her mother was jumpy at the best of times. Knowing she had a fugitive American in her potting shed might well tip her over the edge!

"You never did say what happened to the rest of your crew."

He drew deeply on his smoke and shook his head.

"When the plane went down, six had life jackets, three didn't. Those with the jackets swam to safety, I assume, please God. But those that didn't…" He trailed off.

"I tried, Miss La Mottée, but the tide was so strong and we kept getting flung against the rocks. Their hands kept slipping from my grasp, until finally, I lost sight of them. Somehow I got lucky and made it to shore."

He swallowed sharply.

"I just keep thinking of what I'm going to say to their mommas when I make it home. And I will make it home. I have to." His jaw stiffened. "Let them know their sons died as heroes."

Grace felt tears gather at the thought of the sea claiming those strong young men.

"You will, Red." She bumped his shoulder with hers. "You have all the hallmarks of a survivor to me."

"Oh, I nearly forgot." She fished in her pocket and pulled out Mrs. Moisan's piece of cake.

She grimaced. "Sorry, no bread and it's a little squished, but I hope it fills a gap."

"Thanks, Miss La Mottée. You're an actual angel on earth, I swear."

"Hush now," she laughed. "And please, don't you think it's time you called me Grace?"

"Very well. Angel Grace." He winked, his equilibrium restored. "This might sound strange, me a grown man and all, but would you read to me again? Your voice is very soothing."

"Only if you answer two questions that have been nagging me."

"Like I'm gonna say no to you."

"What are you doing here, Daniel Patrick O'Sullivan from Boston?"

"Well, I've always had this odd thing for sheds."

She batted him playfully on the arm.

"I'm serious. What are you *really* doing here, fighting our war?"

He laughed. "Oh, you're going to like this, being a librarian and all. I was a faithful listener to Ed Murrow, the CBS correspondent who used to broadcast nightly from London during the Blitz.

"'This is London,' he always used to start. He did a report about a mobile library set up in London—Books for the Bombed they called it. I figured any country civilized enough to do that is worth fighting for, me being a bookworm and all."

He glanced over at her.

"Not boring you, am I?"

"No, not at all. Please go on," she urged.

"My mom turned to me. She didn't need to say a word: I already knew I was going to enlist."

Grace found herself mesmerized as he talked, describing experiences which seemed so far away from her tiny Channel Island.

"I came on the *Queen Mary*, loaned by your Churchill, sailed right outta Boston filled to the brim with doughboys. I walked up the gangplank fully laden, and I never looked back. Besides," he shrugged, raking about in an old pouch for more tobacco, "*your war is our war*, as they say."

"You really believe that?" she asked, curiously.

"Sure I do. I always wanted to travel. Visiting London's been my dream since forever." A shadow passed over his face. "It's not the London I expected mind you."

"How so?"

"You listen to reports on the radio, you read about it in *Stars and Stripes*, but nothing can prepare you for the devastation of the Blitz up close."

He shook his head. "Pulverized houses, folk forced to sleep underground, beautiful old buildings wrapped up in sandbags and yet, here's the thing, Grace—everybody just gets on with it."

Red whistled under his breath.

"Boy, those folks are plenty tough too. Not just the men either. We were warned that if we saw a girl in khaki or air-force blue with a bit of ribbon on her tunic, she didn't get it for knitting more socks than anyone else in Ipswich."

"If ever one needed a reminder why we must fight fascism," she murmured.

"It's a beautiful city, perhaps even more so for showing its mettle."

"I've never been," she admitted, embarrassed. "I'd like to go someday."

"*Someday* is a disease that will take your dreams to the grave with you, Grace."

Now it was his turn to nudge her shoulder. "Maybe we could go together one day?"

"Perhaps." She blushed. "So after all the excitement of London, you must be jibbed to find yourself in this damp old shed."

He looked up from rolling his cigarette, his eyes dancing with satisfaction.

"From where I'm sitting this old shed is just about the prettiest darn place on earth."

Grace rolled her eyes.

"What?" he grinned. "I'm not joking. You're beautiful."

She pretended to yawn and he burst out laughing. "Come on, give a fella a break."

Grace lifted one eyebrow.

"What do you want me to say?" he grinned, holding up the cake. "You got a face like a piece of squashed cake?"

"Daft lummox."

"What in the hell is a lummox?" he laughed.

"Second question," she replied, ignoring his own. "Why Red?"

He ran his fingers over his air-force-regulation haircut.

"You wanna see the color of this hair in peacetime. I got seven brothers, all just the same. When the O'Sullivan brothers are out, boy, Boston lights up like a Belisha beacon."

"You must miss them so much."

"You have no idea."

"And your mum?"

His face broke open into a wide smile and he whistled under his breath.

"Mavis O'Sullivan. Once met, never forgotten. Best summed up with three words. Loudmouth. Irish. Matriarch. Do you know the difference between a terrier and my mom?"

Grace shook her head.

"The terrier eventually lets go. I swear to God she'd strangle the German who shot us down with her bare hands." Red winked. "Now, if I've survived the interrogation, how about we have that story now, my Angel Grace!"

"*Your* Angel Grace. Really?"

He grinned lazily. "What? You are to me."

Grace smiled, picked up the classic children's adventure book and began to read.

Moonlight spilled through the shed window and Red began to hum a Glenn Miller song she'd once heard played on the wireless. That tune she supposed was the difference between them. He'd visited the big London dancehalls, jitterbugged to Big Band Music and was living a life of action and adventure she had only read about.

She knew exactly what Ash would say. *You're waging your war with books, not bombs.* Ash's manifesto had always been clear. Before he had been taken, he had transformed the library from a mausoleum of dead and moribund books to a decent cultural asset for the community. A place for *all*. Surely that was also a battle worth fighting?

Two chapters in she placed the book down and stifled a yawn.

"I'd better turn in."

Red picked up her hand and kissed it gently.

"What was that for?"

"To say thanks. I'll be gone by tomorrow evening."

"What? W-why?"

"I think you know the answer. I can't abuse your kindness any longer. Every night I'm here I'm putting you and your family's safety at risk. I know the penalty for harboring me."

Grace fell silent.

"Those patrols are nightly now. It's only a matter of time…"

"Where'll you go?"

"I'll take my chances. I've got the address of another safehouse on the island."

She nodded. "Very well. In that case, go safely, Red. Godspeed."

"What about the book?"

"Take it. I'll write it off as a casualty of war."

"Thank you, Angel Grace. I'll never forget what you did for me."

Grace blew out the candle she'd been reading by and almost immediately the inky darkness wrapped itself around them. An owl called nearby. Something rustled in the hedgerow.

In the sudden gloom she became more aware of the visceral presence of him. The wide sweep of his shoulders, the faint dimple on his chin. The autumn night was warm and still, lacing the ripe country air with an intoxicating fragrance. Lavender, roses and evening primrose still bloomed, bravely waiting for the first frost.

A part of her ached to stand on tiptoe. Find the warmth of his lips in the darkness. See what all the fuss was about. His mouth was just inches from hers. What would it take to close the gap between them, a touch, a sigh, a lingering look?

Instead?

"Good night," she said as briskly as if she were stamping a library book.

Grace shut the shed door softly, unable to work out what was worse as she tiptoed through the wet grass. The tiredness or the crushing disappointment.

3

Bea

BANNED BOOK

Oliver Twist *by Charles Dickens. Banned by Nazi Germany for featuring Jewish characters.*

Bea lay awake in the darkness imagining every creak and rustle to be an intruder. Three hundred thirty thefts reported last month alone. Locals blamed the Germans, the Germans blamed the slaves, the slaves were voiceless.

Next door in Jimmy's parents' room, she could hear the soft *cluck* of chickens in a box under the bed. In this climate of fear, Mrs. La Mottée, like most of her neighbors, had started taking her rations and chickens to bed with her. It was a far cry from the pre-war days when they'd never even bothered to lock their doors.

Horror mingled with excitement crashed over her at the thought of what lay ahead. It was total madness. England was 85 miles away, through a treacherous tide and lethal reefs. The chances of success were infinitesimal. A vivid image sprang into her mind of the slave, his feet dangling between the two Germans, of her father's blood on the planks of his fishing boat. She knew what he would say. It was better to die in pursuit of freedom than live a life of degrading subjugation.

Finally, at 3 a.m., Bea heard a tap on the door. Silently she pulled back the covers. She was dressed and bundled up in an old pair of Jimmy's trousers tightened with string, and his old jersey, which he'd instructed her to put on.

He held up a finger to his lips, the whites of his eyes vivid in the gloom. They crept down the hall, past Grace's bedroom and Bea fought the urge to wake her.

The guilt was overwhelming. She, Jimmy and Grace did everything together. Bea had come so close to telling her last night but something had stopped her. Grace wouldn't consider leaving in a million years. Her friend was cautious and measured in everything. She couldn't jeopardize Jimmy's plans and yet the longing to knock gently on her door, pull her from her sleep to say goodbye and hug her one last time choked her. Jimmy took her hand, led her on.

Outside they drew out their bikes from the barn. Bea froze.

"What was that? I swear I heard talking from the shed."

"You're imagining it. Come on. We can't afford to hang about."

Mounting their bikes they began to cycle down the road, through St. Ouen's, heading in the direction of the beach. The darkness was like a velvet blanket, muffling her senses. Bea swore she could almost hear the sea breathing like a siren's call as they pedaled in the direction of the coast. She felt the comforting sea mist shroud her face and form droplets on her eyelashes. The mist was so thick it would help keep them hidden, but they would now have no chance of knowing about the enemy until they were on them.

The Germans were increasingly paranoid since Denis Vibert's escape and regularly patrolled the coastal areas by night. Like an automaton Bea kept on cycling, keeping her gaze fixed firmly on Jimmy's back, ignoring the iron fist that was gripping her heart. Twenty minutes later she heard the suck and rush of water on shingle.

"Follow me. Stay close," Jimmy ordered as they dismounted by the coast path. They tucked their bikes in a clearing in a small wooded area before making their way on foot down the path which spilled onto the beach. They walked in silence, their feet crunching on the shingle, past the barbed wire, past the *verboten* sign and onto the forbidden beach. Bea was shaking so much, her legs seeming to move of their own accord.

"Courage is not the absence of fear, but rather the judgment that something else is more important than fear," she repeated as they walked, but as they spotted the boat, Bea was so terrified she could feel her heart smashing against her ribs.

They reached the far end of the rocky cove where a wooden rowing boat, painted green, was waiting by the water's edge.

"You're late," said Jimmy's old school friend Francis, and then his anger turned to disbelief. "And what the hell is she doing here, Jimmy? We don't need any bloody women getting in the way."

"We have space and Bea's stronger and fitter than most of you." Jimmy's tone brooked no argument, but she felt hostility crackle from the group of young men. The tension was so thick you could taste it in the salt-brined air.

"Where's this fisherman then?" Bea asked.

"He'll be here," said Francis.

"He'd better be," Jimmy muttered. "We've got no hope of navigating our way to England without him." Bea's thoughts turned uncomfortably to François Scornet, the paroled French soldier who had escaped from Brittany in an attempt to join the Free French Forces, and landed on Guernsey, mistaking it for the Isle of Wight. The Germans had executed him before a firing squad not five miles from here.

"I don't like this," Jimmy said, drumming his fingers on the side of the boat. "Why isn't he here?" They scanned the high black cliffs, looking for the faintest sign of life.

Just then the mist cleared a little and broken moonlight spilled onto the beach, illuminating the group.

"I say we go now," said Jimmy. "It's madness to wait any longer."

He placed his hand on the small of Bea's back, urging her to get in the boat.

"No, we must wait," Francis urged. "We've no hope without him."

Bea was struck by the most horrible feeling of terror. It drenched over her like a wave. Rather than being an escape group, it suddenly occurred to her they were more of a sitting target.

"How well do you even know this fisherman, Francis?" she demanded. "How do you know he's not an informer, or an undercover—"

The shot rang out like a full stop, bouncing off the cliff face.

"*Halt! Hände hoch!*" A guttural German voice tore through the darkness, followed by a sweeping beam of light from further up the cliff path.

"We've been betrayed," Jimmy cried. Bea felt like she might crash to her knees from the fear.

"Come on, everyone," Jimmy urged, pushing the boat. "Get the boat in the water."

He and the rest began frantically hauling the boat toward the water's edge, but then a second, more powerful arc of light caught him in its beam.

"*Halt!*" They heard the sound of an engine roaring up the slipway.

"Jimmy, put your hands up," she begged. "We're surrounded."

For a moment his body stilled. His eyes flickered toward her and she saw desperation, a wildness which vacillated between fight or flight.

He raised his hands slowly, playing for time. "Bea," he murmured, "get on your hands and knees and crawl. Go now. Save yourself."

"I can't leave you, Jimmy," she sobbed.

They heard the sound of heavy boots crunching on the shingle. The Germans were on the beach.

"Leave now, Bea!" he ordered. "If you love me, you'll go."

She pressed her fingers to his face, hoping to convey the fierceness of her love through that one touch, but it was all futile. The game was up.

Wordlessly, she slipped to her knees and began to crawl up the beach, the rocks cutting into her flesh, tears streaming down her cheeks, choking from the unmitigated horror of it all.

She made it to a small rocky outcrop and hunkered down behind a rock. Five, no, seven black figures were running up the beach with dogs, torches bouncing.

As they got closer, Jimmy lowered his hands, slipped his right hand into his pocket and pulled out the gun.

"*Legte die Waffe nieder!*" screamed a voice.

Jimmy threw the gun backward and it landed near her foot with a crack. Bea stuffed it in her satchel.

All was chaos. Screams, barking dogs. The shriek of bullets.

Jimmy was pushing the boat once more, with all his might, alone now, as the figures closed in.

Surrender, surrender, she urged under her breath, but even as she said it, she knew he never would. All of a sudden his body seemed to jerk and then bounce back onto the shingle. An explosion like a great crack of thunder reverberated off the cliff top. Jimmy's head hit the edge of the boat and he slithered, face-down at the water's edge.

Then the Germans were on him. One roughly kicked him over and horror clogged her throat. The color had drained from his face. A hole had been punched clean through his cheek, oozing red and gelatinous, his eyes clear and vacant.

There was a high-pitched whining in her head, like someone fiddling with the frequency of a wireless. The Germans were yelling, their mouths like black maws spilling demands into the darkness, as they cuffed the rest of the group. Then suddenly the noise burst back to life.

"*Den strand durchsuchen.*" Search the beach.

For a moment she was frozen in indecision. Her legs felt like they were being dragged through a thick treacle of fear, but then something primal kicked in. Bea slithered her way toward a bank of pine trees at the far end of the cove. She knew of a steep path that zigzagged up the side of the cliff. As a kid she and Grace had shimmied up it many times, pretending they were the children out of *Swallows and Amazons*, prowling Wild Cat Island on the hunt for stolen treasure. How ridiculous those childhood games seemed now as she climbed.

Taking the cliff path she scrambled up. She was unaware of anything but survival, not the barbed wire ripping her shins to pieces, nor the sting of thorns as she smashed through gorse bushes and over boggy marshland. Had they seen her? Were they chasing? At the top of the cliff, she hurtled headlong into the woods and finally she reached the clearing where she had hidden her bike. She climbed the lower branches of a tree and waited immobilized by terror.

Bea waited for the stentorian voice of a German, the trampling of jackboots. God knows how long she waited there, rigid among the treetops, while with every creak of a branch, images came to her like awful snapshots. Jimmy's head, the spongy crimson mass, the awful look of his surprise on his face. Her fingers were like claws, clinging to the bark, and she was shaking violently.

The clean, sharp smell of pine seemed to bring her to her senses. If she waited here they'd find her. She scrambled down the tree, survival penetrating the fog. She had to get out of there and fast. Once word got out there would be patrols. This place would be crawling with Germans before long. She had the advantage. She knew these fields and footpaths like the back of her hand. If she was careful she could make it all the way back to St. Helier.

Bea pulled her bike out and pushed it fast to the furthest end of the wood that met a small track she knew would take her back and connect her to St. Helier. As she cycled, tears streamed down her face, the wind whipping her hair loose. The split-second awfulness of it consumed her. Just an hour before life had been filled with hope, bravado and the promise of the rewards that come with great bravery. Jimmy's name in the same breath as Denis Vibert's, a homespun hero, a tale that would be repeated to their grandchildren. Now there was nothing. No future.

Bea made it to a field on the outskirts of town and waited for the nightly curfew to pass, sliding Jimmy's tin ring compulsively round and round her finger. Why had she not told Grace? One word from his cautious younger sister and she would have talked him out of it.

A rim of crimson slid over the horizon and the birds began their dawn chorus. She thought of Jimmy's mum, discovering their disappearance, the confusion and pain that would explode in the hours and days to come. The total dismantling, not just of a family, but of multiple lives. Bea picked up her bike and slid through the shadows back into town. Avoiding the barbed-wire checkpoint at Havre des Pas, she left her bike in the alley at the back of her home and shinned over the wall.

The kitchen was dark and smelled brackish. Something smoldered on the fire.

She crept toward the door, but a hand wrenched her back.

"You dirty stop-out!" Her mother delivered a stinging blow to her face. "I've been out of my bleedin' mind all night. I..." Her voice trailed off.

"Bea, what's happened?"

"It's Jimmy. He's dead." She peeled off her wet jumper and satchel.

The gun dropped between them and fell on the floor with a dull thud.

"Oh, Mum. What have I done?"

4

Grace
Eleven weeks later

BANNED BOOK

Friedo Lampe's At the Edge of the Night *was seized by the Nazis for its "damaging and undesirable" content. The disabled and gay author and librarian somehow managed to survive, only to be shot by a Red Army patrol six days before the end of the war.*

It was late autumn and the air was crisp, the sky like blue glass. A good day for a burial. As the coffins passed, Grace gripped Bea's hand so tightly in hers it felt like they were welded together. The sight of so many coffins was more than Grace could bear. She needed to be back in the safe sanctuary of the library, surrounded by books, not bodies. "Come on," she urged. "Let's go back to the library and have a cup of tea."

"Not yet, Grace," Bea replied quietly. "I need to see this."

Grace nodded, understanding. It had been nearly three months since Jimmy's death and the ripples of trauma hadn't even begun to surface. The repercussions had been swift and savage. Jimmy's old schoolmates were in prison awaiting trial. Jimmy's body had been released for burial, but the Germans had banned anyone from attending, save for close family members. Her brother's murder on the beach had stirred up high tension on the island. Aware of this undercurrent of feeling, the German authorities wanted to avoid mass demonstrations and civil unrest. Even in death Jimmy was under orders by the occupiers.

That wasn't the worst of it. Nor the anger when the Germans brought curfew forward an hour and revoked fishing rights to punish the whole community, or the sparse little family group by his coffin. No, what had really clotted Grace's throat with a deep anger, that day they had buried Jimmy under an occluded sky, was that Bea hadn't been allowed to attend. Grace and Jimmy's mother had refused to let her come, even though she'd been Jimmy's fiancée. Try as she might, she had not been able to assuage the deep anger her mother felt toward Bea. Her golden boy was gone and it seemed the Germans weren't enough to blame.

Grace felt nothing but empathy for the friend she had loved all her life. It was not Bea's fault that Jimmy had been gunned down in cold blood. Her brother had been head-strong and when he set his mind to something, nothing on earth would have stopped him trying to escape off the island. But that hadn't stopped her friend from blaming herself and no matter how many times Grace begged her not to, she bore the full crushing responsibility for his death.

"Grace, think of all those mothers who should be here to see this," she whispered as the coffins passed, tears running down her cheeks. Twenty-nine British naval ratings were being buried in Howard Davis Park, the Island of Jersey War Cemetery, after the British cruiser HMS *Charybdis* had been torpedoed off the French coast. In addition, three American airmen, who'd drowned when their C-47 transport plane had been shot down off the north coast, were being buried. Bodies had been washing up like flotsam on the Jersey and Guernsey beaches for weeks.

"They died for us," Bea murmured, not bothering to wipe away her tears. Grace knew her tears had accumulated from the funeral she had never even been allowed to attend and now they seemed to flow unchecked from a heart brimming over with grief.

"It's an extraordinary turnout," Grace said, casting her gaze about. People were pressed into every crevice of the graveyard. She spotted the bailiff, the attorney general, the Constable of St. Helier, alongside farmers, shopkeepers and fishermen. She spied many of her patrons in the crowds too. Ordinary people had turned out in their hundreds for the funerals of people they had never even met. After three years of occupation, islanders were making it clear that their loyalty to the Crown was undiminished.

The Germans were in full attendance too, though not this time to suppress, but astonishingly acting as a guard of honor drawn from members of the army and navy. Unlike her brother, these young British sailors and American airmen were getting full military honors, she realized, as a gun boomed into the air, sending a murder of crows flapping into the cloudless skies.

Lurking at the back of the crowd Grace spotted the man they called "the Wolf." The names Heinz Carl Wölfle and

Gestapo were synonymous. In fact, he was deputy head of the Geheime Feldpolizei, the German Secret Field Police, but given that he styled himself "the Wolf of the Gestapo" and was the most notorious German on the island, it mattered little.

Bea flinched.

"Bea, are you all right?" She looked as if she might keel over at any moment.

"I…I'm fine. It's just the gun, I wasn't expecting it."

As the blur of the crowd shifted again, Grace caught a glimpse of another familiar face at the furthest end of the graveyard, standing with his back pressed against an old yew tree.

"Bea, can you spare me a moment?"

She nodded, staring at the coffins, but not really listening.

"Don't move. I won't be long."

Grace skirted the graveyard, until she was next to the tree.

"Red, are you out of your mind?" she hissed. "What are you doing here?"

He turned and his green eyes lit up. "Angel Grace, I didn't expect to see you here."

"Nor I you. Most of the German top brass are in spitting distance."

"Those goddamn kraut bastards?" His smile slipped. "They ain't looking for me here. More interested in this fake show of military honor. 'Sides, that commandant's so stupid, if his brains were dynamite, he wouldn't have enough to blow his own hat off."

He stared at the group of German High Command, eyes narrowed in hatred.

"Jeez. What a nest of vipers."

Red's uniform had been replaced with rough workman's clothes and a flat cap, but she could tell in the eleven weeks since she'd last seen him in her shed, his hair had grown and was now a muddy brown.

"I got a little help and a strong bottle of hair dye," he whispered in her ear. "The people of Jersey are pretty darn amazing. My name's Phillip Harris now by the way, according to my new registration card." He grinned. "My own mom wouldn't recognize me."

"I do wish you'd be more careful," she said, picking a piece of wet bark from the tree and crumbling it between her fingers. She'd never expected to see him again and it felt overwhelming. "The Secret Field Police are here somewhere."

"You worried about me?" he asked, one eyebrow lifted.

"I'm worried about that."

She glanced at the poster pinned to the noticeboard, not five yards from where they were standing.

WANTED

There are several American aircrew at large on the island. They will attempt to obtain shelter and help from the civilian population. It is expressly announced that anyone who takes in, or extends help in any way to our enemy will be punished by death according to Paragraph 9 of the Order for the Protection of the Occupying Forces.

"You underestimate them."

"They underestimate me. Besides, I'm not here to cause trouble, I'm here to pay my respects to my buddies." Red shook his head.

"They were only just out of short trousers, kids really. Billy, he only joined the air force instead of the navy 'cause he hated water. My boys are a long way from home."

A mist started to drift in off the sea, shrouding the graveyard as the German military began the solemn task of committing the bodies to the earth.

Red reached down and scooped up a handful of earth from the ground, shoving it in his pocket.

"I'm going to give this to their folks back home, so they have a little piece of their sons' burial place." His hands clenched into his fists. "Goddamn it! It's all wrong. I swear to you, Grace, one day, I'm going make sure my comrades rest on American soil."

It suddenly struck Grace—the awful loneliness of being buried on an island you had no connection to, with no one near to mourn you or tend your grave, save for a centuries-old yew tree. Out of nowhere tears began to flow.

Red passed her a handkerchief. "Don't cry, Angel Grace," he said softly.

"Sorry. Only my brother died. Shot by the Germans. The same night I said goodbye to you last."

"Jesus, Grace, I'm so sorry. I don't know what to say."

"There's nothing anyone can say," she said quietly. "We… we just have to endure this hell, survive it somehow."

Silently, he slid his hand through hers, squeezing her fingers in solidarity. It was the briefest of gestures, but she felt her whole world tilt.

Red began to murmur something under his breath as the bodies were lowered into the ground and she listened, spellbound.

"Out of the night that covers me,
Black as the pit from pole to pole,
I thank whatever gods may be
For my unconquerable soul."

She stared at him in amazement, her throat clogged with emotion.

"What? You think us American doughboys can't recite poetry? 'Invictus' is my favorite poem. Reminds me to hold on to my dignity."

He reached his hand into his coat and pulled out *Huckleberry Finn*.

"Thanks for the loan. That was like medicine. I'll be needing another dose soon."

The ceremony was nearly over. Grace scanned the crowds and in alarm saw Bea heading toward them.

"I've got to—" she began, but Red had already left, his tall figure sliding through the throng.

"Who was that?" Bea asked when she reached her.

"Him? Oh just one of my library patrons."

"You seemed awfully close."

"Come on," Grace said lightly. "Let's get out of here."

Clutching Bea's hand, she turned and they eased their way back through the crowds. Once they reached the gate to the graveyard, Grace became aware of a disturbance.

A handful of young women were being barred from entering the graveyard by a small, angry crowd. The tension was palpable and shoves were being traded.

"What's going on?" Grace demanded. "Why won't you let them in?"

"These Jerrybags have no right to come to the funeral of these courageous souls," said a woman Grace recognized from the library. "How dare they show their faces!"

"How dare you deny us entry?" called back a voice. A young, dark-haired woman pushed her way to the front of the group.

"We have every bloody right to come and show our respects, the same as you." She thrust her chin forward, her dark eyes flashing defiantly.

Grace felt Bea stiffen beside her.

"Nancy, go home."

"Says who?"

"Says your older sister. You're making a show of yourself."

"You heard her," jeered the older woman.

"That's enough!" Grace took herself by surprise, but she felt incandescent that this tawdry saga was playing out while the earth was still fresh on the graves. "I buried my brother a little under three months ago and I can tell you now this is the most outrageous thing I've seen, even in the midst of an occupation."

She swung open the gate. "In you come, girls."

The girls traipsed in, but as Nancy passed the older woman reached across and muttered in a spiteful low voice.

"You're Number One on the list for a haircut once your Boche boyfriend's in prison."

Grace stared flabbergasted at the crowd. She knew that, after so long, nerves had been stretched to breaking point, but this wasn't who islanders were.

"Where's your humanity?" she asked in shock.

She didn't wait for an answer. Instead she got on her bike and pedaled off, Bea in hot pursuit.

"Gracie," she said, catching up with her, "you didn't have to defend her on my account."

"I didn't, Bea. I just think it's wrong. We all make mistakes and now, of all times, we need a little understanding, not judgment."

"Have you time for a quick cup of tea before you go back to the library?" Bea asked, changing the subject. "I'm not due at the post office for an hour. Mum'd love to see you."

"Why not," Grace agreed. "Most of my patrons were at the funeral so the library will be quiet for once."

St. Helier was indeed strangely silent. Bea ripped off her headscarf, letting her long dark hair flow behind her and fell in next to her.

Grace shook her head. Of all the many tedious rules and regulations which her best friend despised, the one she hated most was being forbidden to ride two abreast, and the other to cycle and drive on the opposite side of the road.

"Bea," she warned.

"Oh, sorry, am I breaking zee rules of mein Führer?" she retorted in a very bad German accent. She flicked her an impish grin and Grace didn't know whether to feel annoyed at her impetuousness, or pleased that a glimmer of her old friend had surfaced.

In a flash, Bea swung onto the other side of the road. "Come on over and join me on the right side of the road."

They were nearing the harbor where they were always guaranteed to see a German. Sure enough, two were standing sentry at the entry to the quay.

"Pustulant, arrogant, impotent," Bea muttered out of one side of her mouth. Bea and Grace had a game they played where they had to sum up every German they saw with three adjectives, without ever using the same one twice. It was surprisingly hard. Ulcerated. Frustrated. Blond. Bored. Vulpine. Arrogant. Narcissistic. Mocking them stole a little of their power. At least, it always used to. Now it just seemed pointless.

"Come on, Grace," Bea urged. "Play the game."

They pedaled closer to the harbor.

"Humorless. Sexless. Pox-filled," Bea called, her voice on the other side of the road dangerously loud.

"Cut it out, Bea. Get on the right side of the road before you get us both arrested."

Bea stared back, her dark eyes challenging her.

"I think you'll find you're on the wrong side, Grace, and I'm on the right side."

She shot her a look then cycled on faster, her postal uniform jacket billowing up around her.

A flash of green canvas streaked toward them. A green German-army truck had rattled round the bend of the French Harbour at terrific speed. Grace just about had time to make out the surprised look on the face of the driver as he swerved to avoid Bea. The truck impacted with the harbor wall. The crack of metal. The hissing of steam. Grace and Bea stared at the crash scene in shock.

A moment later the door was shoved open and the dazed driver staggered out.

"Quick," Bea hissed. "We've got to get out of here."

They cycled as fast as they could up Mount Bingham, the incline burning Grace's legs, before speeding down the other side of the hill straight into the small beachside neighborhood of Havre des Pas. Bea pulled breathlessly to a stop outside Bay View Boarding House, where she lived with her mother and Nancy.

"Did you see his face?" she laughed. Her eyes were glowing, her cheeks flushed.

"Bea, that was reckless. You could've been killed," Grace gasped. "The driver could've been killed."

Bea shrugged.

"After Jimmy, I'd call that an eye for an eye."

She banged down the bike stand and let herself in the house leaving Grace speechless on the doorstep. Something was happening to her friend. She'd always been what her mother would describe as "a caution." Grace had preferred to think of her as free-spirited, as if somehow the island wasn't big enough to contain all her chutzpah, but now, since her father's and Jimmy's death, something else was happening. A thick leathery crust was growing over Bea's heart that seemed to make her immune to danger. A dark and unsettled feeling uncurled deep in Grace's gut.

"Hello, Mrs. Gold," Grace called as she followed Bea into

the kitchen. The small room was filled with the fug of potato peelings and ersatz tobacco.

"Grace, how's yourself, sweetheart?" Queenie Gold embraced her warmly. Grace had such a soft spot for her best friend's mum. A Cockney by birth, she'd married a Jersey man and moved from the congested streets of Whitechapel to St. Helier after a holiday in the 1920s. She had a heart as big as the moon and an ability to barter that could shrivel the resolve of even the steeliest of market sellers. Not for nothing was she known locally as "the Guv'nor."

"Come in, come in," she ushered. "I'll fix you girls some dinner."

"No, please, Mrs. Gold, don't go to the trouble of feeding me."

"It's no trouble and it's Queenie to you."

"What's for dinner, Mum?" Bea asked.

"Shit and sugar," she shot back.

"You can take the woman out of the East End, but you can't take the East End out of the woman," Bea joked.

Queenie pottered round the kitchen, like Mrs. Tiggywinkle. Tiny little terra-cotta pots seemed to be dotted on every surface wherever a weak pool of sunlight fell.

"I've been transferring little bean and gourd plants. I'll plant them out when they're big enough. They'll do well in my allotment."

"Mum gives away more than she grows, don't you, Mum," Bea teased, flicking her on the bum with a tea towel.

"Saucy piece," she chuckled. "Neighbors are as close as friends and you'd do well to remember that, my girl."

Queenie sat back at the kitchen table where she'd been grating potatoes.

"They reckon ten pounds of potatoes make one pound of flour," she remarked, wincing as she caught her finger on the grater. "And by that time I'll have no ends to my fingers."

Grace smiled sadly as she took in Queenie's red-raw fingers, not so dissimilar from her own mother's. It was the women of this occupation who were the real heroes to her mind. Most of them had an alchemist's gift for rustling up meals from nothing.

"How's the library?" Queenie asked, pushing a cup of nettle tea in front of her.

"It's my sanctuary," she replied. "I don't know what I'd do without my books truth be told."

Her thoughts strayed to the indeterminable days after Jimmy's death. Her mother's refusal to leave her bed, strangled by her sorrow. Her father's absence from the home. Only the library had remained unstained, a beacon of warmth and escapism, calling her in.

"I dare say." Queenie gently placed a work-worn hand over hers.

"I'd love an Ethel M. Dell if you could set one aside for me," Queenie continued. "One of these days, I might actually finish a page at bedtime without falling asleep. Ooh," she lowered her voice, "I heard on the grapevine of a new book from America. *Forever Amber*. Bit mucky by all accounts. That would keep me up all right." She patted the side of her turban. "Any chance?"

Grace raised an eyebrow. "Can't see it getting past Nazi censorship, Mrs. Gold, can you? They don't go wild for scheming strumpets." She hesitated. "But also, I'm not sure we should be talking about grapevine subjects, even behind closed doors." Grace realized in a moment of disquiet, that it was some measure of how far they'd sunk that even discussing hidden wireless chat and controversial books in the privacy of a home made her feel unsettled.

"Last I heard the bloody Boche ain't fitted a listening device to my pinny, but yeah, I see what you're driving at," Queenie replied. "How's your mum, ducks?"

"Not great. Jimmy's death has hit her very hard."

Queenie reached out and squeezed her shoulder. "We all miss him a great deal."

"Not Nancy," Bea interrupted, her voice scalpel sharp. "She doesn't seem to give two hoots."

"Bea, don't create," Queenie replied wearily.

"She was at the funeral of those sailors earlier, Mum! The front of her. Dad'll be turning in his grave."

"Oh, go easy, love. It's not easy on her either."

"She's a selfish cow and I don't know why either of you are defending her."

"The more of a fuss you make over it, the more attractive you'll make the relationship seem," Queenie protested. "Forbidden love seems desirable when you're seventeen, but it rarely ends well."

"It's embarrassing, Mum," Bea protested. "You know I heard someone in the post office the other day joking that when the Germans came and we all hung out the white flags, the girls at Boots hung out their white knickers. My little sister's a Jerrybag!"

"No, she's not," Queenie insisted. "There are women who consort with the enemy to get extra rations and improve their situation, I'll grant you. Then there are young girls who see a handsome young German and think they're in love. There's a difference between the two."

"Oh please. She's as shallow as a soup bowl."

Bea banged her cup down and stormed up to her room. Grace went to follow but Queenie caught her arm.

"Leave her for a while to calm down. She goes by the moon that one."

"It's this anger though," Grace replied, remembering the crunch of hot metal on stone from the accident earlier. "I worry her rage will land her in trouble with the authorities."

"She's got a hot head and she's grieving for her father and now her fiancé. Time is the only healer." Queenie patted her on the hand and stood creakily. "Least she's got you."

After a small dinner of vegetable soup thickened with carrageen moss and yesterday's gray occupation bread with a smear of margarine, Grace took a bowl of soup up to Bea's bedroom. A sharp hunger gnawed her insides as she walked up the stairs, feeling lightheaded. What she wouldn't do for some fluffy white bread, slathered with salted butter and apricot jam, washed down with coffee, *real* coffee, made from beans and not acorns. How quickly her thoughts seemed to slide to food these days.

Bumping open the door with her hip she set down the soup bowl and braced herself for tears, but instead Bea was hard at work.

"What are you doing?"

"Shut the door," she ordered. "I don't want Mum to hear. I was covering Mr. Luce's round up at Trinity last week, when I started spotting these in the hedgerows."

She stuck one of the pamphlets in Grace's hand.

"I can't read it. It's all in German." Grace puzzled. "It's probably another proclamation."

"No, Grace, it's not. It's gold dust. I took it back to the post office and one of the boys has a friendly German on side who translated."

Grace pushed down her irritation that had it been a woman with a "friendly German on side" she'd be quickly branded and made to feel the wrath of society's disapproval. 'Twas ever thus.

"And?" she sighed.

"They're from an RAF leaflet drop. It's a message from the British Government to say they have begun blanket-bombing Germany and that the Allies are winning. It's to demoralize the Wehrmacht."

"But what on earth have you done all this for? Making some bunting for the next fête?"

The leaflets were strung up all round Bea's room from a washing line.

"They were wet when I collected them so I've been drying them out, and I've translated some of them into English on the back. I thought we could distribute them round the island—you know, to raise morale?"

"We?" Grace said warily. "I think I'm already taking enough risks at the library, don't you?"

"Oh, come on, Grace," Bea urged. "It's great what you do, delivering forbidden books, but this is the same when you think about it. It's words on a page that raise morale."

Grace shook her head.

"I…I don't know, Bea. It's risky."

"Look, I'll do half on my next round, posting them alongside letters, and you do the other half."

Grace hesitated.

"Please, Grace." She fixed her with a look. "For Jimmy."

Grace exhaled. "I'll see what I can do, but no promises. I'm a librarian, not a member of the Resistance!"

"This is important. Morale is at rock bottom." She touched Grace's cheek, her beautiful dark eyes shining with intensity. "They're more than leaflets. They offer hope."

Bea was right. Other than their hidden wireless offering up the lifesaving BBC, they were totally cut off from the world, with very little to counter the tidal wave of misinformation churned out by the Nazis. It had occurred to her then how very powerful words were in a time of total war. And that, she realized in a blinding flash, was the worst of it. The Germans had stolen their truth.

Grace tapped the bottom of her teeth with her tongue.

"I suppose as a librarian my job *is* to dispense trustworthy information."

"Precisely," Bea said. "Knowledge is power, right?"

Just then a gust of wind breezed in and playfully picked up a leaflet from the top of a pile. Grace and Bea watched in dismay as it twisted and turned round the room like a kite before sailing out of the open window.

"Quick!" Bea blurted. They thundered down the stairs and out onto the seafront where they realized the leaflet had plastered itself to the windscreen of a black Citroën motor car.

Grace's heart plunged as the vehicle slowed and a familiar figure got out and peeled it off the car window.

"Oh, fuckety fuck!" Bea murmured under her breath.

Grace knew why she was cursing. It could scarcely have been worse if it landed on Hitler's windscreen.

He walked toward them, all sharp angles and high shine and had she not been so terrified, Grace could have laughed out loud. Bea had a theory that you could always hear or smell a German before you saw one. If it wasn't the heavy thud of a jackboot on the cobbles, it was the powerful odor of the enemy troops, a curious mix of the linseed oil they used on their boots and a heavy, spicy cologne.

"It's the Wolf!" she mouthed.

"Leave this to me," Bea muttered as the Wolf summoned them to the motor car.

He leaned casually against the gleaming car, impeccable in a tailored suit, his foot resting lightly on the top of the swastika on the running board. He wasn't as obvious as some of his fellow operatives in the secret police, many of whom swanked about the island in leather trench coats and ridiculous alpine hats. Bea could never fathom why a department set up to be covert and secret drew so much attention to themselves.

"Is this yours?" he asked in a strange accent, more Canadian than German. Rumor had it he'd spent many years in Canada before the war, lending him a charming, urbane air, entirely at odds with his real personality.

"Ummm." Bea stumbled for words.

"Let me save you the bother. I saw it come out of the window of that house. I presume you live there."

"Grace doesn't live here," Bea blurted, finding her voice. "She's just a friend. That is mine, sir."

He fixed his gaze on Bea and looked her slowly up and down.

"This is very dangerous material to have in your possession."

"Is it, sir?" Bea asked, widening her eyes.

His eyes lingered on the skin above her breasts. "Do you like to play with fire, Miss—What's your name?"

Grace felt excruciatingly uncomfortable by the exchange.

"Beatrice Gold."

"Pretty name. Are you Jewish?"

Grace closed her eyes, felt the blood thudding in her skull.

"No, sir," Bea replied.

When she opened her eyes, the Wolf was still staring at Bea.

"So, we are neighbors it appears. My headquarters are up there: Number 2 Silvertide." He nodded back toward a pretty cream Edwardian villa the secret police had requisitioned from poor old Mrs. Scott. "This leaflet is from the RAF and is nothing more than pernicious, pervading propaganda."

Grace watched in astonishment as Bea smiled demurely.

"Please sir, what's pernicious?"

He smiled broadly, showing off a gold tooth. "You left school a little too early, I think. You know, they are teaching German in Jersey's schools now. You should have stayed on."

"So it's from the RAF?" she asked, continuing to play dumb. "Only I don't speak German, so I didn't know."

"In which case, why did you keep hold of it? What were you intending to use it for?"

Grace swallowed uneasily, but Bea didn't miss a beat.

"Well, to be honest with you, sir. Toilet paper. My mum reckons it would come in handy to wipe our arses on, what with the paper shortage."

The Wolf tipped his head back and roared with laughter.

"That's all it's good for, Miss Gold."

He ran his hand along the black bonnet of his motor car and gave them an oily smile. "I like you, Beatrice Gold. You know I spotted you at the funeral earlier. You have one of those faces that stand out in a crowd."

"Face of an angel. Least that's what my mum says," she said smoothly.

He opened the door and gestured for his driver to leave, but at the last moment, wound down the window. "Where do you work?"

"For His Majesty's Postal Service," she replied.

"Actually, Miss Gold," he replied, his voice dangerously soft, "you work for us now, not the Crown. I'll be seeing you around." He chuckled and screwed up the pamphlet. "Toilet paper indeed."

The car slid off and Bea slumped down onto the low wall in front of her house.

"Bea," Grace gasped, "are you determined to give me a heart attack today?"

"That was a close call. What an odious little shit. Did you see the way he was staring at my tits?"

"Listen, I've got to get back to the library. Please, Bea, stay out of trouble." Grace shook her head. "Face of an angel? Where do you get these things from?"

"What was I supposed to say?" Bea grinned, all mock innocence. "Is this a face which harbors seditious thoughts?"

"I'm not answering that," Grace sighed, reaching for her bike.

"Wait one moment." Bea dashed back indoors and returned with the satchel of forbidden leaflets. She pressed it into her hand. "Who are we to deny islanders hope?"

Grace swung her leg over her bike, sighing heavily.

"I don't know why you put up with me," Bea said, a slow smile spreading over her face.

"Nor do I. You're a bloody caution." She grinned, poking her in the ribs.

"But you still love me, right, Gracie?"

"Always."

Fortunately the rest of the afternoon passed in a more peaceful way. The library always had a calming effect on Grace as she lost herself in the soothing rituals of shelving and cataloging. All the petty restrictions, the fear, hunger, suspicion and anger seemed to melt away within this majestic wood-paneled ode to books.

While she had been gone, another box had been left on the library steps. It was extraordinary. Before he had been deported, Ash had put an appeal for book donations in the *Evening Post*. Since then, barely a week had passed without a box of books being delivered by grateful islanders. In 1940 it had been a trickle, but by late 1943 it was a veritable deluge. It seemed no one was more grateful for the spiritual food store of the public library than Grace's patrons.

She undid the string binding from the box and inhaled the mildewy smell of old books, which had been heaved from attics and shelves across the island.

"*A donation, with literary love.*" Grace smiled as she read the card out loud. What treasures. A P. G. Wodehouse, a Vita Sackville-West, a Georgette Heyer, *The Masqueraders* and Jack London's *The Call of the Wild.*

These would fly off the shelves. Fiction was a rare gift. Most of the donations were nonfiction. From *Birds' Eggs of the British Isles* to *Pot Pourri from a Surrey Garden*. At first, these had been largely untouched, but as islanders exhausted her stock of fiction, even *Pot Pourri from a Surrey Garden* held a certain kind of escapist appeal.

Underneath *The Code of the Woosters* lurked an intriguing title.

"*Is Sex Necessary?* by James Thurber and E. B. White," she read out loud. A quick flick through the Penguin title quickly revealed it to be a satirical look at the intimacy between man and woman. Often, Grace had to use her judgment on whether the book was likely to be uncongenial to the regime. She decided quickly that this one would. From her brief exchanges with the commandant, she could see that he and satire weren't well acquainted. And as for *The Call of the Wild*, you didn't need to be a librarian to know that one had made it into the Nazi bonfires.

Grace hated having to censor her own stock, but rather she did it than a heavy-handed Nazi.

"Watch the desk, would you please, Miss Piquet," she called to her library assistant. Grace took the stairs to the galleried Reading Room and checking no one was looking she moved aside a beautifully illustrated tome on birds of the Channel Islands in the Nature section, to reveal the small locked cupboard behind. Deftly she unlocked the cupboard and slid in the Penguin paperback and *The Call of the Wild* with *the others.*

"Sorry. You can come out after the war," she whispered. Grace paused, breathing in the alkaline tang of books, savoring the feeling of safety in her sanctuary.

It struck Grace that all these banned books inside the dome were like thoughts floating around inside a forehead, which made the library a brain. The gentle, questioning, curious brain of the island, entreating all to tread the granite steps in search of knowledge. How satisfying that was!

On the lower half of the library Miss Piquet was up on a ladder busy shelving.

"How many books have we issued today, Miss P?"

"I think the question, my love, is what *haven't* we issued?"

Grace and Miss P worked back to back at the round central table, issuing books and discharging them back in on return. "The nerve center of the island's literary life," Ash used to joke.

The library was on the first and second floors of a States of Jersey public building, next door to the Royal Courts. It was one of the oldest libraries in Britain and it was breathtaking.

Grace's desk was underneath an enormous glass-domed roof with dazzling stained-glass windowpanes, through which fractured light poured down, like thousands of dancing yellow and blue diamonds. To her left and right ran the east and west wings, lined with 8-foot-high, graceful wooden stacks. Science, philosophy, religion and art to her left, fiction to her right. At the end of each wing sat two plush red leather chairs where a book lover could sink into the stacks and escape into the pages.

"Do you know?" Miss Piquet remarked, "I think every historical fiction author we stock is out on loan."

"People seeking reassurance from the past, I suppose," Grace ruminated. "You know, and so too this shall pass." She held up their donated Georgette Heyer and Agatha Christie. "There'll be a stampede when word gets out about these."

"I dare say." Miss Piquet yawned.

"Why don't you come down from that ladder before you slide down and go home?" Grace called. "It's been a long day."

"Thanks, Grace, I will," she said. "Oh, by the way, a charming gentleman came in earlier wanting to enroll."

"Could you not do it?"

"Oh no," said Miss Piquet, buttoning up her coat. "He was most insistent you be the one to do it. And he left something for you. It's over there on the counter."

Grace picked up the brown paper package containing a single slice of cake and a note.

More carrot than cake. But you're sweet enough. R x

"Was his name…?"

"Phillip Harris," they said at the same time. Miss P smiled and gave an almost girlish chuckle. "Delightful fellow."

"What sort of accent did he have?"

"Strange question." Miss Piquet thought. "Cut-glass home counties I'd have said. As English as bowler hats and bread and butter."

Grace looked down at the copy of Georgette Heyer's *The Masqueraders* and smiled at the irony. Was it her imagination or did the beautiful masked woman on the front wink at her?

"All right, Miss Heyer, don't be getting ideas now," she muttered.

First Lieutenant Daniel Patrick O'Sullivan, Red, Phillip Harris, or whatever name he went by, was clearly not a man scared to have found himself abandoned on a tiny island, stuffed full of the enemy.

After Miss Piquet left, she readied herself to lock up the library and deliver a few books on her way home. Grace delivered to the twelve parishes of the island, from the north with its dramatic rocky coves, to the gentle, sloping, fertile south. Roughly speaking, the island was a rectangle, 9 × 5 miles, with St. Helier, its only town, nestled on the eastern tip of the southern coast.

As the island librarian of the only library on the island, Grace was well known in all the parishes and she hoped never to betray the position of trust she was in. Grace had built a reputation of steadfastness and hard work, preferring books to dances, not that there were many of those to attend these days. She knew some younger women thought her dull, but what did she care? The library was her first love. It represented safety and security, a sense of order that the world outside its granite walls could never offer. No. Not once had she craved the recklessness of love. So why did her thoughts keep tugging back to the American?

The pale autumn sun was dipping over the rooftops by the time she'd delivered a Barbara Cartland to Mrs. Wilmslow who ran the hairdresser's, *Gone with the Wind* to Edna Channing at the cleaners and the new Georgette Heyer to Audrey, who sold lotions and potions from Roberts Dispensing Chemist on Bath Street. Each little nugget of joy was received with enormous appreciation, especially when the accompanying RAF leaflet was revealed tucked inside the dust jacket and its contents digested.

Her last stop took her to her father's friend, Albert Bedane, who ran a thriving physiotherapy practice from his imposing townhouse on Roseville Street.

She knocked softly. "Librarian calling." There was a stirring of the blackout blind then he ushered her in.

"Good evening, Grace. What a welcome sight you are." He massaged a stiff neck.

"Long day?"

He nodded. "Occupation aches and pains are many and varied."

"I bet. Hopefully this will help take your mind off things."

Albert had a penchant for Agatha Christie and had been on the waiting list for *Evil Under the Sun* for some time.

"You might want to pay close attention to the inside sleeve," she added casually, taking his library card and making a note of his loan.

"You're a veritable facilitator of joy, my dear."

"And I took the liberty of bringing two more." She pulled out a Dorothy L. Sayers, and a Denise Robbins. "One thriller, one romance. I wasn't sure which genre she favored."

He stared at her cagily and she chose her words delicately.

"Don't worry, Mr. Bedane. You can trust me. Dr. McKinstry came to see me in the library. He mentioned you have a houseguest and given that they may be here for a while, he felt they could use some reading material to while away their time."

She glanced at the small door which led down to the basement, feeling her pulse quicken.

Most of the island's Jewish population had fled when France had fallen to the Nazis and taken the opportunity to evacuate to England. *But not all.*

"Thank you, my dear," he said, visibly moved as he stroked the spines of the books. "What an incredibly thoughtful thing to do. I know how much these books will mean to my houseguest."

She nodded. "A chance to escape, if only for a few chapters."

Grace turned to leave but almost as an afterthought... "What makes you do it, Mr. Bedane? Take the risk, that is."

"I won't lie, Grace. The worry over who I'm helping keeps me awake at night." He shrugged. "But if I'm going to be killed I might as well be hanged for a sheep as a lamb."

Grace smiled, full of admiration for a man prepared to put his neck on the line to help the persecuted and opened the front door.

Outside a black Citroën swished past, showering them with a fine spray of water.

"The Wolf." Grace scowled.

"Not ideal having him live on one's doorstep," Mr. Bedane replied, wiping his trousers in irritation. "Beware of that Nazi, Grace. He's bad news."

"I had worked that out for myself," she replied.

"I'm serious. Grace. He's a shape-shifter, a chameleon, who'll do whatever it takes to impress his Nazi superiors. He's stumbled into a position of power and he's determined to use it." He grimaced. "You get on home now."

By the time Grace reached her village the rain had died off and the Milky Way stretched overhead like a chiffon scarf. A feeling she had never experienced before, like the fanning of a book's pages fluttered in her chest.

Red had never been her favorite color. It was the color which symbolized blood, danger, heat, anger, but also, undeniably, love.

Her hopes of seeing out this war quietly were fast slipping away. A man, especially a handsome, flamboyant, devil-may-care Yank, was a complication she could most certainly do without right now. Sometimes she wished she could just fold herself away in a library book and wait out the war. What a comforting thought that was, to nestle inside the historical fiction stacks, where she knew the ending to every single story.

5

Bea

"I hardly need tell you we are under close scrutiny. Feldkommandantur Colonel Oberst Knackfuss is breathing down my neck." It was dinnertime on a chilly Wednesday, the first in December, and a light snow was dusting the rooftops of St. Helier as Oscar Mourant, Acting Head Postmaster, gathered all the staff of Jersey General Post Office into the large sorting office at the Broad Street depot.

He eyed them all in turn, counter clerk to postie, the air so cold his breath pooled like smoke.

"Apparently there was a collision between a German truck and a civilian cyclist two days ago and the driver believes the bike had the Royal Mail Cipher on it."

Bea swallowed sharply, studying the brown-and-white-tiled wall intently.

"Any injuries to the Boche?" the most senior postman, Arthur, called out.

"The truck is a write-off, but the driver escaped injury."

"What a shame," Eric Hassell called out. "Have to try harder next time, lads."

A ripple of laughter ran through the sorting office.

"This is not funny," Mr. Mourant said sharply. "The commandant also warned me that every single piece of mail which is delivered to Victoria College House is carefully looked at to check it hasn't been interfered with. If anyone here is tampering with letters destined for German Field Command you aren't just risking your life, but that of your colleagues too."

At this, an uncomfortable silence draped the room. The staff at Jersey GPO were in the main an older and deeply patriotic bunch, many having already fought in the Great War. Bea looked round the room and felt a deep swell of pride and admiration. Arthur Blisset, the wise old owl of the group, had a wooden leg to match his Victoria Cross. Billy Matson, Nobby Clark, Eric Hassell and Harold "Peddler" Palmer, who'd been delivering island mail before Bea could walk, had been among the first men to sail over to Dunkirk to help in the rescue efforts. Then there was poor old Phil Warder, the Royal Mail engineer, who by rights shouldn't even be here. His wife Trix, a telegraphist, had evacuated to Bournemouth and he had stayed behind to cut the cables to France and been trapped here by the sudden invasion. He hadn't seen Trix and his three kiddies in over three years.

Then there was dear old Doris, Winnie and Gladys on the front desk who hadn't missed a day of work in over 20 years; game old birds who'd turned down the chance to evacuate to England so they could stay at their posts behind the post-office counter. They might have been a depleted, some might even say somewhat *creaky* group, but they were fiercely loyal.

Within just a few weeks of the occupation beginning, the following announcement had been made in the *Evening Post*:

LETTERS FROM JERSEY

Letters may now be sent from Jersey to countries allied to Germany, under German occupation, or friendly neutrals.

The De Havilland aircraft *The Gifford Bay*, which delivered all British mail to Jersey, had stopped coming. The mailboats vanished and the telegraph room at the top of the building had been sealed off by the Germans, compounding their sense of isolation. All communication with Britain was forbidden, save for Red Cross messages, so for the most part their days were spent delivering inter-island mail, but given that their fleet of twelve Morris 8 vans were now down to four, it took all day to collect mail from the fifteen rural sub-post offices and postboxes by bike.

"I know there has been a marked increase in the number of letters to the commandant in recent months, which is…" he pressed his lips together, "*regrettable*."

"Bloody traitors," Billy said and a murmur of agreement ran round the room.

"That's as may be, but it's not for the Post Office to take matters into its own hands. One day this war will be over and those who collaborate will be dealt with in the proper manner, but while you work for Jersey's Royal Mail you will behave in an exemplary fashion. Need I remind you the vans and bicycles we drive and the postboxes we collect from bear the Royal Cipher. We work for His Majesty, not the States of Jersey. A fact that miraculously seems to have not occurred to our occupiers. If they realize we serve the Crown, they could decide to shut us down tomorrow. We must be beyond reproach."

Bea felt a heavy blanket of despair fall over the sorting office. Mr. Mourant wasn't spelling it out—no one ever did—but it was largely known how informers' letters were dealt with by the Jersey Post Office. Their poisonous contents were either chucked on the boiler-room fire or the letter was steamed open and those who had been informed upon quietly warned. Bea felt her stomach twist. These pathetic epistles were gathering in pace. It used to be one every fortnight, now every day there seemed to be another one.

Empty bellies led to loose tongues spewing information for the food it might bring, or worse, to settle an old score. Bea simply could not countenance denouncing a neighbor, but the cold and ugly truth showed up every day on her sorting table.

"We are postal workers," Mr. Mourant declared, "not vigilantes. Back to work."

The group dispersed and shuffled back to the facing tables to sort the afternoon's mail.

"Not you, Bea. A moment of your time." Mr. Mourant summoned her to his office.

She followed, feeling her tongue dry up.

"I promise I've never tampered with any mail," she blurted as soon as his door closed.

"I believe you, Bea," he said wearily, removing his spectacles and rubbing his bloodshot eyes.

"But I do know the person that caused that accident by reckless cycling was you. I lied, told them one of our Royal Mail bicycles had been stolen. Fortunately they believed me as there's been a spate of bike thefts across the island this week, otherwise you'd be halfway to Germany by now."

Bea felt as if all the air had been sucked from her lungs.

"Thank you," she managed at last. "I'm so sorry, Mr. Mourant. I'll be more careful in future."

He stared at her, his kind eyes shot through with exhaustion.

"I was so proud to make you our island's first postwoman, Bea. Indeed my wife applauded me for it."

"Not quite the first, sir. Don't forget Jersey's first ever postman was in fact a woman, Mary Godfray in 1798…" She tailed off, aware that she was babbling with nerves.

"I'm aware of our history, Bea, and your own personal history too, my dear," he said softly. "I know you've been through a tremendous amount. Losing your father and fiancé is beyond my comprehension."

Bea felt grief corkscrew through her again.

"And that's why I am making allowances for you, but please, my dear, don't ever make me have to sit opposite that odious man again. Silvertide is not a place I wish to visit again in a hurry." He replaced his spectacles, signaling the end of the meeting.

Bea nodded. "Of course." She made to leave but stopped.

"Wait. Did you say Silvertide? Why didn't you go to Victoria College House, instead of the Secret Field Police?"

Victoria College House in St. Saviour was the headquarters of the Civil Affairs Unit, responsible for the military governing of the island. The German Secret Field Police was a different branch of the German Army, and a brush with them rarely ended well.

"For some reason they appear to be quite jiggered about this and that dreadful man, the Wolf, or whatever ridiculous name he goes by, seems to be keen to stamp down hard on *acts of sabotage* as he called it."

Fear began its slow crawl up her spine.

"He actually mentioned you by name, Bea. Asked whether you worked for the Post Office. Said he'd met you recently."

Bea blew out slowly.

"Please, my dear. Avoid that man like the plague."

"I will," she replied and she meant it.

Outside, Arthur was waiting for her. "This way," he ordered, grabbing her by the scruff of the neck. Out in the yard, Eric, Billy and Harold were waiting by the bike sheds with a cup of foul acorn coffee and an Island Gem cigarette.

"Drink, smoke," Billy ordered gruffly, pressing the hot cup into her hands.

"We weren't sure about having a girl delivering mail," Arthur said, striking the match against his wooden leg, and lighting the cigarette before handing it to her. "We never thought you'd manage to cycle up Pier Road without falling off."

"Or manage a round without stopping every two minutes to gossip," Harold added.

Bea thought back to when she'd started soon after the invasion. Of the disbelief at the sight of a woman delivering mail and the endless practical jokes they'd played on her.

"I remember you saying as much," she said drily, drawing nicotine deep into her lungs before blowing out two perfect blue smoke rings into the yard. "Was that before or after you had me on errands to fetch seagulls' milk and rubber mallets, you old sods?"

Harold chuckled, his old face creasing into a network of lines.

"Or the time you tied kippers to my exhaust until the smell drove me round the bend?"

"Very peculiar thing that," Arthur laughed, his voice softening. "But you proved us wrong, girlie. You're a grafter, my love. Just like your old man. In fact, you're like a daughter to us now."

They sat in silence, smoking and drinking bitter coffee. A line of seagulls sat lined up on the handlebars of their postal bikes, eyeing them beadily. Skeins of smoke drifted over the frozen yard and Bea shivered. How was it December already? The prospect of yet another icy winter under the jackboot deflated her mood further. Hundreds more islanders would die this winter from a lack of warmth, food and medicine, forgotten victims of the war, while the authorities slurped brandy by roaring log fires. The simmering, toxic rage resurfaced, squeezing through the cracks, blooming like gas.

"Don't be getting yourself tangled up in trouble," Arthur warned. "Leave the poison-pen letters to us. We've got used to your face in the sorting office, and we've decided we rather like it."

"I've already lost my local priest over there." He made the sign of the cross over his chest. "Please God keep Canon Cohu safe and bring him home to his flock. I ain't losing you an' all."

He squeezed her arm and turned to go back inside.

"Come on, it's cold enough out here to freeze the balls off a brass monkey. Back to the coal face."

The warning was implicit. Leave the dangerous stuff to the men. Something clicked inside Bea and the memories tumbled in. Jimmy and his dirty blond hair covered in sand, his slow smile, the gentle rumble of his voice and his warm breath as he covered her in salty kisses.

Bea twisted the tin ring around her finger and looked at the stain it had left on her flesh. She would never again know the feeling of being held in his arms or imagine the kind of life they could have carved out for themselves had they made it to England. She was blistered with grief, but instead of dragging her into a dark morass it punched inside her chest like a jack-in-the-box, needing a release.

Overhead gulls wheeled, their mournful cries filling the air and silent tears slid down her cheeks, her chest shuddering as the exact moment Jimmy's body had splayed back onto the rocks replayed again in her mind.

She touched her tummy. Her insides felt like they'd been scoured with carbolic acid and quite suddenly she retched. These episodes came upon her sometimes so sharply the light seemed to fade and she felt close to passing out.

Arthur had been waiting for her at the doorway and without a word passed her his handkerchief. She was grateful to him for not making a fuss.

The next hour passed in a blur of banter as letters were date-stamped and filed away by street into the thin slots of her sorting frame, so that they could be organized into the correct sequence for her postal round. The names and streets of her 552 delivery addresses passed swiftly beneath her fingers. She might have passed over it altogether had it not been for the name. *Silvertide.* Such a pretty name, conjuring images of shoals of fish flitting through azure waters.

It was in her pocket before her logical brain caught up.

"Here, Bea, what comes after S?" Arthur called.

Bea rolled her eyes. It was the same routine, the same old joke day in, day out. Actually she found the inevitability of it quite comforting.

"T?" she replied.

"Oh, go on then, my love." Arthur winked.

"As you're offering," Billy said, "that'd be smashing. Me stomach thinks me throat's been cut. We just got time before afternoon delivery."

"Silly old buggers," she laughed, flicking an elastic band at Eric.

In the tiny kitchen along the corridor she waited for the kettle to boil and felt the envelope burning a hole in her pocket. She glanced up the corridor, before shutting the door and pulling out the letter.

"Please forgive me for this," she murmured, holding it in the cloud of steam. If this was a genuine letter without malice, she would never do it again.

The edges wrinkled and the seal released. Heart hammering, she eased it open and unfolded it.

Sir.

I have good reason to know that Mrs. Eileen Dark of Rose Cottage, Havre des Pas, hears the English news very often in the morning at 8 a.m. Watch where she goes.

Yours helpfully.

Mrs. Richards

Bea felt a stab of fury as she carefully folded the letter and replaced it in the envelope. Mrs. Richards had always been a tittle-tattle. Living on a small island did that to you, but this—this was a simply unforgivable thing to do. She lived two doors up from them in Havre des Pas, quite often availed herself of her mother's hospitality in fact. She had to warn Eileen. The fact that it was signed would earn Mrs. Richards 100 Reichsmarks. The fact that it was actually addressed to "Silvertide," the notorious secret police, was reprehensible. No one on the island could claim they didn't know the ramifications of that.

Bea pedaled on her town rounds, stopping for a chat, exchanging goods with her friend Audrey at the pharmacy, an old comb for some more toothpaste, painfully aware of the contents of the incendiary letter she was carrying.

Her heart thumped as she bumped past the scrawl of barbed wire and the soldier at the sentry point that marked the entrance to the seaside military zone. This neighborhood had once been so magical. Before the war it had been the center of tourism, a bustling area full of hotels, which in the summer season lit up along the front with strings of fairy lights.

Bea's home, Bay View Guest House, was sandwiched smack bang in the middle of this seething rat's nest of Germans. You couldn't escape them in Havre des Pas. All strands of the German hierarchy, from your average soldier to blond upper-class Luftwaffe officers to the Secret Field Police were based in their small bay.

But even here in this snakepit nothing was quite as it seemed. The old aquarium, bought before the war by a charming Scotsman, had quickly been turned into an old junk yard to prevent the Germans requisitioning it, and Bea knew fine well, canny Mr. Harris had hidden at least two automobiles in its oily depths. Behind the Wehrmacht barracks at the end of the bay was her mum's little allotment, where alongside tomatoes and beans, she hid at least two crystal wireless sets and black-market tobacco. Now it seemed the locals weren't as they seemed either.

Bea paused outside Mrs. Richards's house and fought the urge to spit on the ground. How could she? Especially as she had a husband away fighting with the British. In the small front yard her son sat playing with a brand-new wooden train.

"Bit cold to be outside, sweetie," she called.

He looked up, little face puckered from the wind. "Mum's with her friend, I'm to stay outside."

"Where did you get that?" she asked casually.

"Mum's friend give it me."

"Did she? That's nice."

"He. Mum's friend is a soldier," he said proudly.

Softly she knocked next door, Rose Cottage, shaking her head.

"Oh hello, my love," said Eileen, smiling as she wiped her hands on a tea towel. "You needn't have troubled yourself to knock. Could've just popped the letter through the door."

"I don't have any mail today." Eileen looked confused and Bea lowered her voice.

"But I do have a message. You've got twenty-four hours to get rid of your wireless."

Eileen's face blanched. "B-but I don't have a wireless, my love."

Bea touched her gently on the arm. "I come as a friend, Eileen. Get rid of it. You'll be searched the day after tomorrow. Make sure your house is in order."

She turned and walked back up the path before Eileen could ask her any more questions. Poor Eileen. She might as well have just slung a hand grenade in her corridor. Bea could picture her still standing there open-mouthed with her tea towel slung over her shoulder, working out whether to believe her. Well, she'd delivered the message, now she had to hope Eileen did as instructed. As Bea cycled off her heart was rattling against her ribs. Fear—or was it excitement?—burned in her chest.

Tomorrow morning she would date-stamp the letter and then it would be posted to Silvertide. Eileen would suffer the indignity and fear of a search by Wolf's men, but if Eileen heeded her warning she would avoid a spell in prison, her children would have their mother at home.

Bea pedaled up the seafront, her back that bit straighter.

"Fuck you, Nazis," she murmured as she pedaled past Silvertide, the HQ of the so-called "Gestapo," lifting her fingers off the bike handle and forming them briefly into a V for victory. Her triumph bubbled over and she bottled her glee, tasting it in her mouth, like sweet wine to be savored all evening.

She pedaled back into town past a small park where a German band was gathered in the bandstand for one of their endless parades and concerts. The conductor had finished and was packing his baton away.

"*Eins! Zwei! Drei!*" she yelled. All at once, the soldiers began to sing again. Bea laughed out loud and cycled faster. It was amazing the difference tiny acts could make.

With her afternoon round finished, she decided to drop in on Grace at the library. Bea turned the corner into Bath Street and was about to draw level with Boots the Chemist when something she saw brought her up short. Instinctively she drew back into the shelter of a doorway.

Her younger sister Nancy and two friends were leaving. They'd changed out of their shop-assistant uniforms and were dolled-up in their best frocks and fancy hats. It was a sad sight really. They were as skinny as the rest of the population but had rouged over their rough edges with black-market cosmetics.

Bea's stomach turned as three immaculately dressed Luftwaffe pilots swaggered up Bath Street, clearly tight.

"Heinz," Nancy said, draping herself against one of the men's chests. The immaculate uniform did little to disguise the fact that he was short and broad, reminding Bea of a toad.

The toad leaned over and whispered something in her ear which was clearly hilarious as she laughed uproariously.

"Oh, please," Bea murmured. After the pathetic court-ship ritual was over the girls and their dates strode back up Bath Street, arm in arm. She was 17, for goodness sake. Would she really give up her virginity for extra rations?

Bea ran her fingers through her hair, full of despair and shame. What was the point in helping to thwart the enemy if her sister was lying down with one? Their good family name would be stained by this. When the war was over and the day of reckoning came for those who had collaborated, would she and her mother be tarnished with the same brush?

She reached into her postal sack for a piece of chalk. Checking no one was about she hastily scrawled on the Boots slate sandwich noticeboard outside the pharmacy.

BOOTS FOR BAGS

Was it childish? Undoubtedly. Was it satisfying? Immensely.

"Well, that's not very friendly, especially as one of those bags is your own sister."

Bea froze, then turned round to face Heinz Carl Wölfle. That damn man must have felt on the soles of his shoes because he had appeared out of nowhere and was leaning against the wall of the butcher's opposite. Had he been following her?

"You know, Miss Gold, we really must stop meeting like this."

She said nothing, just tapped her tongue against her teeth, frantically trying to gather her cool. Last time she had acted dumb, not a ploy that would work this time.

"You owe your sister an apology."

"How do you know she's my sister?" Bea replied.

"I've been doing my homework on you since we last met. You are not quite the innocent you had me believe last time." He wagged his finger. "Rumor had it your fiancé was killed for breaking the law."

"*Your* law. Not ours."

At this the Wolf smiled, slow and dangerous. He stepped closer to her, so close she could see his gold tooth and the web of broken veins that spoke of a fondness for spirits.

"You should take a leaf out of your sister's book and make friends with the Third Reich because we are here to stay," he said softly. "These islands will be the blueprint for the model occupation. Your sister's children will one day speak German as their first language, they will be proud to be the master race and it all happened here first, before England."

He reached over and teased a curl of her dark hair between his stubby fingers and Bea realized she was holding her breath.

"Quite a coup for the Channel Islands, wouldn't you say?"

"Last I heard your attempt to bomb Britain into submission didn't go according to plan. So forgive me if I hold off on the German lessons."

His smile stretched further, but his eyes were cold, full of the sort of feral intelligence that made her realize this man was ruthlessly ambitious.

"Aah, now we get to the real Beatrice Gold. But you know, I still like you. I find your spirit challenging. But we still have this little matter to clear up."

He pointed to the defaced sign.

"You will write to your sister and the Luftwaffe officers to apologize and pay a fine, and no more shall be said on the matter. Or... or I could make it all go away."

He touched the top button of her blouse.

"We could be good friends you and I, Miss Gold. You intrigue me."

She stared at his oddly feminine, fleshy lips, his soft, lumpy body clad in a pair of ridiculous plus fours, and felt her stomach heave as she imagined him naked.

"That's funny because actually you repulse me." She gave him an acid smile. "I wouldn't be your Jerrybag even if your bollocks were dripping in diamonds."

He stepped back.

"Very well, then you must be prepared to face the punishment. You will hear from me."

Bea cycled home, furious tears pricking her eyes. How would she break this to her mum? A fine was the very last thing they could afford, especially as another winter of hardship was upon them.

As she rounded the harbor and took the narrow road to Havre des Pas, Bea felt her heart twist at the sight of all the higgledy-piggledy cottages which hugged the bay. All packed together like wheat in a field. All with their own secrets.

A light snow began to fall, dancing in flurries from the sky, whitewashing the bay and settling on the steel helmet of the German soldier huddled in his sentry box.

Every day this occupation injected more poison into their once-tight community. It seeped through the cobbled streets and country roads, invisible and malign as a cancer. It was up to her to act as the antidote.

She spotted the bailiff, alighting from his well-polished motor car as it slid up outside the Soldatenheim. The man who'd advised them not to evacuate, promised them equal sacrifice. It certainly didn't feel that way from where she was standing, out in the cold.

Bea headed for home, pausing only briefly to trace a V through the snow settling on the bailiff's car window. This island was simmering with dirty secrets that would haunt them all for a long time to come. She would be the one to let them loose. Her thoughts spiraled like the ever thickening snow. The problem was, she couldn't do it alone.

6

Grace

BANNED BOOK

All Quiet on the Western Front, *by Erich Maria Remarque.*
Banned in Germany because of its depictions of German
military experience in World War I. All works consigned to
Nazi bonfires.

Winter came to the island gently as a rule. Not in 1943. As if jumping to a German decree, it came on a stiff northerly, a mad hooting wind that rattled shutters and froze islanders to their core.

By Christmas Eve the town was crowded with shoppers trying to put on a brave face while battling their fourth Christmas under occupation. Grace thanked God she wasn't a mother as she watched women scour the shops in vain for anything to fill Christmas stockings and put in the pot.

"Hello, Grace love, what can I do you for?" asked Molly.

Grace surveyed the sorry collection on her barrow. There was nothing on offer but a few tired looking chrysanthemums.

"Let's have a bunch of those please, Molly. Did you enjoy *Gone with the Wind*?"

"Ooh, I should say, it was right in my lane. Do you know, when I've got my nose in a good book I can almost forget I haven't seen my husband in over three years." She put her hands on her hip, a sure sign she was in for a good jaw. "Do you know, the characters felt so real I thought they might leap off the page and start walking round my house!"

She screeched with laughter.

"Always a sign a book's got under your skin," Grace chuckled.

"The laugh of it is, Grace, I never read so much as a bleedin' word before this war. My George didn't like it, but now I can't get my nose out of a book. You must think me ever so peculiar."

"Not at all, Molly. You'd be amazed how many of my most enthusiastic patrons never set foot in the library before the war, and now are avid bookworms."

"Stands to reason, I s'pose. Not much else to do in the blackout hours."

"True. Let's just hope you all keep it up when peace returns."

"Did you hear Jerry's extended curfew? We're allowed out until 1 a.m. New Year's Eve. How about that?" Molly's voice was bright as she wrapped up the flowers.

"Not that I'll be up to much. So bleedin' cold with no coal I had to resort to wearing my nan's knickers last night. Just as well Rhett Butler ain't in my bedroom," she hooted. "This'll be our last occupation Christmas, you mark my words." She lowered her voice. "The tide is turning."

"Let's hope so, Molly."

"Well, I hope whoever receives these enjoys them," Molly remarked, handing her the flowers.

"Actually, I'm going to lay them on the beach for Jimmy. It'll be our first Christmas without him." Her voice cracked and to Grace's mortification she realized her eyes were wet.

"Oh, my love, I'm sorry. Here, on the house." She pressed the bright blooms into Grace's hand. She stumbled away, murmuring her thanks. It was only when she glanced down did she notice that Molly had arranged the newspaper the flowers were wrapped in into the shape of a V for victory.

Grace had hoped to get away from the market, but librarians are like teachers, known by all. The hand was light on her shoulder.

"Dr. McKinstry."

Dr. Noel McKinstry, Jersey's Medical Officer of Health, had a strong Irish accent and a quick wit. A veteran of the Royal Navy, he was held in high regard by islanders for his heroic care and resourcefulness.

After the invasion he had sourced crutches and bandages. Goodness knows how but he'd arranged free inoculation for children for outbreaks of diphtheria after obtaining vaccines from France.

Rumor had it he passed intelligence to the British through transmitters hidden in the basement of an isolation hospital at Les Vaux. But it was only rumor, Grace reminded herself. This occupation made the truth as slippery as kisses in the rain.

"Grace, my dear, season's greetings. I was waiting for Molly to finish warming your ear." He steered her to a quiet side street. "Albert's houseguest has asked me to pass on her gratitude for the books you were able to loan her."

"I can drop round more books if you think she'd like it."

"It won't leave you in a fix? She doesn't have a library card at present."

Grace shook her head. "The authorities don't check my list of patrons, but should they, I'll just tell them that library books regularly go missing."

"I wish everyone had your conscience and humanity."

"It's nothing," she said, looking down at the pathetic bunch of flowers.

The doctor looked exhausted, scrubbing his face with his hands.

"Tough night?" she asked and he nodded.

"This diphtheria and TB outbreak is out of control. We lost another child last night."

"Oh no. Anyone I know?"

"Little Dolly Moisan up at St. Peter's."

Grace gasped and her hand flew to her mouth. "She was one of my regular patrons."

"Oh, Grace, I'm sorry to break that news."

"Her mother must be devastated."

"There were no words I could offer to comfort her," the doctor agreed. "We just don't have the medicine. It's a travesty. In peacetime I could have cured her."

They stood alone, Grace's thoughts cartwheeling.

"I wish I could help more," she blurted.

He smiled wearily. "But you are, my dear. Books are medicine."

"Here," she said, thrusting the flowers at him in impulse. "Would you pass these on to Mr. Bedane's houseguest? I dare say she'd rather have food, fresh air, or better yet, freedom, but in the absence of any of those, perhaps these will cheer her."

Dr. McKinstry gazed at her, his face doughy with exhaustion.

"You're a good woman, Grace. If ever I can help you, you know where to find me."

Grace headed back to the library, the doctor's words spiraling through her mind.

To her surprise, Bea was sitting on the library steps blowing perfect smoke rings up to the sky.

"The library closed? I thought hell would freeze over before that happened!"

"Ha. I gave my assistant the day off and I just nipped out on an errand," Grace replied. "Besides, you can talk. Sitting here won't get the Christmas post delivered."

Bea leapt to her feet and hugged her tightly. Her best friend smelled of ersatz tobacco and the peculiar smell of the postal room.

"What's that for?" Grace laughed, untangling herself and unlocking the library.

"Have I ever told you how much I love you, Grace La Mottée?"

Grace arched one eyebrow.

"Come on in and tell me what it is you're after."

Grace lifted the library counter and started sorting through the books for her delivery round.

"Grace, I know you're on your rounds this afternoon. Will you be anywhere near Trinity?"

"Yes, it's on my round."

Bea breathed out. "Oh thank goodness."

She lifted the library counter and joined Grace on the other side.

"Whatever's wrong?"

"Will you please pass on a message to Mrs. Noble at Trinity Hill?"

"As it happens, I'm delivering her a copy of *A Christmas Carol* so she can read it to her grandson. I'm not sure if you heard, but her daughter's been jailed and she's been left to look after the grandson *and* run the farm."

"I know and trust me, if you don't deliver this message, her life's about to get a whole lot worse."

"What's wrong?"

Bea pulled out a letter from her postal bag and slid it over the counter.

It was an envelope addressed to *The Gestapo. Silvertide. Havre des Pas.*

"Bea," Grace said warily, "why isn't this envelope date-stamped? You are going to deliver it, aren't you?"

"I will, in good time, but first read it," Bea urged.

Grace's hands shook as she slid open the envelope.

Mrs. Noble has a pig in the soot house in her garden and a wireless under her floorboards. <u>Search and you'll see!</u> Why should she get away with it???

"Isn't it disgusting," Bea exploded. "What kind of depraved person denounces their neighbor for this?"

"Keep your voice down," Grace hissed, glancing about. Fortunately no one had followed them into the library.

"Sorry, but really, Grace. Can you believe it?"

Grace's thoughts were in freefall as she stuffed the letter back in the envelope and thrust it back at Bea as if it were a hand grenade.

"Bea, how long have you been doing this?" she asked quietly.

"This is the first one."

"I can tell when you're lying."

"Very well, two, maybe three now. But I don't regret it." She rested her chapped hands on the counter top. "If I don't warn these people, what do you think would happen if they're discovered?"

"I know that, but it's so dangerous. Need I remind you, you were fined twenty Reichsmarks last week for insulting a member of the Feldpolizei and your own sister?"

"Don't talk to me about that Jerrybag cow. Least she's been sacked from Boots now. And as for the bloody Nazi, how will he ever find out? He's a dimwit in an alpine hat." She picked at a loose flap of skin by her thumb.

"I think you're underestimating him, Bea." Hadn't she said exactly the same to Red? It struck her then how alike he and Bea were.

"No, trust me, that man's so slow it's hard to believe he beat 100,000 other sperm."

Bea grinned at her own joke.

"Look. In two days' time this letter will arrive on his desk, and he'll dispatch his henchmen to Mrs. Noble. If you let her know in advance, then they won't find anything to pin on her."

Grace shook her head.

"Please, Grace. I'd do it myself, you know I would, but it'll take me an age to get up there and my boss is already watching me like a hawk."

Grace stared round her calm and ordered library. All the spines of the books were lined up like a jury, all those authors looking down at her, wondering which direction her story would take. Agatha Christie seemed to be urging her into danger. Jane Austen looked down, coolly advising caution. Grace had the queerest feeling that the rest of her life would unravel from the choice she made at this precise moment.

"But I'm a librarian," she said lamely.

"Exactly. Who'll suspect you? You know, it's perfect the more I think about it. This letter's not been signed. In fact, the majority of them aren't. Spineless cowards."

"The majority?" she spluttered. "I thought you said it was three."

"Never mind that. You've worked in the library for years," Bea persisted, her eyes feverish with excitement. "You've looked at the handwriting of everyone who has ever filled in a library card. You can compare it against their hand-writing. Together we can work out who these denouncers are."

"But then I'll be like a Nazi myself," Grace protested, "deciding who has to be punished, judging my patrons. It's one thing to warn others. That is quite another thing."

"But it's wrong, Grace. Why do they get away with it while my father and Jimmy are dead?"

Grace shook her head in disbelief, stunned at the direction the afternoon was taking.

"Let me put it to you in a language you'll understand," Bea pleaded. "Throughout history, the post office and the library have been intertwined."

Grace raised an eyebrow. "How so?"

"A Jersey postal surveyor came up with the idea for trialing the first postbox in the British Isles in 1854, did he not?" Bea said.

"So?"

"So that man was Anthony Trollope, who later became a famous novelist."

"I'm aware of that. We stock him in the library. What's your point?"

"My point is that letters and literature depend on one another. We are both tasked with getting knowledge into people's hands, keeping the written word flowing."

Grace's brain was aching.

"You'd happily loan Mrs. Noble a book, so why not deliver a warning? You yourself told me your job is to dispense trustworthy information."

Grace rubbed the library counter as she thought.

"Think of that poor boy, Grace! First his mother *and* then his grandmother in a Nazi prison because of a poison-pen letter!" Bea urged.

"Oh, very well. I'll let Mrs. Noble know, but I draw the line at rooting out denouncers."

Bea flung her arms around Grace.

"You're a wonderful woman, Grace La Mottée. You could be saving that woman's life." Her eyes shone in triumph. "I better get back to my round." She slung her postal bag over her shoulder and headed for the door. "History will judge us by our actions today."

The door banged shut behind her and Grace felt like her legs might go from under her.

"Yes and what on earth will they say?" she whispered.

Her head was spinning at the speed with which Bea had somehow drawn her into this web of subterfuge. She didn't buy that the Wolf was a nincompoop.

How could Bea be so reckless as to open the German authorities' mail? But in truth, she knew how, because this was who Bea was. That swagger which in peacetime might have found an outlet in mischief, had, in wartime, given her a cause. Bea could no sooner turn her back on injustice than not draw breath.

"What's a poison-pen letter? Is it a new German invention?"

Grace jumped and clutched her chest. The voice belonged to Peter Topsy, a local lad.

He peeked behind the science stacks, his wide blue eyes unblinking.

"P-Peter, what are you doing here?" she gibbered. "I thought the library was empty. Did you sleep in the Reading Room again last night?"

She grabbed his arm and fought the urge to shake him. "You can't, you mustn't keep sneaking in here to sleep."

Almost immediately his hands started to flutter compulsively by his side. "Sorry, Miss La Mottée. Sorry…sorry."

Grace tried to take a long steadying breath.

"I'm sorry. I'm not cross with you. You startled me is all. How long have you been listening?"

"Wehrmacht strength believed to now be at 11,000, 12,000 cubic tons of concrete fortification, 300 pound shells with a maze of wires and a…" He started up his usual forensic listing of German fortifications and weaponry in his strange monosyllabic voice.

"Please, Peter. You must stop. You must stop spying on the Germans."

She crouched down and tried to meet his gaze. "I know you find it interesting but they will not like it. They'll put you in prison if they discover it." He said nothing, just stared into the middle distance, his hands doing their strange rhythmic dance.

Peter was widely regarded as a being a halfwit, but Grace knew he was a long way from that. In her opinion, he was bordering on genius. Peter had gifts she couldn't even fathom. He could look at a fortified beach or a street scene and half an hour later recreate it in a pencil drawing down to the minutest detail. His intricate drawings of the library stacks were so lifelike they could be photographs. Unfortunately, he lacked any social skills, which meant that most on the island saw him a simpleton, including his own mother.

Grace wasn't sure of his real age. She guessed he was around 13 or 14 and had been coming to the library since he could walk. It was, Grace had long ago realized in sadness, the only place where he found acceptance and safety from the bullies. Lately, though, since his mother had taken up with a German, he had started hiding under tables in the Reading Room and sleeping there overnight.

"Tell you what. I have to go on my rounds, but once I've closed up, if you like you could stay here for a few hours

and do some repairs on some books we've had donated."
One of Peter's other gifts so it transpired was his meticulous ability to repair old and damaged books, carefully stitching the spines, removing stains and breathing new life into them.

He nodded.

"Good. Yes, that's good." She breathed out to steady her heart rate. He hadn't heard anything and even if he had, she doubted anyone would listen to anything he had to say.

"You stay here then." *Where you're safe, away from prying eyes. Away from people who will judge you.*

Grace pedaled out of the Royal Square, her satchel laden with her books. Buried at the bottom, hidden under newspaper, were the *verboten* ones. An Ernest Hemingway, Aldous Huxley and Walt Whitman. Precious forbidden cargo. She delivered a copy of *The Secret Garden* to Albert Bedane's Jewish "houseguest" before swinging west and past People's Park.

Finally, exhausted, she knocked on the farmhouse door of Mrs. Noble. She came round the side, carrying a plate and cup.

She jumped, startled.

"Grace, my love, you gave me a fright." She stared down at the plate. "I was just…um…Do you want a cup of tea?"

"Why not," Grace replied, puzzled at her behavior.

Grace ducked her head under the low door of the whitewashed cottage and followed her up a low-beamed corridor and into a smoky kitchen. Her grandson Tommy was making paper chains out of old copies of the *Evening Post* at the scrubbed kitchen table.

Mrs. Noble poured them both two mugs of carrot tea from an old chipped pot before sitting down with a groan.

"By crie, this Christmas'll be a strange one," she sighed, blowing the steam of her mug. "But at least we will have *A Christmas Carol* to read to while away the hours. You did bring it, didn't you?"

"Oh yes," Grace assured her.

"Smashing. I'll fetch my library card once I've drunk this." She stroked the book like it were a cat, a nostalgic smile crinkling her face. "My Enid used to love me reading this to her at Christmas. It's a family tradition now. It's a bloody crying shame she's not here this year to read it to her own son." The elderly woman broke off and made a heroic effort to compose herself.

"I'm sorry. Only we miss her so much, don't we, Tommy?"

"Nothing to apologize for, Mrs. Noble. I heard she ran into some trouble."

She laughed caustically. "You could say that. Chucked a bucket of horse shit over some German troops as they marched past the farm, the little minx. She's a hot head that one."

"She'll be home in three months, will she?" Grace asked, sipping her tea.

"I wish," she snorted. "She got three months at the original trial. We couldn't believe it, so appealed against the sentence and would you believe it, it's been doubled. She won't be home until June."

Grace's mouth dropped open. "That's—"

"Vindictive, I know. Jerry's getting worse, more paranoid." Mrs. Noble drummed a fist on the tabletop. "It's because they're losing and they know it."

Grace hated herself for the chaos she was about to unleash.

"Tommy," Grace said, "why don't you go and play outside for a bit? I need to talk to your grandmother."

Mrs. Noble raised an eyebrow. "What's wrong? Is it because I dropped the last book back late? I'll pay the fine, only…"

"No," Grace interrupted. "It's not that, I wouldn't dream of fining you."

She waited until the boy was well out of earshot.

"Someone's denounced you, Mrs. Noble. The day after tomorrow, you'll have a visit from the Secret Field Police."

Mrs. Noble's face emptied of color. "Wh-what? How can you possibly know that, Grace?"

Grace closed her eyes. "I wish I could tell you, but I can't, but please trust me. If you have a pig in your soot house, or a wireless under your floorboards, then you must get rid of them immediately. You have twenty-four hours to make yourself purer than the driven snow."

Mrs. Noble rose sharply to her feet, the chair skidding from under her and crashing to the floor.

"Sweet Jesus!"

"Calm down, you've a small window of time, but you must be thorough and pack away all your valuables and breakables; from what I've heard they leave no stone unturned."

Mrs. Noble nodded, regaining her composure.

"The thing is, Grace, it's not that straightforward."

"Can't you slaughter the pig and hide it?"

"I do have something in my soot house, but it's not a pig."

She walked outside and a minute or so later the kitchen door opened and a blast of cold air breezed in.

"We gotta stop meeting like this."

"Red!"

He smiled at her, all twinkling green eyes and easy swagger.

"Angel Grace! Boy, are you a sight for sore eyes. Sure as hell beats sitting in a soot house at Christmas. No offense, Mrs. N."

"You two know each other?" she exclaimed, looking from one to the other.

"It's a long story," Grace replied.

"So what are we to do with the lad?" Mrs. Noble exclaimed. "If they're as thorough as you say they are, he can't be here. I only agreed to have him here until New Year's Day."

Grace racked her brains. She could cycle back into town and track down Dr. McKinstry and get him to locate another hiding place, but that was precious time they could ill afford. The words were out of her mouth before she could stop them.

"You could come back into town with me and hide at the library? It's closed until New Year's Eve. It's a huge risk you going into town, though."

"From where I'm standing, I don't have a whole bunch of other options. I'll go fetch my things."

"Well, you're a dark horse," said Mrs. Noble, when he left.

"I could say the same about you," Grace retorted.

"Good to know there are some decent people on this island," Mrs. Noble replied, her face darkening. "And to think, I must know my denouncer, and they know my daughter's in jail."

She reached for Tommy when he walked back into the kitchen.

"Those Boche bastards might have robbed my grandson of his mother, but they sure as hell won't steal his nan. Thank you, Grace." She shook her head. "And here's me thinking you were just a librarian."

Red returned, hugged Mrs. Noble and then little Tommy.

"No such thing as just a librarian, heh, Grace?" He looked at her over Tommy's head and smiled in a way that seemed to reach a part of Grace's heart that had been sealed off since her brother's death.

"Thank you, Mrs. N. You're a wonderful woman. I'll miss you." He winked. "And your delicious cooking."

The usually reserved country woman flushed and came over all twittery.

"Anything to help out an American, especially as your lot are helping us take it to the enemy. Take my daughter's bike to get yourself into town. And stay safe, my love."

As they bade their farewells Grace was beginning to see *the Red Effect.*

"Stay close and keep your eyes on me," she ordered.

"Oh, I'll always keep my eyes on you." He hoisted a rucksack over his broad shoulders and pushed back a lock of his hair from his face. Mrs. Noble had clearly been looking after him well. Drifts of woody cologne filled the soft country air between them and his newly dyed hair shone.

"Does nothing ever fluster you?" she asked.

"Sure it does. But right now, I just need to keep a cool head and survive." He tugged the edge of his cap and grinned. "Take me to the library!"

They cycled the longer, quieter route back into town, past ancient whitewashed country cottages slumbering in valleys, woodsmoke curling from their chimneys.

The sinking sun painted the island's broad, sweeping fields in a wash of gold.

"It's so pretty in Jersey," Red called.

"It was," she replied, "until the Germans arrived and desecrated our countryside and beaches." She gestured to the left. On one side of an ancient wildflower meadow rose a truly horrendous sight. Nine-foot posts rose from the ground around the perimeter of the field, and in the middle, suspended from a wheel spoke of wires was an enormous 300-pound spider bomb, ready to snare any unsuspecting parachutist.

He whistled under his breath as they cycled slowly past. "Sure glad we didn't crash-land in that."

"A question that's been puzzling me," she called over her shoulder.

"Shoot."

"How did you fool Miss Piquet into thinking you were English when you dropped that note off in the library for me?"

"Easy, my dear lady. One only need think of the rules for cricket and the accent simply slides into place. Tickety-boo what!"

Grace stopped and turned, just to be sure.

"That's astonishing. How do you do that?"

"My old English teacher was originally from Buckinghamshire. I think he spent more time teaching us about cricket than Chaucer!"

Grace smiled and pedaled on, but her ease was short-lived. As the rooftops of town hove into view she felt every muscle in her body tighten.

It was late afternoon on Christmas Eve which meant hopefully most of the garrison would be installed in drinking and gambling establishments.

They cycled slowly through the darkening streets of St. Helier, hosepipe wheels slithering over the ancient cobbled streets. Most folk had hurried home to light stubby candles and to pray for peace.

They had just turned into the Royal Square when a group of four Wehrmacht soldiers strode noisily toward them.

Grace could tell by their flushed faces they were well-oiled and looking for some sport.

"Got your papers?" she muttered, slowly getting off her bike.

He nodded, his eyes narrowing in hatred, the way she'd seen in the graveyard.

Grace felt the blood begin to pulse in her ears. *Please God don't let him do anything rash.* An awful prickly sense of panic was slithering up her spine.

Suddenly Red pushed her up against the granite wall of the library.

"Pretend to kiss me," he whispered, his breath hot in her ear.

"Pardon?" she gasped, pulling back.

He pressed his forefinger to her mouth. "Sssh."

"I...I don't know...I..."

But her words fell away, as suddenly his warm lips were on hers, soft and gentle, he cupped her waist and pulled her body close. Grace closed her eyes and felt the world tilt.

A roar of drunken whoops and catcalls went up from the soldiers.

"*Küsse sie für mich!*" Kiss her for me!

To her disbelief, Red swooped his cap off and bowed as if he were a showman on a stage. The soldiers loved it, roaring and whistling their applause.

"Just smile and unlock the library," he said through gritted teeth.

Inside, Grace leaned her back against the door, clutching her chest.

"What on earth just happened?"

"Not sure I know. But that was a helluva first kiss."

She gazed at him in disbelief, her heart still thudding.

"You going to show me this beautiful library of your or what?" he asked, utterly unflappable.

Red's eyes were drawn up to the book-lined mezzanine and domed glass roof.

"Wowee!" He whistled under his breath.

Grace allowed herself a smile and felt her heart rate come down.

"Thank you, we are rather proud of our library."

"You should be. I've seen some beautiful libraries in my time, but boy, this is something else."

"But you have Boston Library, the first public library in America if I'm not mistaken!" she protested. "It's a masterpiece."

He nodded in agreement. "For sure, but each library is so unique, with its own personality. When we had furloughs in London my buddies laughed at me. They'd head off to Rainbow Corner in Piccadilly and I'd go and look round all of Carnegie's libraries. I tell you, Grace, I love London so much. Every time I mailed a letter home I could use happiness for a return address."

"You're not like anyone I've ever met," she marveled, wondering whether she'd ever had such a passionate conversation with a man her own age about libraries.

"Libraries are our greatest invention, right? Leastwise, that's what my mom used to say. She'd take me and my brothers to our local library every week for a book club."

"I like the sound of your mother."

He tore his gaze from the domed roof and fixed his green eyes on hers.

"Oh, she would *love* you, Angel Grace."

A small cough interrupted them and they looked up to see Peter watching them from the door to the Reading Room.

"Peter!" she exclaimed. In all the drama, she'd forgotten he was here.

"Please don't judge, Red," she murmured under her breath. "Peter is a little, um, quirky."

"Hello, buddy," he said affably. "Good to meet you."

"Would you like to see my drawing?" Peter asked, his face expressionless as stone.

"Peter, where's your manners?" Grace gently chastised.

"It's all right," Red grinned. "Small talk is overrated. I'd love to see it."

"You two go on through to the Reading Room and I'll make tea."

In the small staff room, she lit a match under the kettle and leaned back against the wall with a deep sigh of exhaustion. What a day. Just when she thought life couldn't surprise her anymore. This time last year she was celebrating at home with her family and Bea, all of them vowing 1942 would be their last occupation Christmas. This Christmas she was in the library about to drink tea with an extremely charming, fugitive Yank and a lonely, misunderstood boy.

By the time she carried a tray with tea through to the Reading Room, Peter had spread all his drawings out over the tabletop.

"You're a gifted boy," Red said. "The detail on these is exceptional. Could have used you when we flew over those German military bases. Tell me how you got the shading so exact over this tree," he asked Peter.

Grace sat back in contented silence watching as they talked. Peter was clearly at ease in his company. Oddly, his queer little tics didn't seem to manifest themselves this evening. Red was kind and patient, asking him questions and properly listening to Peter's answers.

"I can tell you've got younger brothers at home," she said.

He smiled wistfully and for the first time she saw a chink in his armor.

"Can't wait to see them, I miss them something rotten, and my mom."

"The terrier?"

He laughed. "You remembered. Thanksgiving is her favorite time, all her boys round the same table, cooking up a storm. Who knows when I'll see them next."

"I don't believe the Third Reich will win," Grace said softly. "No one with any sense does. Justice will prevail."

She held out her hand, her fingers stretched toward his. The kiss, for its all fakery, had forged an intimacy between them that had taken Grace by surprise.

"With all its drudgery, and despair and broken dreams, it's still a beautiful world."

He smiled at her curiously and she felt his eyes drink her in.

"It is with women like you in it."

"She likes you," Peter said without looking up from his book.

"That's good, buddy, because I like her," Red replied without taking his eyes off Grace.

Grace was grateful that the library was suddenly plunged into darkness.

"Gracious, is it that time already?" The gas and electricity went off at 6 p.m. in the library, as in all commercial premises to save on fuel.

"Right, Peter, this is our cue to leave. I need to catch the last bus home before curfew."

She fetched a small candle.

"There're some spare blankets in my office, help yourself to whatever you can find in the staff room and I'll get Dr. McKinstry to drop a food parcel round by the back door soon, which should last you until New Year's Eve. Oh, and feel free to read whatever you'd like, as long as you don't mind reading by candlelight. You shouldn't run out of reading material."

"Christmas in this library," Red mused. "How lucky can a fella get?"

"Just be careful," Grace warned.

"That's what the other man said," Peter remarked, as she went to fetch his coat.

"What other man, sweetie?" she asked, as she wound a scarf round his neck.

"He called himself the Wolf."

Grace felt like her heart had been scooped out with a blunt instrument.

"Th-that man, the Wolf, was here, in the library?"
Peter nodded.

"W-when?" she stammered.

"After you left."

"What did he ask you?" she demanded.

"He asked to see you. I informed him you were out delivering messages."

Grace closed her eyes. "Why did you say that?" Her voice came out high-pitched, queer.

"Because you said so to Miss Gold earlier, that you would deliver the message. He said he would return after New Year and see if he could catch you then."

For a terrible moment, Grace thought she might faint.

"Grace, are you all right?" Red's hand was at her arm, steadying her.

"Yes…yes. It's that man, I just don't know what business he has with the library."

Grace tried to calm herself. There was no possible way he could know what she and Bea had done, delivering a message was harmless enough surely.

"Please, Peter. If you see that man again, don't talk to him unless you absolutely have to. Don't show him your pictures."

"And, Red," she said turning to him, "you absolutely have to be out of here by dawn on New Year's Eve."

"Relax." He smiled. "I swear there'll be no trace of me when you reopen the doors. I'll just lay low here until it's time to move on."

He leaned over and his lips brushed her cheek as outside a light snow began to dust the Royal Square.

"Happy Christmas, Grace." She felt his lips so close to hers, his breath, warm and tingling in her ear. "And thank you for coming to my rescue... *again!*"

"You're welcome. Bye now."

"That's it?" he laughed. "Bye now? That's so British."

"Don't give me the puppy dog look," she warned.

"Angel Grace," he breathed, stepping closer to her. "I've never met anyone like you before in my whole life. This can't be goodbye. When can I see you again?"

"You hardly know me, Red."

"We're at war, Grace. There's no time to be coy."

Moonlight filtered through the domed roof, bathing them in a soft silvery light.

"Happy Christmas," she whispered, turning quickly. "Don't take down the blackout blinds. I'll be back New Year's Eve."

She and Peter walked through the Royal Square, their footsteps echoing off the grand buildings and she wondered why it was she had just masked her own heart in an impenetrable blanket. It wasn't just because of the inherent danger of being in a relationship with a reckless man wanted by the Germans. When the war was over he would return to Boston, to his formidable mother and her tribe of sons, leaving Grace heartbroken and alone. No thanks.

She had never once craved a romantic relationship. All the love and adventure she needed was contained within the books in her library. She could pick love up and slot it back onto the bookshelf. Real life was too messy. Authors made it easy for her to live a rich and full life, without having to experience the actual emotion herself.

They reached the bus stop and Grace touched her mouth. Despite the cold her lips tingled and she indulged in the memory. *Stop it, Grace. That kiss wasn't real, none of it was, even Red's hair color was fake.* And yet, his kisses were like a cherished book her mind kept returning to.

The arrival of the bus jolted her from her reverie. Reluctantly, she turned her back on the library and headed for home.

7

Bea

Bea pulled back the blackout blinds. It was 7:30 a.m. on New Year's Eve and a pale winter sun was struggling to rise. A delicate lace of frost embroidered the inside of the kitchen window. It was so cold the iron railings along the seafront glittered with icy diamonds. Bea turned on the tap and as it spluttered to life she offered up a silent prayer of thanks that the old lead pipes hadn't frozen.

The door opened, bringing a freezing blast of air and her mother walked in clutching a large parcel. "Blimey, it's colder than a witch's tit out there. Stick the kettle on, ducks."

Bea shook her head as she lit a flame under the kettle. Cockneys had a rich and spirited vernacular; she suspected it was one of the reasons her father had loved her.

"Where have you been at this hour, you old scoundrel?" She laughed. "You've even painted on your eyebrows."

"Early bird catches the worm. I've been up since 4 a.m. pulling the bleedin' lavatory chain and running taps to stop the pipes freezing up so my darlin' girls can have a wash and a cuppa." She planted a big sloppy kiss on Bea's cheek. "Then I paid a visit to old Mr. Rossi who used to run the café up the road. He was trying to get rid of this old ham slicer," she said, setting it down on the table with a thump. "He's no need of it since they've shut up shop so I swapped it for a pair of your father's old shoes. Fair exchange is no robbery!"

"And what exactly are you going to do with a ham slicer seeing as you ain't got no ham to slice?"

"Necessity is the mother of invention, sweetheart. I've been growing tobacco down my allotment and I can use this to slice it and package it up to sell."

She sat down with a groan then a grin. "Sweet as a nut!"

"How do you do it, Mum? Always manage to stay so relentlessly upbeat?" Bea yawned as she set about preparing cups and the coffee pot.

"It's in the genes, love. I've been making do and mending since I fell out the cradle. A few bloody Jerries on my doorstep ain't going to change me now. Mind you, having lived through the Depression, I never thought I'd see the day we'd be queuing up at communal kitchens again, or see fascists marching in the streets. And yet, here we are again."

She sniffed and raked about in her old leather pouch for her tobacco. "You forget, I was bombed in the first show. They didn't get Queenie Gold then, they ain't gonna now."

It was true. Queenie had been 15 when a German Gotha airplane bombed her school in Poplar, East London during the Great War. Queenie had clawed her way out from under her school desk and walked home. The story was a family legend now.

Bea was proud of her mother's stoicism, but she worried that she was so busy *getting on with it* that she hadn't allowed herself the space to grieve properly.

Bea kissed her mum on the head, gently kneading her shoulders.

"Ooh, that's hit the spot, love. Don't stop."

"I love you all the money in the world and two bob," Bea said softly, repeating their favorite saying.

She felt her mum relax as she worked into the knotted muscles cording her neck.

"I miss Dad. He used to love New Year's Eve, didn't he."

Every New Year's Eve Bea's father had thrown a party and invited the whole street, setting off fireworks and mixing cocktails so strong they'd blow the roof of your mouth off. It had been three and a half years since he'd been machine-gunned by the harbor, but Bea could still summon the warm comforting feel of his barrel chest, the deep rumble of his laughter.

"Do you miss him, Mum? Only you never talk about him."

Her mother tensed under her touch and she turned to face her.

"Oh, love, you have no idea. We were married for so many years. I uprooted my whole life to move here away from my people. But your father helped me to form new roots." She rubbed her work-worn hands down her apron. "I don't need to talk about him to remember him."

"But talking is good, Mum, surely? Grace reckons that if you don't talk about the dead, they'll never leave you alone."

She lifted an eyebrow.

"Does she now? Talking won't bring your dad back though, will it?" she said bluntly. "We're all gonna die. That's a fact, darlin'. It's what you make of life that counts."

She reached up and caught the tear that trickled down Bea's cheek with her thumb.

"If there's anything you need to tell me, love, I'm good at fixing things." Her perceptive gaze roamed over Bea's face.

Bea was so close to articulating her fears, but speaking them aloud might make them true. And if she was honest, if she started to talk about Jimmy, of the grief which swelled inside her, wild and frightening, unfathomable and seemingly without end, she might never stop.

The absolute truth of it she was shattered, her heart shredded. Crawling through the days. She remembered his death, the blood pumping through the hole in his cheek, so viscerally. She could still smell the blood mingling with the salt, the look of utter astonishment on his face. In many ways she had never really left that blood-soaked beach. The woman who had run for her life up a cliff path was someone quite different. She had been carved into a sharper, more cynical version of herself. Grief had changed her mentally and physically. Her mother's words hung between them.

Anything you need to tell me, love?

But how could she tell her she had missed three, or was it four, monthly bleeds? No. No. No. She battened down the thought. She had read once in one of the women's magazines in the library that shock and stress can do strange thing to a person's body. That was it. Grief had stopped the curse.

"I'm fine, Mum," she said instead. "Best to live with memories than speak of regrets."

"Good. Now what say we have a few drinks this evening? See in the New Year? I've a drop of brandy I've been saving. Invite your Grace too."

Bea wanted to continue the conversation but her sister had come into the kitchen, looking irritatingly as fresh as a daisy. She looked at Nancy, with her silk stockings and lavender scented silk scarf, and in that moment she hated her.

"Morning, love. Sleep all right?"

"Like a log, thanks, Mum."

"I don't know how you sleep at night at all," Bea snapped.

Nancy rolled her eyes.

"Not this again. Mum, tell her to give it a rest, will you."

Queenie shot Bea a warning look.

"Don't needle her."

She turned back to her youngest daughter.

"You look nice, love. Where you off to?"

"I've got a job interview, just a bit of waitressing up at Fort d'Auvergne."

"It's not bad enough you're sleeping with the enemy, now you've got to work for them?" Bea exploded.

"Well, what choice have I got? It was thanks to you I lost my job at Boots, don't forget. The manager said he didn't want no trouble."

"Well, if you work for them, you realize you'll be in contradiction of the Hague Convention."

"Serving coffee hardly constitutes military work."

"You're still taking their dirty Reichsmarks. I hate all those pigs getting rich working for the Germans. There are many on this island significantly better off than they were before the occupation. Judgment day is coming for the lot of you."

"God, you're so holier than thou," Nancy retorted. "It's all academic anyway as three-quarters of the population are working for them directly and indirectly anyway."

"How?"

"Every gallon of water, every pint of milk is of benefit to the garrison. A lot of islanders are working for the Germans whether they realize it or not."

"Not me," Bea said proudly. "I work for His Majesty's Post Office. The Germans have their own post office, so the way I see it, nothing I do benefits the Germans. Unlike you. You seem to be servicing them on all levels, Nancy."

"Meaning?"

"Meaning when you're done frothing their milk, perhaps you're keeping them happy in the sack? You could end up servicing the whole bloody hotel for all we know."

Nancy slapped her so fast she didn't even see it coming.

"I love *one* man," she said, shaking with anger.

Bea stood in shock, clutching her cheek.

"Stop this," Queenie ordered. "What's become of us?"

"So-Sorry, Mum," Nancy stammered, before grabbing her bag and running out of the door. "I won't be home later. I'm out with Heinz."

Queenie looked wearily at Bea and without a word, left the room, disappointment clouding her face, mouth as tight as a white-knuckle fist.

Bea walked to her shift at the post office feeling wretched, not because of rowing with Nancy, but because of upsetting her mother. The truth of it was she and Nancy had never been close. They were very different people and the gulf between them had widened since their father's death. Grace had always felt more of a sister to her.

Bea walked past the Pomme d'Or Hotel, the headquarters of the German Naval Command, under its fluttering swastika and slipped in the back door of the Broad Street post office.

"Sorry I'm late," she called.

The facing tables were full, all the posties already hard at work sorting their individual rounds in the freezing sorting room.

"Last one in makes the tea," Nobby Clark called out, his breath hanging like smoke in the cold air.

Bea hadn't been sure about working in such a male environment, but now she'd rather come to like it. These weather-beaten old men were relentless in their teasing and prolific demands for tea and they never discussed "feelings," which right now suited Bea nicely.

She made a round of nettle tea, marginally more drinkable than carrot or parsnip, and brought the tray through to find them all assembled around Billy Matson's facing table.

"Come here, girlie. Summat to show you," Ronnie Richards yelled. Ron was renowned for having the largest stride of any postman. It took Ron just 15 minutes to reach the top of Mount Bingham and he was always first back from his round.

"You must think I was born yesterday, Ron," she laughed. Last week one of them, she suspected Ron, thought leaving a dead seagull in her postal bag would be a terrific wheeze.

"No, really. Come and take a look at the new stamp that's been issued."

She ventured over to find them all chuckling like a gang of schoolboys.

"What's so funny? It's an improvement on a swastika over the king's head surely?"

"Major Rybot, the fella who designed it, is a brave man."

"I don't get it."

"Look closer," Nobby urged. "See the four As at the top corner? *Ad Avernam Adolf Atrox*. To hell with you, Atrocious Adolf, I reckon."

Ron roared with laughter. "He's chancing it."

"Aren't we all in some way," Bea said, casting a knowing look round the group.

She picked up the pile of mail Billy Matson had brought in from the rural regions that morning.

"Your round's a bit light today, isn't it, Billy?"

"It's tomato paper, ain't it," he replied. "Paper shortages mean folk are having to improvise and produce their own envelopes. They barely weigh a thing."

"I didn't mean that, Billy, and you know it. I mean you've clearly had a lot of poison-pen letters you've already disposed of. Where are they? In the boiler-room fire?"

Billy's smile slipped.

"Please let me help," she begged the group of older posties. "I'm not the only one surely to have noticed there are more informers' letters than ever! If we work together, we can become more efficient."

"Look, love," said Arthur, "you've narrowly avoided arrest once after that scrape with the van."

"He's right, ducks," said Harold, his voice low and gravelly. "You leave it to us, young 'un. We're old men now. We've lived our lives. It don't matter if we get caught, but a fresh young thing like you, all your life still ahead of you…"

He tugged at his beard. "And I don't know about you, lads, but I don't fancy taking on the Guv'nor."

The group all hooted, until Nobby coughed. "The boss is coming, look lively."

They dispersed back to the station at the facing table.

"Take my advice, girlie," Billy murmured. "Hear nothing, say nothing, see nothing."

Bea returned to work and one by one the chatter of the sorting room died down as the posties bagged up their mail and drifted out on their morning deliveries. Frustration beat in her chest.

Bea scooped up the last letter and the breath caught in her throat.

The Commandant. College House. St. Saviour. Jersey.

The scrawled capitals were written in crayon. Glancing about she slipped it into her waistband and casually walked out.

"Just nipping to the girls' room, boss, before I start my round," she called to Oscar Mourant, Acting Head Postmaster, busy on the other side of the large room. He waved her on distractedly.

In the toilet her hands tremored a little as she eased open the envelope.

The envelope ripped. "Bugger."

"You all right, Bea, my love?" called out a voice in the next cubicle. It was Winnie from the front desk.

She waited a beat, trying to calm her voice before replying.

"Fine, just started my curse is all."

"Poor you. Let me know if you need a pad."

"Don't worry, I'm fine," she lied.

Silently she unfolded the letter and Bea realized she was a long way from fine.

SEARCH THE ALLOTMENT SHED OF WIDOW QUEENIE GOLD, BAY VIEW BOARDING HOUSE. I HAVE GOOD REASON TO BELIEVE SHE IS GROWING TOBACCO TO SELL ON THE BLACK MARKET AND LISTENS TO THE BBC FROM A WIRELESS HIDDEN IN HER SHED. FOLLOW HER AND YOU'LL SEE. YOURS HELPFULLY. PS. POSSIBLY JEWISH? HER PEOPLE ARE FROM WHITECHAPEL.

Bea leaned forward and rested her head against the cubicle door as the room spun. She knew her mum had been too trusting.

"Get a grip," she told herself. "You have the advantage."

The letter was unsigned, written in childish handwriting so as not to reveal the sender. Breathing out slowly, she flushed the toilet, stuffed the letter back under her waistband and opened the door.

Winnie was still there, drying her hands on the roller towel, as Bea splashed her wrists under icy cold water.

"You sure you're all right? You look ever so peaky, love."

"Thanks, Win. Bleedin' monthlies. You know what it's like."

"I'm a long time over that, thank goodness," she chuckled. Winnie patted her on the shoulder and glanced down. "Be safe, dear," she said softly. The letter was poking out of her waistband.

"Fuck it!" she muttered as Winnie left. She really had to get a hold of herself.

Somehow Bea managed her morning round, her knuckles as white as wax on the bike handles, as she peddled through clouds of freezing fog to deliver the town's last postal round of 1943. Fog like this was a postwoman's worst nightmare, lacing toes with chilblains and welding frozen fingers to bike handles. When she finished she took a detour past the Royal Square and hopped off her postal bike.

"Here, sonny, guard that bike with your life." She handed the delighted boy an old toffee she had found at the bottom of a jacket pocket and went in to seek Grace's counsel.

Her friend was diligently shelving books in the furthest corner, her face lighting up when she spotted Bea.

"Hello, you. You can't believe what a rush I've just had on. I reckon most folk plan to see in the New Year with a good read." Her smile slipped.

"Bea…?"

"What'll I do?" she whimpered, shoving the letter at Grace.

Grace put on a pair of reading spectacles and read.

"Follow me."

In the safety of her small office, Bea's bottled-up fear found its release.

"Mum's been denounced. Do you recognize this handwriting from any of the library tickets?"

"Bea, calm down," Grace urged. "Hold it back forty-eight hours. That should buy her enough time to clear out her shed."

"This might buy her even more time." Bea ripped the letter in half, then ripped it again, and carried on until it was nothing but confetti.

"I can't believe you just did that," Grace gasped.

"It's my mum, Grace. What else am I to do?"

"Let them search the house and the allotment, see she's innocent and then leave her alone?"

"But it's not that simple, is it? Once he works out she's my mother, she'll be guilty by association."

"Yes, you might well have tarnished me with that same brush." Grace looked stricken. "I wasn't going to tell you so as not to alarm you, but the Wolf visited the library on Christmas Eve, when I was out visiting Mrs. Noble. Said he'd be back. I'm waiting for his visit, Bea."

The silence stretched out between them, no sound but the ticking of the old clock on the wall, counting down the seconds of this agonizing occupation.

"Oh, Grace. How can he know?"

"We don't know that he does, but he's watching you and everyone associated with you." She laid her palm down on the desk. "I understand about wanting to protect your mum, but it...it's just so dangerous! I'm a librarian and you're a postal worker. I just want to survive this occupation and keep this library going. That's what I care about, Bea—this place."

She looked at the piles of old books which had been donated by grateful islanders, crammed into every corner, awaiting cataloging.

"This library speaks its truth and I am answerable to it."

"But what about helping human beings? They're what count, surely, not dusty old books?"

Grace's face softened. "Books are what get me out of bed each day, Bea. It's how I continue the fight, because they are the last bastion of democracy."

"But it's so wrong! How could anyone denounce their neighbor? It's repugnant."

"Not everyone has your scruples, Bea," Grace said wearily. "Starvation makes animals of us all. It's complicated."

Bea shook her head "Well, it's simple to me. You don't sell out your own. Jimmy shared my beliefs."

Grace touched her face, her beautiful green eyes shining in the dim light of the office. "Maybe but doing this won't bring him back. You can't save everyone. It *has* to stop." Her eyes filled with tears and Bea saw herself reflected in them. She felt a sudden shame for dragging Grace and her library sanctuary into this tawdry mess.

Bea nodded and Grace hugged her tightly.

"Thank you. You're a total nit at times, but I do love you."

Bea felt her tears soak into the cotton of her friend's blouse. "I love you too."

"I'll come to yours after work. Stay out of trouble until then."

"I'll try."

"Oh and by the way, do you mind me bringing two friends this evening?"

Something about her friend was different today.

"Why, Grace La Mottée, are you wearing lipstick?"

Grace touched her mouth and flushed. "Just a little. Beauty is your duty—that's what Churchill said on the wireless, wasn't it?"

"Oh, you're making an effort for Churchill, are you?" she teased. "Come on. Spill the beans."

"There's nothing to spill. They're just a couple of bibliophiles. I trust them."

"Very well." She popped a kiss on Grace's cheek. "You know, I've not said this, but one of the saddest things about Jimmy's death was that it stole the chance to call you *sister*."

Grace smiled sadly before reaching for Bea's hand and placing it on the space over her heart. "You're my sister in here. Now off you go. I've a library to run."

Grace's words echoed in her head as her threadbare bike tires bounced and slithered up St. Helier's narrow streets. *I trust them.*

Before this, Bea trusted most of her neighbors. She'd have staked her life on some of them, but not now. War, she realized sadly, was the greatest killer of trust in the world.

Bea was halfway down Beresford Street, drawing level with the German Field Post Office, when something caught her attention. One of the German postal workers had left his bike outside, complete with a pile of bundled-up mail inside the wicker basket at the front.

She dismounted and walked toward it. Jersey Post Office had nothing whatsoever to do with the Germans' mail, thank goodness. She'd have to have been court-martialed before she delivered the Jerries' post. Their post was delivered by Junkers 52 aircraft to the island's airport then transported to Victoria College House, from where it was delivered to Beresford Street.

"What an imbecile," Bea muttered. "Leaving letters unattended like that. Anyone could come and nick them."

She listened. From deep inside the post office she heard the German love song "Lili Marleen" being sung with guttural gusto. They must have started on the sauce early. She glanced at the letter on the top of the pile.

Engelbert Bergmann, Feldpost, Kanalinseln.

A strange sensation crept over her. Rage. Curiosity. Jealousy. She couldn't put a name to it. She pictured Engelbert's wife, some fat frau, well-fed and sitting pretty in her German farmhouse no doubt, wishing her victorious husband a Happy Christmas in his cushy Channel Island posting. Maybe Engelbert was the one who'd squeezed the trigger, or hunted her down on the beach? In that moment, she hated this faceless soldier and all he stood for with her whole being. Why should he get news from home, when her home had been torn apart and trampled under the jackboot?

She glanced about. Skeins of fog drifted up the empty street. Somewhere further up the road she heard the clopping of hooves on stone. Long angry fingers unfurled inside her, a vengeful voice muttered in her ear.

They took something precious from you. Now it's your turn.

The bundle of letters was in her own postal bag before she could help herself. It was so easy, nothing more than a sleight of hand. An incredible feeling of liberation burst inside her, so she grabbed the second bundle. What the hell! She might as well take the lot.

She chalked a V for victory on the seat of the bicycle for good measure. Given that most men's brains were in their pants, she reasoned the German postman might stop to consider the symbolic sign of resistance.

Bea cycled up the street with 90 pieces of stolen mail in her postal bag, her heart doing cartwheels in her chest. The fog consumed her by the time she reached the end of the street. All those soldiers who wouldn't receive news from home this festive season. Good. The damage to morale would be as insidious as the fog shrouding the window-panes.

Thankfully her mum was out when she got home. Bea safely stowed the stolen letters in a box in the attic, next to Jimmy's stolen gun and the other letters. In the musty gloom Grace's words hurtled back to haunt her. *You can't save everyone. It has to stop.* It was a little too late for that.

Sadly the letter denouncing her mother had been far from an isolated incident. Since she'd intercepted the poison-pen letter about Mrs. Noble on Christmas Eve she'd opened a dozen more addressed to the commandant. In one week! Each day more had turned up on her facing table, sprouting like bindweed and trickling venom. In an occupation, the Christmas period had become the season of ill-will. She understood that people were starving and desperate, sick of heart at having no food to put on the table or presents in their children's stockings, but it was no excuse. Spite was spreading like gangrene through the guts of Jersey.

There simply hadn't been the opportunity to warn everyone, and she couldn't expect Grace to help her every single time, so it had seemed easier all round to just not deliver them at all, and hide them instead. Admittedly it flew in the face of everything a postal worker was entrusted to do, but she simply would not allow herself to view it as theft. How could she in all consciousness allow those letters to go to their intended recipients knowing the consequences of such an action? How many lives would be left in ruins by their delivery?

Surely, as a postal worker, that would make her complicit. To Grace it was a moral quagmire, but to Bea it seemed straightforward. She hated the subterfuge and lying to her best friend, but she had begun now. There was no choice but to see it through to the bitter end—alone!

Downstairs she heard a bang and Bea jumped, cracking her head on the low attic beam. "Bugger," she cursed, rubbing her head.

"Mum, you home?" Nancy's voice called up the stairs. "I got the job."

Bea heard the jangle of her sister's keys land on the hall table.

Head throbbing, she covered the letters over with a cuddly toy her father had won for her at a summer fair what felt like a hundred years ago. Kicking the box to the furthest reaches of the attic, she clambered down the thin wooden ladder and managed to replace it back in the loft hatch, just as her sister emerged onto the landing.

"Bea." Nancy paled and stepped back. "I thought it was Mum. What are you up to?"

Bea's nerve endings were screaming. Up above their heads was enough evidence to get her sent to a German prison camp for years. And all it would take was a few well-chosen words from Nancy in her boyfriend's ear.

"Fetching some old clothes out of the attic."

"So where are they then?" Nancy asked, gesturing to her empty arms.

"Mum must have taken them down already," she snapped. "Not all of us resort to sleeping with the enemy to get new clobber."

She wiped the dust off her postal jacket, her fingers stained with ink. "Now, if you'll excuse me, some of us have decent work to do."

Bea swept from the house and cycled back to the post office, blinking back angry tears. What a bloody mess. She would need to move those letters to a safer place and soon.

At Broad Street, the postmen were gathered in the sorting room, having a drink of toxic homebrew. The air was filled with the smell of homegrown tobacco and spicy apple brandy. Bea swallowed sharply as she felt her meager dinner of boiled turnip threaten to make a sudden reappearance.

"There you are, girlie," called Ron. "Come and have a drink with us to see out the year."

"Go on then," she laughed, ignoring the acid churn of her stomach as she took a gulp.

Billy slid his arm around her shoulder. "Sorry about earlier, Bea, but you understand—all we want is to keep you safe. It's what your dad would've wanted. He loved the bones of you."

Bea looked up into his kind, craggy old face and nodded, blinking back tears.

"I understand. Thanks, Billy."

"That's my girl."

"Oi, this isn't a Mother's Union meeting," yelled Nobby, raising his glass. "Time for a singsong. I'll start us off…

"Underneath an air raid, somewhere over there. Adolf in his bunker…" His big voice filled the sorting room.

"We've got the Reich on the run, so stick your bloomin' searchlight up your bum," Bea finished and the lads fell about.

After one more drink and a couple more patriotic songs Bea managed to extract herself and head for home, the freezing air sobering her up. She paused outside her home and stared out over the vast inky tract of moon-polished water, over to occupied Europe. Far behind her stood England.

Compared to Fortress Europe, the Channel Islands were like pebbles scattered in the ocean. Never had Bea felt so isolated on this tiny island. They were nothing but a pimple on the backside of the British Empire. She knew her view on the world had changed since Jimmy's death, shattering her innocence. Her grief sat like a hot lump in her chest, spawning a terrible anger which bloomed and unfurled inside her. She regretted getting Grace involved, of course she did, but somehow, she was entirely power-less to stop herself either. The danger was creeping closer to home, all her secrets coming home to roost. Bea pictured the stolen letters in the attic, sitting there fester-ing like an unexploded bomb. She rested her hand lightly on her tummy and stared at the incoming tide. *Breathe, Bea. Breathe.*

Inside, her mum had been hard at work. The table had been dressed with a fine tablecloth Queenie had crocheted herself. A bean crock (minus juicy pork) was warmed through, and a milk blancmange made with potato flour for afters.

"Smells lovely, Mum," she said, shrugging off her tatty coat.

"It ain't much, but it's made with love," Queenie remarked, surveying the table.

"God, I'm sick of this," Bea remarked.

"Sick of what?"

"This. How are we supposed to get by on four ounces of meat a week, four of butter and three of sugar?"

Queenie rolled her eyes.

"Behave. You don't know the meaning of poor. When I was growing up, me mum couldn't take the curtains down until me dad had read 'em."

"Huh?"

"Newspaper, darlin'." Queenie laughed at her daughter's confused expression. "We couldn't afford curtains so every night Mum had to hang the *East London Advertiser* up at the windows instead."

She flicked her on the bum with a tea towel.

"Your generation ain't got a clue. Now shut your cake-hole and go and get the door. That'll be the library contingent."

Chastised, Bea opened the door.

"Happy New Year—"

Her words caught in her throat when she flung open the door and surveyed the group on her doorstep. "Grace," she said cagily. "Who's this?"

8

Grace

"Peter you know and this is…This is…" She fumbled over her words, unsure who to introduce him as.

"My papers say I'm Phillip Harris, but my real name is Daniel Patrick O'Sullivan, though my friends call me Red. I crash-landed in the sea off the north coast of Jersey, August 8 last year. I'm having what you could call an *extended stay* on your beautiful island until I can rejoin my unit." His voice softened. "And I owe my life to this beautiful lady right here."

He turned and smiled at her so brilliantly that for a moment Grace found she couldn't breathe. Was this what love felt like? All the authors she'd read over the years had weaved tales of big, important love, and though she'd enjoyed the stories, she had never really believed in them. It had seemed so implausible that Romeo and Juliet would go to the grave for each other. And where had love got the characters from some of her favorite novels—*Tess of the D'Urbervilles*, Cathy in *Wuthering Heights*, Scarlett O'Hara?

And yet…all Christmas all she'd been able to think of was Red alone in the library. She'd reached the library at dawn that morning only to discover his new safehouse had fallen through.

"I hope you don't mind me bringing him here. The people who were supposed to be sheltering him got cold feet."

Queenie wiped her hand on her apron and stuck it out. "Queenie Gold. And may I say, lad, what a pleasure it is to have a member of the American Air Force in my home. I have a spare shed on my allotment you can sleep in and this evening you'll be our guest of honor."

Instead of shaking it, he kissed Queenie's hand.

"Thank you, ma'am. Boy, do you remind me of my mom in Boston."

Queenie glowed. "Come in, lad, and warm your cockles by the fire. You must be freezing." She linked her arm through Red's and led him into her home.

Bea raised one eyebrow.

"Don't say it!" Grace said, seeing the glee on her friend's face.

"And I thought I was the risk-taker." Bea laughed.

"I hope you don't mind me bringing him here. I just didn't know where else to turn."

"Of course not! If you can't trust me, who can you trust?"

"But hiding Red in your mum's allotment shed, it's just so risky! Someone's clearly watching her."

"Relax. If any nasty poison-pen letters turn up, I'll see to it that they never make it into the enemy's hands. Now come. Let's get lubricated, it's New Year's Eve after all!"

Bea took her coat and her eyes twinkled with mischief. "Now I know why your lips are the color of a postbox!"

Bea had batted the thorny issue of Red's safehouse away as if it were nothing more than a harmless fly, instead of a merciless totalitarian regime, but what else could Grace do? As Red would say, they didn't have a bunch of other options.

The rest of the evening was as nourishing and joyous as any evening Grace could remember.

Red charmed Queenie and Bea as she'd known he would. They were fascinated as he shared details of a life so different to their own. Turned out he was a pilot embedded with the United States Army Air Forces in Essex, where he'd slept in a Nissen hut which smelled like a "badger's ass." The diet largely consisted of "stuffed marrow" and "warm beer." His jaw had "hit the floor" when he'd visited the whispering gallery at St. Paul's Cathedral and his favorite book was Jack London's *The Call of the Wild*.

Grace smiled as he fielded question after question from Bea and her loquacious mum.

"You're welcome to stay in my allotment shed as long as you like, son," Queenie said, as she topped up his glass. "I'd have you in the house only my other daughter..."

"Is a Jerrybag," Bea interrupted.

"Is having a silly fling with a German, so you can see how difficult that could be. But the shed is yours. What's your longer plan?"

"That's kind of you, ma'am," said Red. "Ultimately my plan is to escape Jersey and rejoin my unit."

"Escape how?" Bea asked. "The voyage to England is treacherous. Trust me, I know."

"But not impossible," Red pointed out. "Or I sit tight and wait for France to fall to the Allies and head there. Either way, it's a hell of an adventure ahead."

He looked at Grace and winked. A silence fell over the tabletop and Grace felt her face heat up as Bea and her mum looked on with interest.

"I feel as if I'm in a romance novel," Queenie said. "Talking of which, Grace, I finished *Pride and Prejudice*, last night. Bleedin' hell," she laughed, pretending to fan herself. "That Mr. Darcy's no better than he ought to be! Reading that novel took me right out of myself. I actually forgot the war. I was standing in that field, wanting to bash their heads together."

Grace laughed. "Reading will do that to you. A book gives you wings, takes you to places."

"Like a kind of time machine, you mean?" Queenie asked and Grace nodded.

"Well, what about that then? Queenie Gold, international time-traveler."

Red laughed. "You should start a book club in the library, Grace. I'm sure more people would love to hear you read. I know I did."

"That's not a bad idea, Red," she agreed. "I wonder if the authorities would agree."

"You'd need to seek permission to start a club and be exempt from rules of group gathering, but you could argue it raises islanders' morale," Bea suggested.

"I could do it once a month, maybe on a Saturday afternoon when people come into town for market," Grace mused. "I'd have to read an extract because we wouldn't have enough books to go round."

"That's an excellent idea, Grace. I'm sure folks would travel if they got to sit and listen to you reading," Red said.

"Pure escapism. I'd come," Queenie said.

"And maybe I could persuade Mrs. Moisan, and maybe my mum too," Grace said.

"I'd come," Peter said.

"You're always in the library every day anyway," she chuckled, ruffling his head.

"Would you come?" Grace asked, reaching out to take Bea's hand. "It might be a good way to reconcile you and my mum?"

Bea nodded, looking tired in the flickering candlelight. "If you really think it would work. How about we call it the Jersey Toads?"

Red looked puzzled.

"Islanders call themselves *Crapauds*, after the Jersey toad," Queenie explained. "I know ... they have some funny ways. It took me a while to work it all out."

"I think we should keep it simple. How about the Wartime Book Club?" Grace suggested.

"I like it," Bea said. "And it's formal enough for the commandant to probably agree."

"That's settled then. Ooh, nearly midnight," said Queenie, reaching for the bottle of brandy and charging glasses.

"To the Wartime Book Club," Grace said and everyone

held their glasses aloft, a fragile sense of hope weaving its way round the table.

"And to liberation for us all," Bea said.

"Liberation," Red agreed, clinking his glass against Grace's.

As 1943 slipped into 1944, how she hoped that this year would bring peace.

"Say, how about you read something for us now, Grace?" Red suggested. "If I'm to start another year in hiding at least let me begin it in a book!"

"I would, but I don't have one."

"Just as well I brought one then!" He pulled *The Complete Works of William Shakespeare* from a satchel. "I didn't think you'd mind me borrowing it from the library."

"Oh no, I don't think so," she blustered, suddenly feeling inexplicably self-conscious.

"Listen, love, if you're gonna lead a book club, you need the practice," Queenie said bluntly.

"Yes, I suppose you're right. Which part?"

"Read whichever pages it falls open on?" Bea suggested.

"Very well." Grace's slender fingers fanned the pages and stopped on page 220.

"Gold Clasps and a Golden Story," she read.

"*Romeo and Juliet* if I'm not much mistaken," Red remarked.

Queenie winked and Grace blushed.

"Very well. Here goes.

"This precious book of love, this unbound lover,
To beautify him, only lacks a cover;
The fish lives in the sea, and 'tis much pride,

For fair without the fair within to hide:
That book in many eyes doth share the glory,
That in gold clasps locks in the golden story."
In those few sublime verses Grace forgot herself.

"Beautiful," Red breathed, unable to tear his gaze from Grace. "Just beautiful."

"You talking about Grace or the writing?" Queenie teased.

"Stop it, Mum," Bea laughed, before glancing up at the clock. "Listen, I hate to break up Romeo and Juliet, but it's forty minutes until curfew."

"You're right, darlin'," Queenie concede.

"Red, come with me, son. You're about the same size as my late husband. I'll sort you out with some of his clothes and then we'd better get you down to the allotment."

"Much obliged, Mrs. Gold, and may I just say, that was the finest meal I have tasted in a good long while." He sighed, casting a sideways look at Grace, who blushed, her eyes sparkling in the candlelight. "Every mouthful a velvet kiss."

"A velvet kiss indeed," Queenie chuckled, leaning back in her chair. "How do you like that, Grace dear? The boy's a poet."

Reluctantly, she heaved herself to her feet and immediately staggered backward.

"Woah there," Red said, catching her. "Are you all right, ma'am?"

In the candlelight, Queenie's face was pale as chalk. She held her hand to her chest and breathed out slowly.

"Mum, you don't look too clever," Bea exclaimed.

"Don't fuss. I'm fine. Too much brandy and not enough food is all."

"Here, lean on me," Red said, holding out his arm.

After they left, Grace went to collect the dishes, but Bea caught her hand. "Leave it. I'll do it later."

Bea glanced over at Peter, but he was utterly absorbed in a drawing he was working on of the small bay outside the window.

"I'm happy for you, Grace."

"What do you mean?"

"Oh, come on, Gracie. You're clearly potty about him. And he is *definitely* head over heels for you! Even a blind man could see that!"

"You're being ridiculous," she scoffed, tracing a pattern through some crumbs on the table.

"Am I?"

"Of course. I scarcely know him."

"You know him well enough to risk helping him!"

Grace shrugged.

"Meeting a man. Falling in love. It's allowed, you know." Bea smiled. "Despite what the Montagues and the Capulets say!"

A loaded silence seeped through the room, the only sound the crackling of the flames and Peter's pencil softly scratching the paper. Bea's hair was backlit by the glow from the fire, lit up the color of amber, but her face was bathed in shadows.

Grace reached for her hand.

"Oh, Bea. You're crying."

"I'm sorry. I swore I wouldn't do this." She wiped her eyes angrily. "Must be all this talk of Romeo and Juliet."

"I miss him too, Bea."

Bea's body seemed to deflate, buckling under the weight of her grief. "I'd do anything to turn back the clock," she wept, her eyes haunted. "Lock him in if needs be. Anything that meant we weren't on that bloody beach."

Grace leaned over, grasped her cold fingers. "Don't you think I wish I'd done that too?" She hesitated, but then remembered that secrets unshared only festered.

"I've never told you this, but that night I wasn't asleep in my room. I'd sneaked out some food to Red. He was in hiding, you see. That's how we met."

Bea's cinnamon eyes widened.

"You see," Grace continued, "if there's blame to be shared then it's only fair I shoulder some too. I had a feeling something was wrong, but I was anxious to get to Red."

"You couldn't have stopped him, Gracie."

"Exactly! Jimmy was never going to sit this occupation out quietly."

Bea's tears seemed unstoppable. "I just miss him so much." She shuddered. "He should be here...here with us."

There was nothing Grace could say to assuage her friend's grief. All she could do was hold her tight in her arms, try to hold back the avalanche of pain. A tarry block in the fire popped, spitting out a red-hot ember onto the hearth.

"I'm scared, Grace," she confessed, her voice barely above a whisper.

"I promise you we'll get through this," Grace vowed,

kissing her forehead tenderly. "We'll face it all together. Like we've always done."

★★★

The Bailiff's Chambers
Jersey
20 January 1944

With the Bailiff's Compliments is enclosed a copy of the Order of the Field Commandant with regard to the application of your Organization, the Wartime Book Club, for exemption from the Order of 26 August 1940.

A translation of the decision is as follows:

In accordance with Paragraph 8 of the above mentioned Order, permission is hereby granted for your activity in accordance with the rules submitted.

Instructions.

1. *The holding of meetings shall in every case be reported one week in advance.*
2. *An advance copy of the reading material shall be submitted to Field Command for approval.*
3. *No books shall be read by the Wartime Book Club which are uncongenial to the Third Reich, or of an offending nature.*
4. *A censor from Feldkommandantur 515 will be in attendance at every meeting.*

She'd done it! It took Grace another three weeks to find enough paper to advertise the inaugural meeting of the Wartime Book Club and get the idea rubberstamped by the States and Feldkommandantur 515. And so it was, on a blustery gray Saturday afternoon at the end of January, that Grace nervously tidied up the library.

"Come on, Peter. Let's arrange the chairs in the Reading Room into a circle."

She had chosen *Rebecca* by Daphne du Maurier.

"What if no one turns up?" she worried. So far the only person who had turned up, a stickler for punctuality, was a German Sonderführer from College House, who announced portentously that he was the "Zensor" from the Feldkommandantur.

"They will," Peter replied, shooting a nervous look at the censor.

"What if I fluff it?" She chewed her nonexistent fingernails.

"You always know what to say," Peter said, staring back at the floor, hands fluttering. "How do you do it?"

"Do what, sweetie?"

"Find the right words." His eyes flickered up and all around the library, anywhere but at Grace. "On New Year's Eve, when Miss Gold was upset, you made her feel better, just with words."

"Well, I guess reading helps. All my life I've read books. I think about what my favorite characters would say and that helps." Grace smiled, warming to her theme. "I suppose you could say I have hundreds of people whose shoes I can step into. Whose words and language I can use as my own."

Peter nodded solemnly and sneaked a shy glance at her.

"Thanks, Grace." His eyes flickered back to the floor.

"You know, it's also worth considering that sometimes talking is overrated. People can talk for the sake of it."

"And say things they don't mean."

"Precisely, Peter. And don't forget, you do your talking with pictures."

"Cooeey," a loud voice interrupted them. "Hello, ducks, is this where the book club is?"

"Mrs. Moisan. You came."

"Wouldn't miss for the world, eh. It's only you that could get me to come into town."

She paused, her breath heaving as she gripped the staircase up to the mezzanine Reading Room.

"Closer to God up here, isn't it, my love."

Grace rushed forward to greet her, resting her hand on her forearm.

"I'm so very sorry about Dolly."

The bluff country woman lifted her chin. "Nothing anyone can say or do is the truth, I have to get on with it." She touched her chest. "She's here, in my heart. I'll do my grieving when Liberation Day comes."

Grace smiled sadly as Mrs. Moisan took her seat. She had the strongest suspicion that she wasn't alone in bottling up her emotions and that come Liberation a tsunami of tears would sweep the island into the sea.

Suddenly the Reading Room was alive, voices echoing off the domed roof. Mrs. Moisan was followed by Bea's mum Queenie, Louisa Gould, who everyone knew was still harboring her runaway slave—a mistake as far as Grace could tell. Bea came, bringing with her Winnie, Doris and Gladys from the post office. Mrs. Noble came with her grandson Tommy and a Lord Woolton pie.

"For you, my love," she said, setting down the pie and her returned copy of *A Christmas Carol*.

"How was your Christmas, Mrs. Noble?" Grace asked.

She shot a sly look at the censor sitting in the corner. "Purer than the driven snow. Thanks for asking, my love."

Grace smiled. "That's wonderful to hear."

The group had settled when finally the library door opened and a figure stood hesitantly at the door. She sensed Bea stiffen next to her.

"Mum, you came."

Mary La Mottée looked like she'd rather be anywhere than the library, but Mrs. Noble and Mrs. Moisan rose and made a great fuss of her, moving chairs so that she could sit between them.

"I'm...I'm not sure I should be here," her mum said, "I've far too much to do at the farm."

"Come now. One chapter won't hurt, Mary," Mrs. Moisan said, reaching for her hand. Mrs. Noble reached for the other. "You've already been through the worse, eh."

"Well, it's terrific to get such a good turnout for the first meeting of the Wartime Book Club," Grace said nervously. "The aim of this book club is to share our love of reading and books. Do you know the very first book club opened in London in..."

"Just get on with it, my love, eh," Mrs. Moisan interrupted with a friendly wink. "We've come here for a story, not a history lecture."

Grace glanced at Bea. "Breathe," she mouthed silently.

"Yes, yes, of course. I'm going to read from Daphne du Maurier's *Rebecca*."

As Grace unlocked the door to a truly spellbinding story she felt a softening of the group. Limbs relaxed, bums sank further into seats. Miss Du Maurier had given these hard-working women permission to switch off and escape their lives. What was it about truly great stories whose words had the ability to pass straight through blood and bone and lodge in the soul? Mrs. Noble had got her knitting out and Grace read to the rhythmic clacking of her fingers working the needles. She glanced up and saw her mother had crossed her arms and had her eyes closed. Scattered diamonds of light danced on her face, streaming down from the stained-glass windows of the dome above them. For the first time since her brother's death, her mother looked at peace.

The problem came halfway through Chapter One, when Grace realized whoever had borrowed the book last had clearly tried to read while cooking, as the pages looked to be stuck together with stew.

"Bother," she muttered. "I shall have to clean this book before we go on."

"Miss La Mottée, I can read it," Peter chimed in.

"But the book's damaged, Peter."

"I know it off by heart."

The group looked incredulous.

"Very well," Grace said, setting down the book.

Peter closed his eyes and just like that, the exact words fell from his lips. The group watched in astonishment as he recited verbatim from his memory. Mrs. Noble put down her knitting and listened incredulously as he took the group back to Manderley again, walking them through the charred ruins of the once-beautiful mansion.

Grace swore she barely breathed as he read. Peter's odd usually monotone voice had changed, the book had given his voice timbre and character. He *had* listened to what she'd said. He'd stepped into the shoes of another and it was then she realized, readers weren't reading a book, they were inhabiting a whole new world.

When he got to the end of Chapter One there was a silence, broken only by the soft snores of the German censor.

"Bravo, sonny. You did a cracking job. How did you memorize all those words?" Queenie asked.

"I can barely remember my shopping list," Winnie chuckled.

He shrugged. "I'm here all the time. It's not so hard."

"Don'cha have any friends, lad?" Doris asked.

"Books are my friends," he replied, without a trace of self-pity.

Grace gave him an enormous thumbs-up, feeling ridiculously proud of him. "Well, I think that was a very successful first meeting," she announced.

"I should say," said Mrs. Moisan. "I nearly forgot the mountain of shit I need to shovel when I get back to the farm."

"And my lumbago," Gladys from the post office piped up.

"And the bloody Hun on every street corner," Mrs. Noble whispered so as not to wake the censor.

"Any questions before I call an end to our first meeting?"

"I have one," came a voice from the back of the room. "I love your passion for reading, but it was Thomas Edison, the great American inventor, who said, 'Not everything of value in life comes from books—experience the world.' Do you agree?"

All heads swiveled to take in the handsome stranger with the cut-glass accent at the back of the room.

For a moment Grace was speechless, before recovering herself. "The same man also said, 'Never stop learning. Read the entire panorama of literature.' Now, if that's all there's tea and cake downstairs."

She made her way quickly to where Red was buttoning up his coat.

"Are you barmy?" she hissed. "There's a German censor not ten feet from where we're standing."

"And the chump's fast asleep." Red's mouth twitched in amusement.

"Please, Red, you've got to go. You can't be here."

"Not until you promise to come and see me and bring a book. But mainly just bring yourself."

"Red, you are utterly incorrigible, but honestly, this… this is a step too far."

He held his hands up in surrender, a wicked smile curling the edges of his mouth. "I'll go when you promise to come and see me."

The German censor grunted, a terrific snore rocking his body, and for an awful moment, Grace thought he was about to wake.

"Yes, yes, very well."

"Can you bring me a copy of *The Call of the Wild*?"

He stepped closer to her, so close she could see herself reflected in his green eyes.

"It's a banned book," she murmured, feeling lightheaded.

"That's all right. I'm a banned man."

"I'll do my best."

Out of the corner of her eye she saw Bea approach her mother.

"Now go, before you give me a coronary."

The Call of the Wild indeed. Trust him to love that book. She kept her eyes on him until she was sure he was on his way out. At the top of the staircase he turned and blew her a kiss before vanishing.

"Grace, your mum and I are going for a cup of tea," Bea said. "Do you want to come?"

Grace blew out slowly and tried to force her thoughts from Red.

"No, you two go on. It's good to see you both talking."

Grace smiled as they left the library together. Who knew whether *Rebecca* had helped to restore a fragile kind of peace. Possibly, but it was a start, wasn't it?

Bea and her mother left, along with the rest of the Wartime Book Club, and Grace began to stack the chairs.

Wordlessly, Peter began to help.

"You don't have to do this, sweetie. Why don't you get on home? Your mum'll be worried about you."

He shook his head. "She's out with Kurt."

"Kurt?"

"Her German boyfriend."

Grace swallowed back her anger. "Very well, in that case, there's always jobs here for you to do."

Together they worked in amicable silence, cleaning up the library, and it occurred to her how comforting she found his presence.

Heavy footsteps shattered the calm.

"Red, if that's you…" she began, turning around.

"Sergeant Wölfle," she said uneasily.

"Miss Grace La Mottée, acting Chief Librarian. You are everywhere and nowhere."

"Peter, time for you to go home," she said warily.

"But you said there was always jobs—"

"Please, sweetie," she interrupted, trying to keep the fear from her voice. "I'll see you Monday."

He picked up his coat and she could sense the Wolf watching him intently as he walked from the library.

"Interesting child. A simpleton, so my informers tell me, but he, like you, is not quite as he seems."

He pulled a chair off the pile and sat down, crossing his legs. Just five yards away from him, tucked behind *Birds of the Channel Islands*, the *verboten* books were hidden. Forbidden authors H. G. Wells, Leonard Brown, Duff Cooper, Ernest Hemingway and Winston Churchill, among others, were simmering in the darkness, biding their time, demanding to be let out.

Grace felt her stomach knot into a tight fist.

"I'm sorry. I don't understand. How may I help you?"

"I was sad to miss you on Christmas Eve when I visited the library and you were out delivering messages."

"Books actually. Not messages."

He eyed her up and down and shot her that oily smile. Bea was wrong about him. He wasn't an ignoramus. He was sharp as a fishhook and she had the most awful feeling she would end up impaled.

"You were out delivering books when I visited, not just on that occasion but on two others too. But wherever my men go, it seems like you have been there first."

He lit a cigarette.

"Sorry, it's no smoking in the library."

"Everywhere and nowhere," he repeated, blowing a stream of blue smoke in her direction.

"I'm afraid I don't follow," she snapped, pushing down the tide of irritation that he had refused to extinguish his cigarette.

"My men searched a premises on Havre des Pas following an anonymous tip-off, and we found very little of interest, but I did discover a book from this public library."

She swallowed. "That's not unusual, this library is especially well frequented since the outbreak of war. Books aren't outlawed, are they?"

"The right kind of books, no."

"All our stock has been checked by the commandant's office."

"Is that so?" he asked, looking around the stacks.

Her heart began to pick up speed.

"Yes."

"Then two days after Christmas we searched a house up in Trinity. Nothing of note, but I did find a copy of, what was it…"

He made a show of racking his brains, tapping his forehead.

"Aah yes, *A Christmas Carol*, date-stamped Christmas Eve."

"I don't understand."

"Your friend Bea used that line on me once before and I fell for it then, but no longer. She is no innocent and neither I suspect are you."

He stood abruptly scraping back the chair. "It seems that where we go, you have been there just before."

"A coincidence," she murmured, scarcely able to breathe as he walked toward her, his face so close she could smell his hair oil.

"The funny thing with coincidences, Miss La Mottée, I have come to understand, is that they are rarely as innocent as they seem. On this tiny island everything is linked. Everyone knows everyone. Someone in the post office, say, might be old friends with the butcher, the baker... *the librarian.*"

Grace felt fear dripping down the back of her throat, as he ran his hand along the nature bookshelf, inches from the banned books.

"If I discover you are tipping off people and breaking the law, the penalties will be severe. Your family will never see you again. Do you think you could do that to your mother, Grace, especially after Jimmy?"

She tried to keep her expression unchanged but her face betrayed her and he smiled maliciously.

"Oh yes, you see, I've done my homework. I know your brother was the one shot for attempting to get information to the British and he was engaged to be married to your friend Beatrice Gold, who has shown such hostility toward the Third Reich. You see, everything is connected on this island."

Her world tilted closer to the edge of insanity.

"You have me wrong, sir. I knew nothing about my brother's escape attempt. I am a small-town librarian who wishes to live in peace."

He drew deeply on his cigarette. The tip glowed red and crackled.

"I'd hate there to be an accident. Imagine if the library were accidentally to catch fire. It would go up quickly, would it not—all this paper?"

An expression of almost girlish glee lit up his face.

"We've done it before, Miss La Mottée. The Jersey Masonic Library…" He tailed off. How could Grace forget the day a German wrecking squad had arrived from Berlin and swarmed all over the Masonic Lodge in St. Helier, seven months after the invasion, looting and destroying. It had taken troops two days to rip out every book and bookshelf. The contents had been burned in the garden of the lodge, covering St. Helier in a cloud of ash for days after.

"Do you remember the flames?" He edged closer. "Didn't those books burn beautifully?"

Her thoughts strayed to *Ulysses* by James Joyce and *All Quiet on the Western Front* by Erich Maria Remarque, already a pile of black ash in some Nazi book-burning pyre.

"Why are you so afraid of words on a page?" she trembled. "You've spent all this money building fortifications to keep the Allies out and yet you consider my library to be of greater threat."

"Trust me, your library is no threat to the Third Reich. We are cleansing the world of *Untermenschen*, creating a better world. It's as easy as tearing pages from a book, Miss La Mottée."

His words crawled over her skin like vermin. He turned to leave but turned back to her almost as an afterthought.

"Oh, and from now on I shall require a list of every single person who attends your book club."

He left and the roaring in Grace's ears reached a crescendo. In an uncharacteristic fit of anger she walked up and slammed the door shut. Then she placed a hand against the wall and let out a loud anguished sob.

"What is happening?" She held on to the wall. This library was her entire world, her feelings wrapped up in the spines of the books, her soul in the stacks. But now it seemed that her last haven was at risk—and there was nothing she could do.

9

Bea

Bea smelled them before she saw them. She had delivered her postal round to Havre des Pas, and was cycling under the shadow of Fort Regent, back into town when the stench hit her. Hot, marshy gusts of something deeply rotten washed over her.

Her sense of smell seemed so acute of late.

"Oh, Jesus!" She pulled over by a granite bollard at the edge of the French Harbour.

"Not a pretty sight, is it." Dr. McKinstry was standing a few feet away and together they watched the spectacle.

A pathetic, shabby group of prisoners trudged along the side of the quay next to the high barbed-wire fence.

Barefoot, despite the freezing February fog and icy winds, feet black and raw, they trudged like walking skeletons.

One of them—he could have been 13 or 30, it was hard to tell—staggered suddenly to the right. The OT guard nearest to him raised his rubber truncheon and brought it crashing down on his head.

Bea cried out loud and buried her face in her hands.

"Where's your humanity?" Dr. McKinstry shouted at the guard.

"Keep out of it, old man."

"And this is the superior race?" Dr. McKinstry intoned, his voice as dry as dust.

"Why are the ones at the back wearing striped clothing?" she asked and he shook his head.

"They've shipped them over from Sylt and Norderney."

"Where's that? Russia?"

He looked down at her, his eyes bloodshot from exhaustion.

"No, dear girl. They are the names of camps in Alderney, just forty miles from here."

"Oh." She was ashamed at her ignorance.

"No reason for you to know. They keep it well hidden. There're only a few civilians left, so fewer prying eyes. They do as they wish—and believe me they do. That island will reverberate with screams for many years to come."

"How do you know this?"

"A patient's son was sent there for six weeks after he refused to step off the curb to make way for a German officer. His mother says the child who has come back is not her son. Here on Jersey they work them like beasts of burden and if they stop for a minute they beat them. But in Alderney, if they stop work..." He trailed off. "Not for your ears."

Bea swallowed, felt a strange whirring start in her head. Jimmy had been right. The Channel Islands were prisons without walls.

"Where are they sending them now?"

"I should imagine they're packing them off to Germany in case the Allies invade. They want to hide the evidence of their crimes."

Bea composed herself, pushing down the acid bile that threatened to spill over.

"Are you busy, doctor?" she asked.

"You cannot imagine. Every other person on this island has scarlet fever, flu or diphtheria. Do yourself a favor, Miss Gold, don't get ill."

Her stomach folded. "Doctor, might I ask a question? If a person's malnourished might it be possible for their monthlies to stop?"

"Yes. But it could also mean they're with child. Make an appointment to see Dr. Lewis. He's your doctor, I believe."

"No, it's not for me," she said quickly. "I'm asking for a friend."

He looked down at her searchingly. "Advise your friend to see a doctor without delay."

He touched the tip of his hat then strode on.

Bea stared out at the empty ocean beyond the barbed wire. The flat surface of the sea never failed to amaze her. It was like the skin of a mackerel. Sometimes gray, sometimes purple, or pink, but today, as dark as a bruise. If she did this, kept her mind focused on other things, everything would be well.

In the distance, something astonishing happened. A giant silver barrage balloon had broken free from its moorings by the harbor and was sailing out to sea in the direction of England. Her thoughts leapt to Jimmy.

"Why did you have to leave me?" she whispered, holding her tummy. She glanced down at his cheap tin ring on her ring finger. Bea had never felt so achingly alone or so afraid. Her secrets were stacking up like a precariously balanced house of cards.

Bea watched as the barrage balloon faded to a pinprick on the horizon. One day soon, the Allies would come over that same horizon and free them all from this living nightmare. Then she would pass her letters to the British and leave them to hand down justice on the traitors who had denounced their own.

Her secret stash of stolen letters was growing, horrifying and thrilling her in equal measure. If she was honest, she was proud of how good she was getting at it. She'd developed a magician's sleight of hand. One in the sorting frame, one slipped up the sleeve of her jacket. Most envelopes these days came from recycled tomato-packing paper so were light and easy to conceal.

Barely a day had passed without another piece of poison making its way into the box. After her brush with Nancy, she'd moved them to the allotment for safe keeping. And there, tucked under a carton of weed killer and a manual on how to grow summer fruit, was enough evidence to either get her deported to a Nazi prison, or the senders of the letters arrested for war crimes, or better yet, treason. The question was, what would come first? Liberation or her arrest?

The sickness surged through her again, blooming and unfurling. The air was a ripe stew of smells. The savory stench of diesel and unwashed bodies churned her guts and stirred up her hormones. A few spots of rain began to fall and the wind snapped the swastika at the end of the pier.

"Just keep going," she told herself, picking up her postal bag and mounting her bike. "Come what may."

After she'd finished her Saturday round, Bea collected her mum as promised and they headed to the Wartime Book Club.

They had to push their way through the door to the library.

"Blimey," said Queenie. "It's heaving in here."

It had been five weeks since their first meeting and word had spread round the island faster than a fever. Bea had to hand it to Grace. She had tapped into a need most islanders weren't even aware they had—the simple pleasure of being read to. Half the post office was here. She spied Dr. McKinstry, Albert the physiotherapist, Molly from the flower stall. Extra chairs had been squeezed into the elegant, galleried Reading Room.

The rain drummed on the glass-domed roof, but inside Grace had made it so cozy. Tealights flickered from the corners, keeping the darkness at bay.

"Why do you think it's so popular?" Bea puzzled as they eased their way through the crowd toward Grace. "Aside from the fact that it's somewhere dry and moderately warm?"

"It's free?" Queenie shrugged. "And let's be honest, it's the only way most people'll escape from this island." She looked stricken. "Oh, darlin' I'm so sorry, that was tactless of me."

"Bit late to be apologizing for being tactless, Mum," Bea said, nudging her with her shoulder.

"Me and my cakehole. It'll get me into trouble one of these days."

"You're not wrong there, Mum. You could talk the leg off an iron pot."

"The apple didn't fall far from the tree," she flashed back.

"Over here." Mary La Mottée and Mrs. Noble had saved seats for them near the front.

"Hello, girls. Bea, are you well? You look ever so peaky," Mary commented.

"Charming," Bea quipped. "I'll have you know I was Miss Havre des Pas 1939."

"Who here's gonna win any beauty competitions?" Queenie remarked. "We're all a right shabby show."

"Ignore Mum. I'm fine, thanks for asking, Mrs. La Mottée. It was a long round this morning and I got a chill."

Mary picked up her hand and rubbed it between hers. "Why don't you come to ours for your dinner tomorrow, and you, Queenie." She lowered her voice. "We've got a bit of pork. My husband slaughtered a pig we've been keeping on the sly."

Bea thought of roast pork and crackling and felt her mouth water.

"Mind you, we had a close shave. Germans came knocking last week. They were doing random house searches in the area. We got wind of it and we bundled the pig up, put her in a bonnet and put her into our bed under the covers."

"You never," Queenie breathed.

"We did. When the patrol come through, I told them it was my elderly mother, in bed sick with scarlet fever. They couldn't get out fast enough."

The group hooted with laughter and Bea relaxed. Being on speaking terms with Mrs. La Mottée was one blessing at least.

Grace cleared her throat.

"I'm impressed at the turnout and in such filthy weather. Today I'm going to read from *Pride and Prejudice* by Jane Austen. It's a classic, and I think sometimes, we all need the reassurance of the past." She smiled as she stroked the cover.

"Despite being written at the time of the Napoleonic wars, Miss Austen very cleverly never mentions war at all. This war has changed the literary landscape and now quiet classics that portray a calmer, more certain age provide solace." She smiled and gestured to the tealights. "There's a certain irony that the classics, which were written by candlelight, are once more being read by it."

"Interesting perspective," said a voice Bea vaguely recognized. He stood at the entrance to the door, bundled up in a winter coat, hat pulled down low, his voice disguised as English, but there was no doubt it was him.

Grace's eyes lit up at the sight of him and Bea realized that she had been right in her assertion that her friend had strong feelings for the American. A fact that would have delighted her in peacetime, but now left her worried. It wasn't just risky. It was downright dangerous, especially as he seemed to have such a cavalier attitude toward risk— not that she was one to judge! She had waited so long for her friend to fall in love, knowing that he would have to be something special, but never guessing that this would be the man to claim her friend's heart.

Grace and Red exchanged a secret smile and she began to read, her voice strong and soothing and Bea had to admit, despite her fears, it was like having honey poured into her ear. Fading light filtered through the domed glass panels over her head, casting Grace in an ethereal glow. The Wartime Book Club had captured the hearts and minds of Jersey folk, desperate to escape. Grace was taking her patrons to rhododendron-splashed valleys, sunlit Hampshire drawing rooms and misty Cornish bays. There was no barbed wire or hunger in these books.

In its own way, it was bibliotherapy. Bea cast her eye over this little huddle of souls suffering from all the fury of the war, hunkered in the top of this ancient library. If books were medicine, then Grace was the medic.

Bea heard the soft tread of footsteps behind them and glanced back. Her gaze turned to the top of the staircase. Louisa Gould tiptoed her way in, whispering apologies for her lateness. Behind her was a young, dark-haired man in a suit and Bea nearly fell off her chair.

"She's taking a bloody risk, bringing him into town," Queenie muttered darkly.

Forty-five minutes later, Grace put the book down on her lap.

"That's all for now, but please do all stay for tea. I wish I could offer you biscuits, but alas, my rations do not permit. I can leave you with this, though, my favorite quote from *Pride and Prejudice*: 'I declare after all there is no enjoyment like reading! How much sooner one tires of anything than of a book! When I have a house of my own, I shall be miserable if I have not an excellent library.'"

"And we should be miserable were it not for Grace and her excellent library," Queenie called out. "Three cheers for Grace."

The library was filled with applause and Grace blushed modestly.

When the crowd around Grace dispersed, Bea weaved her way over.

"That seemed to go well, it's proving terrifically popular," Grace said.

"I'm proud of you, Grace," Bea said quietly. "This is exactly what people need right now."

"Are you well?" Grace puzzled, holding her hand to Bea's forehead. "You don't look good. You must've got soaked on your round earlier."

"No, us posties are made of tough stuff. Occupation collywobbles most likely," she said, referring to the gripey tummy many islanders now suffered with, due to excessive consumption of vegetables!

Louisa Gould appeared by their side, clutching a box.

"Grace and Bea, have you met my nephew, Bill?"

A loaded silence fell round the group.

"No, I don't think we've had the pleasure," Grace said, holding out her hand.

Bill said nothing, wisely, just smiled at the group and shook their hands.

"I've been going through Edward's things, and I've dug out a lot of his old books," Louisa remarked. "Always had his nose stuck in one. Anyway, I should like you to have them, Grace my love. I think…" Her voice caught. "I think he would have approved of my donating them to the library."

Grace opened the box. Unimaginable riches: *The Three Musketeers. Wuthering Heights. The Happy Return.*

"Have a look underneath," Louisa urged. "All his favorite books as a child."

"Oh, Lou *Swallows and Amazons, Robinson Crusoe, Moonfleet, Dickon among the Indians.*"

"Say, *Swallows and Amazons,*" Bea exclaimed. "You'll laugh, Mrs. Gould, but Grace and I used to pretend Jersey was Wild Cat Island. The scrapes we got into. Or rather, *I* got Grace into."

"How innocent and precious our childhoods seem now," Louisa replied.

"Precisely why I can't accept these, Lou," Grace insisted. "This is your son's childhood in a box."

"You can and you will," Louisa stated flatly. "They'll bring so much pleasure to other children. Reading these is what gave my Edward such a taste for adventure."

"But don't you want them to remember him by?" Bea asked.

"The best way to honor my son is by actions not words," Louisa said pointedly, smiling at the young man by her side.

"Edward was a moral man, it's what made him sign up to fight in the first place. I think he'd approve of what I'm doing."

Bea wasn't sure whether she was referring to the books, or providing sanctuary to the runaway slave.

"Very well then, Lou," Grace said. "St. Helier Public Library is very grateful for such a generous donation."

"I'm glad they're going to a good home," said Louisa. "Talking of which, we'd best get going if we're to make our bus."

She clutched both of Grace's hands in hers. "Before I go, I want you know that coming here, listening to you reading, it takes the sharp edge off my grief."

Bea and Grace watched Louisa Gould and her young friend leave. Bea felt so choked at the widow's generosity and courage.

"That's a brave woman," Red murmured.

Dr. McKinstry appeared at their side. "I was waiting for Louisa to leave. There's a matter of some urgency to discuss. But first…" He turned to Red.

"Sir, I cannot help you if you refuse to help yourself. You're taking an enormous risk being here, not just to yourself but to Grace. The censor is downstairs checking people's papers."

Red looked chastened. "I apologize, I didn't mean to cause offense, only I'm going stir crazy cooped up in that shed."

"Just as well I've located a new safehouse for you then, on the north of the island. I'll take you there in one hour. Meet me at La Vaux Sanatorium."

His face darkened as he glared at the group. "No more unnecessary risks." His Irish accent, usually so soft was cutting.

"Leave now and for God's sake, man, just show them your papers and keep your trap shut."

Red left and Grace looked crestfallen.

"Grace and Bea," the doctor went on, lowering his voice, "you are playing with fire."

Bea had a feeling she wasn't going to like what the good doctor had to say. "I have intelligence, from someone close to Heinz Carl Wölfle of the Geheime Feldpolizei. He thinks there's a Resistance cell operating within the library and the post office and that the book club is involved somehow. He's trying to make connections between all three."

Grace's face emptied of color.

"Why can't he just leave us alone? I told him when he came in that I am just a librarian. Resistance cells? What kind of nonsense! This is Jersey, not France."

Bea felt the blood in her veins run cold.

"Why does he think that?"

"He thinks informers' letters are being intercepted at the post office and that somehow the library is involved is passing on information."

"Bea and I are not doing anything to attract the attention of the Wolf," Grace said. "We just want to live quietly now and get on with our jobs, don't we, Bea?"

The doctor scrutinized her.

"I'm not passing on warnings any longer," Bea whispered.

It wasn't a lie exactly; an omission of the full facts perhaps. *I'm not passing on warnings any longer, because I'm stealing informers' letters instead and hiding them in my Mum's shed. Like I stole the Germans' mail.*

The air in the library seemed to thrum with intensity, as if all her secrets had leapt up and were chuckling and rustling through the stacks.

Dr. McKinstry breathed out deeply. "That's all right then. Because the Wolf has a spy on the payroll, someone who has been sending fake letters to him. He says not one has reached him at Silvertide."

Bea felt her lungs empty.

"Bea," Grace said slowly, watching her carefully. "Havre des Pas is your round, isn't it?"

She nodded. "It doesn't mean a thing. That man's got bats in his belfry, sending letters to himself. Honestly, he's barking mad."

"Yes, that might well be true," the doctor agreed. "But he's dangerous. He won't stop at anything and for some reason, he has his sights on you both."

"He's a sneaky rat." Bea seethed.

"He is," he agreed. "And rats are masters of survival."

Wearily they all stood.

"I have to close the library now," Grace said. "Thank you, doctor. And, please, don't be too cross with our American friend. He's frustrated being cooped up instead of out there with his unit."

"He'll be a lot more cooped up if he's not careful," he replied. "Good day to you both."

Bea tried to leave too but Grace pulled her back.

"Are you in trouble?" she asked, her voice laced with concern.

Bea longed to fold herself away in Grace's arms. Instead she shook her head.

"Grace, this isn't a plot in one of your novels. My life is far more mundane. I'm fine."

"I'm always here for you, you know that." Grace's gentle green eyes were entreating her to open up. "I know I can't ever replace Jimmy, but I can love you enough for the both of us."

Bea grabbed her hand, squeezed it tight.

"I know that, Gracie."

She left quickly so Grace wouldn't see the hot tears gathering behind her eyes, or hear the scream of panic that threatened to burst out of her.

Thrusting her papers under the nose of the censor, she got on her bike and pedaled out of town. She didn't even stop to think where she was going. She just needed to put distance between her and Germans. One thought drummed repeatedly through her mind. Some of the letters she had hidden were fakes, sent by the Wolf. She had played straight into his hands!

Skirting St. Aubin's Bay, she cycled on to St. Brelade's Bay. Fields and beaches scarred with ugly fortifications flashed past. Scrawls of black cloud dirtied the sky and a rattling wind sent dry leaves spiraling into the air.

Finally, exhausted, she stopped at the cliff overlooking Devil's Hole, the path down sealed off by barbed wire. This was the place where Jimmy's and her new life was supposed to have begun. The fact that she would never see him again, *ever*, was impossible to comprehend.

She closed her eyes, imagined the two of them before the war, dancing under a red summer moon at Billy's Lido. She in her best green summer frock, he all done up "like a swell"—two young people in love, whose only concern had been where to swim or dance.

Her eyes snapped open. The weather was turning wild. The wind roared. Needle-sharp hailstones hammered her face.

"Oh, Jimmy," she moaned, "if you can hear me, I'm in a terrible fix."

She stared out at the black ocean. The waves swirled and boiled before exploding onto the rocks in a crash of white foam.

"I'm scared, Jimmy," she whispered. The wind snatched her words away.

The future stretched out like a vast unbearable void.

10

Grace

BANNED BOOK

Ernest Hemingway's writing was viewed by the Nazis as a "corrupting foreign influence" and his books banned.

After a long hard winter at war, Grace's thoughts turned to spring. It was the first Saturday in March and a sense of hope blossomed among the stacks.

She'd come in that morning to find dozens of donated books, so many in fact that she and Miss Piquet had to pile them up high in her office.

Grace and her library assistant had been working flat out all day recommending, stamping, shelving and dealing with the queue that at times threatened to snake out the door. 1943 had been busy, but 1944 was proving to be even busier.

As the occupation clamped its jaws ever tighter round islanders' necks, it felt like everything was short but books. There was the cinema of course, but no one with a shred of self-respect would dare pass under the swastika, which now hung over The Forum on Grenville Street, to watch what amounted to German propaganda.

West's cinema was where the locals went, but sometimes it felt as if the only thing they'd shown over the past three years was *The Wizard of Oz* and Grace had decided there was only so many times she could follow Dorothy up the Yellow Brick Road. So the library it was—a refuge for tattered souls.

Grace took a moment to appreciate the book tower in her office.

One book caught her eye. *The Book Lovers' Anthology: A Compendium of Writing about Books, Readers and Libraries.* Usually their donated books were a little on the tatty side, but this hardback looked like it belonged in a rare-books archive. Its burgundy embossed-leather cover and gold-tipped pages made it easily the most divine book she had ever seen. Grace picked it up, her fingers fanning the soft cream vellum pages. She held it to her nose, breathing in the musty tang of old paper. A note slipped out. Elegant looping words etched on tomato-packing paper.

I'll never forget the sight of you reading Jane Austen by candlelight. R x

Grace smiled. *How on earth?*

The door opened a crack and Grace slid the note in her skirt pocket.

"Hallo. Sorry to disturb. Do you have a moment?"

Albert Bedane, the physiotherapist, hovered at her office door.

"For you, Mr. Bedane, always."

"Gracious, look at all these books."

"Donated, would you believe."

"It's your book club, Grace. It's igniting a fire."

"I'm not sure about that, but I hope it offers a little solace, the chance to escape the churn of one's thoughts."

"Which is why I'm here. Might we talk in private?"

He shut the door.

"How can I help you?" she asked, clearing books off chairs so he could sit down.

"I'm after more books for my houseguest, please," he said, pulling out *The Secret Garden.* "She romped through this."

"Of course. She's almost exhausted my stock of romantic fiction."

"Have you anything more in the vein of *The Secret Garden?* Something about the the loneliness of the protagonist and the vivid descriptions of opening a secret door to a hidden-away garden...well, it spoke to her. She said it made her feel less alone somehow, reminded her of the beauty of nature."

Grace felt her heart buckle. She couldn't imagine not breathing country air, witnessing the magical twilight hour when bats flitted from the eaves of their old farmhouse. Of all those hazy summer hours reading under the apple tree in her garden. What must it be like to be hidden away in a cellar, breathing the same stale air, month after month?

"She needs another world to roam. A metaphorical door to open."

Her eyes alighted on the nearest box. Serendipity.

"*Alice in Wonderland!*"

"Isn't that a children's book?"

"I'd say it's a book for book lovers of any age. Alice falls down the rabbit hole and uncovers a strange subterranean world, filled with doorways she has to find a way to open."

She sighed. "I adored this book growing up. I used to explore under my bed hoping to find a loose floorboard, a portal to another world."

"What did you find?"

"Dust mainly."

He laughed. "This'll do nicely."

"I do hope it works, Mr. Bedane, until the day comes when she can open her real front door."

"Please God that day comes soon."

He looked up, Grace thought in deference to Him.

"Allied planes flew over St. Helier last night, Grace. British or American, I'm not sure. They were just visible to the naked eye. There were eighty-eight of them—I counted."

"Maybe that day will come sooner than we think," she ventured hopefully.

"Here's hoping." He picked up the book and tapped it. "Until that day, we have Alice."

"Tuck it in your bag," she advised. "I haven't cataloged it yet, so it's off the record. Actually, half a mo. If you get stopped with this book, it'll look iffy."

She glanced around her office and the idea suddenly came to her.

"Here." Grace picked up a donated copy of *Wayfaring Life in the Middle Ages*, slipped off the dust jacket and popped it over the top of an indignant-looking Alice.

"If you get stopped and searched, this'll look an awful lot less suspicious."

"You're a wonder, Grace!"

He hesitated, clearly something else weighing on his mind.

"I…um…I don't suppose you have anything else off the record, if you catch my drift."

"I'm afraid your drift must have slipped from my grasp, Mr. Bedane."

"I'll speak more plainly. I was happily making my way through some of Ernest Hemingway's fine novels when the invasion happened and they just seemed to have, well, *vanished* from the stacks."

"Yes, apologies for that. Our uninvited guests decided Hemingway is an author uncongenial to the regime."

"I was hoping to read *A Farewell to Arms*…" He tapped the book on his lap. "Should the occasion present itself."

She stared at him for a very long time, her thoughts ticking over.

"I think we know that we can both trust each other, Grace. You must know that I, of all people, would never betray that trust. I have far too much to lose."

Grace nodded, understanding.

"Very well. Why don't you bring back the cover of *Wayfaring Life in the Middle Ages,* and I'll see what opportunities present themselves."

He smiled as he rose to his feet. "You're an enlightened librarian, Grace."

"One would hope all librarians are," she replied.

Fifteen minutes later, Mr. Bedane left, happy with a concealed *Alice in Wonderland,* tucked in his physiotherapist's bag.

When Grace emerged from her office she was startled to see the library even busier than before, with every seat and spare patch of space in the mezzanine Reading Room full.

"Book Club time, Grace," Miss Piquet reminded her.

"Gracious, already?"

"You look how I feel, my love." Molly the florist laughed.

"I'm so sorry," Grace said, flustered to have been caught on the hop. "We've finished *Pride and Prejudice*, haven't we, but I haven't had a chance yet to think about what next."

"Might I make a suggestion?" piped up Mr. Warder, the post-office engineer. "It might sound a bit silly."

"You wouldn't believe the requests I get," Grace replied. "This morning, an elderly gentleman came in and asked me to look after his pet ferret while he went to market. Our Bibliothèque Publique certainly gives me a wide insight into the peculiarities of man."

The library crowd fell about. The grumpy looking German censor in the corner looked confused.

"Don't worry, Grace. I'm not smuggling ferrets," Mr. Warder chuckled. "I had a Red Cross message delivered from my wife Trix in Bournemouth. She used up her twenty-word allocation would you believe to tell me not about the children, but that she's reading *Footsteps in the Dark*, by Georgette Heyer, and would I read a copy too, so we could feel together."

He looked embarrassed. "Sounds like terrible sentimental piffle if you ask me. I'm more of a P. G. Wodehouse man myself. Could we possibly read it together in book club?"

"What a wonderful idea of your wife's, and as for sentimental, not a bit of it. Georgette Heyer is a first-class writer, full of dry wit and charm. Her research on the British Regency period is second to none."

While Miss Piquet hurried off to fetch the book, Mr. Warder rooted around in his pocket, fighting off tears.

"Sorry, sorry... I don't know what's wrong with me."

"Nothing wrong with you," Queenie said, handing him her handkerchief. "You're a human being with a beating heart. You'd have to be made of stone not to be missing your wife and kiddies."

Mr. Warder nodded, rubbing his eyes with the heel of his hands and Grace pushed back her own tears. Every day the horror of this god-awful war showed up in her library.

While she watched the book club's show of solidarity, she suddenly realized two things, both of which made her feel disconcerted.

Firstly, Peter wasn't there. In the franticness of the day she hadn't noticed he wasn't in the library. Usually he was like her little shadow and he never missed book club. Secondly, while they had closed ranks around Mr. Warder, the Wolf had sneaked into the library and was sitting at the back, whispering something into the German censor's ear.

The easy atmosphere of earlier evaporated as one by one the book club noticed the most notorious German on the island, sitting at the back of the library.

"Miss La Mottée, I wanted to see what all the fuss is about," he said, his odd accent piercing the still of the library. "Please, act as if I am not here."

"Fat chance of that," Queenie muttered under her breath.

Grace began to read from the book, feeling as if every word might trigger a timebomb, her anger growing as she turned the page. This book club was supposed to be their sanctuary from the enemy, a safe space to escape from the war.

When she reached the end of the chapter, she shut the book and forced herself to focus on Mr. Warder.

"I bet the author would be delighted to know that, despite being separated by an ocean, you and your wife are reading together. The book is like a bridge between you."

His rich laughter filled the library. "A bridge indeed. I rather like that."

"Let's continue this book next week, shall we. Take care, everyone."

The room was filled with the sounds of chairs scraping back as weary islanders reluctantly reached for coats and bags.

She felt his presence behind her before she saw him, his hand, stained with earth, touched her arm and she froze.

"Grace, I'm in a fix," he whispered.

She turned, the blood in her veins turning to ice.

Red was in the rough workman garb of a country farmer, not so unusual for a Saturday afternoon when many from the rural regions came into town, but there was no way his English accent would stand up to an interrogation.

The censor and the Wolf had positioned themselves at the door to the library, questioning everyone as they checked their papers.

"Get in my office now," she hissed, her heart thundering in her mouth.

Red slipped into the side room and Grace walked as casually as she could through the library, making a point to chat as convivially as she could to everyone as they left.

"You get off now, Miss Piquet," she said as the room emptied. "I'll close up."

Eventually, it was just her, the censor and the Wolf, standing in a puddle of late-afternoon light.

"I've been observing you, Miss La Mottée. You're rather like a priest taking confession."

"I run a library, Sergeant Wölfle, not a church."

"You won't mind if I take a look around, check there are no irregularities."

"Be my guest," she said, as the whirring inside her ears reached a screaming pitch.

She positioned herself behind her circular desk, so he couldn't see her legs shaking as he and the censor made a show of checking round the stacks and under the tables.

"I can't think what you're looking for," she said curtly.

"There are Russian workers on the loose and several American aircrew at large on the island." He smiled at her contemptuously. "It's for your own safety."

He glanced at her office door.

"What's in there?"

"Old books mainly. It's my office."

She closed her eyes as he swung open the door.

Moments stretched out like hours.

The door slammed and she jumped.

"Good day to you, Miss La Mottée. Don't stay too late. I should hate to have to fine you for missing curfew."

He and the censor left and Grace stood rooted to the spot, forcing herself to count to a minute before she dared to move.

The air in the library seemed to crackle as she moved softly to the library door, locking it.

Something fizzled and the lights snapped off, plunging her into darkness.

Cursing, she lit a candle and went to her office, pushing the door open.

Her fear had assuaged, replaced by anger.

"Red," she hissed.

In the far corner of her office, where she had piled up all their donated books, she heard a scuffling noise. Red's face poked out behind the tower of books in boxes.

"Boy, just as well I lost so much weight. I'd never have squeezed behind here six months ago." He shot her a reckless grin. "That was a close shave."

"What is wrong with you?" she cried, slamming the candle holder down so hard shadows danced over the room. "Are you trying to get yourself caught? Why can't you just stay in the countryside like Dr. McKinstry told you?"

Red looked taken aback at the force of her anger.

"This isn't a game, Red," she continued. "This library is my life. Why are you taking these risks?"

Then to her embarrassment, she burst into tears.

He covered the room in two easy strides and pulled her into his arms, so close she felt the warmth of his body pulsing against hers.

"I think you know why, Grace," he whispered. "I'm falling in love with you and there's not a darn thing I can do about it."

He reached down and her eyes flickered shut as his mouth found hers. This time the kiss was real: sweet, tender and searching. Grace surrendered to his touch, kissing him back with a passion she hadn't realized she was capable of.

Finally he broke off and a silence fell over the library like a velvet cloth.

"But why?"

"Only a librarian would ask that," he teased.

"But if you must know, I love the way you're passionate about this library and the people who use it, the way you make me feel when you read." He winked. "Your knockout smile."

"I...I don't know if I can say those words back to you," she said quietly.

His fingers trailed softly down her cheek and she could feel the heat coursing through them.

"I don't need you to say anything."

Red cupped her face and kissed her again, softer this time, slow and deep, his fingers probing the naked skin of her neck.

"You've no idea how many times I've dreamt of this moment," he murmured, his voice husky, his eyes all leaping flames as he lowered his lips back to hers.

After the kiss they both froze, as if movement would shatter something so fragile and precious.

"I've never been kissed in the library," Grace murmured eventually.

For some reason, it made them both laugh.

"Have you had a sweetheart?" He watched her reaction in the flickering light. "Sorry, I'm being too American aren't I!"

"No, it's all right. I've never had a suitor or a gentleman friend." Grace laughed. "I sound like something out of a Mills and Boon."

"Never?"

"All I've ever really loved is books," she confessed.

Grace thought back over what books had meant to her. The time Bea came knocking and she hid under her bed as she was so close to finishing *Black Beauty*. Or the nights she would fall asleep with her cheek pressed against a book, waking up with the spine etched on her face.

"I guess this was a good choice then," he remarked, reaching for the *The Book Lovers' Anthology* on her desk.

"How did you get this?"

"The people I'm staying with have got the biggest library I've ever seen in a house. I told them about your Wartime Book Club and they were impressed."

Grace shook her head, speechless at the gesture.

"I wanted to prove to you that I love you, Grace."

He smiled down at her. "In fact, I want to know everything there is to know about you. Favorite childhood book?"

"Impossible to whittle down to one, but growing up I used to love *Moonfleet*."

She laughed. "I made Bea read it after me and she was hooked. She convinced me there was a shipwreck out by Bouley Bay so we once made a raft and went in search of the notorious Blackbeard and hidden treasure. But the raft broke apart half a mile out and we had to be rescued."

Red burst into laughter. "Did Bea often get you in trouble?"

"Too often, yes," she said ruefully. "She reminds me of you actually."

"I'll take that as a compliment."

He bent down to kiss her again, but this time she rested a finger on his lips.

"Enough excitement for one night. You've got to go. For all we know the Wolf's still outside watching the library."

"You're the boss."

He pulled his cap down low over his face and looked at her longingly.

"You have never looked so beautiful, Angel Grace."

He jerked a finger at the office window. "Where does that lead?"

"An alley and some bins."

Before she had a chance to stop him, he pushed the top of the sash window up and eased his tall body through it until he was sitting on the ledge.

"Before you go, Red."

"Yes."

"Do you remember when I asked you why you signed up and you told me about that mobile library in London, Books for the Bombed?"

"Course."

"I never asked. Did you visit it, when you got to London?"

His face lit up at the memory, his wide smile creasing his cheeks into dimples.

"Sure I did. Oh man, what a kick. I waited outside St. Pancras Town Hall and this big old library bus trundled round the corner. Knocked my socks off to think of it delivering books throughout the Blitz. They even let me borrow a book."

"Don't tell me, *The Call of the Wild*?"

Red's smile stretched wider. "See now. You know me better than you think you do."

He shook his head. "I tell you, Grace. Life is extraordinary. Three years ago I was bumming around Boston, working out what to do with my life. Now I'm visiting all these incredible libraries. And I've met the woman I want to spend the rest of my life with. This is the greatest experience my generation can ever hope to have!"

He laughed—such a big infectious noise of incandescent joy that she realized he wasn't reckless. He just loved being in the thick of life.

The breeze rustled in through the open window, ushering the scent of salt, tobacco and wood smoke into the library. The pocket of air between them shimmered, charged somehow from Red's confession.

He sighed, his heart and head doing battle.

"Go on, shoo," she laughed.

"Oh boy, Grace, you got me hook, line and sinker. Until next time." And then he was gone, his long lean body slipping out the window and clambering across the library roof.

Grace shut the window behind him, her head still spinning at the turn of events.

For a long time she sat at her office desk, running her finger down the spine of *The Book Lovers' Anthology*.

Red's confession had sent a ripple of undiluted joy through her, a gentle thrum that began in her toes and cascaded through her chest. She might not be able to admit it to him yet, but she could admit it to herself. She *was* falling in love with him. Any man that was prepared to risk everything to bring her the essential anthology for biblio-philes had to be worth a punt, didn't he?

But there was something nagging at her subconscious.

Suddenly, in the dark void a grubby voice came back to Grace.

Interesting child, a simpleton so my informers tell me…

A cold feeling slid over her, bursting her euphoria.

Peter!

11

Bea

BANNED BOOK

The works of German author Thomas Mann, recipient of the 1929 Nobel Prize for Literature, were banned by Nazi Germany. In 1933 only his political writing was blacklisted and burned, but after he claimed solidarity with other banned writers, the Nazis stripped him of his citizenship.

"All right, all right, keep you flamin' hair on. I'm coming," Queenie grumbled, standing up creakily and pushing back her chair.

Bea had been darning socks at the table, but at the sudden rapping of the door, dropped the needle and thread, pricking her flesh.

"Who is it, Mum?" Bea asked, wincing as she sucked her finger. Door knocks like that usually came from a German fist. A cold tendril of fear unfurled inside. This was how it would come. The heavy boot tread. The knock at the door. Then she would be dragged down to Silvertide.

"The devil himself by the sounds of it," Queenie said.

But it wasn't the Wolf and his men.

"Grace, love, whatever's wrong?" her mum asked. Any relief Bea felt that it wasn't the Secret Police quickly dissolved when she saw Grace's panicked face.

"It's Peter Topsy. He's missing. I just knocked at his home and his mum hasn't seen him since yesterday morning— not that she cares. That's two visits to the library he's missed now. That's not like him. He's in trouble, I just know it."

"Grace, love, calm down," said Queenie. "He'll be with a pal pinching eggs out in the countryside."

Grace shook her head. "No…not Peter. He's not like most boys his age."

"So what do you want to do?" Bea asked, setting aside her darning.

"We need to get a search party together and start looking before curfew. His mum doesn't even care that her son's missing. It's up to us to find him."

Queenie was already reaching for their coats.

"Come on then. Let's see how many of the book club we can get together. Meet in the Royal Square and we can start the search party from there."

Thirty minutes later they had raised most of the book club based in St. Helier, including Billy, Nobby, Mr. Warder, Eric and Harold from the post office, along with Albert the physiotherapist, Dr. McKinstry, Molly and the counter staff, Winnie, Doris and Gladys.

"We'll split up and go on our usual town rounds and see if anyone's seen the young chap," said Nobby.

"I'll go to the offices of the *Evening Post* and see if they can run a front-page appeal for information," said Mr. Warder.

"And I'll try the hospital, see if he's there," said Dr. McKinstry.

"Come on, Grace," said Bea, tugging her arm. "We'll go to St. Aubin's Bay, search along there. Maybe he was hunting for limpets and lost track of time."

They got on their bikes and cycled down to the coast, backs hunched against the cold. A capricious wind whipped the sea into boiling, frothy white peaks and sent the gulls tumbling inland. The air was charged and static. A queer sulfurous yellow stained the horizon. A storm was brewing.

Bea suddenly felt queasy and pulled over, resting her foot on a bollard. She stared in subdued silence over the wide sweep of bay back to Elizabeth Castle. The brooding Elizabethan castle had been cut off by the tide and stood isolated and alone.

Grace's voice rose over the wind. "I've known you long enough, Beatrice Gold, to know when something is wrong. You're keeping secrets from me."

"Don't be daft," Bea replied, scuffing her foot against the curbstone.

"Please, Bea. You can confide in me. Whatever's troubling you, you don't have to go through it alone."

Just one more comforting word and she'd crack.

"Girls." A figure was running toward them, waving her arms.

"Molly, what's wrong?" Grace asked.

The florist was shaking, her face bleached white as bone.

"A body's washed up on the shore."

Bea and Grace began to run toward the clot of people gathered on the beach.

"Is it Peter? Please let me through," Grace yelled.

Bea's breath was rasping by the time she caught up with Grace.

She touched Grace's shoulder, eased her way through the crowd.

A woman lay sprawled on the sand, her waxy face bloated, her lips bruised blue. She stared up at them with a look of utter surprise on her face. Her peroxide-blonde hair clung to her face like strands of seaweed.

"I recognize her from town," said Molly. "She works at the Victor Hugo Hotel."

"The brothel?" Bea asked and Molly nodded.

"I got chatting to her one day," Molly said. "She was a nice girl, the Germans had her sent over from Paris."

A silence fell over the wet sand as Bea digested this. *Sent over.* Rage crawled inside her heart. From what she could tell, women had always been commodities to be bought and sold like sugar or meat, but war had stripped away the veneer. A dead prostitute on the beach would have caused a scandal in peacetime, but during an occupation, eyes were bound to slide the other way.

"How did she end up here?" Grace asked.

"God knows, but she weren't out for a dip, was she," murmured an onlooker.

"Poor lamb," Molly murmured. "I'd better go and let the authorities know."

Grace choked back a sob and began to walk back up the beach. Bea ran after her.

"Grace, wait," she called. Grace had made it to the road that hugged the bay by the time Bea caught up with her.

Grace was bent over, her hands on her knees. "What world is it that a young woman can be washed up like a shipwreck?" she cried. "And we'll never discover what happened to her, or even what her name is. I can't stand this ... this endless agony."

Grace sobbed as Bea pulled her into her arms. Her friendship with Grace was about the only thing that made sense. Would it really be so calamitous to share her secret with the one person she trusted above all?

"I love you so much, I don't know what I'd do without you," Bea whispered.

They held each other, two tiny insignificant souls in the eye of a storm.

An interior voice urged Bea on. *Tell her. Now.*

Over Grace's shoulder, Bea saw the outline of a black Citroën slide past. She locked eyes with the figure in the passenger seat and shuddered.

"You're cold," said Grace, pulling back. "Come on. We'd better both head home so we're not caught out after curfew. We'll have to resume the search for Peter tomorrow and hope the police find him this evening."

The moment passed. Grace blew her a kiss and pedaled away.

The horizon seemed to tremble as a streak of lightning rent the air, followed by a low growl of thunder that echoed off the sea wall.

★   ★   ★

Grace was right. Bea had built a wall around herself. During the day she went on her postal rounds, numbly, mechanically, but the fear stole up on her. How many times had she gone to the toilet to check, but there was no wetness between her legs. Her body was brewing and fermenting, creating a human being. She had to face facts now, she must be what, five, or five and half months gone?

Bea had always prided herself on her resilience, her ability to push away her feelings. She'd done it with her father and Jimmy. But there was no pushing away this dirty secret, for this one had a life of its own. Fear seemed to loop endlessly round her mind, switchblading between outcomes. She couldn't have this baby, but how could she get rid of it?

There was a woman in St. Helier. She didn't even live in a backstreet like some of the books in Grace's library would have you believe. She lived over a stationer's shop and seemed pretty harmless. But abortion was illegal and it could—and did—go wrong. Besides, how could she even think of such a thing? This life was all she had left of Jimmy, but Jersey was a small island. She'd be a social pariah. In peacetime a woman in trouble would have slipped away quietly to stay with a relative in England, but she was trapped with a secret that in about four months' time would betray her.

This baby was her one hope, all she had left of the man she loved, the bright star in a vault of hopelessness. The picture of Jimmy in her head was slipping away. All those little habits, the mannerisms, the natural smell of him were fading. So much about a person was intangible. This baby was all she had left of their love, or proof that he'd ever existed. She couldn't stand that the bright and handsome young man she'd known, who'd dived from the top board at the lido and delivered free milk to the island's poor, would now forever be known as "that escapee."

As she pedaled through the gloaming and the rooftops of St. Helier hove into view, Bea knew what she had to do. The answer had been staring her in the face all along. First, she would go to the allotment, destroy the informers' letters that were gathering mold among the seeds and pots. Then she would come clean with her mother and face the problem with her. Her mother would know what to do. She always did.

But as she freewheeled down the hill to Havre des Pas her breath froze in her lungs. A black Citroën was parked outside their small guest house.

"You are a ghost, Beatrice Gold." The Wolf stretched back in his chair, his long leather coat creaking as he laced his hands behind his head. Behind him hung the large inevitable framed picture.

Bea tried not to look at the portrait and instead reflected on how the Wolf had changed. Gone was the ridiculous alpine hat and in its place, a more severe look. Perhaps there was a Gestapo style guide in those Nazi magazines in the library. The thought made her smirk.

"You find this funny?"

"Not remotely. So why I am a ghost then? I can see you're itching to tell me. Is this why you've invited me to the not-so-secret headquarters of the field police?"

His smile froze, those reptilian eyes flickered to narrow slits.

"It's what we call islanders who refuse to acknowledge our presence."

"Strange that you should dub me as the invisible presence, when it is I who choose to see straight through you," she said. "Anyway, it's a moot point really seeing as you're losing this war and won't be here for much longer."

"And what gives you that impression, Miss Gold? Did you hear it on your wireless?"

Clumsy. He'd have to work harder than that to trip her up.

"What wireless?"

She smiled and readied herself to twist the knife.

"I heard one of your soldiers faced a firing squad last week for desertion and was buried at the Strangers Cemetery. You're shipping out all your slaves and morale must be low as your troops look as miserable and starving as the rest of us. And you're clearly worried about an Allied invasion. Why else have you started testing the air-raid siren every Saturday at noon?"

"Are you Jewish?" he asked, abruptly changing tack.

"It's a nice place you've requisitioned here," she said, as she surveyed the large room that looked out over the beach. "I can see why you kicked out poor Mrs. Scott," she remarked, putting her hands in her pocket. "Who wouldn't want a sea view?"

The Wolf steepled his hands together and gave an imperceptible nod. The blow left her reeling. Bea realized she had been struck from behind.

She cried out and whipped round in her seat. A large man in full uniform had crept in the room behind her. He must have been standing at the door all the time. He stood staring straight ahead, his eyes chillingly blank.

"*Genug.*" Enough. The Wolf slammed his palms down on the table. "I am getting tired of your games. Take your hands out of your pocket in front of the Führer."

Stunned, she slid her hands from her pocket and clenched them into fists.

"This is my associate, Karl Lodburg. He is here to help you think straight, so I ask you again. Are you Jewish?"

Bea's ear began to throb and she swallowed uneasily. She thought of the life inside her and suddenly felt incredibly vulnerable, a stab of fear piercing her bravado.

"Why would it matter if I was?" she said, feigning innocence.

"For someone who keeps her ear close to the ground you are remarkably ill-informed," he replied, taking out a toothpick from a small box on his desk. "There have been a series of orders in the *Evening Post,* all Jewish people are required to register and are subject to restrictions on their movement." He waved his hand. "Cinemas, theaters... the library. To prevent contamination."

She felt the looming presence of Karl behind her. He was all Teutonic power and muscle, with a bicep where a brain ought to be. He had slapped her as if batting a fly. What would it feel like to be on the end of his fists? A dark cold dread inched through her.

The Wolf was using the toothpick to clean something from under his nail and Bea wondered what it was. Dirt. Sand. Dried blood?

Don't show him you're scared.

"I hate to disappoint you but no, I'm not Jewish and I don't know why you would think that."

"Gold...could so easily have been shortened from Goldberg, Goldstein, no?"

"It could. But it hasn't been." She fought the urge to touch her throbbing temple. "My mother is from Whitechapel. Her people are French Huguenots who came to England in 1718 and founded a Protestant church in London. She can prove it."

Bea jutted out her chin. "And my father was Church of England, born in Jersey."

"Interesting history lesson."

"Not that I would have any problem myself with being Jewish. I don't discriminate against people on the basis of their faith."

He said nothing, just stared at her, gauging that bloody toothpick deep under his nail.

"Can I go now? Only it's getting late and I should hate to miss curfew."

"Take off your clothes," he ordered.

"W-what?"

"I need to ensure you aren't concealing any weapons."

"This is absurd."

"Karl, perhaps you could help?"

"No," she snapped. "I'll do it."

Burning red and blistering with fury, she peeled off her postal uniform—trousers and blouse and jacket—and stood before his desk in her camiknickers and moth-eaten vest.

Her long dark hair was tucked under a chenille fishnet snood.

"That tatty hair net too," he ordered.

She bit back a retort as she pulled it off, letting her hair tumble down her back.

"Your hair needs a wash," he said snidely.

"Who can spare the soap?" she snapped, realizing how quickly a man's lust could turn to loathing once his precious ego had been dented.

The Wolf and Karl looked at her as if inspecting livestock at auction, their gazes intimate and probing. Her swollen belly seemed to stand out, shining and white in the glow of the lamplight. Easy to conceal in clothes and covered by a large postal bag. Not so easy when stripped down to bare flesh. Bea closed her eyes, humiliation scorching through her. When she opened them, a sly smile had spread over his face.

"Naughty, Beatrice. Seems you are concealing secrets after all. You can go now."

He stood up and flicked the toothpick into a waste bin. "Karl will see you out."

The whole thing had been an exercise in power, an attempt to have the last laugh as he couldn't make the Jewish issue stick. Bea knew that, but it made her sick to the stomach.

She dressed quickly and walked out into the hallway, where an orderly sat behind a desk.

"This way," said Karl. Instead of leaving by the front door, he gestured to a small staircase down to the basement. Her heart started to thunder as she walked down the stairs. Karl was right behind her, so close she could smell his metallic breath on her neck.

The stairs led to a small underground corridor and there was a strange, fetid smell down in this basement, like bleach in a butcher's shop.

"This door leads out onto the back garden, follow the path and it will take you back out to steps which lead onto the beach," Karl ordered. Bea said nothing, just walked stiffly in the direction of the light. *Just keep walking. Ten steps, five steps…* All the other doors leading off the corridor were shut, except for the last door on the right. It was partially open, almost as if left open on purpose. She glanced in as she walked past. A figure sat on a bed, hunched-over and hugging his knees. He looked up as she passed, alerted by the noise and immediately his hands started to flutter.

"Peter," she breathed, stopping.

"Out," ordered Karl, shoving her roughly in the back. And then, abruptly, she was outside in the garden.

Bea reached the wooden gate that led to some wooden steps out onto the beach, her heart pumping with adrenaline. She waited, heard the back door slam, before picking up a stone from the beach. Slowly, deliberately, she carved a V for Victory into the back of the wooden door. "Fuck you, Nazi scum." She swore under her breath and hurled the stone across the beach. Then she walked back across the wet sand, her mind reeling as the first drops of rain began to fall. Her fears swirled and bloomed like monsters, growing horns and teeth. She saw the Wolf's gold tooth, his flaccid skin, the map of broken veins across his cheek. She imagined him guzzling brandy at the local brothel, untroubled by the trail of destroyed lives in his wake. A thick treacly hatred clotted in her throat.

How could this man, who arrested civilians for buying on the black market, while buying under the counter himself, and who happily threw schoolchildren in jail, wield power over them?

At least one good thing had come from this disturbing encounter. She would not destroy the letters. She would continue. *Resolve. Courage. Conviction.* She murmured those three words under her breath as she walked up the steps from the beach.

On instinct, she went instead to the allotment shed.

The Wolf thought he had the balance of power now, now that he knew her secret. No doubt he was already planning how best to leverage this against her. She felt sick. The way he had made her undress, the secrets he knew gave him an ownership over her.

Inside the shed, she lit a small stubby candle and listened to the sound of the rain beating down on the corrugated iron roof. Thank goodness Red had been moved on to another safe house in the north of the island, leaving the safe haven of the shed to Bea.

The floor of the shed was compacted dirt, but in the corner, underneath a bench and covered over by an old wooden pallet and gardening manuals, were the letters.

Bea lifted the wooden pallet and reached into the earth, pulling out a bundle of letters. She didn't need to read them out. She knew their contents off by heart.

MRS. GREEN, TRINITY HILL... HAS HIDDEN HER WIRELESS IN THE SOOT HOUSE IN HER GARDEN

Please search Brompton Villa. Gt Union Road for at least 2 wireless hidden under her floorboards.

WHY IS JACK CORNU, 4 GREAT UNION ROAD, ALLOWED TO HAVE RECEIVED 1 TON OF COAL WHEN OTHER PEOPLE HAVE NONE AT ALL? ALSO CALL AND SEE HIS STOCK OF FOOD IN HIS BEDROOM CUPBOARDS. SEE WHAT YOU THINK OF IT???

Bea wondered if any of these people who had been so clumsily denounced had the faintest clue how close they had come to being searched and arrested. There was no nuance or ambiguity as far as she was concerned. It was wrong. In denouncing these people so spitefully, the anonymous cowards who had written these letters were prepared to condemn them to a prison in Germany, and for what? Rage pooled in her stomach. Who were these enemies in their midst?

Her eyes fell to the bundle beneath. The mail she had stolen from the German Post Office on New Year's Eve.

Ninety letters that would never be delivered. Swallowing her fear, she opened one. The front of the card depicted a brilliant red sailboat, heading into the sunset. It reeked of cologne. She turned it over. A scrawl of meaningless German words covered the back. She did however recognize two of the words. *Heil Hitler.* She picked up another and slit it open with her finger.

A photograph fell out. A young blond man, strikingly handsome, depressingly young, stared back. To her surprise the letter was written in English.

My dear fiancée, Emilia. I have been practicing my English, so I hope you will forgive me writing to you in English, ask our neighbor to translate. He used to be an English teacher, didn't he?

So my dearest one. I'll be thinking of you and remember the happy hours we spent together last year at Christmas. I hope you haven't forgotten me. I haven't heard from you in such a long while.

Christmas has not been so happy for me this year, because I'm only happy when I'm with you. God grant that we can spend next Christmas together again. I wish only to be home and reunited with you. What I hope most is an end to this war will come soon so that we can all enjoy life again.

The letter slipped from her fingers as an awful thought dawned on her. In stealing this mail, was *she* being as petty and vengeful as the very people whose letters she had intercepted? This man sounded so normal and as desperate to see an end to this war as she was. Hadn't Grace said as much? Now he might never receive a reply from his sweetheart Emilia. Guilt sneaked in at the edges of her anger. She stuffed the letter back in the hole in the ground and hastily covered it over.

She must remain focused. This choice was the right one. She had taken—no, *purloined* (a far less grubby word)— these letters to demoralize the enemy. So that soldier was lonely. So what? Weren't they all? No more wrestling with her conscious. This foul ideology must be thwarted. Her conviction, her resolve must stay steady.

From her purse she pulled a cracked mirror and a stub of old red lipstick she had been saving for best. She needed to paint on some armor before she went home. Her mum would be all over it if she detected the slightest thing wrong. She loved her mum dearly, but her inherent nosiness meant she needed to know the ins and outs of a cat's arsehole.

By the time she pushed her key in the door, she hoped Queenie might be in bed. No such luck. She could make out her faint outline in the smoky darkness, nursing the remains of a weak fire.

"Where have you been? I thought the search had been called off for this evening?"

She rose like a battleship, hands on hips.

Bea sighed and kicked off her wooden clogs, grateful for the veil of darkness. "I carried on looking for Peter."

"And?" Queenie's shrewd gaze seemed to permeate the gloom of the small parlor.

"The Secret Field Police have arrested him."

All the breath seemed to leave her body in one juddering gasp. Bea stared at her usually well-upholstered mum and it occurred to her suddenly how much weight she'd lost.

"Whatever has become of this island? Still, your sister got her job back at Boots today, so that's one small blessing."

"How?" Bea demanded.

"The German commandant had the manager in and insisted the girls he dismissed be reinstated. And you can debate the rights and wrongs of it, madam, but now she has two jobs, it's much needed coinage coming in."

Bea rolled her eyes. The last thing she wanted was to get

into a conversation about her Jerrybag sister. "I'm done in, Mum. I'm up the wooden hill to Bedfordshire."

She had hoped her mum's old childhood saying might soften her mood, but Queenie wasn't known as the Guv'nor for nothing.

"When are you going to tell me what's really biting you?"

Bea gripped the stair rail, wincing as a tiny wooden splinter sliced under her fingernail. The brackish smell of the smoky fire and the stench of boiled turnip turned her guts.

"Nothing that couldn't be cured by Hitler taking a bullet in the head." Anger iced her voice. "Give me a couple of bricks, a mallet and half an hour alone with that man."

Queenie took her face in her hands, forcing her to meet her gaze.

"Tell me you're not involved in anything reckless at the post office."

Bea felt the small blood blister forming under her fingernail, so small but yet so exquisitely painful.

"Why do you think that?"

"Because you're young, angry and impetuous."

"Perhaps, but I'm not stupid, Mum. Now, please can I go to bed?"

Queenie released her grip and Bea trudged up the stairs, her belly hot and swollen, her world shrinking.

12

Grace

BANNED BOOK

The Outline of History by H. G. Wells. *The British author was best known for his science fiction novels like* The Time Machine *and* War of the Worlds, *but it was his Socialist beliefs and nonfiction work that Nazi Germany objected to most and banned.*

Word of Peter Topsy's arrest spread through the veins of St. Helier, passing from lip to ear as spring cartwheeled in, waking the island of flowers from its winter slumber. But no one was talking about the blanket of daffodils softly spreading across the island. Every person that came into the library wanted to ask her about Peter. *Was it true? Had he been spying and passing information on to the British? Had he been arrested for espionage?* By the time she'd delivered her fifth book on her morning delivery round, according to the rumors, Peter had already been executed by firing squad.

But the facts were grim. Peter had been arrested and charged with espionage and spying, and was in the town's prison awaiting trial. To the Germans, he was a political prisoner, which meant he would be shown no mercy. Only Grace knew that he was a 14-year-old boy with a fascination for drawings and a brain that meant he didn't see the world as others did. She shuddered to think of him alone in his jail cell. It had been seven weeks and four days since his arrest and together, she and Dr. McKinstry had appealed to the bailiff to intervene.

As she pulled off the main road and cycled down a bumpy country track, books juddering inside her bicycle's wicker basket, a horrible feeling unfurled inside her. The Wolf had arrested him on the strength of those intricate pencil drawings of the fortified beach at Havre des Pas, so lifelike they could almost have passed for photographs. And therein lay the problem. The authorities were claiming he'd drawn them for intelligence purposes and had been planning to get them to the Allies. But something else also nagged at Grace—hadn't the Wolf also done it to get at her? Wasn't he waiting for her to make a mistake, setting traps? He was itching to get her library closed down. Grace felt the pressure build inside her head until she felt she couldn't breathe. She dismounted, pressed her hand to her chest and tapped lightly. *Breathe, Grace.*

She glanced behind her. A field of wheat swayed gently in the crisp golden sun. The smell of lavender and wild garlic filled the air. In the distance she heard the rattle of farm machinery. Breathing deeply, she turned and continued on foot up the dusty track until she came to a smaller path that cut through a wood.

"Red," she called softly into the pine-scented air. "Are you there?" She turned a bend and there he was. His broad back was resting against a tree trunk, his eyes were closed, his face lifted to the sun. Her heart dissolved.

Since he'd shinned out of her library window she and Dr. McKinstry had successfully managed to persuade Red to stay away from town, on the proviso she met him once a week somewhere well away from prying German eyes.

"Is that my favorite girl?" he asked, without opening his eyes.

"How did you know?"

His eyes opened and his whole face lit up at the sight of her. "I can tell your footsteps. They're much daintier than some blockhead Boche."

She trailed her fingers up the nape of his neck. He smiled, drowsy as a cat in the sun. "Don't stop," he begged.

"I can't stay long. I've—"

Grace squealed as he grabbed her hand and pulled her down onto the sun-baked earth, covering her neck with kisses and pine needles.

"I'm sorry, Angel Grace," he moaned. "Only you drive me crazy. The days between our meet-ups drag by."

She kissed him back, slower now. "I know," she whispered. "You're bored. I've brought you another book if that helps."

She propped herself up on one elbow and pulled out a copy of Ernest Hemingway's *A Farewell to Arms.*

"Thank you." He sighed. "Hemingway sure as hell wouldn't be sitting around, hiding in haylofts."

Grace could feel his frustration fizzing over.

"W-what are you saying?" she asked, not wanting to know the answer.

"I don't know, Grace, only that I can't keep hiding for

much longer. If our boys don't come soon, I'm gonna have to make a break for it. The fella I'm staying with is a straight-up guy, reckons he can get me a rowing boat."

Talk of perilous ocean escapes felt so incongruous in the still of the glade. A shoal of butterflies danced over the gorse bushes like windblown confetti. Not a puff of cloud interrupted the blue.

It was the most beautiful day. The kind that only a few years ago would have had the bucket-and-spade brigade flooding to the island's wide sandy beaches on the south coast. She thought of halcyon days with her brother and Bea by the bathing pool at Havre des Pas. Bea larking about in a kiss-me-quick hat. White sails patching a pale-blue sky. Dripping lemon ices and squeals of laughter, the sun kissing her library-white skin brown. There was such an innocent, dreamlike quality to those long-ago summers that at times she wondered if they had ever existed at all. And that, she realized, was the worst of it. The occupation hadn't just stolen their freedom, it was leaching her memories.

"Do you really think they're coming?" she asked, shielding her eyes as she scanned the horizon in the direction of England.

"I have no doubt of it," Red said. "The war will be over soon. The crazed ideology has already failed. The dream of the great fatherland is dead. We just need the Allies to push it over the finish post."

Grace desperately hoped he was right. Change was in the air. All German leave had been stopped and the authorities were twitchy. Hardly a day passed without Allied planes flying over the island, followed by heavy bombing on the French coast. Her father's hidden crystal set had crackled out the welcome news that the RAF had led successful raids on targets all over northwestern France. Not that they needed telling. Doors and windows had rattled all over the island.

"I don't want my war story to end like this," he continued. "Hiding in the shadows like a scared kitten until I'm rescued."

There was nothing she could say, but the thought of him leaving, after she had finally admitted her feelings toward him, was annihilating. Her mind cruelly took her to the evening she had kissed her big brother good night, oblivious of what he'd been planning. She hadn't had the chance to talk him out of the escape attempt.

"Please, I beg of you, don't do it," she cried, emotion clogging her throat. "Just hold out a little longer. You must promise me."

"Oh, Grace," he sighed, sitting up and squinting against the sun. "Please don't make me promise that. I can promise to be smart about it. I can promise to love you always, but hiding from the enemy for the duration of the war?" He shook his head. "That's not me."

Grace nodded, defeated. Of course. She knew the kind of man Red was. Surprising herself, she pulled him toward her by his collar. "Very well. If you go, I'll miss you terribly. I-I do love you, you see," she finally admitted in a tumble of words.

She pressed her lips to his, enjoying the solid sensation of Red's broad chest, the sweet oblivion of his embrace.

Everything faded away. A soft breeze fingered her hair as his tongue gently probed hers. She got the feeling that nothing would ever feel as good as this ever again. When she was with him, the eviscerating hunger, the tiredness, the uncertainty that draped her like a scratchy blanket seemed to dissolve. Kissing, it seemed, could be almost as time-consuming as choosing your next read.

"You don't know how long I've waited to hear you say that," he whispered, his hands traveling down to the small of her back. "Thank you for giving me hope."

Grace pulled back from the urgency of his kisses. Not because she was being chaste—although to be honest, she was clueless in that department—but because she had work to do.

"Let me go," she laughed, playfully batting his hands away.

"I'm sorry," he groaned. "But you drive me crazy, Grace. I can't wait to be with you, properly."

"I...I can't consider that, Red, not yet."

His smile faded. "I didn't mean to pressure you. I mean, obviously I want to—you are the most beautiful woman I've ever met—but what I meant is I can't wait to be in a world where I can walk down the street hand in hand with you. Be free to tell the world that you're my girl."

"Please God that day will come soon."

"So what are you throwing me over for?" he asked.

"I'm a busy bee. I've got to finish my book rounds, then it's book club and after that I have to my write my annual library report. I have to document the last year." A sense of hope unfolded inside her, pushing back the darkness. "This is history in the making. Our library issues have soared. Over 100,000 issues last year and 1944 will top that. That's double the issues in peacetime."

"Impressive."

"It is, but these dry numbers and lists don't reflect the esteem and love islanders feel for our library. I have to find a way to express that."

"Well, if anyone can, you can."

Grace gathered her satchel and pushed her bike along the sandy, sun-baked path which led back to the road. Every particle of her longed to stay. The shushing of the leaves and the silken air were begging her to stay a while longer, but the library was calling louder.

As she reached the main path that led back to the road she glanced back and blew Red a kiss.

Diagonal pillars of sunshine had crept through the canopy of leaves, casting his face in a gentle peach hue.

"Bye, Grace La Mottée." He waved and returned her kiss. "I knew I loved you from the moment I first set eyes on you."

"Stop it!" She laughed. "Someone will hear."

"I don't care. I'm crazy about you. Tell me you're my girl."

She smiled, a soft spring breeze feathering her blonde hair. "Yes, Red, I'm your girl."

From the corner of her eye she saw a motor car slide away from the small country road at the end of the track, but her head was a kaleidoscope of books, her heart too full of love, to pay it much heed. High above Red a lone bird of prey hovered.

Back on the road into town, the shadow of a motor car swallowed her and pulled to a halt in front of her.

The Wolf emerged from the back seat. "A word if I may, Miss La Mottée."

Grace pulled to a wobbly stop and nearly crashed into him. He gripped her bike handles.

"Oops-a-daisy. You see, I am picking up your British sayings, no? What a beautiful day. The sun has got its hat on for our Führer."

She nodded, desperate to get away, but he had her bike handles firmly clamped.

"It was our great leader's birthday two days ago, and this weekend the celebrations continue."

"I hadn't noticed," she lied. They could hardly escape Hitler's 55th birthday. *Victory in the West* shown on repeat at The Forum cinema. Forty troops brandishing torches had led a flame-lit procession around the island, with two military bands performing in the parade. To say nothing of the nauseating propaganda displayed in the window of the German bookshop around the corner from the library.

"You should come for some cake this afternoon at the town hall."

She knew what Bea would say to the outrageous suggestion they celebrate Hitler's birthday. *Not as long as I've got a hole in my arse.*

But she didn't have her friend's bravado or sass, instead she replied: "No, thanks. I'm leading the book club."

"Aah yes, the popular book club." His eyes sparkled with malice. "Our censor tells me it is a lifeline for many on this island."

She said nothing. Entering into conversation with the Wolf was like poking a rat trap.

"Wouldn't it be a shame if it were to close?"

"And why would that happen?" she retorted.

"If it were to emerge that you are loaning *verboten* books."

"But I'm not," she said, in a voice like cracked ice.

His smile slipped. "Prove it. Empty your bag."

She handed him her satchel and closed her eyes, knowing what he would find if he was thorough.

"As I suspected," he crowed, his voice triumphant. "You have concealed one book inside another. Loaning books that are forbidden is a breach of German rule."

But as he pulled out the book from its dust jacket, he looked confused.

"The book is *The Serpent in the Garden* and yet the jacket says *Knitting Patterns for Beginners*. What is this?"

She smiled, despite her thumping heart. "My patron's husband isn't keen on her reading romances, in case she gets ideas, so I conceal it inside another book jacket. Last I heard, loaning romance novels isn't breaking your rules."

She took the book from him and tucked it back in its jacket. "Costume romances of the past offer escape from the disagreeable present. Now, if that's all, I'll be on my way."

Books can you make curious, impudent even. That was the only thing Grace later reflected, which could account for what she said next. She went to push off from the curb, but suddenly stopped. "Do you like reading, Sergeant Wölfle?"

He looked at her suspiciously, as if it were she now trying to catch him out.

"I don't have time."

She nodded. "Of course you don't." *You are far too busy locking up schoolboys.*

The man's soul was sterile. What redemption could there possibly be for a man who was already dead? No wonder he hated her library so much. It represented freedom, enlightenment and tolerance.

"I ought to be getting back to the library."

"Good day, Miss La Mottée. Pass my regards to your friend Miss Gold." A malevolent look slid over his face. "I wish her well…in her condition."

Grace pedaled off fast, her thoughts in freefall. What an odd thing to say. This encounter had ended well, but it could so easily not have. Had he stopped her this time last week, he would have discovered *The Time Machine* by H. G. Wells, wrapped up in a copy of *Alpine Flora* and *The Sun Also Rises* by Ernest Hemingway concealed in a copy of *Bovine Health*.

The idea had come to her when she'd hidden *Alice in Wonderland* inside the cover of another book and thus far it had worked beautifully. Somehow, she'd managed to convince herself that it was less risky than when Bea had opened letters at the post office.

Every week Grace swore to herself she would stop delivering *verboten* books. But then she'd witness something that made her continue. Fake news in their newspapers. A small boy with his nose pressed against the window of the German bookshop. As a librarian she liked to think she planted seeds she might never see grow, but planting them still mattered. After all, that same boy she'd caught staring at a window display full of Nazi propaganda was also now learning German in school. His fresh young mind was being slowly conditioned to hate.

Islanders needed access to uncensored books. It mattered. Reading was their last form of freedom.

But…this encounter had proven that she could no longer afford to take those kind of risks. What good was she as a librarian if she was behind bars?

After she had delivered *The Serpent in the Garden,* Grace rode along Roseville Street back into town and mentally scanned the inhabitants.

At number 12 was Clarissa Fleetwood-Bird, a spinster who used to run the Chess Club before the Germans shut it down, who had a formidable appetite for bloodthirsty crime novels. Over the road at number 9, was Teddy Bernard, a sailor in his time, who would have loved to have lived in Paris—as a woman. Next door to Teddy lived Mrs. Barclay-Miller, committed Christian, who loved nothing more than a bodice-ripper after Bible Club.

People were a little like book covers. What you saw on the outside rarely coincided with the true contents. Grace wondered whether anyone could tell that the island's perennially single librarian was finally a woman in love?

The unpleasant encounter with the Wolf meant by the time she got back to the library Grace was 15 minutes late for the book club. A small cheer erupted from the Reading Room as she hastened up the stairs.

All the familiar faces were settled, doughy with exhaustion, but with the light of hope she often saw in people's eyes as they gathered under the domed library roof.

There was her mum, in her usual place between the

matriarchal pillars that were Queenie Gold and Mrs. Moisan. Next to them, busy unraveling her knitting, was Mrs. Noble chatting to Louisa Gould. Dr. McKinstry was talking shop with Albert Bedane the physiotherapist, while Molly the florist gossiped loudly with Winnie, Doris and Gladys from the post-office counter.

Bea sat on the other side of the Reading Room with her tribe of "old fogeys" as they called themselves from the sorting room. They were clearly winding her up about something as they were all giggling like naughty schoolboys.

A bored-looking German censor sat in the corner, looking like he'd rather be anywhere than policing a book club in the library.

She looked about. Was it her imagination or were more people wearing as much red, white and blue as they thought they could get away with? Pieced together they could almost make up a complete Union Jack. The penny dropped. Tomorrow was St. George's Day.

Grace felt a sudden rush of affection for this disparate group of fiercely patriotic islanders who made up the hotchpotch book club.

Despite his advancing years and wooden leg, Arthur the postman rose quickly and pulled back Grace's chair for her to sit.

"Through primrose tufts, in that green bower,
The periwinkle trailed its wreaths;
And 'tis my faith that every flower
Enjoys the air it breathes."

"I didn't know you were a poet, Arthur," she smiled.

"Alas not my words, my dear. William Wordsworth."

"A poetic postie," she grinned. "Which is timely as this week I thought it would be nice to read some poetry, if that's agreeable to all."

"I should say," winked Lou Gould. "I've the perfect thing." Lou fortunately was unaccompanied by her "house-guest," but she had pulled the lining of her coat through her button hole like an impudent tongue poking out at the Germans. Grace cast a nervous glance at the censor but he appeared to have fallen asleep, his head slumped forward, a small bubble of spit glistening at the corner of his mouth.

"May I go first? I'd like to read out a little ditty I wrote," said Bea's neighbor Eileen. It wasn't on the pre-authorized list she had already cleared with the commandant, but the censor *was* asleep. What harm could a poem do?

"Yes please, Eileen."

She cleared her throat.

"We are all quite well, though getting thinner,
Not much for tea, still less for dinner,
Though not exactly on our uppers,
We've said adieu to cold ham suppers.

In peacetime there are those who wish to slim,
Tried diet, massage, baths and gym,
Though tell the scout of every nation
The secret's solved by occupation.

Little Jersey bombed and mined,
For us, warfare has proved unkind.
But after all the stress and strain,
A great height we will rise again."

A ripple of appreciative murmurs ran round the room, not too loud so as not to wake the censor.

"Eileen, that's smashing. Did you write that yourself?" asked Louisa Gould.

"Yes, my love. I like writing poems, keeps my mind occupied."

"Might I read something?" asked Queenie.

"Grace, don'cha dare turn down the Guv'nor," Nobby from the post office joked, holding his fists up in a joke fight stance.

"Watch it, you," Queenie laughed, taking a swipe at his head, "you're not too old for a clip round the ear."

She pulled out a Red Cross letter from her handbag.

"Not a poem as such, but it's poetry to my ears. It's from my sister in East London, who says, and I quote: 'Alf's condition worsening. Family watching day and night, awaiting end. Happy release.'"

Knowing looks and grins were exchanged round the group. Everyone knew who Alf represented.

Queenie's offering seemed to unlock something in the group and soon all were sharing some of their favorite poems, verses bubbling from lips like burst damns.

Louisa read a bewitching rendition of Dylan Thomas's *Under Milk Wood*, beguiling them all with her soft, lyrical voice as she took them through rabbits' woods and black, moonless nights. Her voice swept through the library like a clean, crisp wind.

Molly rattled off a magnificent Emily Dickinson and Mrs. Noble closed her eyes as she read her favorite Shakespeare sonnet.

That warm and drowsy spring afternoon, they read as if their lives depended on it and Grace felt more at peace in that moment than she could ever remember. Reading was helping them *all* to make sense of the unimaginable, with the library now a community refuge.

It was veteran postman Arthur's offering that finally dug up the pent-up grief that Grace knew so many of her group had buried. He recounted his poem with his eyes closed, as if transporting himself to Grace knew not where.

"If I should die, think only this of me:
That there's some corner of a foreign field
That is for ever England. There shall be
In that rich earth a richer dust concealed;
A dust whom England bore, shaped, made aware,
Gave, once, her flowers to love, her ways to roam;
A body of England's, breathing English air,
Washed by the rivers, blest by suns of home…"

Arthur rarely talked of his experiences in the Great War, which had earned him his medals and his false leg, but "The Soldier," by Rupert Brooke, seemed as apt in 1944 as it was when it was first published in 1915. His gravelly voice hung in the dome-like space above their head as they soaked in the truth of the words.

Everyone sat alone with their losses. For too long people had plastered over their smashed dreams with stoic smiles. Finally, Queenie began to cry for the husband she had lost, comforted by Louisa Gould, whose son Edward would never return home from the Royal Navy, and Mrs. Moisan, whose daughter Dolly's life had been cut down by disease before it had even begun.

Grace blinked back her tears and glanced over at Bea, but her expression was unreadable. Silently, Grace moved to her side and slid an arm around her old friend's shoulder. She felt the tiny bones in Bea's neck, as fragile as a bird, flinch at the touch.

She needed to write her annual library report, but she had a feeling that her friend needed her more.

"Bea, why don't we go for a cup of tea once I've locked up the library?"

"Stop! Your time is up!" The censor had woken, his guttural command slicing through the still of the library. "Please evacuate the library."

"I think he means *vacate*," Bea laughed. "Go on then." She hesitated. "I-I could use your advice."

Grace had never seen her friend look as vulnerable as in that moment. The beauty and truth of poetry had opened them all up, sloughing away the varnish of their reserve.

"I knew something was wrong. Don't worry. Whatever it is, we'll work it out together. Like we've always done."

Bea's face crumpled in relief. "Thanks, Grace."

A tap on her shoulder and Grace turned.

"A word in your shell-like, Grace," Molly muttered. "I hear you're trying to visit Peter in prison?"

"Trying and failing. They're saying family only, but his own mother has no interest in visiting."

"I might have a way. But you'll have to come with me now."

Grace glanced at Bea and then at her watch.

"Can it wait an hour?"

"Not if you want to see Peter. It has to be now."

"You go, Grace," Bea urged. "Our chat can wait, especially if you've got a chance to see Peter."

Grace kissed her softly on the cheek. "Thanks, Bea. But we will have that talk soon, I promise."

On the way to St. Helier's Public Prison on Newgate Street, Molly filled her in.

"My sister-in-law's a ward sister. She's treating Peter for a broken rib and influenza and she's due to see him today at five p.m. She has said if we visit, she'll let you have ten minutes on your own with Peter."

They walked quickly, dodging an emaciated pony barely pulling a trap as they headed to the island's only prison. The old prison and hospital were adjoining. Grace allowed her gaze to travel up the tall granite wall to the jagged glass protruding from the top. Fear clamped her heart.

In the hospital, they followed a maze of carbolic-scrubbed corridors into the casualty department, until they came to a door.

Molly knocked softly.

"Enter," called a strong Scottish voice.

Sister Morgan turned out to be a powerfully built Scottish matron, with pink cheeks and an air of invincibility.

"This is my friend," Molly ventured and Grace found a set of shrewd eyes drinking her in.

"I'm trusting you because you're the Chief Librarian and I hear good things about you," she said in a powerful Glaswegian accent. "But if I hear you've blabbed about this meeting, then it will never happen again. Do I make myself clear?"

Grace couldn't find any words in the presence of such a formidable matriarch so simply nodded her compliance.

"Good, because I'm putting my neck on the line here."

She pulled out her fob watch and a moment later there was a knock on the door.

"Stay back," she whispered, pulling open the door. Grace and Molly pressed themselves back into the shadows of the room.

"You're no coming in here with your dirty gun," Sister Morgan barked into the corridor. "Sit yerself oot here. He'll no be running away."

Grace and Molly exchanged smiles. Even the steeliest German soldier wouldn't dare answer this woman back.

A second later Peter walked into the room. He had his back to Grace. Sister Morgan reached into her sterilizer and a hot bowl of stew appeared as if from nowhere.

"Now then, sonny boy. You're to eat this all up while I nip out to fetch some more dressings." She raised a finger to her lips. "You've a friend come to see you. Ten minutes," she whispered as the door clicked. And then she and Molly were gone.

Peter turned and Grace's hand flew to her mouth. He was a mess. One eye was swollen shut where clearly a German fist had rammed into it.

"Oh, Peter, what have they done to you?" she wept. As she hugged him fiercely he began to cough uncontrollably, spasms shooting through his skinny frame.

"Sssh, my love, ssh. It's going to be all right."

When the coughing fit passed, she guided him to the bed, and picking up the bowl of stew, tried to coax him to take a mouthful.

"Please eat, Peter." He ate slowly and finally he seemed to come to his senses, fixing Grace with a watery gaze.

"I don't know why they have done this to you, but I promise you, I am doing everything I can to get you out."

"I didn't do the things they say I did," he whispered at last. "They hurt me, Grace."

He pulled up his prison tunic and Grace inhaled. His skinny torso was a patchwork quilt of bruises.

"I didn't do it and the more I say I didn't do it, the more they hurt me."

"Everyone knows you're not a spy. I'll get you out of here."

"Do you promise?"

Grace hesitated.

"I can't promise that, Peter, no. But I won't rest until I've done everything in my power to get you home."

"The library is my home," he said quietly, and Grace's heart shattered.

"Talking of libraries. I have books." She pointed to her satchel. "*The Hound of the Baskervilles.*"

"I was reading *Advanced Mathematics and Calculus of Observations,* before they arrested me. Could you bring me that?"

"Perhaps best not, sweetie, under the circumstance."

Peter's intellect was beyond anything she could comprehend, but his common sense was somewhat lacking.

"Stick with Conan Doyle. Maybe the lovely ward sister will hold on to it for you, perhaps let you read it when you come here."

She felt a soft hand on her back.

"Don't worry, Miss La Mottée. I'll see that the bairn is safe. The two blockheads outside have gone for a cigarette, so go quickly now. Come back the same time next week."

Peter stared after her and Grace wanted to wail at the injustice of a regime that locked up and battered schoolboys.

Outside, Grace leaned against the high prison wall and wished in that moment she smoked. She closed her eyes, tried to blot out images of Peter in his cell, the fists and boots raining down on him in the hopes of making him "confess."

Bastards.

She felt a hand on her arm and started.

"Grace."

"Red."

"I went to the library and Miss Piquet told me you were here visiting Peter."

He stared down at her, his open face so handsome and she saw herself reflected in his gaze.

"I just had to come and see my girl, even if it's only for five minutes. I can't wait another week."

He laughed. "*My girl.* Reckon I'll never get tired of saying that."

At first she thought the noise was a pony and trap but when the clattering grew louder she realized it was footsteps. The pounding of jackboots. The smell of linseed and German cologne stained the air. A gloved hand gripped Red's arm like a vice.

"Phillip Harris. Or should I call you First Lieutenant Daniel Patrick O'Sullivan?"

The Wolf's voice was high, almost trembly in its triumph.

"You are now our prisoner of war."

The look on Red's face demolished her. Shock turned to a flash of fear, then white-hot anger. She could see him weighing up whether to run, but the Wolf had them surrounded on all sides.

"I advise you not to try anything stupid," he remarked casually.

Grace held on to the granite prison wall in a state of disbelief. In the compressed silence, noises became amplified. The Wolf's excited shallow breath. A shop sign creaking in the wind. The sound of clogged feet hastening past them on the street.

"Mummy, isn't that the librarian—" a girl on the other side of the road began.

"Keep moving, don't look," urged her mother.

"It is good that I am able to make this arrest so publicly," the Wolf declared, the sunlight flashing off his gold tooth. "Nothing pleases the public more than to know the authorities are working hard to keep them safe from dangerous fugitives. Handcuff him!" he ordered his aides.

"This is ridiculous," Grace cried. "He isn't—" she began,

but Red cut over her as two men from the Secret Field Police snapped handcuffs on him.

"I don't know this woman," he insisted. "I approached her for food but she said she couldn't help me."

"Don't worry, lieutenant. When we find out which islanders have been hiding and feeding you, believe me, the penalties will be severe."

The Wolf's face twisted into a smile of almost girlish glee. "I've been hunting you for a very long time now. My sincerest hope is that you will be deported to a German prisoner-of-war camp. I shall be making a recommendation, along with my arrest report, that you represent a significant escape threat." He pushed his face closer to Red's. "I should so love for you to experience the camps of the Great Fatherland."

"Your fatherland is finished and you know it," Red said. "It won't exist by the time the RAF and my buddies are done."

The Wolf curled his lip in contempt. "Take him away."

Red was swallowed into the back of a German military vehicle, the doors slammed shut.

"Wait. Please, wait," Grace pleaded, hammering on the back of the van.

"Don't make a scene, my dear," the Wolf muttered, lifting his hat chivalrously as two ladies hurried past on the other side of the street. "The only mistake was to befriend our enemy."

He turned back to Grace, his eyes as keen as a rodent.

"You see, I was right. I knew eventually he would come out of his hiding place. All we had to do was follow you."

He reached out and trailed his finger along her jawline. She flinched and jerked her head away. "And you still expect me to believe you are a small-town provincial librarian? It is only a matter of time before I uncover the whole truth about you, Miss La Mottée."

His black Citroën pulled up at the curb and he lowered himself into the back seat. Grace knew his ego would not permit him to leave without a parting shot.

"By rights I should have you in for questioning." He smiled, supremely confident in his power. "But isn't it more fun to give you enough rope to hang yourself?"

13

Bea

BANNED BOOK

Power *by Lion Feuchtwanger, a popular Jewish author of historical fiction. The Nazis ransacked his library and burned his works. Because he spoke out openly against the Third Reich, Hitler made him a personal enemy. Feuchtwanger fled first to France and was then smuggled to Portugal (disguised as a woman), before making it to the safety of America.*

Bea locked the cubicle door behind her, pulled down the toilet lid and sat down heavily. With trembling fingers she yanked down the waistband of her slacks and rolled down the thick rubberized corset, until the pink swollen flesh of her bump was revealed. The relief was immense. Also immediately the fluttering began, a drum roll of kicks as her baby squirmed inside her. Relief gave way to guilt as she took in the thick grooves across her flesh where her waistband had been digging painfully into her compressed abdomen.

She placed her hand on the delicate skin. "I'm so sorry," she whispered.

What a god-awful mess. How could she have been so impossibly stupid? It wasn't like her mum hadn't warned her and Nancy enough times about the shadowy fate of girls who found themselves "in trouble."

Bea closed her eyes and tipped her head back until it was resting against the cool green-and-white-tiled wall. She had to tell someone and soon. But who? How could she tell Grace the truth now of all times? Since Red's arrest two days earlier she'd walked about as if in a trance, convinced somehow it was her fault.

Bea had already had to let her waistband out twice. People had begun to notice. At the last book club, Molly had asked how on earth she'd managed to put on more weight when all around her people were nothing but skin and bone. Admittedly Bea was clueless when it came to the details of a confinement, but even she knew that in roughly two months' time, a rubberized corset would no longer conceal this baby.

Her heart began to pick up pace as she imagined, what then? Her baby would be taken from her, that much she knew. No matter that she could love this child, that it was all she had left of Jimmy, in the eyes of society this baby would be illegitimate. A bastard. An occupation secret to be shunted off quickly to a cold and loveless institution, then quickly forgotten.

In peacetime, she'd have been packed off to the Weymouth Home for Wayward Girls across the water, but that was no longer an option. Now she'd have to give birth on the island and live so close, yet so far from her baby. Her and Jimmy's baby. In that moment the longing to see Jimmy was exquisite. She pictured him loping over the fields toward her after a day's toil, face filthy with dust, hair flecked with hay, his lazy laughter as he grabbed her and kissed her neck. Like a lantern show the image slid away to be replaced with him bleeding to death on the cold stone beach, surrounded by Germans with guns.

A horrific thought struck her. What if the occupying authorities got involved? What if, as the child of an enemy of the Third Reich, they could lay some claim over her baby and take him or her? A terrible vision of the Wolf plucking her baby from her stole though her mind.

"You all right in there?" called Doris and Bea jumped.

"Fine. My nose is awful stuffy is all."

"That'll be those gas-combustion engines they're using on the busses now. One hell of a noisy, smelly affair."

"Yes you're probably right, Dor," she called back.

Bea stood up, reluctantly pulling up the thick sheath of rubber, and made herself a promise. No more carrying on. This afternoon, she *would* tell Grace. And Grace could come with her while she broke the news to Queenie. Grace would be a calming influence when Queenie Gold flipped her lid.

Her heart raced as she stood up quickly and for an awful moment thought she might faint. She held on to the back of the door and in the darkness her mind tumbled. Poison pens, secret babies, stolen letters . . . it was a tangled web of such deception and complexity. And nestled right in the heart of it was that bastard Wolf, who would love nothing more than to sign her arrest warrant.

Bea made her way back to the sorting room when Winnie called through to her.

"A visitor at the counter for you, Bea."

Monday dinnertime and the queue for postal orders, stamps, pensions and savings snaked along the middle of the post office. Standing nervously to the side of the queue was a young couple.

"What are you doing here?" Bea said coldly to her sister, ignoring the Luftwaffe pilot by her side.

"Please, sis," said Nancy softly, "can we talk?"

"I've nothing to say to you. You're a bloody disgrace. And as for you," she said, finally addressing Nancy's boyfriend, "the German Post Office is on Beresford Street."

Bea looked at the man who had captured her sister's heart. She could understand if he was some sort of strapping blond Adonis, but all she saw was a smallish man— a cigarette paper over 5 feet 5 inches—with slightly too fleshy lips and hair the color of wet sand.

"Would you please deliver this to your mother this afternoon?" he asked, sliding a brown paper package over the counter.

"Do it yourself," she said, turning to leave.

"Please, Bea," Nancy called after her. "I'd deliver it myself but I'm due back at Boots, and it's urgent."

"We really would be most grateful," said her boyfriend.

"Oh it's the royal *we* now is it?" Bea felt the anger surge up inside her. Hormones, hunger and grief were a heady mix.

"Did Nancy tell you our father was killed when your lot bombed the harbor?" She was aware her voice was shrill and people in the queue were staring, but she couldn't stop.

"Take your package and get out before I get called a Jerrybag too." She pushed the package back at him with all her force. It skidded over the polished counter before landing on the floor with a smash.

Nancy looked horrified as a stain of damp seeped over the brown paper. "Oh Bea, what have you done?" she breathed.

"What have I done? I never asked you to come in here."

"Do you know what was in that?"

"No and I don't want to."

"It was a vial of insulin," Nancy persisted. "Precious insulin. For Mum." She broke off as tears filled her eyes.

"What are you talking about? Mum's not ill."

Nancy sighed and gripped the counter. "She has diabetes. She's had it for years apparently."

"Wh-What? Why keep it a secret?"

"You know Mum. Never one to make a fuss. Dr. Lewis has been getting her insulin but all his supplies have run out now. Heinz has a friend who works for the German hospital and he's been sneaking supplies of insulin for Mum, but even they're running short."

The room seemed suddenly to empty of oxygen.

"Mum desperately needed that medication."

Bea felt as if her legs were crumbling.

"I don't understand," she managed at last. "How come you know and I don't?"

"Because she didn't want to upset you further after Jimmy died. She's trying to protect you. That's all she ever does."

Nancy shook her head, judgment clouding her face. "But the only person you think about is yourself. Haven't you even noticed how ill she looks? Come on, Heinz."

Bea stared after them open-mouthed as they left the post office.

"Show's over." Mr. Mourant took Bea's arm and led her back into the sorting room. "What did I say to you, Bea?" he murmured under his breath, his voice barely containing his anger.

"If that Luftwaffe pilot decides to report you, you could be court-martialed for that insolence. You could land us all in it."

"I'm sorry, Mr. Mourant. It won't happen again."

"No, you're right. It won't. Next month we have an opening at the Red Cross office. You can start work there, after the Whit Sunday bank holiday."

"But... but I'm a postwoman. I deliver letters."

"Do you?" he said, challengingly. "Deliver the letters, that is?"

"Y- yes, of course I do."

"Well, still, all the same. You can finish this month, then that's it. I'm relieving you of your duties. Better you be there." He looked at her searchingly. "Out of temptation's way."

"But I love working for the post office," she protested.

"And when the occupation is over you can return. Besides, the Red Cross isn't all bad. You'll still be helping people. Those messages are islanders' only link to the outside world. It's a very important job I'm entrusting you to." And then in a softer voice, "Believe me, Bea, I'm doing you a kindness. I'm protecting you."

"Who from?"

"Yourself, my dear."

Bea stormed into the sorting room and grabbed her post-bag, shaking from the force of her boss's approbation.

"What's biting you, girlie?" asked Harold as she swept out the door into the yard.

Bea pedaled hard in the direction of Havre des Pas, finally flinging her bike down in her small front garden. She found her mother in the kitchen.

"Oh hello, love. Come home for your dinner?" She tailed off. "Whatever's wrong?"

"Why didn't you tell me you were sick?" Bea demanded.

"I'm not."

"Not yet you're not, but what happens when the insulin runs out?"

"Well, it won't, because Nancy's boyfriend has a supply." Her face softened. "You know, Bea, he's really not a bad lad."

"I . . . I just can't believe you've kept this a secret from me all these years," Bea cried.

"It's not a secret. Your father knew, but it's not for you and your sister to know."

Queenie wiped the table down with vim and vigor, like she always did when she was agitated. "'Sides. I've coped with it most of my bleedin' life and would have carried on doing so were it not for this occupation."

Bea's anger deflated and she sank down into a seat.

"Oh, Mum, I'm so sorry. Nancy's right. All I've been thinking about is myself. I didn't stop to see what was happening in front of me."

"Heh, heh. Come here," said Queenie, pulling her roughly up out of the chair and into her arms. She laid her head against her mother's wrap-around apron and thought back to simpler times, when the most trouble she got into was for stealing jam tarts. How far away those childish pursuits seemed now.

In the silence, a voice urged her. *Tell her.*

"I'll be all right," her mum said, her chest gently heaving against Bea's ear. She smelled of cinnamon and Sunlight soap. "Takes more than that to finish Queenie Gold off. So now you know the truth. Your turn."

Bea's eyes snapped open and she drew back.

"What do you mean?" she asked, her voice a hoarse whisper.

"What are you—six months?"

Bea stood statue-still.

"Do you take me for a fool? In my old neighborhood they reckoned I could smell a pregnancy. I know a girl in trouble when I see one. I've been waiting months for you to come clean."

Bea had no more strength left to deny it. What was the point? And as she nodded all she actually felt was relief. She closed her eyes, waited for the slap, the screaming. It was what she deserved.

Instead, her mother laid both her hands gently on her tummy.

"A boy I reckon."

"A...aren't you cross?"

"And what would that achieve? It's Jimmy's I take it?"

Bea nodded. "The night he was killed."

"How many times did I tell you to keep your hand on yer ha'penny?" Queenie sighed as she sat down at the table and began rolling a cigarette. "You aren't the first unmarried girl to let a boy cross the dotted line and I dare say you won't be the last. I knew that quick tongue and velvet smile of yours'd land you in hot water!"

"Does that I mean I can keep him?"

Queenie said nothing as she licked the edge of her cigarette paper and Bea felt a soft feathering of hope for the first time since Jimmy's death. Could she actually be a mother? She didn't know the first thing about babies. In fact, they terrified her. *And yet.* This was her child, hers and Jimmy's.

She stared at her mother, anticipation stealing her breath.

"Of course not, love," Queenie said gently. She lit her cigarette and sighed out the smoke.

"We'd never survive the scandal. Illegitimacy is a stain that never washes off." Her words hung heavy. "And what about the poor baby? Think of the life you'll be condemning him to. The same folk who go around branding homes with swastikas will quickly be branding him a bastard," she said shrewdly and, with brilliant clarity, Bea suddenly realized she was right. She and her child would be despised, cast out, social pariahs in a goldfish bowl.

Her throat locked. "So what do we do?"

"I know a small maternity home in the north of the island. In about a month, you'll leave your job. I'll go in and say my friend needs help on her farm."

"No need," said Bea miserably. "They're making me leave to work at the Red Cross office. I just need to work a month's notice."

"Even better. You won't take the new job. We'll move you up to the home instead. I have a discreet friend who can make inquiries. She's helped plenty of girls who found themselves in trouble with their German boyfriends. There are women on this island who might be prepared to foster a child, until we're liberated. Then the baby can be adopted in England."

Bea looked out of the window. Outside, the sky looked like it had been freshly painted, blousy clouds scudding through the blue like sails on a ship. The truth was out and the sky hadn't fallen in. Just like that her mum had a plan that made it all sound so easy. The trouble was, Bea knew it would be easier to hand over her heart than her and Jimmy's baby.

Tears began to slide down her face.

"In a year or two, when it's all over and the Germans have left, you'll move on from all this. I promise," Queenie said, stroking her head. "You have to 'cause you've no other choice," she said with brutal pragmatism. "I'm from the *no choice but to get on with it* generation, and now, my love, so are you."

"I better get back to work," said Bea, feeling like the ceiling was shrinking down on her head.

"That's the ticket. Just one more thing. Tell no one about this. The fewer people know that you're in the family way, the better. That includes Grace. Especially Grace." She picked a strand of tobacco from her tooth. "This can't get back to Jimmy's mum. It'd destroy her."

Bea nodded.

"Not good enough," she said, a chill lacing her voice. "You have to promise me."

"I promise."

Queenie's face softened, compassion returning to her features.

"Good girl." She rummaged inside her handbag and pulled out a stubby tube of Yardley's Renegade Red. "Paint your face on. Show 'em your flag's still flying."

But even with her lips stained vermilion red, Bea still felt utterly defeated. How could she not have seen what was plainly staring her in the face? She reached for her mum and wrapped her arms around her as if love alone could hold back sickness. "I'm so sorry, Mum."

"Hush, child. I'm the parent. It's for me to worry about you, not the other way round."

Bea went on her afternoon round, deliberately leaving the library to last. She parked her bike against the steps of the Bibliothèque Publique and went in search of Grace.

She found her studying something on the desk, a frown etched over her face.

"What's up? Someone not paid their fine?"

Grace looked up, her face bleached of color. She had pinned her long blonde hair back into a chignon with a pencil and most of it had escaped, tumbling down her shoulders.

"Grace? What's wrong?"

"I've been absolutely out of my mind with worry over Red and now..." She choked back a sob. "They're closing down the book club!"

"What? They can't do that!"

"They can and they are." She held up a letter. "This was just delivered from the commandant's office."

"But why?"

"Because your book club broke the rules." The voice seemed to come from on high. The girls looked up to see the Wolf leaning over the mezzanine railings.

Casually he walked down the stairs and came to join them at the desk.

"You read poetry that was offensive and uncongenial to the Third Reich."

"We did no such thing," Grace protested.

"Really?" He pulled out a notebook from his pocket.

"'The Soldier' by Rupert Brooke?"

"But that's about the last war, not this one. I consulted with the Feldkommandant's office on this very issue. I was told that books which are disparaging and provocative against the Third Reich are *verboten*. It does not apply to texts that are objective representations of battles or historical events."

"And what about this one? '*Little Jersey bombed and mined, For us, warfare has proved unkind, But after all the stress and strain, A great height we will rise again.*'"

"That was a spur of the moment poem written by one of my patrons," Grace protested. "I didn't even know she was planning to read it."

"It is deeply offensive to the Third Reich and damaging to morale. I do not blame the commandant for shutting down your group."

A shadow passed over Grace's face.

"It was you, wasn't it? That censor who was on duty reports to you. He was never asleep."

He smirked. "Amazing how people let down their guard when they think they're not overheard." He turned to Bea and she felt the blood in her veins turn to ice. "Amazing too how many secrets people are keeping on this parochial little island, isn't that right, Miss La Mottée?

"Your American boyfriend is behind bars. Your book club is over. I suspect there is more, but don't worry. I will uncover the truth."

Grace's head slumped into her hands.

"Please. Whatever you may think of me, I beg of you not to shut down the book club. You don't know what it means to islanders. It's a lifeline."

"Then you should have censored your reading more effectively."

"Censor my reading?" Grace repeated in a daze. "I'm a librarian. If I censor people's reading, I may as well steal their thoughts."

The Wolf shrugged then snapped his fingers. As if on cue three men dressed in black appeared from behind the stacks.

"Search the library," he ordered. "And her office."

"No, please," Grace cried, opening the counter hatch and running out. "Please stop. We've already surrendered all the books on your list. There is no point."

Grace wept as his men went round, sweeping books from shelves, pausing from time to time to shake loose their pages.

"Many of these books are old and fragile, please be careful. You'll ruin them."

"Continue," the Wolf ordered before turning to Grace. "I do admire your carefully constructed amiable bookworm disguise, Miss La Mottée. Now please close the library until we have conducted our search."

Bea held Grace as she choked back sobs.

"How can they do this, Bea?" she wept. "First Peter and Red, now this! What more do they want from us?" She held her hands to her eyes to block out the sight, but at the sound of tearing pages, Bea knew they may as well have ripped out her friend's heart.

"Everyone OUT!" the Wolf ordered, turning to Bea. "That includes you."

"Go," Grace said quietly. "Don't make it worse."

Bea felt a thick hatred clot in her veins. "Very well. But I'll come back later to help you clean up."

She left, tears blurring her eyes and followed the stream of stunned people as they filed out of the library.

Outside, her heart began to hammer in her chest as the scales fell away. She knew what she had to do. She had been fooling herself to think that the Wolf was an idiot. He was a dangerous man, hell-bent on ruining them both.

Bea cycled to the allotment, and stuffed the stolen German letters, along with the informers' letters she hadn't delivered, into her postal bag. It was a risk, but one she knew she had little choice but to take.

At the post office yard she found Arthur tinkering with one of the delivery vans.

"Can I have a word?"

"Whatever's wrong, girlie?"

"I've got a big problem and I know I'm risking both of our lives, but you're the only person I can turn to. My father always said you were a man you could hang your hat off."

Arthur's craggy old face fell and Bea prayed her leap of faith wasn't misplaced. She opened her bag enough to let him peer in.

"I need a safe hiding place for some unwanted post. I'd destroy them but I think they'll prove useful after the war."

She clutched her tummy, her heart pounding so hard she could hear it pulsing in her ears.

"Calm down, girlie."

His rough voice was barely above a whisper as he drew her back behind an old Ford van.

"I know somewhere the Germans will never look."

"Where?"

"Les Vaux Sanatorium. It's only used for TB patients. There's a room in the basement there. I'll move the letters there."

"And they'll be safe?"

He nodded. "I reckon so."

They paused as a pair of old men in crumpled caps passed by on the street outside, well out of earshot, but you never knew.

"But how can you be sure?" she whispered once they'd passed. "This is my doing. I don't want this to come back on anyone else here."

"The Hun are terrified of tuberculosis. Trust me, they steer well clear of the place."

Bea had so many questions. What else went on in the basement of the TB sanatorium? Who else knew about it? But she knew better than to ask. The relief that she had spring-cleaned her own business was immense.

"Thank you, Arthur."

He nodded as he took her postal bag from her, his face grim.

"I warned you not to get mixed up in any of this business, girlie."

"I'm sorry, Arthur. I couldn't stand by and watch such a diabolic thing going on."

Arthur raised his eyes to the heavens.

"No, I dare say you couldn't. God knows your father would have done the same. But," he raised his finger, "I hear you're off to work at the Red Cross office soon and I'm glad of it. You keep out of trouble. Please God we are close to victory."

She reached up and kissed his weather-beaten cheek.

"Don't worry. Nothing bad'll happen to me."

"The invincibility of youth," he sighed.

"How can people turn on each other?" she asked on impulse.

He shrugged. "Spite. Hunger. Rewards. Who knows. But what you have to remember, Bea, is that those who denounce are in a small minority."

"P'raps. Trouble is, you begin to doubt everybody."

"Be cautious with your trust and keep your trap shut. A still tongue…"

"Keeps a wise head. I know, I know. That's what my mum always says."

He laughed. "Saucy piece you are, Bea Gold. Go on, be on your way."

She turned and cycled back to the library to help Grace with the clear-up and despite the banter with Arthur, a terrible unsettled feeling seeped over her like hot oil.

Outside the library she paused on the steps to catch her breath. Local stonemason Joseph Le Guyader was re-laying some of the paving in the Royal Square. He worked diligently, scooping up sand and patting it down to lay foundations, rolled-up cigarette glued to the side of his mouth. Wouldn't it be wonderful to have a straightforward job like that? He must have sensed her watching as he glanced up and smiled. Slowly he drew a V in the wet sand, before placing a thick slab over the top. Bea returned his smile and opened the library door.

She found Grace on her knees in the middle of the library, like a fallen angel, surrounded by piles of scattered books. The search had shaken free the dust from the stacks and motes spiraled in the prism of sunshine streaming down from the glass dome above. You could taste the adrenaline and shock in the air.

Grace looked up, her beautiful green eyes puffy from crying. It was hard to tell which was the most wounding to her, Red's arrest or the closure of the book club.

"Where do we even start?" she cried, looking around at the piles of books.

Most of the shelves had been swept of their books. The library had been trashed.

"Look at my library. Just look. How could they?"

"Did they find anything?" Bea whispered, sinking to her knees beside Grace. Grace took a juddering breath and shook her head.

"I don't think so." She pulled a key from the sole of her shoe. "The others are still locked in the secret cupboard behind the nature stacks."

She managed a slight smile.

"Clearly *Birds of the Channel Islands* don't represent a threat to the Third Reich."

Bea gently pulled Grace to her feet.

"That's my girl. I know it's awful that they've closed down the book club but at least they haven't found anything to warrant shutting the library down."

"But where do we start?" Grace asked, surveying the chaos.

"We start at the beginning. Come on. You picked me up after Jimmy's death, now it's my turn."

She gave her an irreverent grin. "Besides, I know you're dying to teach me the finer points of cataloging."

A rumpled smile crossed her friend's face, halfway between a sob and a laugh.

"That's the spirit," Bea laughed. "Don't let that Nazi bastard get to you. He's only doing this 'cause he knows they're done for. His control is slipping away."

"I suppose I should be grateful they didn't find my hidden books. Oh and the best of it is, every single book we are donated now needs to be sent straight to them to be read and cleared before I can loan it out, to check it's not uncongenial to the regime. My library feels tainted."

She pushed trembling fingers through her hair. "It's all my fault."

"What? Why?"

"I told Red I loved him. I should have known he would have appeared in town *and* I should have protected my book club. I failed to see the danger I was putting us all in."

She touched the delicate skin at her throat. "It's as if I have a noose round my neck which gets tighter by the day."

Bea hugged her tightly, swallowing her own pain. Grace had eloquently summed up precisely how she herself was feeling.

"I'm sorry, Bea. Some friend I am. I haven't even asked you yet what it was you wanted to talk over with me."

Bea remembered her mum's warning. "Oh, Mum's not well is all. She's got diabetes. She's had it for years apparently. I just can't fathom why she didn't tell me."

"Your mum's a proud and stubborn woman. Like someone else I know."

Bea felt Grace studying her, reading her like a book. "Are you sure there's nothing else?"

Bea bent down to pick up a book so she couldn't see her expression.

"No, nothing else. Come on, let's get your library back in apple pie order."

They worked in silence and Bea could tell Grace was freighted with despair over the events of the past 48 hours. Every book those barbaric men had torn from the shelves was wiped gently with a soft cloth and replaced to its rightful spot.

"How long has this library been going for?" Bea asked as they worked.

"Over 200 years."

Bea gazed up at the glittering dome roof and was struck by the enormity of its history.

"It strikes me that an institution which has already survived for so long will be around long after the Nazis have left, long after you and I have popped our clogs."

Grace ran her finger up the spine of the beautiful burgundy-and-gold hardback she was holding and finally a smile curled the corners of her lips.

"You're right. Wars will come and go…"

"But the library remains," Bea finished.

She reached for Grace's cold fingers and squeezed them tight.

14

Grace

BANNED BOOK

Bambi, a Life in the Woods, *by Felix Salten. This is a sweet story about a young deer who finds love and friendship in a forest, but the original tale of Bambi, adapted by Disney in 1942, has much darker beginnings as a novel about persecution and antisemitism in 1920s Austria. The Jewish author's book was banned by the Nazis in 1935, who burned it as Jewish propaganda. Salten fled Austria in 1938. He sold the film rights for $1,000 to an American director, who sold them on to Disney. He never earned a penny from the adaptation and died in Zurich in 1945, alone, with no safe place to call home.*

Four weeks on Grace was still reeling from the savagery of her losses. Nature was her consolation. It was a Monday morning at the end of May and spring had merged into bright, sun-sharp days. In the fields the corn turned brown to butter-blonde. Thick clumps of purple heather and yellow gorse glowed in the sunshine, the air filled with its coconut scent. Grace savored its tang in her mouth as she pedaled to and from the library each day.

Most people were more concerned with what was happening in their home than the passing of the seasons. Mealtimes were what her mother had dubbed "SOS"— soup or spuds. Nothing of any flavor passed their lips these days. But nothing had scoured Grace more than Red's arrest and the closure of their book club. Their absence over the past month had felt like the removal of a limb.

When it came to the club, it wasn't so much the books themselves, as book issues were at a record high. It was the feeling of companionship, the collective act of reading, which had made them all feel as if their suffering were a shared endeavor. The sense that somehow, their literary gatherings were protecting them from the occupation. Nestled in the sanctuary of the library, words flowing over and around them, had kept real life at bay.

Every week without fail Grace had secretly managed to visit Peter in hospital, thanks to Sister Morgan. If it hadn't been for those precious encounters, she would have doubted he were alive at all. It was if he'd been swallowed into a vacuum of darkness. Without his continual, calm presence it felt like the library was missing a precious book.

Sighing, she pulled the *Evening Post* from the newspaper rack and turned to the section which reported sessions at the Royal Court. It was the usual fare. A farmer fined £30 for having an unregistered pig. A four-and-a-half month prison sentence for Winifred Green who worked at the Royal Hotel in Guernsey, where the chef was an ardent

Nazi and to his frequent "*Heil Hitler*," she had replied, "*Heil Churchill.*"

But *nothing* on Peter.

Red's arrest had been a far splashier affair. The Nazi authorities had gone to town on that, ensuring that most of the front page of the *Evening Post* had been dedicated to the capture of "a most dangerous enemy of the Third Reich." Fortunately they were no closer to working out who had offered him sanctuary, but the warning to islanders was implicit. Grace hadn't even bothered to read the article. It was nothing more than bragging propaganda. But the photo they'd used of him had nearly toppled her. Red in irons being taken to the prisoner-of-war camp in St. Helier. She couldn't make out his face in the grainy photo but his broad shoulders stayed strong, his back unbowed. God, she loved him. There wasn't a moment when she didn't find herself thinking back to their last tender kiss in the woods. Just knowing he was near was some comfort until she remembered the Wolf's threats.

I should so love for you to experience the camps of the Great Fatherland.

Everything she held dear was slipping away from her, everything she touched turned sour. She sensed Miss Piquet watching her and realized she was standing in a trance by the newspaper rack. Grace swallowed. *Pull yourself together. You aren't the first woman in this war to have a loved one behind barbed wire.*

She busied herself with tidying the newspapers. In peacetime they'd stocked 11 English dailies, plus 80 periodicals and magazines. Now *The Times* and *Daily Mail* had been replaced with *Die Wehrmacht* and *Signal* magazine.

The sight of Nazi propaganda in her library, a space that has always been the last bastion of democracy, was more than she could stand. On impulse she tossed *Signal* magazine onto the floor. It skidded across the parquet, landing at a pair of well-polished brogues.

"You better not let the authorities see you doing that."

"I'm so sorry," Grace gushed to the unfamiliar gentleman standing in front of her.

"Quite all right," he said, amusement twitching at his lips. "I confess, I feel like doing the same myself." He held out his hand. "I'm Dr. Hanna. I'm a representative of the Red Cross."

"Good morning. How may I help?" she asked.

"I'm acting as an intermediary between the Germans and the American prisoners of war, housed at South Hill, St. Helier."

"Oh." She faltered, feeling as if a tiny bird was trapped in her chest.

"I've persuaded the occupying authorities that some form of entertainment and diversion should be provided for the prisoners. There's a variety concert this afternoon in the gymnasium in the compound. One of Jersey's postal workers, Eric Hassell, has agreed to sing."

"That's a wonderful idea," said Grace, confused, "but please don't ask me to perform. I'm a lousy singer."

"No, don't worry," Dr. Hanna chuckled. "I wondered if you could spare some books? One of our prisoners has requested a prisoner-of-war library." He smiled wryly. "He's terribly well read. Never has the Geneva Convention been quoted quite so much."

Grace felt a glow emanate from somewhere deep within. It was him. It had to be.

"But of course. I'd be happy to provide some. As a matter of fact, I've a large number of books donated to the library, which I haven't had a chance to catalog yet—at least a hundred. I'd be happy to donate those? I can't see my patrons objecting to offering these books to our American friends."

"Marvelous. They'd all be so grateful. In fact…" He looked about and lowered his voice. "The prisoner who has volunteered to run the library has requested a brief meeting with you to ask your advice. Is that something you'd feel comfortable with?"

"Of course. I'd be happy to offer him some insight."

"Naturally it's nothing like on this scale, but run properly a prisoner-of-war library has been proven to be a great morale boost. Might you be free now?"

"Now?"

"Between you and me, Miss La Mottée, if we take this through the official channels, it will get snarled up in red tape. If you slip in while the concert's on, we should be able to give you five minutes in the prison library to… er, deliver a few books and a little morale. Do you understand what I'm saying?" He spoke slowly, emphasizing the word *morale*.

Grace smiled knowingly. It seemed the Red Effect worked even on gentlemen.

"Give me five minutes to gather some books."

"Certainly. I'll meet you out at the front of the library."

"Miss P, can you hold the fort for an hour?" she called. "Just a little errand to run."

Grace's heart was galloping as she ran to her office and piled up her books in a box. She hardly dared allow herself to believe that she might actually see Red.

Perhaps it was the sense of hope which kindled a little mischief, but on impulse she ran up the stairs to the Reading Room, withdrew the key to the secret cupboard and pulled out *The Call of the Wild*. Taking care to tuck it under her blouse, she secured in her waistband and ran outside to join the doctor.

Dr. Hanna insisted on carrying the box, as they walked the short distance to the prison compound.

They walked past the old French Harbour and a sign pointed up a steep hill to MILITAR ARREST-ANSTALT. Seeing this caused a flood of adrenaline to pump through her. She was about to smuggle a *verboten* book into a German prison to her American sweetheart. This war had changed her in ways Grace suspected she wasn't even yet aware of. A few years ago, she had been such a timid, compliant thing. She hadn't even dared return a book a day late from her own library.

"Here we are. Put this on," Dr. Hanna said briskly, giving her a Red Cross armband and handing her the box of books.

Inside the compound Grace looked about. The camp was laid out in a rectangle about 150 feet long, at the top of the hill overlooking the harbor. The doctor led her to the gymnasium at the far end of the compound.

"There's a small annex at the back of the gymnasium that's been earmarked for use as the library. I've some other matters to tend to. You have five minutes to arrange your books before I return."

He smiled and touched her softly on the shoulder. "Relax."

Then he was gone. Grace's heart thumped as she looked around the compound. It was deserted. Most people, warders included, were crowded in the gymnasium for the concert. The sounds of applause and cheers drifted out.

Grace slipped into the room, using her shoulder to bump open the door. The room was cold and empty, save for some makeshift shelves knocked together and nailed to a wall and a small table in the middle of the room. The disappointment was profound. She must have got the wrong end of the stick. She was supposed to just deliver books and leave.

Grace placed the books on the table.

Behind her the door clicked and she froze. The scent of tobacco and boot polish filled the room. A hand touched her shoulder and turned her around slowly.

She had forgotten how tall he was, how much his presence filled the room, like the sun muscling out from behind a cloud.

"Red," she wept, feeling her heart smash against her ribs.

He pulled her into his arms and kissed her greedily and all Grace felt was a scalding relief. Tears slid down her cheeks as he lifted her off her feet and hugged her so tightly she swore she could feel his heartbeat against her own.

"Oh, Grace, you don't know how good it is to see you."

Gently he placed her down and held her face in his hands.

"Let me look at you." The sounds of music drifted in from the concert next door.

You smile, and the Angels sing.

"Apt," he murmured, tracing the outline of her lips with his finger.

"Thank you for coming. This is going to sound terribly corny, Grace," he sighed, "but I've seen stars and sunsets that'd make you believe in God, the Alps by moonlight... But nothing, I swear, is as beautiful as the sight of you walking across that yard carrying books."

He kissed her once more.

"*You* are my reward for staying alive, Grace."

"Red, I'm so sorry—" she blurted.

"What the hell for?"

"I feel like I'm to blame for your capture. Like somehow I encouraged you to follow me into town that day."

"I'm a big boy, Grace. I make my own decisions." He grinned and a flash of the old irreverent Red was back. "Besides. It was worth it to see you one last time."

"But you're a prisoner of war. It must be awful being cooped up in here."

"It's boring and demoralizing, to say nothing of a blow to the ego. But at least I've got the library to focus on until..."

He trailed off when he saw the books.

"Grace, these'll go down a storm with the fellas. Reading staves off the boredom." He laughed at a sudden memory.

"Our colonel has a nightly session of storytelling, reading out loud from Shakespeare, with each of us taking a part. The guards think we're crazy!"

"There's one more," she said, slipping *The Call of the Wild* out from her waistband.

"You remembered!"

"Of course. But please keep it hidden."

He crossed his heart. "On my life."

For a moment they simply stood facing one another and Grace wished she could bottle this perfect moment and keep it forever.

"Grace, there is so much to say and I'm aware we're running out of time. Dr. Hanna'll be back in a moment and I can't abuse his kindness."

His gaze flickered out of the grimy window, beyond the barbed wire around the prison compound.

"To know that you love me makes any amount of suffering worthwhile."

"And you really think that you and I have a future together after the war?" Grace asked. "That we can live peacefully with our books, grow old together?"

She laughed at the notion. "Lose our reading glasses and bicker over who feeds the cat?"

"I really do, Grace. But it will be dogs, not cats."

"Two cats, two dogs," Grace asserted.

"Whatever you want, Grace."

"But where will we live?"

"I don't know, Angel, but somewhere there has to be place for us. There's so much out there to see. I want to take you to London. To see the traveling library."

Hope kindled. "And the Whispering Gallery? Oh, and I'd love to visit the London Library. In fact, all the great libraries of Europe."

Red laughed at her enthusiasm. "Sure. Hell why not? Let's visit all the libraries in the world."

He hesitated.

"And Boston Library? Maybe one day, you might consider coming home with me, as my wife."

"Oh, Red." She leaned her forehead against his.

"I've finally met someone who I'm not afraid to die for," he said into the warmth of the space between them. "You and me, Angel Grace, it's meant to be. Will you marry me?"

He pulled back, scanned her face.

"I know I'm no catch right now. I'm a goddamn prisoner of war, but one day I'll offer you the world, I promise."

"Let's concentrate on surviving this war and if we do," she looked up at him, feeling like she'd swallowed the sun, "then of course I'll marry you."

Grace closed her eyes and rested her head against his chest. Did she even dare allow herself to indulge and share in a dream that big?

A soft knock at the door reluctantly dragged her back to her senses.

"Time to go," Red said.

"I love you so much," she whispered, tracing her fingers along his jawline, over the faint dimple in his chin, trying to commit every detail of his face to her memory, before turning.

Grace reached the door. His voice pulled her back.

"One last thing," He pulled off his prison cap and revealed a shock of tufty red hair. He wrinkled his nose as he mussed his hair, his green eyes all the more vivid. "No hair dye in prison. This is me. The real me."

She half-sobbed, half-laughed. "I still love you. Cheer up, Yank. Won't be long."

As Grace strode out across the yard, her heart was full.

Back in the library she was surprised to find the book club assembled around her desk. Molly, Mr. Warder, Mrs. Moisan, Bea, Queenie, Mrs. Noble, Louisa Gould, Albert Bedane and many more.

"Hallo, everyone. Have I missed something?"

"We had an idea, Grace ducks," Queenie said. "We know we can't gather in here as a book club no more, but what's to stop us meeting outside?"

"I don't understand."

"We know how worried you are about Peter," Bea chipped in. "We thought we could maybe stand on the street outside the prison, read in solidarity and support."

"He might not see us," said Louisa. "But if he can, then he'll know the book club is waiting for him. That's got to lift his spirits surely?"

"I love it," Grace said. "But wait—we're not allowed to assemble in groups of more than five."

"We thought of that, Grace," said Mr. Warder. "We split up into groups of three and stand apart. What do you think?"

"I think I don't know what I've done to deserve such wonderful friends," she said, her voice catching in her throat as her eyes filled with tears.

Queenie pulled out her hankie.

"Doing something, no matter how small, is better than doing nothing at all," she said and the group nodded their agreement. "The only thing I used to read was my ration book. Now I'm a regular bookworm."

She swayed a little and Grace grabbed her arm. Queenie seemed to have shrunk over the past month and didn't look at all well.

"Don't fuss," Queenie whispered.

"You're right," Grace said, releasing her grip on Queenie. "We might not be a proper reading club anymore, but we can be a literary support group."

Grace gathered some of Peter's favorite books, and leaving poor Miss Piquet to hold the fort once more, they made their way to the town's prison. The pavement on the street outside the prison was narrow, but there was so little traffic these days they easily found three separate spots to gather in.

Discreetly the groups huddled in their small circles and took it in turns to read excerpts. They drew curious looks as they read out their favorite passages, but Grace didn't care. Falling down a rabbit hole, being swallowed by a whale, galloping through a frosty night on the back of a black horse was mind-expanding joy. How she hoped that somehow, in some way, Peter could feel the strength of her love. Or better yet, was looking down from those dark and mournful windows above. She willed the words off the page and up, up and in through the bars of the windows.

They stayed for 40 minutes before the group dispersed, back to work or the drudgery of keeping a home in wartime.

Back in the library, Bea handed Grace a letter.

"Read it."

*The widow Louisa Gould. La Fontaine. Harboring a Russian
POW and flaunting him at the library. Search and you shall
find.*

Grace closed her eyes.

"I thought you'd stopped."

"I had. I have," she stumbled. "I promise. I just delivered
some mail to Victoria College this morning and the vice
principle, Pat Tatam, called me in. This was delivered to
him by mistake instead of the Commandant at Victoria
College House."

"He opened it?" Grace asked.

"Told me the seal had come loose. Left me alone in his
office and then told me to redirect it. But never mind how
it came to be opened. The most important question is,
what do we do?"

Grace closed her eyes, felt her heartbeat drumming as
she turned over the consequences. The library had been
named in the letter. The Wolf wouldn't need any more
evidence than that to shut down the library and arrest them
all.

"Mr. Mourant is watching me like a hawk," Bea persisted.
"I've only got until Friday then I'm leaving. I can't leave
without making sure Lou's safe."

"You're leaving the post office?" Grace exclaimed. "What?
Why? You never told me."

"I've had enough of all them early starts. Mum's got a
friend up in Trinity who's sick and needs some help with
her farm."

Bea shifted her post bag over her tummy.

Grace stared at Bea and knew without a shadow of doubt her friend was hiding something from her.

"But the point is, Grace, none of that's important right now." Bea drummed an impatient finger on the letter. "This piece of poison needs dealing with and fast. I'll have to post this letter to the commandant this afternoon, tomorrow morning at the latest. It's already been date-stamped which means if I hold it back any longer it'll raise suspicion."

She looked at Grace, wide-eyed with fear, and already Grace knew where this was leading.

"Lou needs telling today. The Wolf will turn her house over the minute this lands on his desk."

Grace felt Bea's hand on her arm. "Please, Grace, you can tell her on your way home tonight. I can't make it to St. Ouen's and back without raising suspicion."

Grace let out a sigh that seemed to wrap itself around the library. "Very well. But only if you tell me why you're really leaving the post office, because I don't buy all this nonsense about helping out your mum's friend. Your mum is sick. She needs you at home."

Bea stared at the floor. "I know. Look, I'll tell you everything. I promise. But not now. First, let's deal with this."

"Very well. I'll go now."

Bea threw her arms around her and hugged her tightly. Grace felt a tremor run through her friend's body.

"Bea, you're shaking," she whispered, drawing back. "Please tell me you're all right."

"I will be. In time. Did I ever tell you how much I love you?"

"You're scaring me, Bea"

But her friend had already left, the heavy library door banging shut behind her.

Outside, Grace pulled on her raincoat and called out to Miss Piquet.

"I'm so sorry to do this to you again, Miss P. But I've something of a family emergency at home. I swear you've earned yourself a place in library heaven."

"Go on with you," Miss Piquet said, rolling her eyes. "Library heaven indeed!"

Half an hour later, Grace and Dr. McKinstry were heading west, bumping along the island roads in his old boneshaker. Thank god, as a medic, he was still allowed a vehicle, and was still in his surgery when she called.

"I've arranged another safehouse for Bill," he said. "He'll need to leave tonight." The doctor frowned. "She won't like it one bit. She's come to look upon that young man as something of a substitute son, but we must impress the danger of this situation upon Mrs. Gould."

They pulled to a stop outside the small whitewashed country shop, surrounded by green rolling pastures. It could have been one of a thousand such stores run by middle-aged matrons in Britain's sleepy countryside villages. Women like Louisa were the everyday heroines of this war, stalwarts who knew every single one of their customers by name and were rooted in the communities they served.

"Who could do such a despicable thing to Lou?" Grace murmured, as he turned off the ignition. Over the road, curtains twitched at the home of two old maids, the Vibert sisters.

Dr. McKinstry shrugged as they sat in the silence of the motor car, listening as the engine ticked and cooled.

"And why?"

"Jealousy. Hunger. A chance to settle old scores?"

"What separates Louisa from the people who write these letters?"

"A refusal to believe her own hardship is more important than others," he replied wearily, taking out his keys. "Come on. Let's do this."

15

Bea

Four days later Bea had finished her last round and went back to the post office to collect her final pay packet at 5 p.m.

She had hoped to slip away. No such luck. As soon as she pushed her bicycle in through the yard, she could see it was filled with postmen and counter staff.

"Surprise!" yelled fifty or so voices.

Homemade bunting in the shape of letters was strung across the yard. A trestle table had been laid with a half-passable spread.

"You didn't think you was gonna slip away without a fuss, did you?" said Nobby, popping the lid on a bottle of beer and guzzling the foam as it spilled out.

"Come on then, girlie, let's be having you," said Arthur, pushing a drink into her hand. "I've been saving this calvados for a special occasion."

"We've pooled our rations," said Winnie, gesturing to the trestle table. "It's not much, but we didn't want you leaving without a decent send-off."

Bea felt her throat close up with emotion. Leaving here was breaking her heart. It was just one more sacrifice to make.

"You're a gobby piece, but we won't half miss you," joked Harold.

"Yeah only 'cause you old buggers will have to make your own tea now," Bea retorted and the crowd fell about.

"Jokes aside, we *will* miss you. A great deal," said Arthur softly. "When this occupation is over, you can hold your head up high."

"Three cheers for Bea," said Mr. Warder. "*À ta bouonne santé!* Your good health.*"

"Speech," the crowd clamored.

"*Té v'là, vièr bougârron, tu n'as pon acouo mouothi don. Prend tan temps, n'y'a pon d'prêsse,*" she replied. The yard fell silent. "You old sods, you're not dead yet, I see. Take your time. There's no hurry." She grinned and translated.

"I thought you didn't speak Jèrriais," Winnie exclaimed.

"You don't know everything about me," she said, winking at Arthur.

As the yard erupted with laughter, Bea spotted Grace slipping in at the back of the crowd.

When the cheers and backslapping had finished, Winnie tapped her on the arm.

"A little present for you," said Winnie, drawing her over to the privacy of the bike shed.

"Just have a peek in, but be a good girl and don't pull it out. You won't want anyone seeing."

Bea moved aside the tissue paper and saw soft white wool bootees.

"I had to unravel my son's old jumper to make it, but it should do you in about a month or so time by my reckoning."

Bea passed her hand over her mouth.

"It's all right, you don't need to say anything. I've known for months. I won't say anything. You have my word."

Bea leaned over and hugged her.

"Thank you, Win," she whispered. "I'm touched...and scared."

"I dare say. You aren't the first and you won't be the last."

Bea pushed back the tidal waves of tears that threatened to swamp her at the act of kindness. If Jimmy were alive then this baby would be a cause for celebration. She'd have a proper ring on her finger, be about to start a new life as a mum. Instead, she was slinking away in shame, her precious baby a dirty little secret. A tear escaped and ran down her cheek as she brushed her fingers over the bootees, imagined 10 little pink toes in them. Up until now, her child had remained faceless, but the closer the birth drew, the more she found herself fantasizing about her baby. Would he look like her or Jimmy? The thought of meeting this little person, conceived from an act of love, so very much wanted, *needed even*, and then having to hand him over to a stranger was almost more than she could bear. She inhaled sharply, the pain of what lay ahead was excruciating. The heart-rending enormity of having to give her child away crushed down on her like a physical weight.

"I don't know that I can do this, Win," she confessed.

The elderly counter clerk touched her cheek.

"Us women are bred to be tough, born to encounter disappointment. You'll survive. You'll see."

Bea nodded.

"That's what Mum said."

"And she's right. You're still young. You'll have your family in time."

But it won't be Jimmy's baby.

Winnie smiled sadly. "Be of stout heart, my love."

She looked around the yard at the tough old posties she'd worked alongside all these long occupation years and realized that, in the finish, it would be the people she missed the most.

"Come on, girlie," bellowed Harold, beckoning her with an avuncular smile. "Why the long face? It's Friday, it's a bank holiday weekend, the sun's shining and the Hun are on the run. Let's charge these glasses."

Through the crowds she spotted Grace talking to Mr. Warder and felt a powerful rush of love for her friend and all that they had been through together. This baby would be Grace's nephew, her blood. Bea knew her mum didn't want her to, but she couldn't keep this a secret from Grace any longer. It wasn't fair. Grace had risked her life to help. Delivering the warning to Louisa three days ago. Arranging with Dr. McKinstry for Bill to be hidden in another island safehouse. Disaster had been averted and it was all thanks to Grace. She owed her the truth, before it was too late.

"Grace," she called and waved. Grace turned, her green eyes lighting up. She was so beautiful and radiant she looked as if she'd been lit up from within. Bea recognized that look: she was in love, she realized with a pang.

"Wait there," she called. "I'll come to you." Grace made her way toward the bike sheds, weaving her way through the throng, glass in hand.

Then a peculiar thing happened. The light snapped off. Revulsion and fear clouded her face. She stumbled back, shaking her head.

Faces all around her seemed to freeze mid-conversation.

Slowly, Bea turned around and even before she saw him, a sixth sense told her exactly what was about to unravel.

"Beatrice Gold, I need you to accompany me to Silvertide for questioning."

The Wolf was flanked by three men, all holding fixed bayonets.

"Is this really necessary?" said Mr. Mourant. "We can all talk in private in my office. I'm sure we can iron out any little problem."

"I assure you, this isn't a little problem. Miss Gold is in serious trouble."

Bea's legs went from under her and all hell seemed to break loose. She saw mouths opening and closing, yelling words of protest. She saw Grace fighting her way through the crowds, Winnie making a grab for one of the Wolf's men as he moved toward her. But it was as if someone had turned down a dial on a wireless. Her ears buzzed, everything went blurry and then she was falling.

"Who are you working with?"

Bea came round at Silvertide. At least she assumed it was Silvertide, but the room was dark. Underground? She was slumped in a chair. The Wolf was sitting across from her behind a desk, alongside another man. Her head throbbed and she felt something moist at the corner of her mouth. She tasted the sharp metallic tang of blood on her lip.

"No one," she croaked.

"You expect me to believe that? If there is a Resistance cell operating at the post office, we will uncover it."

Bea closed her eyes and felt a powerful tightening across her belly, like she was wearing a metal belt. A gripping sensation squeezed her abdomen. She groaned.

"Don't think because you are carrying a bastard baby, I will go easy on you. In fact, this might well be a blessing in disguise for you. Wouldn't you say, Bode?"

Something in his demeanor told Bea the man he was with was his superior.

"Hauptmann Bode. I don't believe we've had the pleasure."

He smiled. Bea stared at him. Everything about him was viscerally repulsive. His lips were moist and fleshy, his fat neck seemed to spill over his collar and his hair was an oil slick. She said nothing, trying very hard to breathe through the gathering wave of pain.

"If you are found guilty, you will be deported and your baby will be removed from you," he continued. "I should imagine under the circumstances that would save you the bother of trying to find a mother for your illegitimate child." He drew out the word *illegitimate*, rolling it out through glistening lips. She turned away in disgust. The Wolf motioned to the back of the room and for the first time she noticed his associate, Karl Lodburg. He crossed the room in two easy strides and slapped the side of her face.

"Look at Hauptmann Bode when he addresses you."

Pain and fear exploded inside her but she forced herself to look the Nazi in the eye.

"Why am I here?"

"Your friend Louisa Gould, her brother and all the rest said the same when we arrested them."

"How long have you known about the slave she has been harboring?" said Wolf.

"I don't know what you're talking about."

Bode slid a letter across the table.

"You opened this, didn't you, and warned Mrs. Gould."

"I don't know what you're talking about," she repeated.

"We know everything. You should have stayed behind to oversee the clean-up."

"I don't know—"

"Yes, yes," Wolf interrupted. "You don't know what we're talking about. But don't worry, Miss Gold. We can be patient while you remember. We have all the time in the world." He leaned back and lit up a cigarette. "Unlike you."

He pulled a crystal wireless set and a Russian–English dictionary out of a drawer. Bea's heart plunged.

"Recognize these?"

She shook her head and gripped her tummy, her mind spinning out of control. Could it be true that Louisa and her family had been arrested, or was he lying? Did those things belong to Louisa, in which case her fate was sealed? But surely, he had no actual proof that she had intercepted this letter, or any others? Anything that could point to her guilt was safely hidden in the basement of a TB isolation hospital.

"I have men searching your mother's house and allotment as we speak," the Wolf said. "I wonder what we'll turn up."

"You can't do this," she yelled. "My mother is sick. You leave her alone."

Bony fingers crawled up her spine as she imagined her mother opening the door to them. The Germans' sense of *justice* meant that all associated with her would be made to suffer. If the Germans on this island loved anything, it was a show trial, with the more people in the dock, the better.

"Please leave her out of this," she begged. "She is not a well woman."

"We will when you tell us the truth. Who are you working with at the post office and the library?"

In the distance a boom sounded, and the fetid air in the basement seemed to shudder. The Wolf flinched. Ash dropped off the end of his cigarette into his lap.

The sound of the Allies bombing France offered up a slender shaft of hope. Surely they were getting closer?

"So, what have you to say?" Bode asked.

Bea met his gaze and lifted her chin. "Long live the King." Then she snubbed her nose at the portrait hanging over his head. "And fuck you, atrocious Adolf."

The Wolf's jaw twitched and he gestured to the lump of muscle standing behind her.

A fist snapped across her left cheekbone and sent her reeling. For a while all she could do was hang in his solid arms and watch as blood dripped from her nose onto the carpet.

"She is making a mess," Bode sniffed. "Take her to the prison."

Outside, Bea was marched through Havre des Pas with her hands handcuffed behind her back and a bayonet positioned between her shoulder blades. Before they left Wolf had ordered she remove her jacket and stomach girdle.

There truly was nowhere to hide anymore. Her distended stomach went before her. Tears of humiliation burned her eyes, the left-hand side of her face pulsing with pain. All along the seafront she saw the twitching of net curtains. You could almost hear the tremor of the jungle drums. As they drew level with Bay View, Bea prayed her mother wouldn't see.

No such luck. Queenie Gold was standing in the small front garden smoking a cigarette while inside, Wolf's men ransacked their home. She saw their dark figures behind the window pane of her bedroom. She imagined them swarming like vermin, trawling through her things.

"You leave my daughter alone, you rotten bastards," Queenie screamed when she spotted them.

"Mum, get inside," Bea warned.

A vein bulged in her mother's neck when she spotted the dried blood caked around Bea's nose. "I mean it. You harm one hair on her head and I'll fucking strangle you with my bare hands!"

But her escorts just kept marching her on, their jackboots cracking off the pavement like a whip.

Mr. Bedane the physiotherapist was walking the other way and realized with alarm what was unfolding.

"Please, Mr. Bedane, help," Bea yelled, tears running down her cheeks.

"Mrs. Gold, this won't help your daughter." The physio-therapist restrained her mother. "Come with me."

He managed to get her mother back inside the garden but Bea's humiliation still was not complete. They marched her straight through the center of town. Past the library and then along Broad Street, past the post office, where her colleagues were gathered outside, still in a state of shock over her arrest. As they marched closer she saw their unfolding expressions. Anger turned to dismay at the sight of her.

It was a walk of shame, designed to humiliate and warn. They did this to most of their prisoners, but none had been quite so cruelly exposed. Anger pierced the dull fog in her head. All she had ever tried to do was help.

"Hold your chin up, girl," Arthur called, his mouth tight with fury. The last face she saw as she was marched through the prison gate was her sister Nancy's.

Jersey's prison belonged to an earlier war. Its thick, solid stone walls had been built in 1811 to house prisoners at the time of the Napoleonic War. Bea had often gazed up at the blackened 30-foot high wall separating the prison from the street, but never once been inside it.

"Welcome to the Gloucester Street Mansion," called a woman from the cell next door.

"Lou? Is that you?"

Silence, followed by a rustle. Bea imagined her running her fingers over her rough skirts.

"I've been here two days now. They've arrested us all."

"Who, Lou?"

"My brother, my sister, my maid, two of my friends. Everyone bar the budgerigar."

The left-hand side of Bea's face started to throb. This was exactly as she feared.

"Did they find anything during the search?" she asked, hardly daring to breathe.

A cough.

"A radio set, a Russian–English dictionary, some gift tags with Bill's name on."

Even worse than she'd imagined.

"Don't worry, Bea. I didn't say anything about who tipped us off. It will all be all right, you'll see. We'll just have to serve our time until liberation."

Her words sounded hollow and tinny. Louisa's false sense of security had already been her downfall and Bea didn't share her belief that this would turn out to be an adventure.

"But listen to me. This is important. They'll have you back and forth to Silvertide."

"She's right," piped up a voice from the other side.

"George Fox, is that you?" she called.

"For my sins."

Bea would have recognized that gravelly voice anywhere. She'd got to know George and his wife Cecilia from her postal round. He was a tough old bugger, who slaved in a hot kitchen despite the grief it gave his *gippy lungs*, as he called them.

"What are you doing in here, George?"

"Caught stealing food from the Hun."

Bea nodded. Made sense. He had seven hungry mouths to feed.

"Take my advice, love. Say little as you can. Keep it to yes and no. They'll try and trip you up. They wanna break you." He began to cough; it sounded like a motor car backfiring. Poor bloke. He'd been gassed in the first war. Had he not suffered enough?

"One minute I'm sitting there, next I'm spitting teeth on the floor," he wheezed. "But hopefully they'll go easier on you, being a woman and all."

"Thanks, George. I'll be all right," she replied, unconvincingly, touching her throbbing cheek.

"Keep the faith," called Louisa. "We just have to bide our time."

Bea stroked her swollen abdomen. Trouble was, time was not on her side. She felt her baby squirm and kick, a powerful reminder that she must be strong, for it was not only her survival in the balance.

George and Louisa were right. The Wolf was trying to break her mentally. Bea lost track of how many times she was woken from her sleep and dragged to Silvertide at all hours of the night. The left-hand side of her face had mushroomed into a vivid purple bruise from where she had been punched after her arrest. They held back on further violence, but the threat of it was always there, pulsing in the interrogation room. Karl Lodburg was a constant presence, positioned strategically by the door, arms crossed, hands idly caressing his biceps. He was a blond mountain of a man who smelled of bacon and muscle rub. Bea wondered how many of the island girls he'd seduced and lain down with. The thought made her blood boil.

Back and forth. Back and bloody forth. And always the same question. "What network are you working with?"

They genuinely seemed to believe she was a part of an organized network of resistance. As if they could scarcely believe a bunch of old postmen and a librarian with a conscience would risk everything. On George's advice, Bea kept her answers to as few words as possible—*yes, no, don't recall*—remembering the pain of that punch after she'd insulted their Führer.

The walks there and back were psychologically more grueling than the interrogations. The smell of sea air, the tantalizing glimpse of greenery, before plunging back to an underground room and prison cell were torturous.

Day bled into night, into day. Soon Bea was so exhausted, disoriented and hungry that she lost all sense of time. She'd eaten precious little more than a jam jar filled with a watery brown substance, purporting to be soup, and dry black bread. Her skin crawled and she desperately needed a hot bath.

Three days on from her arrest, by Whit Monday evening, the weather was so hot and stifling in her cell that all she could do was lie motionless on her bed, staring at the bruised sky between the bars of the window. Streaks of lightning flickered over the horizon. Now that her secret was out she swore the baby had grown, her bump like a round ripe melon and her breasts full and tender.

Outside, she heard an enormous roar. She struggled to sit upright.

"Lou, did you hear that?" she called breathlessly, gripping the edge of her bed.

The noise rose like a massive wave and permeated the thick prison walls. It sounded like hundreds, if not thousands of people cheering.

She pressed her face to the bars of the window. "Maybe they've heard news? Perhaps this is it, Lou. They've surrendered! Our liberation is coming." Immediately her baby started to kick. Oh, thank God. The relief was like a switch being flicked inside her body.

"Don't get your hopes up," intoned George. "A guard let slip there's a football match on. There are huge crowds by all accounts. The Hun are down there now breaking it up. Looked too much like a patriotic demonstration to their eyes."

A football match? The disappointment was so tangible it was like a stab to her heart.

"How can people be out there enjoying sport when we're locked up in here?" she cried.

"Life goes on outside," Louisa sighed.

Bea's forehead hit the prison wall and she started to weep, great shuddering tears of despair which rolled down her cheeks. The tears were like a gigantic release and she shifted, wobbly, holding on to the walls for support. A gush of warmth sprang from between her legs and liquid spattered onto the concrete floor of her cell.

"Lou," she whimpered, "I think my waters have broken!"

16

Grace

In the three days since Bea's arrest, Grace had alternated between pragmatism and outright panic. As it had been a bank holiday the library had been closed so she hadn't even had the escape of work and her fears churned on an endless loop around her mind. Her mother was so terrified, she'd insisted that Grace not leave the farmhouse all weekend, leaving her to do nothing but pace and fret. Pace and fret.

By five o'clock on Tuesday morning, the weather was so muggy, with thunder rumbling over the island, that she abandoned any notion of sleep. Grace dressed and cycled to the library, relieved to be out from the oppressive house. Lightning split open the dark skies over the ocean as she pedaled along the bay into town. In the distance she could smell burning.

When she reached the library, to her surprise, a lone figure sat hunched on the steps.

"Thank goodness you're here," said Molly. "Grace, you must come with me to the hospital."

"It's Bea, isn't it?"

"We need to hurry. We might already be too late."

"Too late?" she gasped. "Is she sick?"

"Just come with me."

They ran through the deserted streets, a sense of foreboding building inside Grace with every step, but instead of the General Hospital, Molly led her to the Dispensary, the maternity hospital on St. Saviour's Road. An armed German guard was posted outside the entrance.

"What's going on, Molly?" she panted, groggy with exhaustion. "Please just tell me. Is Bea sick?"

She felt a roaring start in her head as Molly gripped her wrist and shook her head.

"No, you ninny. Look at where we are! She's giving birth!"

"Giving birth?" Grace repeated in a daze.

Molly led her up a maze of corridors then pointed to a door.

"You knock. I'll wait here."

Grace knocked softly and then pushed open the door, her heart going like the clappers. This was madness, insane. Bea wasn't having a baby. She couldn't be.

Inside, Dr. John Lewis, a medic well-respected on the island for his formidable work ethic, was looking at his stopwatch and counting.

"That's good, my dear. The contractions are about a minute apart. It won't be long now. I'll tell you when to push."

Bea was on the hospital bed on all fours. Her face was waxy and pale, save for a livid yellow and purple bruise on her cheekbone. The image was so shocking, Grace stumbled back.

"I can't give birth, it's too soon," Bea whimpered.

"Your baby certainly doesn't seem to think so," Dr. Lewis replied calmly. "He, or she, is ready to come out and meet you."

"I can't." Bea wept helplessly. "I can't do this."

"In my experience, that's usually a sign that the baby is about to make an appearance. Now rest and gather your strength for the next contraction."

In that moment a silence stretched over the while tiled room and Bea turned, her eyes widening.

"Grace . . . Oh, Grace. You came." She shook her head. "I'm so sorry. I'm so, so sorry."

Snapping out of her torpor, Grace threw her bag on the floor and ran to Bea's side.

"What for?"

"Aren't you shocked?"

"Well, yes, a little, t-this wasn't what I was expecting to find," she stammered.

As understatements went, it was a whopper.

She coughed to clear her thickening throat.

"Good grief, you're having a baby." She stroked back a strand of wet hair from Bea's forehead and a sudden thought dawned on her and the emotion nearly floored her.

"Oh, Bea, is it—?"

Bea nodded. "It's your niece or nephew."

"Oh, my love. I don't know what to say."

Bea looked spent. Her cheeks slick with sweat, her wet hair plastered to her face.

"You must hate me for lying and I'm sorry, so sorry, I never planned any of this."

"Never mind all that. I'm here now, Bea. What can I do?"

"You can help me get her off this bed for starters," Dr. Lewis said through gritted teeth. "Believe me, this baby'll come a lot quicker with gravity on its side."

Together they heaved Bea off the bed and almost immediately another contraction seized her. Grace watched wide-eyed, breathless with admiration, but terrified for her friend as the pain seemed to take her away to another place.

"Take my hand," she urged, cupping her palms. Bea rammed her fist into it and bore down, her eyes squeezed shut as she tipped back her head and bellowed with all the fury and might she possessed. Her face was etched with a feral fury, her eyes were tightly shut, as if she might find the strength she was looking for in the darkness.

"That's it, push … push … Now stop," Dr. Lewis ordered.

"I can't do this," Bea roared.

"You can and you are," Dr. Lewis replied, getting down on his knees. "I can see baby's head. Now on the next contraction one last big push."

Bea's wild screams seemed to bounce off the tiled walls as the room filled with a fecund smell.

Grace cried helplessly as her friend's eyes rolled back in her head, her fingernails tearing into the skin on her palm. "Come on, Bea, come on."

And then the brutal, bloody, beautiful business of birth was done and Dr. Lewis was wrapping a baby in a white towel. "Pass me that clamp in the dish," he ordered Grace.

Grace watched, stunned, as he cut the cord between mother and child.

"Oh, Bea, you did it," Grace cried, tears unashamedly rolling down her cheeks. "You have a baby boy."

One hour later, with her baby son sleepily feeding at Bea's breast, the entire thing felt like a surreal dream.

"I'm going to see if I can arrange for you both to have a nice cup of tea," said Dr. Lewis, discreetly leaving the room. Grace waited until the door softly closed and she heard footsteps squeaking up the corridor.

"I can't get over this, any of it," Grace murmured. "I'm ashamed that you didn't feel you could tell me."

Bea couldn't even tear her gaze from her son and his tiny scrunched-up face.

"Never mind that, Grace. What does it matter now? He's here and isn't he the most exquisite thing you've ever seen? I can't believe me and Jimmy made something so beautiful." She shook her head in disbelief. "He has my whole heart in these hands."

His tiny little pink fingers were clutched around Bea's so tightly it was as if their bodies were drawn together like a magnet.

"He is—" Grace swallowed. A spear-thrust of tangled love and grief rippled through her. She couldn't find the words to express what it felt like to be looking into the eyes of her brother Jimmy. "He is perfection."

Finally Bea looked up at Grace. She had never seen such bittersweet pain etched on her friend's face and it knocked the breath from her. "It's as if Jimmy has returned to me. How can I leave him? It'll kill me."

It was a dramatic statement but one which Grace believed. How could any mother be expected to part with the helpless little person they had just delivered into the world?

Bea looked around the room, fear exploding on her face as if she had suddenly remembered the fate which lay outside the door.

"They'll come knocking for me soon, Grace, to take me back to prison."

She could see almost see the unraveling of her friend's thoughts.

"I bet there's a guard on the door, isn't there? How long before that black Citroën pulls up outside? Oh God."

Grace scrubbed her face wearily. The idea came to her from somewhere deep inside her self-conscious, tangling her shattered brain with the complexity of it.

Her memory reached back for a precious offer, shored away for a time when she would need it.

If ever I can help you, you know where to find me.

"I think there's a way, Bea," she said quietly. "Please God it'll work. You have to trust me."

She passed her finger lightly over her best friend's brow. "Do you trust me?"

"Grace," she said warily. "What are you going to do?"

"What needs to be done. I have to go soon, but before I do, might I have a cuddle with my nephew?"

"Of course. But, Grace, please tell me what you're planning. Don't do anything you might regret."

Gently Grace scooped up Bea's son and held him as if he were made of porcelain.

He lay perfectly still, swaddled in a white blanket, only his little face peeking out from the nest. He stirred and yawned, his eyelashes fluttering in a dream. Grace was spellbound. Hadn't she had hoped one day to have a baby of her own? With Red. In dreamier moments in the library, hadn't she imagined such a life for herself?

She squeezed back bitter tears as she realized that even if his dream of their life together after the liberation had been possible, it would surely never happen now. Not after what she was about to do.

"Hello, little chap," Grace whispered. "You've got a grand-mother at home who needs someone like you to lift her up. And we will make sure you hear all the stories there are to tell about your brave daddy."

She bent down and kissed his velvet cheek and felt her heart clench with pain and fear at the dark abyss that lay ahead. One which she must walk in to, in order to save her family.

From the maternity hospital, Grace walked slowly back into town via Havre des Pas, seeing the beauty of the ocean as if for the first time. The sound of the waves rushing in, usually so calming, sounded like a giant mournful sigh.

The smoke from the bombings which had drifted over from northern France was clearing and the sun was burning through. The sunrise was spectacular, like someone had rolled out a bolt of shimmering orange silk across the ocean.

Grace stood for a long time on the jetty to the bathing pool, playing out endings to her story, alternatives to what she knew needed to be done. But in truth, if she were to save her best friend and her nephew, there was only one course of action.

Her heart cruelly took her mind to Red and the pain of losing the only man she had ever loved threatened to demolish her. He would need an explanation. But how to explain that she was putting her best friend's future ahead of theirs, sacrificing her safety for Bea's? Would it be cleaner, easier, safer all round, if his love could be turned to hate?

One hour later, she was resolved as to what needed to be done. She walked through the maze of back streets to the doctor's door.

He answered quickly.

"Dr. Hanna. I'm so sorry to disturb you so early, but I need your help. Do you think you can get me into the prisoner-of-war library today? I urgently need to speak with Red—I mean, Lieutenant Daniel Patrick O'Sullivan."

He was shaking his head before she'd had a chance to finish.

"Not possible, my dear. Visits are strictly forbidden. We managed it before on account of you delivering books, but it's not a chance I'm prepared to take again."

The disappointment was like a blow to the solar plexus.

"But I can tell you that prisoners are permitted to take a short daily walk in a fenced-off park next to the compound at 11 a.m. There's a spot, I believe, by the barbed wire where one could, if one were determined enough, converse with a POW without being seen."

She breathed out. "Thank you, doctor."

Back in the library, Grace went about her morning duties like an automaton, counting down the minutes to 11 a.m. She laid out the morning newspapers, managed some shelving and dusted down the stacks.

The soothing daily rituals provided no comfort this morning. How could they when they might be her last and that, Grace realized with an enormous tearing wrench, was the worst of it. She was about to give up the two great loves of her life.

At 10:30 a.m. she tidied her desk, and checked for the hundredth time she had the key to the cupboard where the forbidden books were stored. Next she wrote a letter to Dr. McKinstry.

When she'd finished, she picked up *The Book Lovers' Anthology* and let the pages drift open. A passage was lightly underlined in pencil, written by a past bibliophile for a future book lover. It could have been written for her.

I would rather be a poor man in a garret with plenty of books than a king who did not love reading. Thomas Macaulay.

It was oddly comforting.

"Miss Piquet, I need to pop out." Her voice cracked and she stumbled on the words. "Run an errand. Not sure when I'll be back."

"Grace, my dear, are you all right?"

"I'm fine."

She looked at her loyal library assistant, an unassuming, dependable woman, the kind who almost never put herself first and wondered why it was, in war, it was so often women who bore the brunt. When this terrible occupation was over, would historians ever study the home front in the way they were bound to with the battlefront?

Would they ever appreciate the relentless suffering of working-class women like Queenie Gold, the solidarity shown by women like Louisa Gould, or the quietly heroic battle of public servants like Miss Piquet? She supposed not.

"You're a real treasure, Miss P, and I adore you. Shame on me for not saying it before now."

"Grace, are you sure you're all right?"

She swallowed. "Perfectly. Won't be long," she lied.

Grace turned quickly and forced herself to walk out of her library. She knew if she made the mistake of looking back at her beautiful book-lined palace she'd never find the mettle to carry out her plan.

As she passed under the granite BIBLIOTHÈQUE PUBLIQUE sign she felt her heart cleave in two.

She slipped like a ghost out of the Royal Square, quietly posting her letter to Dr. McKinstry into the mouth of a red postbox at the top of Broad Street.

All around her people went about their morning business with a weary sense of inevitability, picking up rationed gray bread from the bakers, queuing up outside the communal bakehouse with that evening's tea in a clay pot.

Nothing was quite as it seemed anymore in St. Helier. The bric-à-brac antiques shop a few doors up from the post office was now a front for the black market. The hairdressers up the road offered news from the BBC from a crystal set hidden behind a drier. Outside a paperboy called out fake news from the censored *Evening Post*.

Grace felt oddly detached watching the daily routines of town life play out, knowing the chaos that lay ahead.

At the park next to the prison, she found the place the doctor had mentioned by the barbed wire. Children's footsteps were stamped in the soil. This spot was doubtless a magnet for curious local kids.

At precisely 11 a.m. the prisoners filed blinking out into the park and her heart simultaneously soared and plunged when she spotted Red's lean figure lope out.

"Red," she hissed. His pal nudged him and she saw him mouth something in his ear, clearly lewd, as immediately the other POWs started wolf-whistling.

Red bounded over to the perimeter fence.

"Grace. God it's good to see you. Ignore those chumps. They're only jealous 'cause I have a beautiful fiancée and the best prisoner-of-war library. Boy, you oughta see how popular it is, Grace. Why only yesterday…" He tailed off. "Grace, what is it?"

In a trance she reached her hand out to the wire.

"Ouch, careful, Grace. It's sharp, that wire." She didn't even feel the pain.

"Grace, you're bleeding, what's wrong?"

"I'm sorry, Red. I thought I could do this, but actually I can't."

"What? Why?" She never heard him sound this panicked before. "Wait, if it's location I'll move to Jersey. I don't care where I live as long as it's with you."

She shook her head, breathed out as the pain began to stab at her finger. Good. She deserved it, for it was nothing compared to the pain she was about to unleash.

"No, it's not that. It's us. I... I've been thinking and it's all too complicated. Better we end it now before any real harm is done."

"Before any real harm is done?" he repeated in astonishment. "Baby, it's a little late for that. I'm in love with you."

She closed her eyes so she didn't have to see his expression. "We're just not compatible. I'm..." She readied herself to stick the knife in. "I'm not even sure I really love you."

"Please, Grace, don't do this," he begged. "Don't break my heart."

She opened her eyes. The agony on his face was more than she could bear and she reminded herself why it had to be this way. It was easier to get over someone you could hate. Better he think she simply didn't have the guts to see it through. That way he could rail in anger, tell his buddies he was led on by some flighty young woman.

He stumbled back from the barbed wire.

"No, no, no! I don't believe you. You *do* love me. I know you do. Why are you doing this, Grace? Why? What's changed?"

"I got carried away by the romance of it all and now you're here and I'm on this side of the fence," she said coldly. "It doesn't take a genius to see it was never going to work."

Grace didn't even recognize her own voice.

"Please don't go. I beg of you, don't leave like this...I don't understand."

In the distance a whistle sounded and tears filled his eyes.

Grace turned around, his pleas stabbing like tiny knives as she ran from the compound, her soul screaming. She had just broken a good man's heart as well as her own. Actually, she'd done more than that. She had crushed a hero's hope beneath her heel.

What a thing to do.

How quickly a life spent in pursuit of happiness, literature, culture, service to others could be dismantled. It took her less than an hour to leave the library, scoop out Red's heart and then arrive at Silvertide.

By now Grace was so numb, she scarcely felt anything as she knocked at the headquarters of the Secret Field Police.

She captured the memory of Bea cradling her baby—Grace's nephew—and held it in her mind as she requested a meeting with the Wolf.

An orderly pointed her to a wooden chair in the corridor reception area and she sat down and crossed her legs with her handbag perched on her lap, looking for all the world as if she was waiting for something as mundane as a dentist's appointment. She fought the urge to get up, wrench the door open and run.

Think of why you're here, Grace. Bea's happiness. The future of such a fresh and innocent life. All this was more important than her suffering. Family came first. It was such a universal truth.

That baby changed everything.

Her brother's son was just hours old. She smiled as she remembered the sweet snuffling noise Jimmy's son had made, the musky biscuity smell of him. Grace felt she could buckle under the sheer weight of love and the responsibility that came with that.

"Well, this is a surprise." The Wolf's odd, half-German, half-Canadian accent dragged up her spine like a cheese grater.

She sat up straight. "You were right."

He smiled coldly. "You better come into my office."

"I hear you enjoy deals, Herr Wölfle," she said surprised at how confident she sounded despite her thundering heart. "You have my friend in custody for intercepting mail and warning Louisa Gould."

He said nothing, just reached for a cigarette and lit it.

"We both know that you don't have a shred of evidence on Bea to get a clean conviction," she went on, knowing that if she didn't play this right, they would both end up in the dock.

"Go on," he said, blowing out the smoke. A blue haze hung between them. A ridiculous Alpine cuckoo clock ticked on the wall.

"What if I were to give you information that could lead to a triumphant outcome for you? I should imagine your Nazi superiors would be impressed with a confession that could wrap this whole case up nicely."

"You want to cut a deal?" he said at last, picking a shred of tobacco from his lip. "The librarian is about to turn informer? I confess, I'm almost disappointed in you."

"I'm not here to inform on my fellow islanders. Now are you interested in what I have to say?"

He leaned back, his leather chair creaking, enjoying the game.

"Yes, Miss La Mottée. If you give me something concrete, I will consider releasing your friend."

The words came out cleaner than she could ever have imagined.

"In that case, it was me who warned Louisa Gould. Not Bea. Me who gave Louisa the Russian–English dictionary." A slight tremor, but still the words came as she unhooked the key from a chain round her neck and slid it over the desk. "Me who's hiding *verboten* books and distributing them around the island." She smiled contemptuously. "I've been doing everything in my power to thwart your Nazi regime."

And it struck her then that it was all true.

The only secret she omitted? The one hiding in a basement not two minutes' walk from here. That she would take to the grave.

"So I guess that makes you right about me all along."

He leaned back and steepled his fingers. The silence dragged out as he processed her confession.

"Drink?" he asked suddenly, pulling a bottle of black-market Scotch from his drawer.

She shook her head.

"It's a pity really," he said as he poured. "I had you down as having more guile. I never bought the prim librarian act."

He drank deeply from the glass and sighed, his stale breath turning Grace's stomach. "I confess too. I'm almost disappointed this all turned out to be so easy." He laughed, lifting one finger from the glass and pointing it at her. "But note the word, *almost*."

The alcohol colored his cheeks to a high shine. "This is a very fine moment for the Third Reich."

In true bureaucratic fashion, he pulled a piece of paper from his desk and slid it over to Grace. He pressed a pen into her hand and patted her gently on the shoulder. Grace's soul shriveled. All the effort and dedication to her library, all the hours spent reading and wrapping islanders in the solace and sanctuary of books. Four years of surviving. All distilled into this one agonizing moment.

"If you will write down your confession in full and sign it your friend will go free."

17

Bea

BANNED BOOK

Not so much a banned book, as a book snub. When The
Hobbit *first appeared in print in 1937, its author, J. R. R.
Tolkien, received interest from a German publisher, keen
to put out a German edition, but first they asked for proof
of Tolkien's "Aryan descent." He allegedly wrote an elo-
quent reply chastising them for the "Impertinent and irrele-
vant inquiry," later calling Hitler "a ruddy little ignoramus."*

Attorney General's Chambers
Jersey
28 June 1944

Dear M. Le Connétable,

I have been informed by the Court of Field Command 515
that, by decree of that tribunal dated 22 June 1944, the
following convictions and sentences were imposed:

LA MOTTÉE, Grace, Acting Chief Librarian, single, born
22.5.1918, aged 26, of St. Ouen, Jersey. Sentenced to five

(5) years' imprisonment for aiding and abetting breach of the working peace, concealment and issuing of forbidden literature and inflammatory material likely to cause offense and embarrassment to the Third Reich. Sentence to be served in Germany.

GOLD, Beatrice, Postmistress, single, born 14.8.1918, aged 25, of St. Helier, Jersey. Sentenced to one (1) year imprisonment for illegally intercepting and opening mail bound for the occupying authorities. Sentence suspended. Tuberculosis certified.

TOPSY, Peter. Born 2.1.1929, aged 15, of St. Helier. Found not guilty of espionage, after medical report and intervention plea by our bailiff, Alexander Coutanche. Child to be released to the care of Jersey Home for Boys.

GOULD, Louisa, née Le Druillenec, of St. Ouen, born 7.10.1891, aged 53, sentenced to two (2) years' imprisonment for failing to surrender a wireless receiving apparatus, prohibited reception of wireless transmissions and aiding and abetting breach of the working peace and unauthorized removal. Sentence to be served in Germany.

Would you please have these sentences inscribed in the local police register?

Yours faithfully
Attorney General
C. J. Cuming, Esq.
Constable of St. Helier.

28 June 1944

Bea sat under the shade of an apple tree in Mary La Mottée's back garden while her four-week-old son slept in his coach pram next to her. The sun blazed high in a sky as blue as harebells. The air smelled of apples and cordite.

Nothing could come close to expressing the crawling horror she felt at Grace's sentence. Five years! *To be served in Germany.* Six days on from the end of the bombshell trial, she was still no closer to processing the sacrifice Grace had made for her. The German tribunal had made an example of her. They didn't need evidence to convict, they'd already proved their justice was a sham, but in Grace's case, they actually had it by the bucketload.

A whole secret drawer of *verboten* books in the library. Grace's signed confession that it was she who'd sourced and loaned the Russian–English dictionary from the library to Louisa Gould. She too who'd tipped off Louisa Gould about her denunciation. All of which of course, combined with Louisa's conviction and those of five more members of Louisa's circle, meant that they had all they needed to hand down sentences which would act as a deterrent to the whole island.

Grace was popular, that much was evident by the throngs of people who had gathered outside each day of the trial to show their support. For once, troops hadn't been ordered to send the crowds packing. It was precisely the show trial the authorities wanted.

As for Bea, the Germans had suffered no loss of face in giving her a suspended sentence. Especially as she was "sick."

Nobody had been more surprised than Bea when, three days after she had given birth, Dr. Lewis came and told her she and the baby were to stay in isolation in the Dispensary until after the trial and then be discharged into the care of Mary La Mottée. Dr. McKinstry's production of a swapped medical sample, which proved *without a shadow of doubt* that Bea had "tuberculosis," had guaranteed her passage to safety. But it had also given her so much more. It had given her the chance to stay with her baby.

Dr. McKinstry had confided that Grace had negotiated with the Wolf to secure Bea's release, but fearing that he would renege on it, she'd already asked the doctor to fake Bea's illness in a letter posted before she'd arrived at Silvertide. It was an insurance policy that Grace had been clever enough to take out, because 30 minutes after her confession and subsequent arrest, Bea had also been formally charged. Thank goodness for Grace's foresight. She had outwitted the Wolf and proved that when it came to Nazis, there was no negotiation.

The gate at the end of the apple orchard creaked and Bea looked up. She squinted as a tall figure opened the crooked wooden gate and walked toward her. Her heart leapt into her throat. *Jimmy?* She had barely been able to keep her thoughts from him recently. The swell of longing for him was even more potent since she had given birth. She yearned for him with fresh sadness, as if his death had been only yesterday. How proud he would have been of his son. Their child was the spitting image of him. Every time Bea looked into her son's eyes something inside her soul folded. The ache of love was like nothing she had ever experienced.

There was only one name for him of course, Mary had seen to that. Personally, Bea would have preferred something a little less predictable, but she owed Mary so much she hadn't put up a fight. And so Bea existed in a dream-like space, torn between bliss and heart-battering guilt that Grace wouldn't get to see her nephew, little Jimmy, grow up.

The figure drew closer.

"Arthur. Please tell me you didn't cycle all the way across the island with your leg."

"As if. I got the bus, you daft sod."

He peeked in the pram.

"He's a little treasure, Bea. Wish you'd told us."

She shrugged. "You know what society's like."

"Aye, that I do. I'm glad Grace's parents have seen sense and are supporting you. You deserve to be a mother after everything you've been through."

"Of sorts."

"What do you mean?"

She hesitated. Should she trust Arthur with this information, but in the finish she couldn't really see what harm it would do. She was sure half the island was gossiping about it anyway.

"Mary is passing her new grandson off as her son. Apparently she's telling people she thought it was," she inverted her fingers into commas, "'the change,' but it turned out to be a surprise baby. Little Jimmy is a blessing from God after her son was killed."

Arthur's eyebrow lifted.

"She's told the story that many times I think she actually believes it."

"I suppose such situations are commonplace," he replied. "And you, Bea, don't you mind?"

She shook her head.

"Honestly, if it gives me a chance to be near him then no. Mary has said I can live here as long as I like, and as he grows up he'll be told that I am his big brother's widow." Her voice dripped sarcasm. "Saves the scandal—as if such things matter at times like these. Half you lot at the post office know the truth, but she's banking on your silence and the fact that in time the gossip will fade and people will just see him as her child."

"But that will be hard on you, no? He'll grow up seeing you as the maiden aunt."

"It's a sacrifice worth making and in truth, I have no other choice, not if I want to see my son grow up."

She picked up a bruised apple and rolled it between her palms.

"Besides, my sacrifice pales in comparison next to Grace's."

In Arthur's gentle presence she felt the dam inside her break. Hot tears tracked through the dust on her face. "The awful thing is, growing up, I was always getting Grace into trouble."

"But you can't think that Grace would not have the courage of her convictions. She is the most moral woman I know. She wouldn't have reached her decision lightly."

"Perhaps, but I'll always blame myself. It was me who talked, *no, begged,* her into delivering that warning to Louisa Gould."

Her tears fell faster and harder and she leaned into Arthur.

"I miss her so much."

A tremendous, earth-shattering boom seemed to lift the hairs on the back of her neck. They stared over at the cloud of black smoke muddying the horizon over the French coast.

"There goes another French town," Bea winced. "The Allies are making good progress it seems."

"And that's our hope, Bea," Arthur said. "It's been twenty-two days now since the invasion of France. We've been counting them off on the walls of the post office."

"You think they're coming for us?"

"Unlikely. They're pressing eastwards, with Berlin fixed firmly in their sights. Besides, Hitler won't give up these islands without a fight. He's invested too much in their fortification. He'll insist the garrison fight to the bitter end."

"So why is this a cause for hope?"

"Because the more cities and towns the Allies re-occupy, the less chance Grace has of being deported. With any luck, the prison they've earmarked for her, Louisa and all the others will soon be dust."

"So, are you saying Grace's entire life rests on the battle raging over there?"

"Yes. We have to hope the Allies bomb the hell out of those prisons and work camps, before it's too late. Please God the link to France is soon severed."

They lapsed into silence, both of them staring over at the mushrooming cloud of darkness seeping over the blue. The most tremendous battle was raging 17 miles from them, one which their entire fate rested on, and yet here they were sitting in a sunny apple orchard with a sleeping baby. The dichotomy of life in wartime. Bea closed her eyes and offered up a silent prayer. She had never much been one for church—that belief had been shattered when she'd watched Jimmy die in front of her—but tomorrow, she vowed she would go and pray like never before that the *link*, as Arthur described it, was blown to oblivion.

"Oh, Bea, I'm sorry," Arthur said suddenly. "I am that hungry my brain seems to have melted. I have a message for you. Your sister Nancy's boyfriend gave it to me to pass to you."

"That—" Bea went to spit out the word "Jerrybag," but somehow couldn't summon the anger.

"What does she want?"

"Read it and find out."

Bea missed her mum dreadfully. Queenie Gold had come to Mary's to meet her grandson only once, but the effort had clearly been a tremendous strain and by all accounts she barely left the house these days. Guilt sliced savagely as Bea realized the stress of her arrest would have contributed to that confinement. She opened the note, written on thin tomato-packing paper.

Please find a way to come home as soon as possible. Do not delay. Yours, Nancy

Mary was of course all too happy to take over the care of Jimmy Junior and an hour later, Bea had packed a bag while Arthur waited outside to escort her on the bus back to town.

"Don't try to get back tonight. You can't afford to miss curfew and get into any more trouble," Mary fussed, plucking Jimmy from Bea's arms. "This little one and me will have a lovely cuddle. Get to know each other a little better."

An ugly spike of jealously lanced Bea's heart. *He's my baby, not yours.*

She fought the temptation to take him back and smother him in territorial kisses. The pain in her chest was physical as she watched Mary cooing over her little boy. What kind of bargain had she struck? The chance to watch Jimmy grow up was going to come at a terrible cost if it was Mary he ran to, Mary he called "Mama," Mary who would be the center of his world, while she was relegated to the role of spinster auntie.

A voice hissed in her head. "Take him. He's your child. Run. Before it's too late." But where on earth would she run to? A chain of events had been set in motion now, and with Grace having made the ultimate sacrifice, how could she reject her mother's offer of a home and respectability?

Her arms ached at their sudden lightness.

"I've expressed some milk. It's in a bottle in the kitchen," Bea said, stroking Jimmy's soft hair. "And he gets terribly gripey if he's not winded properly after a feed."

"Stop fretting. I have raised babies, you know. Go on, shoo. Your mother needs you."

The bus ride into town was even more arduous than usual, with many usual routes now closed off by the Germans. Bea hadn't realized, cocooned as she had been in the countryside, the diabolic fate of islanders now that their food supplies from France had been cut off due to the bombing of French ports. Every face she saw out of the bus window was gaunt with starvation. Women trudged along the streets like they barely had the strength to lift their toes.

When the bus finally lurched into St. Helier, Bea could see the town was absolutely crawling with armed Germans on high alert in steel coal-scuttle helmets. Guards had been doubled outside their billets and Red Cross flags fluttered from the hospital.

Bea said goodbye to Arthur and wandered through the streets feeling like a stranger in her own town, her empty arms aching, missing the weight of him, the sweet, milky smell of her boy.

The fish market had been closed down and a communal feeding station set up in its place. All the cinemas and the theaters were shut. Windows and doorframes all over town were cracked and shaken loose.

But it wasn't until she walked through the Royal Square that the changes finally sank in.

Library closed until further notice she read, rooted to the spot. Guilt punched her heart and it took her a moment to remember how to breathe.

Her usual route home past the French Harbour was now sealed off and heavily guarded. Beyond the barbed wire round the docks, Bea made out a morass of slaves and forced laborers being kicked and whipped onto waiting ships—the Germans trying to get rid of more of their vile war crimes before the Allies arrived.

Still, she cheered herself with the prospect of a hug from her mum. Queenie Gold's hugs were legendary and what a treat it would be to curl up in her mother's warm and cozy kitchen.

But when she pushed open the door the house was cold and silent.

"Cooey, Mum, it's me. I'm home." She reached into her string bag and pulled out a loaf wrapped in a cabbage leaf and a paper bag with three precious eggs. "Mary's sent supplies."

She placed the food on the kitchen table and looked up as Nancy came into the room, her face drawn. "She's in bed. Dr. Lewis is with her. Come up."

Bea followed her up the stairs, a dreadful sinking feeling pressing down with every step she climbed.

"Mum, I'm home, I'm sorry I didn't bring Jimmy," she whispered as she walked into the bedroom. "Mum?"

Her mum was asleep, the doctor sitting by the side of her bed, baggy-eyed with exhaustion. The curtains were drawn and a strange antiseptic smell hung over the darkened room, stirring the silt of unease inside her.

"Why she's asleep at this time?"

The doctor looked at her with compassion.

"Bea, you've been away from home for over four weeks now. In that time, your mother's health has deteriorated."

Nancy stood beside her. "Bea, she's not asleep, she's unconscious."

Bea wanted to shake her silly younger sister.

"Impossible. I saw her just after I had Jimmy. She seemed all right…" Her voice trailed off. Who was she kidding? She had looked awful.

"It's her diabetes, Beatrice," the doctor said gravely. "With no insulin, I'm afraid she is dying."

The truth was eviscerating. What planet had she been living on? She had been so absorbed in her own troubles that she had failed to register the severity of her mother's illness. Bea gripped the bedframe.

"Then we must get her some now. What are we standing around here for?"

The doctor and Nancy looked at her with pity, their faces resigned.

"This is ridiculous. Do something! NOW!"

"Bea," Nancy said softly. "There is no insulin anywhere to be had on this whole island."

"It's true, I'm afraid," said the doctor. "Yesterday I received word that a shipment had got though from France. I rushed down to the docks myself to sign for it so that I might administer it immediately, but when I opened the crate, it was empty."

He shook his head in exhaustion and agony. "It'd been raided in France. Insulin reaches a high price on the black market. I am a doctor who can no longer treat my patients."

"But surely there'll more supplies sent soon?" Bea protested. "The Red Cross perhaps?"

"We don't know when we'll next get medicine. It's not just your mother. There are people all over this island dying from preventable disease and malnutrition. It's not just medicine we are now cut off from, but food." He stood up and reached for his doctor's bag. "We are under siege conditions now. The invasion that promised us our freedom is now the very thing that could kill us."

"All we can do is make Mum as comfortable as possible," said Nancy. "That's why I sent word."

The doctor reached the door. "I shall leave you in peace while I check on another patient." He hesitated. "I urge you to say what needs to be said." And then he was gone.

"NO! Please, don't go," Bea pleaded, her voice growing louder as he walked down the stairs, his footsteps heavy. "Don't go! Do something."

At her cries, her mother's eyes flickered open.

It seemed to take a while for her gaze to focus and register Bea's arrival and when she did her hand crept along the bedsheet.

"Love, you're home." Her face was deflated—no, ravaged— and Bea's rage gave way to tears.

"Mum, I'm sorry. I'm so, so sorry."

She looked down in dismay as she realized her breasts were leaking milk, staining the fabric of her thin cotton dress.

"Come closer," Queenie whispered. "I need to see your face."

Bea kicked off her shoes, got onto the bed and cradled her mother's body in her arms.

"You've lost so much weight."

Her mother laughed, a sound as dry as the rustle of autumn leaves and her whole body seemed to shudder from the effort.

"I needed to shift some of the timber. Still I might have gone too far. These old legs are so bandy I couldn't catch a pig in a passage."

"Mum, you don't have to do this—put on the Queenie Show for my benefit."

She ran her hand shakily across Bea's cheek. "No show. I have two things to ask of you."

"Anything, Mum."

"First, kiss my grandson, would you?"

At the thought that her mother would never hold or know Jimmy, tears began to stream down her cheeks.

"All that little mite needs is love," Queenie whispered. "Love him fiercely. Love him enough for me too."

"I will, Mum. I can promise you that."

"Good. Now one more." She gestured to Nancy, who came and sat on the other side of the bed and took her hand.

"What is it, Mum?" Nancy asked.

"You both must promise me to set aside your differences. Make your peace."

Nancy looked over at Bea and she glanced away, studying the faded print of the yellow buttercup flowers on her mother's coverlet.

"Cherish and hold each other tight. You only get one family."

Bea felt her mother's fingers squeezing hers, imploring her.

"No more rows."

A silence stretched round the room and Bea looked over at her younger sister.

"I'm sorry, Bea," Nancy said. "I won't apologize for who I choose to love, but I should have been more sensitive to you after Jimmy died."

Bea nodded and felt a hot, scorching sensation prickle through her breasts, a visceral reminder that her body, which had just welcomed a new life into the world, was now preparing to say goodbye to another.

"I'm sorry too," she choked, "for all the things I said and all the stupid things I did. I wasn't thinking straight after Jimmy died."

Nancy smiled in relief and in that moment Bea suddenly saw with dizzying clarity how she had demonized her little sister, wrongly channeled the vast weight of her grief into blaming her.

She looked down at her mother, ready to smile and reassure her that their peace had been made but her face was still, her eyes oddly vacant.

"Mum?" She bent down and kissed her cold forehead. "Can you hear me, Mum?"

Nancy shook her head. "She's gone."

Gently, reverently, Bea closed her mother's eyes and then kissed her on the cheek one last time. She knew that at any moment the pain and grief would come calling, but for now, it was something to be cocooned in numb disbelief.

"I love you all the money in the world and two bob," she managed. "You go and rest with the angels now, Mum." She reached across her mother's body and threaded her trembling fingers through Nancy's. "I promise, we'll do you proud."

In the distance, heavy bombing rumbled and Bea felt the bedframe tremor. The war was still raging, but Queenie Gold's battle was over.

18

Grace
29 June 1944

BANNED BOOK

The Complete Fairy Tales of the Brothers Grimm *by Jacob and Wilhelm Grimm*. Rapunzel, Rumpelstiltskin, Hansel and Gretel—*these were just a few tales to come out of* The Complete Fairy Tales of the Brothers Grimm *in 1812. The Allies banned the tales in Germany after the fall of the Nazis, who glorified* Little Red Riding Hood *into a symbol of the German people saved from the Jewish wolf.*

In prison, Grace felt close to cracking. She had been in isolation in a cell now for thirty days wrenched out blinking into the light, only to face that sham of a trial. Now that "justice" had been handed down, seven days on from her sentence, she was none the wiser as to when she would be deported to Germany. No one told her anything. No one spoke to her, apart from her prison guard.

She missed her family desperately, but being separated from the umbilical cord of the library and having no books to fall back on was torture. In any moments of challenge in her life, reading had been her balm, helping her search for the light and blot out the darkness. Now her hands felt twitchy and queer, her mind full of fractured thoughts that wouldn't quite connect. Red. Did he hate her for being so careless with his heart? Had news of the trial reached him in his prison?

How she prayed that it hadn't. Her only wish for that beautiful man was the happiness that came with freedom. She knew it might sound perverse to some, the notion of cutting herself off from love in her darkest hour, but this was a path she must walk alone. If Red had known the truth, he would have talked her out of the sacrifice and then Bea might be in this cell now and not her.

Surely in this case, love wouldn't set him free, but shackle him tighter? This way, he could flee the island without looking back in regret. For she had no regrets. She knew that the Wolf would go back on his word and still arrest Bea. How could a Nazi have scruples? But at least her back-up plan had worked, and besides, if she hadn't taken the full blame and pleaded guilty without reservation, who knows whether the TB certificate would have been enough to stop the Germans coming for Bea. It was a comfort to know that Bea was free, but questions burned inside her blood. Would she ever again see the little baby boy who had captured her heart so quickly? And what of Peter? Where was he?

Grace stared around her cell and tried to memorize the details, keep her brain working. The space was small, 6 × 8 foot, with a barred window she could just peek out from to the street below. The thick stone walls were wet and cold.

Her bed was a straw-filled palliasse. Last night she had woken with a rat on her head.

The nights were the worst, when her cries bled into the darkness. As she lay awake listening to the thundering of the guns across the channel, she thought of all the bodies which had lain on this bed before her.

Was it possible for misery and despair to press down into the fabric of the bed? A sort of hopelessness bled from the walls and into the very essence of the air.

Claustrophobia gathered and built inside her chest as she paced her cell. She was stuck in a story over which she had no control, even less understanding and absolutely no knowledge of how it would end. Panic prickled all over her, and a horrible needle of self-doubt slid into her veins.

What if she died in Germany?

Her heart was racing so fast. *Stop this, Grace. Calm yourself. How will you survive five years imprisoned if you can't manage one month in St. Helier jail?*

She forced herself to travel in her mind's eye to the place where she felt calmest.

Grace murmured the words out loud. To remind herself she did still have a voice: "You're walking up the stairs to the library, climbing the wooden ladder to the top of the stacks. Shelving. Cataloging. Issuing. The Hidden Books. Think of them, Grace."

A Farewell to Arms by Ernest Hemingway. *Brave New World* by Aldous Huxley. *War of the Worlds* by H. G. Wells. She pictured the Wolf and his men climbing the stairs to the Reading Room and unlocking the secret cupboard, reaching their greedy hands into the dark sanctuary. Those books were probably already ash. A cold hard fear bit into her bones as she remembered the burning books at the Jersey Masonic Library, their flames leaping into the blue sky.

What was the last bundle of donated books before her arrest? Think. Think.

Agatha Christie, *The Mysterious Affair at Styles*, Margery Allingham, *Police at the Funeral* and *In Defence of Sensuality* by J. C. Powys.

The reminder of these books, donated with love, overcame the panic and she felt the attack subside. Exhausted, she lay down on her bed. At least no one could take away her memories of the library itself. Grace hoped it would be remembered forever by others too as a symbol of resistance.

Please God that would be her legacy, should the worst happen.

At first she thought she had imagined it. But no, it was definitely footsteps, growing louder and clunkier the closer they got to her cell.

It was a guard. Günter.

Over the weeks she had got to know him a little better. Günter had served in Stalingrad and been invalided out of active service and sent here to serve as a guard. His toes had frozen on the Eastern Front and had been crudely amputated. He walked now with wooden blocks pushed into the tips of his jackboots and Grace recognized his heavy gait.

"Hello, Günter," she said politely as he pulled open the door with a scraping sound.

"*Guten Morgen*, Miss Grace." He glanced behind him, then produced a cardboard box, which he placed gently on her bed.

"What's this?"

"As a political prisoner you are allowed a food parcel. Be careful eating it."

"Why?"

He pressed a finger to his lips.

"You see."

The door slammed shut and Grace stared mystified at the box.

She opened it. It was a plum pudding the size of a cricket ball. Immediately her mouth filled with saliva and embarrassed at her primal reaction she scooped it up and ate greedily. It was more carrot than fruit, but the taste of cinnamon and sugar-beet syrup was like nectar of the gods. Almost immediately her stomach protested. After four weeks of watery soup, it was too rich and in frustration she dropped it back in the box. It was then that she saw it. A note. She unrolled it and wiped the flecks of pudding from it.

My dearest Gracie,

There is no space here to tell you my feelings for the sacrifice you made so that I might be a mother, or the guilt I feel. I wish I had not dragged you into my messes. All my life you've been clearing up after me. I fear this might yet be my biggest one. And yet, when I look into my child's eyes, your nephew, I know that self-pity and recrimination are pointless. He needs me to be strong. We all need to be brave and count down the days until you return to our beautiful island.

Who knows how long we may be apart for, but I like to think we are connected by a golden thread. It doesn't matter how far you go, it cannot snap.

Remember in Rebecca *when Mrs. de Winter says that men and women emerge finer and stronger after suffering? This is our moment of trial, Grace, but justice will prevail. The Nazis will <u>not win</u>. They have already lost. Cherbourg has fallen. Next it will be Paris. Then Berlin. Hold hard to that thought.*

I won't breathe properly until the day you walk free. Until then I am at the end of that thread. Keep faith, my beautiful Gracie. I'll be seeing you.

With endless love and devotion,

Your old friend, Bea

PS. Your literary support group send love. Wait for the testing of the air-raid siren at noon then try and look to the street if you can.

Grace held the note and closed her eyes in relief. The swirling morass of darkness inside her receded. It was something bright and beautiful in a world which felt cloaked in evil. Hope was indeed a powerful thing. And that, she realized, was exactly what she had to coat herself in, like armor.

A gentle tap at the door and Günter appeared.

"Anything you would like disposed of, Miss Grace?" he asked quietly.

Grace took a leap of faith.

"Yes please, Günter, if you don't mind. I'm finished with this."

As he left he traced his finger over the grime on the back of the prison door. *"Ich hasse Krieg,"* he whispered, so quietly Grace strained to hear. "I hate war." He shut the prison door and only then did Grace see the initial.

V

At midday, she heard the wailing siren rise and fall over the rooftops of town. Mustering all her strength, Grace stood on her bed on her tiptoes and gripped the iron bars covering her cell windows. She could just about make out the far end of the street beyond the prison walls. With nothing to buy, the streets were empty, just a scrawny dog dozing in the sun.

A succession of Allied planes flew overhead, the stream of their shadows flickering over the bars. Grace watched transfixed, trying to imagine the faces of all those young pilots passing overhead, the Channel Islands scattered dots beneath them. Did they think of the fate of islanders as they flew over?

When they had faded from her field of vision, she looked back to the street and jumped.

There was Bea. She'd recognize that mass of dark curls anywhere. She was leaning against a lamppost reading a book and was that? Oh my goodness—yes it was. Grace's hand flew to her mouth.

"Peter! You're free!" Standing next to Bea, looking up at the prison walls, was little Peter Topsy.

She could have collapsed from the utter relief. *He was out.* The bailiff must have secured his release. It was a bolt of pure, undiluted joy. There was some hope among all this madness.

His lips were moving. She couldn't make out what he was saying but she recognized the green spine of the book. *Rebecca.*

As her eyes traveled along the street she realized there were members of her literary support group dotted everywhere, pretending to be apart so as not to breach the rule of five. Winnie and Molly reading from a magazine. Mr. Warder and Arthur from the post office poring over a pamphlet. Mrs. Moisan and Mrs. Noble reading together.

Pretending to wait for a bus nearby, studying the *Evening Post,* was Albert Bedane the physiotherapist and her library assistant Miss Piquet. They mightn't be able to meet officially any longer, but the Wartime Book Club was alive.

It was an enduring symbol and an image she would carry with her to Germany.

A German truck crawled slowly up the road and the group dispersed. Grace clutched the bars of her cell in silence, hot tears sliding down her cheeks. Bea and Peter were the last to leave and when they did, Bea blew a kiss up at the prison.

Grace returned the kiss, touched her heart and lay back down on her prison bed. They might be able to censor their newspaper, seize their wirelesses and shut their libraries, but they couldn't control islanders' spirit. The truth was irrepressible.

The light eventually bleached from the sky and Grace had just managed to doze off when the prison door opened.

"It's time, Miss Grace."

She sat up and swallowed, her head thumping, her mouth dry.

"What now? But it's getting dark."

He said nothing, just shrugged apologetically.

"Thank you, Günter."

He opened the door for her to pass and bowed his head. It was a gesture of kindness and respect from such an unexpected source that she felt quite moved.

Günter led Grace up darkened corridors then blinking into the light of a courtyard lit up by spotlights. After weeks in solitary confinement it was as if someone had wrenched up the dial on the wireless. Faces and voices, loud and blaring. The stench of stale sweat. Barking dogs. Prisoners everywhere, forced out of cells and being jostled out into the courtyard. At the far end of the yard stood a fleet of German trucks.

The smell of so many unwashed bodies crushed together was overpowering.

She stood shivering, trying to get her bearings as a stream of bodies bumped past her.

"*Bewegung!*" ordered a guard, shoving her between the shoulder blades with his rifle. "*Schneller.*"

She half-climbed, was half-pushed onto the back of the German truck. It was dark. Rows of prisoners faced each other on long benches. Two armed guards guarded the exit. The journey was beginning. Grace was trembling so much she had to lay her palms on her knees to stop them knocking.

Once all the trucks were full, the engines sputtered to life and the convoy of vehicles streamed past the prison gates.

The streets of St. Helier slid past. She closed her eyes. In the darkness she could hear her pulse hissing in her ears. It was happening. It was actually happening.

When they neared the docks she became aware of a commotion. Through the flapping canvas side of the truck she could see civilians remonstrating with the guards at the entrance to the docks. Angry indignant faces yelling in protest.

This was why they were being moved under cover of darkness, like human cargo.

"We're the last transport to be deported," whispered a man next to Grace. "They're worried about an Allied landing. They want to get shot of all the troublemakers."

The truck stopped. A voice tore through the night. "*God save the King. There'll always be an England.*"

Grace closed her eyes and tried to let the words comfort her, but her heart was beating fast.

German voices tore through the night. Searchlights combed the darkness. Then the truck pulled off abruptly, speeding through the gates to the docks, then stopped with a screech at the back of a queue of trucks. The canvas side of the truck flew up and on the other side of the barbed wire, Grace spotted a familiar face, standing by the gates. Distraught. Alone.

"Bea," she cried.

"Grace," she screamed, her face lighting up in recognition. Bea started to run, dodging past the sentry guards, streaking toward the truck. Suddenly the air became electric.

Uniformed arms shot out to grab her but Bea gave a

ferocious roar and slipped by them, dodging and ducking until she was by the side of the truck.

"Bea!" Grace exclaimed. "Go back. You'll be shot!"

"No, no. Not yet." Tears streaked down her face, her hair was wild and windswept, her eyes swollen and red-raw. She looked undone, primal in her intensity.

"Mum died," she blurted.

"Oh, my love," Grace cried. "No!"

Bea gripped her hands, her fingers cold and trembling.

"You're all I have left now, Grace—you and baby Jimmy. You *must* come home. You *must* survive this."

Over Bea's shoulder she saw a flank of guards running toward them, mouths open wide, bellowing orders. Somewhere from the sentry box she saw a flash of metal, a gun was trained on her.

"Go quickly. Your boy needs you alive," she urged, but Bea's fingers pressed hers, gripping so tightly.

"Not until you promise me you'll do everything you can to stay alive. We need you, Jimmy and I. We love you."

Bea's chest heaved with emotion, her eyes beseeching her.

"You must come home." Bea kissed her hand. "I will never stop waiting for you."

"I'll come home," she vowed. "And, Bea—look after my library."

All at once, the truck was swarmed and Bea was wrenched free from her grasp.

The canvas flew back and Bea's face vanished, her cries swallowed by the sounds of sea water slapping against metal.

Maybe had she not seen Bea she might have held it together, but the sight of her old friend uncorked all her pain and fear and it crashed over her. Would Grace ever feel a caring, human touch again? A kiss? A smile? Did humanity exist where she was going? All the things that she had missed so desperately, that had almost seemed within touching distance again, were fading. A breezy walk on an unmined beach. A new cotton frock. Fluffy white bread slathered with salted butter. Curling up cozily in front of a fire with a new book... Her stomach clenched into a solid knot of fear as she imagined the gray bookless world that lay ahead. Camps. Correction. Concrete.

Dark electric thoughts bounced through her mind.

If I die I will never see the sun sink over the lighthouse, the ocean, my wonderful library of books. And it was really only then, when her own mortality was staring her in the face, that she realized she had so many dreams that her head was bursting with them.

To make love to Red. To travel and see all the great libraries of Europe. Maybe even write her own book one day. And all those classic novels she still had to read.

In all her life, Grace had never abandoned a book, believing that if someone had committed their energy to putting words to a page, as a reader she owed it to them to finish it. Now her own story would be abruptly finishing.

Bea's frantic dash through the docks had made the German troops guarding the prisoners twitchy.

Grace and the rest of the prisoners on her truck were shoved and knocked into the greasy guts of the ship waiting in the waters of the harbor. The last thing she saw was the dark silhouette of gunships and barges, scrolls of barbed wire dissecting the darkness.

As the ship's fetid interior consumed them it took a while for Grace to get her bearings and her eyes to grow accustomed to the darkness in the hold.

"Grace, thank goodness it's you."

A hunched-over figure huddled among many bodies had a familiar voice.

"Lou." She breathed in relief. "I thought I'd never see you again."

A long, low blast of noise vibrated through the hold. All at once, all the ships in the harbor sounded their bull horns. After so long in confinement, the noise was a cacophony in her head.

"Some German, high up in the navy, has been killed," said a voice in the darkness. "They're paying their respects."

How was his life so much more valuable than all of theirs, all these prisoners pressed down like rats in the darkness?

Another voice sounded, louder now.

"Nah. They're jibbed because of the breakout at the POW camp."

Grace felt like someone had dashed her face with ice-cold water.

"What breakout?" she called.

"Didn'cha hear?"

"I've been in solitary confinement."

"Some Yank managed to scale the barbed-wire fence using a load of hardback books piled up on top of one another. The one on top was by all accounts *The Call of the*

Wild. Last seen rowing out of Gorey Harbour on a small rowboat in the direction of France. Good luck to him!"

Grace slumped back against the metal wall. She could feel the relief in her bones. For there was no doubt in her mind it was Red. Who else could execute such an audacious escape? An escape she was pleased she'd had some small hand in. Please God let him survive and rejoin his unit. The agony of their departure was tempered by this news. She may have broken his heart but he was at least free, his spirit intact. She thought of him out there right now, somewhere in the dark ocean, slicing through the waves with France in his sights. *Oh, Red. You beautiful, brilliant, brave man.*

The love she felt was matched only by the sudden bolt of fear as the boat's engines rumbled noisily to life. The prisoners held their collective breath.

"Do you realize that four years ago today we were hanging out the white flags, wondering what our fates would be?" Lou murmured. "Little did we know that for you and me our journey is only just beginning."

They'd barely been going 20 minutes when an enormous flash of light lit up the hold.

A colossal boom seemed to lift the boat from the water and the walls buckled. The pressure inside the hold changed, causing a vacuum that left her ears shrieking.

Panic, dark and electric, filled the hold as an eerie creaking sound echoed and rippled down below.

"We've been hit—We're all going to drown—We're free."

Confusion reigned. Lou's fingers tightened round hers.

"If we'd taken a direct hit we wouldn't be talking now."

Once the screams had subsided the sound of throbbing engines filled the sky. Allied bombers by the sounds of it, heading to France.

"The irony if we get killed by our own," Lou murmured.

But then an extraordinary thing happened. The boat started up again and immediately changed course, turning back in the direction of Jersey.

"They've had second thoughts. The raid's forcing them to turn back," Lou cried.

Before long the high granite walls of the harbor loomed into sight. Grace just about saw the outline though the high portholes above. A fragment of hope swelled inside her. Perhaps the crossing had been deemed too risky. Joy kindled and flared. Maybe she could see out her prison time on the island after all.

"Grace, my love." Lou's voice was light with the hope of salvation. "They've brought us home."

But despite the noise and confusion on the quayside, the sound of running boots and agitated voices, nothing happened. No one came for them. The heavy steel door to the gangplank remained resolutely shut.

All night they stayed that way. No water or sanitation. No food. No information. Desperation growing by the hour. Louisa kept hold of her hand, despite falling into a restless sleep. As the first chink of light bruised the horizon, the engines started up. This time no one said a word. Their hope gave way to despair as the boat sailed out of the harbor once more.

A new day had been born and the sun rose, painting the sky a hundred different colors, from a milky orange to pearly pinks. Its staggering beauty seemed the cruelest farewell.

Grace watched as the island slid from view, the fort, the wide sweep of St. Aubin's Bay, trying to commit every last inch of it to memory. She reached out to Louisa and they held one another. Too scared, cold and hungry to cry, just trying to hold back the avalanche of fear.

Grace closed her eyes and the vibration of the boat's engines rocked her.

"Do you know what kept me going, Grace?" Louisa whispered. "That one day we would stand at the harbor and watch the Germans leave. I never dreamt that we would leave before them."

Grace stroked her hair and tried to find words to ease the older woman's suffering.

But in the absence of suitable words of her own, she fell back, as she had done so many times in her short life, on poetry, remembering the words that Ash had always said.

If a book is medicine, then a librarian is the medic, dispensing books like prescriptions to soothe a tattered soul.

"Out of the night that covers me,
Black as the pit from pole to pole,
I thank whatever gods may be,
For my unconquerable soul…"

She trailed off, unsure whether the words of William Ernest Henley's "Invictus" were the comfort Lou needed in this moment of abject fear.

"Please, continue," said a halting Russian voice from further up the boat and heads nodded in agreement. Grace drew in a deep breath.

"In the fell clutch of circumstance
I have not winced nor cried aloud.
Under the bludgeonings of chance,
My head is bloody, but unbowed."

She finished the verse and her fellow prisoners dipped their heads, some murmuring silent prayers, others moved to tears by the truth of those words. The boat and her escorts disappeared over the horizon.

19

Bea

Five months later. November 1944

BANNED BOOK

German Jew Alfred Kerr was a journalist and theater critic whose columns were anthologized in book form. When the Nazis came to power they burned his books and Kerr and his family were forced into exile in Britain. His daughter, Judith Kerr, grew up to be a children's author, best known for The Tiger Who Came to Tea *and the book based on her childhood experience of fleeing Nazi Germany,* When Hitler Stole Pink Rabbit.

"Your daddy could be a rogue at times," Bea whispered. "Did I tell you about the time he slipped a homemade bazooka under the sluice gates at the bathing pool? Brought up a dozen stunned fish and scorched my bathing suit."

She smiled and nestled her face against the top of baby Jimmy's peachy head. Feeling the soft, warm weight of him pressed in her arms as she fed him, she was about as content as it was possible to feel these days.

After D-Day 6 June 1944, the Allies had smashed through the German defenses, first Granville, then by

August 1944, most of Normandy and Brittany was under Allied control.

In the Channel Islands, things were about as desperate as it was possible to get. Electricity and gas supplies were virtually exhausted, as were bread and potatoes. "Food" was whatever islanders could scavenge or scratch from the ground and hedgerows. The Germans were seen shooting seagulls to eat. Islanders' cats and dogs vanished from the streets.

There were *just* about enough rations to support life. Only yesterday Bea had taken a look at herself in the mirror and got a start. Every rib, every vertebra, every single bone in her body was shining through her skin. Only her breasts, slightly engorged and covered in blue veins, reminded her that her body had a purpose. Every spare scrap of food helped ensure that she could continue breastfeeding. If it hadn't been for her precious boy, she doubted whether she would even still be alive.

As the gold and scarlet leaves rustled in with autumn's sweet embrace, it was in stark contrast to the harrowing pain she felt at the loss of Grace and her mum.

They had buried Queenie Gold shortly after Grace had been deported and half of St. Helier had come out in mourning. Bea hadn't realized how popular her mum had been. She hadn't been island-born, but with her salt-of-the-earth Cockney mentality, she had embedded herself in islanders' hearts. Queenie was old-school, always looking out for and caring for people who needed her time, offering tea, roll-up cigarettes and blunt advice.

As her mother's body had been lowered into the hole, Bea had turned away and felt like the crushing pain might just bury her along with her. She had tried to picture her in life, not death, yakking away on her allotment, 5-foot nothing of Cockney sass, shrewd blue eyes sparkling under her turban. How could such an enormous life force be reduced to dust?

Tears began to slide down Bea's cheeks, dampening baby Jimmy's soft hair. This felt different from her grief for Jimmy. This was her mother. Her solid, irreverent rock of a mum. Wasn't she always just a permanent fixture? Getting up at 4 a.m. to make sure there was running water for Bea and Nancy to wash, hatching schemes, bustling about St. Helier in her pinny, smelling faintly of cooking oil, lavender and Woodbines.

The thought that she would never again rest her face against that apron, wrapped up in one her mum's lung-busting hugs was unbearable. And she couldn't even think of Grace's pale face and frightened eyes staring out from the back of that army truck. How had it come to this? How had she lost three of the most important people in her life?

"I still have you, my darling boy," she whispered. "I promise I'll never let any harm come to you."

"Beatrice." The sudden voice at the door made her start and Jimmy's little fingers splayed in shock.

"Have you finished feeding?" Mary probed.

"Yes," she said, feeling instantly guilty. "I was just about to wind him."

"No need. I can do that," she said briskly, plucking Jimmy from her arms.

"But I'd like to," Bea protested.

Mary's face softened.

"Beatrice dear, you are grieving, as are we all, but I think you are becoming too dependent on Jimmy."

"He's my son. He's dependent on me," she spluttered. "He needs me."

"What he needs, dear, is a respectable home. A good start in life. Too many people have seen you walking round with him. Tongues will wag. We must remember our arrangement."

A slight light of desperation gleamed in Mary's eyes.

"I am his mother. Remember?"

She turned to leave but stopped as if on an afterthought.

"Why don't you express some milk and then go and stay at your sister's for a night? I think a break from Jimmy might help you to have some...*perspective*."

Bea felt like she'd been punched in the guts.

She looked at her son, her boy, nestled in Mary's arms, his apple-red cheeks glowing under his white wool bonnet. She took in the gentle rise and fall of his tummy and felt the familiar fold of longing in her gut. It wasn't enough to love from afar. All that mattered was being a mother to her child.

But how was it possible? Society, much less one as small and conservative as St. Ouen's, would never allow her as an unmarried mother to fulfill that role. Sure, she could have pretended that Jimmy had made an honest woman of her before he died, but in a community so small that even a new coat warranted a village inspection, she doubted she'd have got away with it. But in her desperation she'd even considered that, until she remembered the neighbor who'd been there at their engagement drinks—the night he'd been killed!

Her head ached with the impossibility of it all.

"Very well," she said. "I'll go to St. Helier, but only so I can go and help in Grace's library. I'll be back, Mary."

Hunger, pain and pent-up frustration shimmered between the two women. The door of the old farmhouse slammed shut.

In St. Helier, Beatrice walked down the narrow, winding streets with her hat pulled over her head. Not that anyone would recognize her. Most people walked stooped against the cutting November wind, on matchstick legs, nursing colds, flu and other ailments caused by a lack of nutrition. St. Helier was a changed place. Cold. Sickened. Haunted. And like its inhabitants, at its lowest ebb. Food was all anyone could talk about. *When would Churchill send some? Were they to be starved along with the Germans? Had they been entirely forgotten by England?*

She pulled her winter coat tightly around her fragile frame. She'd made it from a length of old blackout material, double-breasted with some velvet-covered buttons she'd taken off her mum's old cushions, but it did little to keep out the bitter wind.

Bea was just about to turn into the Royal Square when she spotted the Wolf striding along with a woman on his arm. He stopped to remonstrate with Joseph the stonemason, kicking at the pile of wet sand.

"When will these infernal paving slabs ever be finished?" he demanded.

Joseph looked up with ill-disguised hate in his eyes. "Soon. Soon."

"See that they are."

The German soldiers on the island no longer looked so smart. Most, resigned to the direction the war had taken, shuffled about in rotting uniforms, as hungry as the rest of the islanders. Bea had recently heard of a German soldier sentenced to death for stealing food. Another bleak brush-stroke of death in a picture of needless despair.

Poor sod. They were, to all intents and purposes, now prisoners themselves, trapped behind their own fortifications. Clearly this had also dawned on the Wolf. He was now wearing a military uniform, instead of his usual civilian attire, and the cynical side of Bea would lay bets that he'd done it in the hope that, upon liberation, the Allies would take him for an ordinary soldier, not the ruthless Nazi operative islanders all knew him to be.

He began walking in Bea's direction. Quickly, she doubled back on herself, turned into a side street and flattened herself against the wall.

He walked straight past, too busy whispering in his female companion's ear to notice her, but something peculiar was happening to Bea; a terrible sense of danger spiked the air. She was back in his interrogation room at Silvertide, the smell of blood and bleach washing over her. The street began to sway and tilt. A prickle of terror ran the length of her spine.

The ground rushed up to meet her and she curled into a ball, shuddering. She pressed her hands against her mouth to smother her sobs. "Please forgive me, Grace, I'm so sorry." She felt as though she was made of stone: unable to breathe, unable to move her body. In the middle of Royal Square, she was paralyzed by fear and grief, run down by this suffocating occupation.

"Bea…Bea…" Slender arms scooped around her and pulled her up. "It's all right. I've got you. You're safe."

Someone held Bea's hands and spoke calmly to her, until finally the edges of the dark tunnel she'd found herself in receded.

"Miss Piquet…I…I don't know what happened to me."

A warmth snaked round her clogged feet. She looked down. To her mortification she had wet herself.

"Oh God."

The older woman shook her head. "It's shell shock. Many left over from the first war experienced this."

"But I'm not a soldier."

"But you've experienced the same trauma. The bombs which killed your father, the bullet which took your fiancé…"

"The arrest which took my best friend," Bea continued miserably.

"Come on, dear. I'll walk you to the library and you can freshen up there. Take my hand, your legs'll feel wobbly. Tell you what, why don't you come and help me in the library for a bit?" Miss Piquet suggested.

"I…I don't know if I can."

Grace's last words came back to her. *Look after my library.*

"Actually…I will. If that's all right?"

"Of course."

Miss Piquet gestured to the sign over the door. BIBLIO-THÈQUE PUBLIQUE. Carved in granite, permanent, immovable, ancient.

"Never give up hope, Bea. There is good worth fighting for in this world. The library reminds us of that."

After she'd cleaned herself up, Bea put in a solid afternoon's work helping Miss Piquet in the library. Since Grace's deportation the authorities had allowed the library to reopen, but only with a guard stationed at the desk to monitor the issuing of books. Bloody ridiculous, that this far-flung outpost of the Third Reich would consider it necessary to put librarians under armed guard.

Miss P mainly had Bea shelving the returned books. It was repetitive work but Bea found it oddly soothing, a good respite from the lonely churn of her thoughts.

She was touched by the flow of library patrons, including all the members of their now disbanded book club.

The Wartime Book Club may have been banned, but the authorities couldn't prevent them from coming into the library and when word spread Bea was in, all the regulars stopped by. Winnie and Gladys from the post office for their weekly Mills & Boon fix and a cuddle that had Bea pushing back the tears.

Molly the florist took *Gone with the Wind* for the fifth time and left news of Allied victories across France.

Mr. Warder from the post office borrowed another Georgette Heyer, protesting (too hard) that it was under his wife's orders. But it was the arrival of Arthur, the postman, who toppled her.

"The post office ain't the same without you, girlie," he said gruffly. "Soon as this bloody war's over, we're petitioning Mr. Mourant to reinstate you."

"Thanks, Arthur, but I don't think I made that good a job of it."

"Don't talk tripe. You made a damn good fist of it."

He looked about the library and lowered his voice. "You saved lives, you can be sure of that." He punched her playfully on the arm. "You belong back with us."

He stomped off with an Agatha Christie and, Bea could have sworn, wet eyes.

By the end of the day, Bea felt humbled as she observed the rhythm of library life play out and realized how hard Miss Piquet worked. She remembered something she had glibly said to Grace long ago. *But what about helping human beings? They're what count, surely, not dusty old books?*

Being here, in Grace's domain, made her realize that actually *dusty old books* did count—they were helping human beings to escape as much as a rowing boat and a compass. Grace had always been so sure of her place, her sense of belonging to the library was what had made her so impressive.

As Bea walked back to her old home in Havre des Pas, she ruminated that half the problem was she didn't know where she belonged anymore.

She went to push open the small wooden gate, but it was missing.

"Bea, I didn't know you were coming home." Her sister Nancy's face lit up as she opened the door. "I've only got a plate of turnips and parsnips but it can stretch to two."

Since their mother's death, Bea had found an unlikely ally in her sister. For so long they had been at war over her sister's choice of boyfriend and now in the finish, it scarcely seemed important. They were all starving and desperate for the war to end.

"Come on in," she said, gesturing to the cold dark room, lit by a Brasso tin she had converted into a small light with a shoelace threaded through the cap for a wick. Electricity was being shut down earlier and earlier. The long bleak winter evenings loomed.

"Where's the front gate gone by the way?" Bea asked.

Nancy looked bashful as she pointed to the wooden log basket by the grate.

"Don't worry, I reckon Mum'd be impressed that you managed to get it off those rusting hinges."

"Necessity is the mother of invention."

"That's what Mum always said."

"True. Do you know I got so desperate I tried to buy a pound of tea on the black market last week. They were asking *eight pounds*, Bea! I only earn three at Boots."

"I thought you were also working at the Soldatenheime?"

"I was, but I thought about it and I decided you were right. Working for the Germans is no good."

"I'm proud of you, Nancy."

"Thanks. I wish I'd always had your scruples."

"And look where that's got me," Bea sighed.

"At least you did something! You can hold your head up high. I have a feeling things are going to get uncomfortable for me when this is all over."

"Why do you say that?"

Wordlessly, Nancy slid a letter across the tabletop.

Watch your back come liberation. When the Boche lose this war, you'll be strung up from a lamppost. The Jersey Underground Barbers.

"Nancy, this is awful. When did this arrive?"

"Someone pushed it through the door this morning while I was at work." She shrugged. "I get one most weeks. I ignore it." Her bitten-down fingernails told another story.

"The irony is, Heinz is gone. I'm not technically a Jerrybag anymore, but it seems a badge I'll probably have to wear for the rest of my life."

She scrubbed her face, her eyes haunted in the dim light.

"Oh, Nancy, where's he gone?" Bea asked.

"I've no idea. He's been shipped out. I'll probably never see him again." A tear broke free and slid down her cheek. The beautiful, blonde, carefree girl of only last year had lost her sheen. Bea burned with shame as she realized how savagely she had judged her sister and how right their mother had been.

"I really loved him, Bea," she continued. "He treated me like an equal, was actually interested in what I had to say. Now I'll probably be left with an islander who'll have me darning his socks and making his tea."

Bea felt ashamed that until recently she had been the one sitting in judgment. Hatred toward anyone suspected of collaboration had intensified in tandem with their hunger pangs.

"I'm sorry, Nancy."

"Don't be sorry. If losing Mum and Heinz has taught me anything it's the fragility of life. Take your chance at happiness. Be a mum, a proper mum to little Jimmy. You'll only get one chance."

"But how? I'd forever be tainted. I'd never survive the scandal." She pushed down her irritation at her sister's naivety, reminding herself she was young and heartbroken.

"Who says you have to?"

"What are you talking about?"

"We received a Red Cross message from Aunty Flo in Whitechapel earlier. The usual stuff—heavily coded hints about the Allies winning the war, condolences over Mum. But she signed off…" She picked up the telegram and read. "Always a home for you girls here in London."

Nancy's face radiated hope.

"Don't you see, Bea? When our liberation comes, you should take Jimmy and move to London. It's a huge and anonymous city. Who'll stop to question a war widow with a little 'un?"

Bea looked down and twisted Jimmy's battered tin ring round her finger.

"It's your chance to start over, Bea—you know, reinvent yourself."

Arthur's words drifted back to meet her. *Do you really want to be a maiden aunt?*

In that dark little kitchen, starving, exhausted and broken, a tiny tendril of hope unfurled inside her. Was it truly possible to reinvent herself?

Nancy stood up slowly. "Now let's eat."

20

Grace

BANNED BOOK

Albert Einstein's The Theory of Relativity *was banned by the Nazis, who enlisted 100 authors and scientists to denounce him. He is alleged to have replied that to defeat relativity, one did not need 100 scientists, just one fact.*

"You want a book? You think this is a library?"

The snub-nosed guard laughed as if he'd said the funniest joke, then slapped her face hard. Grace fell to the ground, felt a blow to her lower back. That one action opened the flood gates. Kicks, fists, feet rained down on her. She curled protectively into a ball. Then came a sharp kick to her spine which sent her back into spasm, just as a steel-capped boot made contact with her tummy. The pain was like nothing she'd ever experienced. Grace felt something break inside her, felt the warmth of blood fill her mouth, then mercifully the walls closed in.

Later when she regained consciousness in her prison cell, Louisa was holding her, her rage simmering.

"Guards, we need water," she cried. No one came. No one ever did, apart from to shove some cup of greasy water with bits of turnip floating in it through the hatch.

From the moment their boat had docked at St. Malo, it had been a filthy, frightening, violent blur. They had been herded onto busses and cattle trains and held in anonymous gray transit cells before being moved again. No one told them anything. Justice was a remote and shadowy concept and in all the time since they had been deported, Grace had realized, as political prisoners, they were numbers, not names. They were lost to the world.

"Why did they do this to you?" Louisa wept, holding Grace as tight as she dared. "I've nothing to clean you up with."

The wounds on her face and body would heal in time, but Grace had the terrible feeling that the kick to her abdomen had done something terrible, something irreversible.

"You must stop speaking back to them," Louisa implored. "Say nothing."

Grace knew she was right, but she also knew she couldn't stay silent, not when she was witnessing so many atrocities. It had come as a genuine shock to see their treatment at the hand of the Third Reich and had made them both realize how civilized their occupation in Jersey had been compared to the violence and depravity meted out here. She thought they had been isolated in the Channel Islands, but that was nothing to the filthy fog of silence they had sailed into. The gloves were off. The ground rules had changed.

"I've been living in a fool's world," she whispered, scarcely able to comprehend the savagery of her downfall.

Louisa took off her cardigan and tied it around Grace's abdomen to stem the flow of blood.

"Hush, my love. Only positive words and thoughts. We can't let these bastards beat us, Grace, we mustn't. We will get through this. As long as we stay together."

Grace nodded, too lightheaded to speak.

"We must stick together," Louisa whispered.

Exhaustion gnawed at her bones, and a tiredness so colossal swamped her. She closed her eyes.

Days bled into weeks and then they were on the move again, this time washing up in Jacques-Cartier Prison in Rennes, Brittany. On the way in Grace had been stunned at the size of the prison. As she and Louisa and the other prisoners in their consignment had been processed and herded up long corridors she'd heard the calls of German, French and Polish women.

Nights were the worst. Sleep never came. Grace looked over at Louisa, sleeping in her small iron bed, her breath ragged, and moved quietly to the cell door. Grace was worried about Louisa. She had withstood the suffering, the cold and starvation with a quiet dignity. True to her word, she never indulged in self-pity, often encouraging Grace to talk about their beloved Jersey, and yet, she was suffering. She had taken to shaking her head involuntarily and her legs were covered with raw ulcers and sores, which had to be causing her immense pain.

Outside the tapping started up and Grace sighed. She'd never guessed how noisy it could be in a prison, especially at night. Prisoners calling to empty their slop buckets, mysterious tapping on the heating and toilet pipes and over it all, guttural German orders. A howl reverberated up the corridor, two women fighting, followed by running footsteps.

"Oi, keep it down," yelled a woman's voice from the cell next door.

Grace felt a ridiculous surge of hope.

"You're English?" she called into the darkness.

Silence.

She climbed on the six-inch heating pipe which ran the length of the cell and used it to hoist her face closer to the small cell window.

"Please. Talk to me. I heard you speak just now. You're English."

Grace rested her face against the cell wall and closed her eyes. "Please, I need…" She tailed off. What did she need? To speak with someone whose language was familiar, to know that she was alive?

"Keep your voice down. The guards'll hear."

Grace's eyes snapped open. "Thank you," she whispered. "Who are you?"

"Never mind that." Her accent was cut-glass, home counties English. "You're *Eingänge*?"

"Sorry?"

"Newcomers."

"Yes, sort of, though I can barely remember a life before this."

A dry rustle of a laugh.

"Yes, a Nazi prison will do that to you."

A tearing pain flashed through Grace's abdomen and she groaned.

"They have quite the penchant for brutality, don't they. God, what I wouldn't do for a smoke."

"We're from Jersey. How did you end up here?"

"Listen. Take my advice. Keep your head down. Stay silent. Use every opportunity to escape."

"But how?" she stammered, her throat locked.

"Look here. I didn't say I knew how. Just keep your eyes open for possibilities. This is your last chance. This prison is the last stop before Germany."

Grace felt a hot lance of terror.

"How do you know?"

Silence.

"I only helped to pass on warnings, a few books," Grace protested. "I'm not a member of the Resistance."

"Doesn't matter. You've made yourself an enemy of the Third Reich."

The mysterious woman fell silent again and something told Grace she had said all she was going to.

Exhausted, she fell back on her bed and stared at the wall.

Graffiti smothered it. Grace reached out and traced her fingers over it, feeling the dent and jagged groove of words written in moments of pure desperation, or perhaps resignation to their fate.

"*Mort pour la France*," she whispered out loud, feeling out the words with her fingers like braille. Despair blanketed her. She thought of the people she loved, her family, Red, Bea and her library friends. Why hadn't she said goodbye properly? She saw Red's face behind barbed wire and the longing to hold him, tell him that she loved him madly, desperately, burst out of her in a shudder of regret.

Grace managed to drift off, but sometime in the dead of night, she was awoken not by a noise, but a vibration. She sat upright, her head spinning, the clenching pain in her stomach almost drowning out rational thought.

She held onto the edge of the bed and felt the thrum of the cool iron.

"Lou, can you hear that?"

Lou stirred groggily and started to shake her head.

"What's that noise?"

Her voice was drowned out by the unmistakable drone of aircraft.

Grace climbed onto her bed, her palms so slippery with sweat she struggled to get a hold on the prison window. Through the narrow sliver of bars she saw in the distance a church spire, a dense jumble of blacked out buildings and chimney pots… above only a dark empty vault. And yet…

"It's bombers," said Louisa. "It must be Allied bombers."

The vibration grew to a roar and though they couldn't see them, the whole prison suddenly seemed to shake. An enormous flash lit up the interior of the cell and Louisa's face appeared, frozen and white, like a tableau against the filthy prison wall.

"They're dropping—"

She never finished her sentence. The force of the explosion was deafening. The air was filled with a thick choking acrid smoke. Grace gripped Louisa's hand.

"I can smell burning."

"Stay calm," Louisa ordered.

Another explosion, this time closer. Then another. It was like being trapped in a metal bin with someone beating the lid with a jackhammer. The walls of the prison seemed to buckle and groan.

"We're trapped," she gasped, feeling in her panic like she could smash the walls down.

"Hush. Breathe," Louisa ordered, pulling her in and encircling her with her arms.

Grace clung to Louisa, her eyes tightly closed, feeling the hammering of Louisa's heart through her ribs.

"I don't want to die here, Lou, I'm not ready to die."

A bomber's moon crept out from its hiding place and the cell lit up with moonlight. It stole across the walls illuminating the graffiti.

"*Mort pour la France,*" Grace repeated.

"What's that? Don't be silly. No one is dying, do you hear me? They sound closer than they really are. And really, why would the Allies bomb a prison?"

Suddenly, their prison door was wrenched open. The glint of a steel helmet, a blank void for a face.

"*Raus jetzt!*" Out now.

Beyond him, they saw more guards, ushering women up the corridor. Bodies bumping, the smell of shit and cordite filled the air.

"Keep together," Louisa urged as they filed out into the tidal wave of prisoners.

Grace felt the hot press of stumbling bodies and a voice in her ear: "Keep your eyes open."

She whipped round but a guard grabbed her arm and twisted it painfully up her back.

"*Bleib in bewegung, Engländerin!*"

Grace and Louisa spilled out into a central courtyard. The cold air and the toxic smell of burning smacked them like icy water.

The courtyard was filled with guards, their necks craned skyward. Searchlights cut dusty ribbons through the sky. Above were the Allied aircraft, RAF most likely, as it was night. They were so tightly bunched, you could scarcely put a pin between them. Grace felt a ridiculous surge of hope, even when sticks began to fall from their undercarriages.

Pandemonium broke out. The prisoners screamed and ran around in circles, but there was nowhere to hide. Dogs barked. Shots were fired.

Grace and Louisa stood in the middle of the chaos, gripping each other's hands, rooted to the spot as great dark waves of fear rose and plunged.

A bomb dropped on the furthest corner of the courtyard. A colossal boom and the sky seemed to rain bricks.

"Get down." Grace pushed Louisa to the concrete floor and draped herself over her. They were enclosed in a hot swirling morass. Grace realized she had been holding her breath and now desperately needed to breathe, but as she lifted her head, her lungs filled with a bitter choking dust.

Eventually, she dared to lift her head a few inches off the ground. As the smoke cleared she felt the last of her breath leave her body.

One side of the courtyard wall had been destroyed and the adjoining prison wall was flattened, as if someone had punched a giant fist through it. Prisoners were disappearing through the hole, a silent steam of bodies, running without looking back.

Grace staggered to her feet, ears ringing, and it was then that she realized Louisa was lying motionless, a rag doll on the cobbles. Had she pushed her too forcibly to the ground?

"Lou," she cried, her voice sounding so far away.

The older woman pulled herself up on all fours and began to cough.

"Lou, are you all right?"

She coughed again, saliva spooling from her mouth.

"Yes…Yes, I think so. Just winded."

"Lou." She looked about, lowering her voice. "This is our chance. We have to go."

"Go? Go where?" Lou looked at Grace as if she'd just suggested popping to the shops.

"See…" Grace gestured to the shattered wall. "It's twenty feet away at most. Then we have to navigate our way past that prison entrance, but it's chaos so we might make it. But we must leave now. Right now!"

Louisa closed her eyes and Grace had a terrible feeling.

"I can't run."

"You don't have to," Grace said, frustration mounting. "You can lean on me, I'll support you. Please get up… please."

For a moment Grace thought Louisa was trying to stand up. She fell back on her haunches, swayed slightly, then sat back, crying in pain.

"Come, Lou, take my arm. Let's go."

Louisa shook her head.

"I can't do it. I can't run. I don't have it in me."

Desperation clogged Grace's throat.

"We made a promise to stick together. Please, Lou. You must get up."

She sat motionless in the prison courtyard. In the distance, Grace could see a group of guards forming.

"You go, Grace. Take your chance. You'll do it on your own, without me slowing you down."

Her lungs burned and throat was raw. Tears and snot streamed down her face. How could it come down to this? Grace gripped her fingers. "I'll carry you if I have to. This is our only chance. I beg of you, Lou."

Louisa crossed her arms. "No, my love. My running days are over. I am too old. I'll take my chances."

"But I can't leave you."

"Go, child. And if you should make it back, you tell them Louisa Gould will be fine. I am a tough Jersey woman."

She stared one last time at the older woman's face and saw the fear radiating out from the edges of her bravado. "Go, Grace. I'll see you in Jersey. I'll be a little bit behind you, that's all, my love."

Tears flowing down her face, Grace turned and ran across the prison yard, legs pumping, heart shattering.

She imagined Red, vaulting over the prison fence, running with ferocity into the black of night, beckoned by the call of the wild. He had taken his chances, and now, so must she.

Grace plunged into the inky blackness. At the gates, a guard lay dead, his torso severed in two by the glass window which had blown out from his sentry box. Behind him another guard dangled limply from a tree, his entrails hanging down from the branches. Grace cried out in horror and carried on running, waiting any minute for a bullet to take her down.

She carried on running through fields of wheat and past bomb-shattered farms, their charred rafters jutting into the sky like bony fingers. Thirty minutes later, maybe more, she came to a village and finally she stopped.

Skeins of smoke drifted across the square burning her throat. Grace was so thirsty. In the center of the square, next to a memorial to the Great War, was a water fountain, but she didn't dare leave the shadows.

Her gaze flickered up the street. A large wooden loaf of bread hung over a shop, creaking gently in the wind. The boulangerie. The sirens carried on blaring, reminding her that she had to take cover fast. She knocked four times on the door.

"Please, please, please, answer." She murmured silent prayers under her breath.

A woman opened the door a crack and on seeing Grace quickly babbled something. A man, her husband, Grace supposed, came to the door. Neither said a word, just stared at her. She looked in the man's face for softness, warmth, some sign of humanity she could appeal to but saw none. Just suspicion.

How she wished she'd learned to speak Jèrriais now. It might not have helped her to communicate with them perfectly, but it would have been a start.

"*Evade de prison…*" she said, overgesticulating with her hands.

The man's eyes narrowed and he shook his head, already closing the door in her face.

Surprised at her own desperation, Grace stuck her foot in the door.

"*Mon nom est Grace La Mottée. Je suis bibliothécaire de Jersey.*"

She looked at the wife imploringly. "The Bibliothèque Publique, St. Helier. *S'il vous plaît aider?*"

The woman's face softened, the door opened wider and Grace stumbled into the kitchen. Inside, away from blaring sirens, in the normality of a home for the first time in months, Grace went into shock and started to shake violently. How queer it seemed to be among domesticity, things, people, the smell of bread, rosemary and thyme. Grace had no idea whether these strangers would turn her in, but they were her only chance of freedom.

The woman wrapped her in a blanket and sat her by the fire, barked incomprehensible orders at her husband, who reluctantly began to pull down copper pans from over the range.

"My name is Madame Josephine," she said in halting English. "You can stay only until the Americans or the British come. We will keep you safe." She pointed to a small door in the corner of the kitchen. "In the pantry."

From his place by the stove came a grunt, then a torrent of angry French. Madame Josephine silenced her husband with a wintery expression.

She turned back to Grace and her whole face softened, an almost shy smile lighting up her eyes. "I like books very much."

As a cup of something warm was pressed into Grace's hands she realized for the first time that one side of the higgledy-piggledy kitchen was absolutely rammed with books. They teetered in piles and ran off like dominoes over the shelves, across the top of the range shelf and even piled up like doorstops on the floor. She was a bibliophile and suddenly Grace realized, she *could* trust this woman.

A horsehair mattress was laid down in the still room and Grace fell exhausted onto it. It was dark and quiet, all she could make out was the glimmer of glass jars on the shelves above her. The smell of bottled fruit, dried herbs and vinegar filled her nostrils. The stench of prison and the wailing of sirens faded. She fell into the deepest sleep of her life.

When she woke, the door had been opened a fraction. The house was silent. She blinked groggily. Her insides felt eviscerated. Now the adrenaline had worn off she felt her body grow rigid with pain as if something deep inside was rotting.

Stacked by the entrance to the still room was a pile of soft blankets, a candle, a baguette with butter and a bowl of café au lait. The coffee had already formed a skin. How long had she been asleep for? Grace reached shakily for the bowl and her fingers brushed paper. Madame had left her something else and her soul leapt. It was a book. She picked it up, felt its well-thumbed pages and slowly felt her humanity restore.

She pushed the door to the still room open as far as she dared, until the milky light of morning poured into her dark hideaway.

"*The Count of Monte Cristo* by Alexandre Dumas." Grace read aloud and half-laughed, half-sobbed. As well as being a bibliophile, Madame had a sense of humor. "A very good choice," she murmured.

A note slipped from its pages: *Another escape for you, Mademoiselle La Mottée. Until la liberation.*

Grace tried to read, but she couldn't follow a sentence. Her thoughts grew jumbled and she began to burn with a fever. Louisa's face slipped into her mind.

I've changed my mind. Please wait for me.

Grace cried out and reached for her face, but she vanished to the touch. Grace's hands groped in thin air and then she was spinning, faster and faster. She felt a mixture of pain and fear so sharp she thought it would kill her. Grace slumped back on the bed, spilling the bowl of coffee. A dark brown stain seeped across the mattress.

21

Bea
Liberation Day

Hostilities will end officially at one minute after midnight tonight, but in the interests of saving lives the "ceasefire" began yesterday to be sounded all along the front, and our dear Channel Islands are also to be freed today.

Winston Churchill, 8 May 1945, 3 p.m.

In the event, the Liberation of the Channel Islands did not come until the following day, 9 May. Bea sank down on the library steps in the Royal Square as the extraordinary scenes unfolded. She had been here since dawn, virtually pushed out of the door by Mary, and had watched as the trickle of people coming into the square turned into a flood.

By noon it was as if someone had turned up a dial after years of quiet. Church bells pealed. Ecstatic crowds sang, laughed and shouted to each other. The island had been holding its collective breath for five years and now the heady sense of freedom surged over them.

Automobiles and motorcycles hidden from the Germans for years had been uncovered from the back of barns and under haystacks. Wireless sets were pulled from their hiding places and placed on window ledges. Girls in red, white and blue ribbons sat hoisted high on young men's shoulders and sang the National Anthem.

The days of fear, privation and hunger were now consigned to history. Through the crowds she spotted a young man kiss a woman—a total stranger by the looks of her stunned face—but instead of slapping him, her grin stretched ear to ear, and she kissed him back passionately. The crowds around them exploded with joy and euphoria.

Bea's gaze slipped down to her scrawny legs, at the battered tin engagement ring on her pencil-thin finger, now so loose it was in danger of slipping off. Her eyes filled with tears and she dashed them away.

"It's all right, my love," said a woman nearby, waving a Union Jack flag with her son hoisted high on her shoulders. "I've shed a few tears of relief myself I don't mind admitting." Bea tried her hardest to plaster on a stoic smile. These weren't tears of relief.

She had hoped coming here would help her feel closer to Grace. For eleven months now she had not allowed herself to conceive of Grace being dead. She was a librarian, not cut out for barbed wire and brutality, and so Bea had filed away the memory of her best friend under "to come." But Liberation Day was here and Grace was not. And that was the awful twisted truth of it. She had sacrificed her freedom for Bea and yet now, when it came to it, Bea didn't feel free. Not even close. She felt like a ghost.

By 2 p.m. a great roar went up as RAF Spitfires flew overhead and crowds started flocking to the harbor as rumors surfaced that the first British Liberation Forces were arriving.

"They're going to hoist the Union Jack from the Pomme d'Or," cried a voice.

Bea could not move from the library steps, her legs weighed down as if encased in concrete. The noise, the color, the renewed vibrancy of life was sensory overload. All too much for her shattered mind and aching heart. Too much.

"Bea." A gentle hand touched her shoulder and made her jump. She looked up through her tears into the face of Albert Bedane, the physiotherapist.

"Mr. Bedane," she said, this time the smile genuine. On his arm was an elderly lady who Bea had not seen before.

"Any news from Grace?"

Bea shook her head.

"Keep the faith. Many things are still unraveling."

Bea looked quizzically at the older woman. She held on to him tightly, squinting into the sunshine. Many islanders wore the pasty look of malnutrition, but this woman looked as if she hadn't seen daylight in years.

"Is this your mother? I haven't seen you about St. Helier."

"My name is Mary Richardson, dear. This man isn't my son, but he is my savior." She fingered a Star of David necklace at her pale throat.

The penny dropped.

"Mr. Bedane, I salute your courage," Bea murmured.

He shrugged and smiled down at Mrs. Richardson. "This lady is the brave one."

She spoke in a voice so quiet Bea had to lean forward.

"Over two years in hiding and do you know what kept me going?"

Bea shook her head.

"Reading. Books became my constant companion."

"Did Grace—?" She inhaled and glanced at Mr. Bedane, shocked.

"Without fail, every week she delivered until she was arrested…" His voice trailed off awkwardly.

"I hope to meet this librarian myself one day and thank her personally," Mrs. Richardson said.

Mr. Bedane smiled down at her affectionately. "Come now, time to build up strength in those muscles."

"Always the physiotherapist," she said, raising one eyebrow, "even on a day such as this."

She grinned and off they went, Mrs. Richardson leaning heavily on his arm. Bea stared after them, stunned.

"So you had your secrets too, Grace," she murmured. How her friend would have loved to have met Mrs. Richardson, her faceless, silent library patron.

Bea sat there until dusk fell and the crowds thinned out in pursuit of parties and free-flowing alcohol. It was then that she realized.

"Why you sly old dog."

Joseph Le Guyader, the stonemason who had made such an onerous task of re-laying the paving in the square, had finally cleared away a pile of sand to reveal the last slabs. A huge V was carved into the granite. He must have been working on it for months, right under the Germans' noses. What had started out as something transient, a hand gesture, a snapped match, was now permanently carved into the heart of the island.

Who knew how many more secret acts of resistance would bloom with the oxygen of liberation? Bea smiled at the realization. It might not have been organized, but it *was* resistance from those who'd risked their lives to help the persecuted, to hinder the Germans, and help the men and women who had successfully escaped. She knew what she had done: to intercept informers' letters was not theft, but an act of defiance and she would argue that with her dying breath. Be damned those who tried to claim their occupation had been a safe and an easy one, for they had not been here and seen what she had, nor suffered her losses.

Finally, stiff and aching, Bea got up and decided to go to her mother's grave. There was plenty that Queenie Gold would have made of this day.

She walked in the direction of the graveyard, threading through the throngs of glassy-eyed revelers. Many a liberation baby would be conceived this evening, Bea realized with a wry smile. She drew level with the Old Harbour and saw something that brought her up abruptly.

A crowd of people were gathered, staring down at something on the ground. Bea hurried over. As she drew closer the crowd's angry taunts reached her.

Bitch. Pin the Jerrybag down. Jerriyte.

Bea pushed her way through the baying crowds and felt horror clog in her throat.

Nancy was lying on the ground naked from the waist up, screaming and writhing as two young men attempted to pull down her skirt.

"Strip her, then string her up," yelled a woman Bea recognized as the butcher's wife. Everyone knew she had traded in the black market with the Germans, but her crimes didn't seem to hit where it hurt. In the heart.

"Please stop," Nancy whimpered, desperately clinging to her skirt. The absolute exposing shame of it. Schoolboys sat on window ledges, laughing, passersby looked the other way, hurried on, while others stopped like they were watching a busker on market day. She even saw the flash of a camera, sunlight bouncing off windows, capturing her sister's nakedness. Laughter, applause, jeers.

Fear, hot and greasy, slid down Bea's throat as she realized someone had tied a rope to a gas lamp nearby.

"Stop this!" she cried. Her voice was drowned out by the crowd.

Queenie Gold appeared in her mind as clear and fully formed as if she was standing right beside her, hands on hips, eyes blazing with fury. A push on Bea's shoulder propelled her forward and she burst into the center of the crowd.

Before Nancy's attacker had a chance to know what was happening, Bea grabbed his testicles in her hand and squeezed them until her knuckles turned white. He whimpered in shock and his legs buckled.

"How do you like it, huh?" she seethed. "Now get your filthy hands off my sister and fuck off before I call the police."

She turned to the crowd.

"Show's over. Go on, be on your way."

She released the man's genitals and he crumpled onto the ground, groaning softly.

"You're mad," he rasped.

A silence fell over the group as Bea took off her jacket and wrapped it around Nancy's shoulders to protect her modesty.

"Come on, sis, let's get you home."

The stunned crowd parted to let them pass.

"None of you lot ever been in love?" she muttered.

Bea took Nancy home, gave her a stiff drink and then led her up the stairs.

"Into bed," Bea ordered, pulling back the coverlet on Nancy's bed. "You look done in."

Bea had wanted to stay but Nancy made her promise she would return home to Jimmy.

"Are you sure I can't stay? What if they come back?"

Nancy shook her head. "I just need to be by myself. Besides, they're hardly likely to return after what you did."

"Fair enough, but I'll be back tomorrow."

"Thank you, Bea," Nancy said softly. "You know, a year ago, it was you wanted to see me strung up."

Bea tapped the door frame. "People change."

"You know who you reminded me of earlier?"

Bea shook her head.

"Mum!"

"I'll take that as a compliment." Bea smiled and tucked the coverlet around her sister. "Get some sleep."

As she cycled eastward, exhausted and emotional, Bea realized she *had* changed. Losing Grace had deflated all her boisterous anger, made her realize that in the finish, the wise woman invested her energy in love.

The day of reckoning she had predicted had come and Bea was surprised to find she wanted no part in it. She thought back to the frenzied mob, infected with hatred, hell-bent on retribution. What she'd seen in their eyes had scared her because she had once been like them. She *had* to let love into her heart now because love was the only thing to disinfect hate. Jimmy had loved her. They should have had more, a lifetime together, to parent their son, to laugh, cry and share secrets. But now there was only her. And that meant Bea must love for the pair of them.

As she pushed her bike up the lane to the farmhouse she spotted Mary collecting twigs from the orchard.

"Mary, what are you doing? You don't need to do this anymore. Fuel supplies are on the way."

Mary seemed to look straight through her, her face doughy with exhaustion.

"Oh yes. Force of habit, I suppose."

"You look jiggered." Bea touched her arm gently. "Why don't you go and have a nap?"

"A nap?" She snorted. "I've all of Jimmy's napkins still to wash." A low wail started up from the pram in the garden. Mary dropped the bundle of firewood.

"Damn it. I'm so tired. He's so restless and been grizzling all day. He just won't sleep."

"He's teething I expect. Let me go to him. I can settle him, then I'll make a start on the washing," Bea offered.

"No, dear. I can cope."

Mary plucked Jimmy from his pram and stalked inside, her back bowed.

Bea's dreams of a fresh start in England seemed to sail further away.

Slowly she gathered the kindling that Mary had dropped and moved to the far end of the garden where she started a small bonfire. When the flames were licking hungrily to the sky, she reached into her bag for the bundle of letters.

Arthur had retrieved them from the TB hospital yesterday and dropped them off to her on his postal round. "Yours to do with as you wish," he'd told her. "If you want to find out the people who sent them, now's your time. The streets will soon be crawling with British Military Intelligence."

But she realized now that what she wished most of all was to see an end to this poison. What good would it do finding the senders of these treacherous letters? It wouldn't bring her parents back, nor Jimmy and Grace.

She pulled the bundle of informers' letters from her bag. They were yellow and musty now, crinkled at the edges. Freed from their hiding place, they polluted the air with spite, nasty crackling words that took her back to the darkest days of the occupation.

Search and you'll see. Why should they get away with it? Possibly Jewish?

She remembered Grace protesting when she had tried to persuade her to help identify the sender of these letters.

But then I'll be like a Nazi myself, deciding who has to be punished.

She had been right. She always was. And in that moment, here in the garden of Grace's old home, yards from where she'd hidden Red, Bea was the closest to her friend that she had felt in months. She saw her beauty in the rosehips tumbling from the porch, felt her goodness in the soft evening light that filtered down through the apple trees.

The fire was mellowing now and would burn out soon unless she fed it. She looked at the letters, frozen in indecision. Fire was so drastic, so irreversible. If nothing else these letters were important documents. Did she not owe it to history to preserve them?

A door slammed at the back of the farmhouse and Bea flinched, dropping the letter at the top of the pile. She watched in shock as the heat of the fire reached out like fingers and consumed it like a living thing.

There it was then.

One by one she fed the letters to the greedy fire, watching transfixed as the flames caught them, turning their hateful contents to ash. When she had finished she felt oddly cleansed, purged of the poison she had been carrying for so long now.

After that, Bea sat by the fire and allowed memories to pour over her. Stolen kisses in the sand dunes with headstrong Jimmy, so sure of his immortality, fizzing over with adventure. Kind, beautiful Grace opening her library to all, reading to them through the boredom and fear. Her father and mother, who she had imagined were invincible and yet in the finish were not. And upstairs, her sweet baby boy already pushing out his first milk teeth, so near and yet never further from her. The five people she loved the most and yet none were within touching distance on this historic day.

Bea sat outside until the fire died down to a soft glow, ashes mingling with her tears, smudging her cheeks. A fragile fingernail clipping of moon appeared over the farmhouse. Reluctantly she stood up and that's when she saw it, bright and dazzling—a meteorite pulsed and blazed through the dark velvet vault.

★　　★　　★

Five weeks later, Bea was summoned to the post office. She cycled into town along St. Aubin's Bay, pleasingly on the left-hand side of the road. It was a glorious June day and Jersey had on her best summer frock of sparkling green sea and intense blue sky. A light mist hung about a mile out to sea. The tide was turning.

Bea paused and turned back to the face the wide sweep of bay, and closed her eyes for a long time, savoring the warm breeze over her shins. When she opened them she started. A group of prisoners under armed guard was marching along the pavement toward them. For a moment, Bea was taken back to the bad old days, until she realized they weren't Russian, French or Polish, but German.

Not all the German troops had been taken back to England to prisoner-of-war camps, some had been ordered to stay behind and clear up the thousands of mines, ammunition and other detritus of war. As they filed past her, she kicked off the stand on her bike and was about to cycle off when one of the prisoners stood in her path.

"Günter!"

It was the friendly prison guard who'd sneaked the note to Grace. It was odd to see him now under armed guard.

"I never got the chance to thank you," she said quietly.

"No need. I hope she makes it."

"No fraternizing," ordered a British Tommy, standing guard. "Keep moving."

"One last thing," he whispered. "The Wolf." Bea's heart thumped at the very mention of him. "I have it on good authority he is hiding from British Intelligence at his mistress's home. The last cottage on Rope Walk in town."

And then Günter was gone, walking stiffly in the direction of the mined beaches. She watched him go, hobbling on the feet which war had shattered.

Back in St. Helier, Bea was stunned at how busy it was. And noisy! People everywhere, laughing and supping pints outsides the pubs. Church bells rang. Children were having boisterous games of football in the street. No one was scared to draw attention to themselves any longer!

British Force 135 was doing a wonderful job of getting the island back on its feet and restoring its economy. Queues of housewives chattered outside the shops and business was brisk now that there was produce to sell and sterling instead of Reichsmarks to buy with. She waved at Molly, busy gossiping at her flower stall laden down with the first crop of sweet-smelling freesias and carnations.

In Broad Street, she pushed open the door to the post office.

"What's all this about?" she asked Winnie.

"Search me, love," she replied, lifting the hatch. "Come on. We're to assemble in the sorting depot."

"But I don't work here anymore."

"Orders from the top. Mr. Mourant specifically mentioned you by name."

In the sorting office a small cheer went up when Bea walked in and as if by magic, Arthur appeared by her side. Gently he bumped her shoulder with his.

"What comes after S?"

"Make your own, you daft sod."

He grinned. "Good to have you back."

A suited man Bea didn't recognize stood next to Mr. Mourant.

"Your attention, please," the postmaster called out. "It's my great pleasure to introduce you to Mr. Payne. He is the representative of the Postmaster General in London and he arrived by mailboat from England this very morning."

Applause echoed round the room, more Bea felt due to the arrival of a boat from England, rather than this bureaucrat.

"On behalf of His Majesty's Postal Service and every single postal worker in England I bring you greetings and congratulations on your Liberation and a warm welcome back to the direction and control of the British Post Office. The trials and sufferings you have undergone during your five years of separation, and the fortitude with which you have endured them, have not passed unnoticed by your mainland colleagues. The waiting has ended and I am proud and happy to find myself at your service. Telecommunications with England have now been restored." Cheers erupted in the sorting room. "British stamps with the king's head are on their way." The cheers grew louder. "Until then, I have 20,000 free postage-paid cards for islanders, which may be sent free of charge to anywhere in the British Empire."

The announcements were a cause of great jubilation.

"With respect," said Mr. Warder, "after years of separation from my wife in Bournemouth, I'd better visit in person and not just send a postcard. She'd have my guts for garters. I only came here for a quick engineering job. That was five years ago."

The room echoed with laughter and it warmed Bea to see. How quick people were to laugh and joke now the cloud of oppression had gone.

"Don't worry. You'll be granted leave, Mr. Warder," Mr. Mourant chuckled, before his tone grew somber.

"I should also like to draw your attention to yesterday's *Evening Post*, which has a tribute section to those who helped make things easier for their fellow citizens during the Occupation, including the post-office workers, who, at considerable personal risk, opened letters addressed to the German Secret Police and Commandant, and, wherever they found the letters were from informers, took the trouble to call on the persons informed and warn them. They saved many a resident from jail and worse."

He paused and let his gaze drift to Bea and Arthur. Then to Billy Matson, Nobby Clark, Eric Hassell, Philip Warder and Harold "Peddler" Palmer. No one said a word. Staying silent had been ingrained for so long that Bea's lips remained firmly closed. She stared down at the floor feeling uncomfortable.

"They go on to praise those who helped escaped prisoners of war, the brave folk who kept hold of their wireless, and the courage of those who made it off the islands. Everyone referred to is deserving of the highest praise, for they helped to brighten a page of local history which unfortunately bears many blots. You can all hold your heads up high. Drinks will be served when we will toast the return to normal service."

Everyone drifted back into the front desk where bottles of bubbly were being popped open.

"Miss Gold…Bea…a moment of your time," Mr. Mourant called over.

"Am I in trouble?"

"Whatever for?"

"You and I didn't exactly leave under good circumstances and I was dragged out of here by the Secret Field Police."

Mr. Mourant's face softened. "Oh, my dear. All I was ever trying to do was protect you. Officially I had to condemn those who intercepted and opened informers' letters. I never knew for sure, but I suspected it was you all along and that's why I tried to move you, but alas I was too late."

The silence hung between them.

"For what it's worth, I think you are a terrifically brave and principled young woman."

Bea's thoughts turned to Grace. "And look where my principles got me."

"Will you come back? Your old job is waiting for you."

Bea smiled then shook her head. "I'm sorry, Mr. Mourant. I'm not the same woman I was before. But thank you, I appreciate the gesture."

A pop and a loud cheer rang through from next door.

"I have a feeling there are a number of postmen who won't leave it there. Look here. Come next door and have a drink and think on it."

He left and Bea picked up one of the free postcards.

REOCCUPATION OF CHANNEL ISLANDS. This card is liable to CENSORSHIP and may be sent only to an address in the BRITISH EMPIRE or to a member of HM FORCES.

A pen sat next to it. Before she could stop herself she picked it up and scrawled a message on it and popped it in her bag. Bea looked around the battered old sorting office and felt overcome with nostalgia. It would be so easy to fall back into her old life, work all the hours God sent delivering island mail. Mary would be pleased to see her out from under her. But there was only one place she really needed to be now. She slipped quietly out of the back door and cycled in the direction of the Royal Square, pausing only to pop her postcard in a bright red postbox. She'd kept the communication brief.

The man who called himself "The Wolf of the Gestapo" is hiding at 48 Rope Walk.

It struck her as deeply ironic that, after years of condemning anonymous informers, actually, that was exactly what *she* now was.

A part of her would have loved nothing more than to be standing outside that little cottage on Rope Walk when the British Military Intelligence Nazi hunters came knocking. But she had seen enough of the Wolf to last her several lifetimes.

In the library she was stunned to find the entire Wartime Book Club assembled under the newly restored chandelier.

"Bea," came a chorus of voices.

"You're in here so much now I might have to put you on the payroll," Miss Piquet said.

She thought of her last vow to Grace, to help keep the library going. "That's all right, I'm happy to keep Grace's seat warm, just until she gets back."

"Any news on who informed on her and Louisa?" Molly asked, her face souring. "Whoever it was they ought to be in irons."

"Huh, fat chance of that," spat Mrs. Noble. "The British Government has set up an investigation into informers. That'll be another whitewash, you mark my words. Everyone might want us to forgive and forget, but I can't. If it hadn't been for Grace warning me, I might well be somewhere over there too."

Gossip and rumor volleyed back and forth with everyone pitching in with their opinions on everything from what to do with collaborators, to whether the States of Jersey needed reform. Their voices seemed to reach a crescendo in Bea's head. The post-Occupation fallout had triggered a maelstrom of complex questions and feelings were running high.

"STOP!" Peter Topsy stood up so sharply his chair crashed back. "We are here to discuss books. Grace would hate to see this arguing."

Peter had been so quiet that up until now they had almost forgotten his presence. A stunned silence fell over the group.

"Peter's right," Bea said, picking up his chair. "We are here for books, not politics or revenge."

"Sorry," said Molly, chastened.

"Yes, me too," agreed Mrs. Noble.

"Now, what are we reading?" Bea asked.

"Well, as we can read whatever we like, I propose Ernest Hemingway's *A Farewell to Arms*," Albert Bedane suggested. "Seems apt. I still have the copy Grace loaned me."

"How about we let the newest member of our Wartime Book Club have a say?" said Mrs. Noble.

"Yes, good idea," said Miss Piquet. "And while we're at it we better change the name of our club. The Wartime Book Club is now an anachronism, thank goodness."

"Thank you," said Mary Richardson, who was looking much brighter after five weeks of fresh air. "Might I be so bold as to make two suggestions?

"How about Grace & Gould Book Club, in honor of the bravery of Louisa Gould and Grace La Mottée. And rather than a book about war, might we read *Rebecca* by Daphne du Maurier?" Her voice stumbled over the silence. "It's a wonderful book."

A moment of reflection fell over the group and Bea swallowed back a knot of emotion.

"I think you could not have come up with two more perfect suggestions, Mrs. Richardson," Bea said, laying her hand over the older woman's. "That is one of Grace's favorite books."

"A toast then," said Dr. McKinstry. "To the Grace & Gould Book Club. And new beginnings."

Peter Topsy was all too happy to oblige the group with a reading and they fell into a soporific silence as the words of the book flowed over them, Daphne du Maurier's prose washing away the hatred and anger of earlier.

Winnie and the girls from the post office slipped in and listened, drowsy from champagne, while the clack of Mrs. Noble's knitting needles worked softly in the background.

June sunshine streamed in through the glass-domed roof, bathing them all in a buttery glow. Never had the library looked so beautiful.

Bea looked at the empty chair, where Grace should be sitting.

I will never stop waiting for you.

Back at St. Ouen's Bea paused outside the farmhouse and nailed a smile on her face.

"Hello, Mary, I'm home. I stopped and got some oranges from the grocers in St. Helier. Oranges, can you ever imagine? I think I'll need a refresher lesson in how to peel—" Her voice trailed off when she realized Mary wasn't alone.

"Mary? What's wrong? Who's this?" She dropped the oranges and watched in a daze as they rolled across the floor.

She didn't need introductions to know this woman had brought news of Grace. The sense of shock was palpable in the room.

"Bea, you'd better sit down. This is Madame Ballard."

A tiny bird of a woman dressed all in black fidgeted with a handkerchief.

"Please, just say it," Bea begged.

"My name is Madame Ballard, I am from Rennes. I am the niece of Marie Gruchy of St. Clement, which is how I was able to trace you and the Gould family."

She swallowed sharply and Bea felt like she might faint.

"I met Louisa in a camp called Ravensbrück. We were in the same block together."

"What is Ravensbrück?" Bea asked. "Is it a prison? Excuse my ignorance, but we are only now getting uncensored newspapers again."

"No, not a prison. It's a death camp. I cannot even begin to describe the atrocities. I survived because I was fit to work and so was taken to an aircraft factory ten miles east of Berlin. But for Louisa…"

Her voice fell to a whisper. "She was not so lucky. She was selected for the gas chamber in the depths of last winter."

"A gas chamber," Bea repeated, unable to conceive of the horror she was articulating.

"She was the bravest woman I know. Right to the end she kept up everybody's spirits, gave English lessons to many of the prisoners." Her voice broke. "She withstood the suffering in the camp with exceptional courage."

Bea choked back a sob. "Oh my God, Louisa…I just don't know what to say." She knew the question had to be asked.

"And Grace La Mottée, did you meet her? She was younger, fair-haired, about my age."

Madame Ballard shook her head. "I'm afraid not. This is what Madame La Mottée asked me also. I never came across a Grace La Mottée, but Ravensbrück was enormous. There were hundreds of thousands of female prisoners there from around Europe. I was split from my people on arrival so it's likely if Louisa and Grace arrived on the same transport they would have been housed in separate blocks."

Bea glanced at Mary, but she was staring in a daze at an orange at her foot.

"I am so very sorry to be the one to deliver this news," Madame Ballard went on. "I will leave you now, but I hope this gives you somewhere to start your search for your loved one."

Bea saw Madame Ballard to the door.

"I just don't understand how they could have ended up in a concentration camp. They were sentenced to a prison term."

She shrugged. "I do not know. I can only guess that the military had more pressing matters to tend to by that stage of the war and so that they had the misfortune to end up being dealt with directly by the SS."

"Ought we hold out hope?" she whispered. "You can speak plainly with me."

Madame Ballard's face softened. She was so tiny, a gust of wind would have blown her over.

"I can't answer that I'm afraid. I have walked through the gates of hell and seen sights I will never recover from. I will pray for your friend."

She slipped off back down the path and for a long while Bea just stood staring after her.

When she turned Mary was bundling on her coat, her face a mask of fury.

"Where are you going?"

"To see the Vibert sisters with some questions." Her fingers trembled as she tried to button up the coat. "If it turns out to be them I'm going to kill them, so help me God, I'm going to actually kill them."

Locals strongly suspected two spinster sisters, Maud and Lily Vibert, who lived close to Louisa's shop, of being her informers, but they were denying it and, without firm proof, it would be Mary who'd end up in trouble with the law.

"No, Mary, please. Think of baby Jimmy," Bea begged, throwing her arms around her, but Mary was wild with anger, her body rigid. Her gaze was so wide all the whites of her eyes glowed in the dim light of the passage. "Dear God, how much suffering can I take?"

In a moment, her body deflated. She slid down the wall, defeated, and the most awful keening wail erupted from her, like a wounded animal.

"My Grace. My darling Grace. How will I live without her?"

"Please, Mary," Bea sobbed. "We don't know that Grace is dead."

"She ended up in a concentration camp, Bea. In hell on earth. I can't stand it." Tortured cries racked her body and all Bea could do was sit next to her on the floor of the passage, holding her tight, until the force of the first wave of agony passed through her. Mr. La Mottée returned home and immediately went to fetch the doctor.

Bea put Mary to bed that fine June afternoon and Mary La Mottée didn't get out for another three weeks. Bea took over all the care of baby Jimmy, tasks she would have relished before but in light of the circumstances were bittersweet. Bea pushed baby Jimmy all over the island to get him out from the blanket of misery that had draped itself over the once-cheerful farmhouse. A carpet of wild flowers spread over the island—nature's irretractable stealth, smothering sentry boxes and covering concrete bunkers. Mr. La Mottée sought sanctuary on the farm and Mary's sisters moved in to help.

By now the news of Louisa Gould's death had spread. News had also broken that her brother, Harold Le Druillenec, had been liberated from Bergen-Belsen, the only British man to have survived the camp. Memorials were planned.

Emotions were running high on the island, with certain collaborators rumored to have packed up and fled to England for fear of retribution.

And Grace's absence burned like a fever in Bea, consuming her every waking thought.

One Saturday in late June, Bea took baby Jimmy into St. Helier for the market. Everywhere she looked people were returning to the island they'd fled or had been forcibly taken from. Evacuees. Deportees. And then she spotted a face she recognized instantly.

"Ash!" St. Helier's Chief Librarian looked at her nonplussed.

"It's Bea. Grace's old friend."

"Bea," he said, his face coming to life. "Please forgive me, I barely recognized you. You look so different..."

"So wretched, you mean."

"No...I..." he stumbled.

"It's all right. I've been on the Occupation diet for the last five years."

"And this little one?"

He looked down at little Jimmy in his pram, stuffing a balled-up fist in his mouth.

Bea thought of "the story" and yet somehow, the words slid out cleanly.

"He's my son," she said proudly.

"Oh, Bea, he's a little smasher..." He trailed off and Bea could see he was struggling not to cry. "I ought to be in the library. So many people keep coming in to welcome me back. To tell me what an astonishing job Grace did in my absence. But it just makes the truth harder to bear."

He pushed up his half-moon spectacles and blinked back at her, bewildered.

"The first place I came when the boat docked was the library, I couldn't wait to see Grace, you see. I couldn't believe it when Miss Piquet told me she'd been arrested and sent to prison in Germany. I still can't believe it."

"She ran that place like a dream, Ash," Bea blurted. "You could never have found a more committed, devoted librarian. She risked her life to take books to people in hiding, she started a wartime book club, but above all she helped islanders to escape. She gave them a kind of freedom through reading."

He touched Bea's cheek. "I had no doubts she would. I will take up the baton of waiting," he said astutely. "Your little boy needs you."

Bea looked at the housewives bustling around the Central Market with purpose and felt drenched by a wave of helplessness.

"What can we do, Ash? Ought I write to the Red Cross, or perhaps to the prison authorities in France? We know poor Louisa ended up in that god-awful camp, but we don't know that Grace did. There has to be something..." She trailed off. "What is it?"

"I...I..." He fumbled for words.

"Please, Ash, speak plainly. This Occupation's infected Jersey with enough secrets."

"You're right," he replied quietly, his voice laced with compassion. "I didn't want to tell you this for fear you might lose hope, but honesty is the only way."

"What do you know?" she asked, fear clamping her heart.

"I've been making inquiries. The last place Grace was

registered at was Jacques-Cartier Prison in Rennes. It was badly bombed by the Allies shortly after her arrival."

Bea gripped the handles of her pram. The market seemed to spin around her. There it was then. Another little petal of hope withered and dropped away.

She felt Ash's hand on her shoulder.

"Can I see you home, my dear?" His voice sounded like it was coming from miles away. "You don't look well."

White spots bloomed at the edge of her vision. "No, I'm fine. I'll be seeing you." She had to get out before one of those awful turns came upon her. She stumbled out of the market, colliding with a shopper, sending her basket of vegetables crashing to the cobbles.

"Oi! Mind yourself."

"Gosh, I'm so sorry," she stammered. Blinking back tears she recognized the face of Mrs. Richards.

Her fractured thoughts crystallized.

Sir. I have good reason to know that Mrs. Eileen Dark of Rose Cottage, Havre des Pas, hears the English news very often in the morning at 8 a.m.
Yours helpfully
Mrs. Richards

Mrs. Richards glanced from Bea to baby Jimmy, her face rigid with condemnation.

"I don't know how you have the front to parade that poor bastard child about!"

Bea felt as if she'd been whipped across the back of the legs.

She pushed the pram out of the market with as much dignity as she could muster. *Just get home. Breathe.*

But moments later she stopped. Actually no. Her blood boiling she turned abruptly and tapped Mrs. Richards on the shoulder. "I hope you choke on your one hundred Reichsmarks!"

Mrs. Richards's face turned the color of a skinned rabbit.

Having the last word was a hollow victory. As Bea pushed Jimmy's pram in the direction of the bus stop she realized that, in the finish, it didn't really matter. Mrs. Richards might be a spiteful traitor, but there would be plenty more who would agree with her judgment of Bea. With an awful sinking sensation, she realized her mum had been entirely right in her prediction.

The same folk who go around branding homes with swastikas will quickly be branding him a bastard.

The realization sounded as clear as the church bell tolling the hour. The bus arrived and Bea boarded it, numb. Mercifully it was empty. She pulled baby Jimmy from his nest of blankets and sat him on her lap and nuzzled his velvet head. His chubby fingers explored her face, his bright green eyes the mirror image of his father. So pure. So heartachingly innocent.

"Oh, my darling boy. I'm so sorry."

As the town slipped away and the bus trundled through the sleepy patchwork of green fields, Bea realized with a terrible sinking sensation that this island she loved was no longer her home.

She'd be rich pickings for gossip in the market by now. They'd be turning her over like a bruised apple. *Did you see that tart who had a baby out of wedlock? What, the one who got us all in trouble for trying to escape? Not that woman from the post office, who steamed open the Germans' mail!*

She didn't just have a whiff of scandal about her. She was drenched in it like cheap perfume. The war was over now and a woman like her would always be out of step on this sleepy little British outpost. The Occupation had become part of her identity. And while she might not have always gone about things the right way—the *respectable* way—Bea would be damned if she would live cloaked in shame and wrapped in lies. Her son deserved more.

Back in the family farmhouse, she put sleeping Jimmy in his cot and knocked on Mary's bedroom door, her tears dried, her resolved stiffened. She peered round the door. Her bed was empty.

"Mary…Mary…" She ran around the farmhouse banging open doors. Please God let her not have done anything stupid.

Eventually she found her in the apple orchard, sitting under a tree.

"Mary, I need to speak to you and I'm afraid it can't wait any longer. This story, it's not wo—"

She held up a silencing hand.

"Bea, I'm glad you found me. I need to talk to you too."

"May I just—"

"Please, my dear. Let me go first."

Bea sank into the thick grass and waited for the torrent of questions: Had she been seen in town? Had she changed his napkin, rubbed a clean finger over his swollen gums? "I think you should take Jimmy to England."

"Pardon?"

"I've been thinking about it and this arrangement can't work, not in the long term. I know you're desperate to start a new life…as Jimmy's mother, not his auntie." Her voice softened. "And after everything you've been through, you deserve to."

"Oh, Mary." Relief flooded through her.

"I've been so wrapped in my own grief I haven't stopped to consider what you've lost. I don't think I can steal the opportunity to be a mother from you because it suits me."

Bea couldn't speak.

"Grief is hardly the right incentive, is it. I love my grandson dearly, but it's not healthy to treat him as a replacement son. Besides, I'm too old now to be a proper mother. The Nazis have taken two of my children and I need to be alone with my grief."

Bea wept for her selflessness, her despair. "Oh, Mary, I don't know what to say."

She took both her hands in hers. "I promise to bring your grandson home as often as I can, to tell him about his proud Jersey family."

She nodded. "See that you do." She released Bea's grip. "Hurry now. Go and start planning. Your new life in London is waiting."

22

Grace
July 1945

BANNED BOOK

It was poet Otto Heine who wrote in 1821, "Where they burn books, they will, in the end, burn human beings too." In 1933, his books were burned on Nazi book-burning bonfires.

Grace clung to the mailboat railing, her eyes fixed firmly on the sight of Jersey, a great lump of granite rock shimmering on the horizon.

It was 1 July and the irony of the date was not lost on her. Five years to the day when the Germans first landed at the island's airport and their ordeal began.

But now she was finally coming home to the beautiful island home she loved. Grace fought to hold back tears and control the lump in her throat.

"You nervous?" asked a lady next to her.

Grace realized she was gripping the railing so hard her knuckles had turned white.

"Yes," she confessed.

"You live in Jersey?"

"Yes…Well, I used to."

"Ah, evacuee returning, are you?"

Grace swallowed. How could she sum up what she had been through when she couldn't even allow herself to sit with the memory for a moment? Her arrest, prison, the beating that had stolen something so precious from her: the escape, hiding, then the terrible sickness.

Instead she nodded. "Yes."

There. She spotted it straightaway. The flicker of disapproval. The woman moved an inch away from her.

"My husband called your lot *rats*, deserting a sinking ship. Course, who am I to judge. Myself," she pressed a gloved hand to her chest, "I could never have left my island. Roots too deeply buried you see. Not that I blame you for leaving. Well, my dear, you won't find the island as you left, I can assure you. Course we didn't have the bombs like you did, but…"

Grace tuned her out. She desperately needed to be alone with her thoughts, to mentally brace herself for what was to come.

As the island came into closer view, the black granite outline of earlier formed tiny white strips of sand, secret coves, rocky outlets and lush green vegetation. Her heart turned ridiculous somersaults in her chest. A Jersey mailboat passed them, chugging its way toward England, steam pouring from its funnels, the outlines of passengers just visible on the deck. All those people on board just like her, making bold steps toward rebuilding their lives. The postwar world was a giant game of chess, each move triggering complex ramifications.

Did they know she was coming? She had written Red Cross messages, plenty of them over the past month, but as she had been warned at the office, the world was still returning to normal service, and it was anyone's guess whether they had got through. The first mailboats from England to the Channel Islands had only been reestablished in the last few days. Grace had glimpsed the bundles of letters in the hold. How astonishing it seemed, all those stories contained within those gunnysacks marked with HM Royal Mail insignia. Next to them was an even more gratifying sight. Something that had given Grace the will to live while she had waited in London for the islands' liberation. Crates rammed full of new books all donated from the Channel Islands Book Committee, formed by the Channel Islands Refugee Club. Grace had volunteered for them for the past few months in London, drumming up donations to replace all the new books they had missed while under Occupation. Now she was personally escorting them to their new home.

The woman was still prattling on. "Don't be offended if anyone's iffy with you for jumping ship. I dare say it wasn't easy over in England."

Grace smiled weakly. "No, we none of us know what the person next to us endured."

"Well, you certainly won't. No offense, love. I know you had rationing in England but it wasn't a patch on our hardships."

"How ridiculous," Grace snapped, slamming her palms down on the railing. "There's no hierarchy in suffering."

"Well, how rude," the woman huffed. "I was only trying to warn you what to expect."

"Excuse me, I apologize, I…" Her head started to spin and she ran to the toilet. The old Grace would never have snapped like that. But this comparison of misery just uncorked all of hers. Her mind spun with the images of it. The howling pain, the fever, the sweat-soaked nights, the blessed arrival of American tanks that meant Madame Josephine could finally bring her out of hiding. Her own liberation had passed in a morphine-induced blur and when she had finally come back to her senses she knew that something precious had been taken from her.

In the dimly lit toilet she ran cold water over her wrists and pulled down the roller towel, then smoothed down her skirt, her fingers lingering over her hollow tummy. The tummy that would never swell with new life.

She thought of *him*. She couldn't ever bring herself to say his name, much less think of his face. It was as if someone had rubbed out all the memories of the happy times she had shared with him. *Reading in the secrecy of the shed. Stolen kisses in the library. His marriage proposal.* All gone. And all that was left in its place were blurry outlines.

Those memories belonged to the old Grace. Life had been carved into the before and after of her ordeal. "Ordeal" was such a dry word for what she had seen and experienced in that Nazi hell hole. The dehumanization, the brutality, the savage destruction of what made her a woman.

With one well-placed Nazi boot, her dream of motherhood had been crushed. Grace knew she should feel lucky. The medics at the Allied Field Hospital outside Rennes had saved her life. At the time she had been so sick she had no idea how close she had come to dying. The infection that had begun in prison and festered while she was in hiding had led to blood poisoning. A hysterectomy had been the only thing that medics could do. That and some of America's new penicillin had brought her back from the dead. Yes, she was lucky indeed. She had breath in her lungs, a beating heart in her chest, while for millions of others, the war had devoured them.

She also knew that, though she was physically frail, she had a toughness that had been tempered in the furnace of the Third Reich. And yet, there was this peculiar numbness, like she was encased inside a sterile bubble.

Grace lightly tapped the skin over her eyebrows to snap herself back into life.

"Come on, Grace La Mottée, you can't hide down here in the toilet."

By the time she emerged the woman thankfully had gone and Grace was able to stand alone with her thoughts.

It was late afternoon by the time the harbor bobbed into sight. The sun was softening, burnishing the windows of the harbor offices orange and stitching their outlines in gold. Grace could have wept at the beauty of her island.

She watched as two gulls swooped and soared past, inches from her face. When she looked back she saw that the harbor was absolutely swarming with people. She hadn't seen such crowds before, all eagerly waving to people up on deck, calling out. Hope and excitement were etched on everyone's faces. Grace was overwhelmed with the enormity of the hours that lay ahead. The questions that needed answering.

What had become of Louisa Gould and her brother? Were her frail parents still alive? Was the library still running? And a bright, beautiful, insolent face topped with a mop of dark hair nudged its way into her mind.

Gripping her small attaché case, Grace made her way toward the gangplank.

"Sorry. Dreadfully sorry," she blustered as she bumped through the crowds surging to get off the boat.

"Grace!" The voice was so loud she felt her eardrums quiver.

"Nancy!" Grace felt all the breath leave her body. "What are you doing?"

"I'm moving to England with…" She was so flabbergasted she trailed off and started frantically pointing down at the quay.

Grace followed her gaze and there on the quayside was Bea clutching Jimmy. Her wild curls had been tamed into neat pin-waves, which looked as awkward on her as the smart green wool suit.

She was being held in the tightest embrace by Grace's mother, while her father stood awkwardly nearby, hands thrust in his pocket, clearly unhappy to have been dragged into the town instead of the country. And in that surreal moment, Grace knew that this was real. That these people, her people, from whom she had been parted for so long, were actually here.

Her lips opened, but no words came as she moved in a dreamlike state, knowing that at any minute her presence would unleash a storm.

"She's back!" Nancy's voice sounded like a siren over the heads of the crowd. "Bea, she's back."

Bea stared up, squinting into the sun. Her face froze. Her mother fainted. Baby Jimmy started to cry as he was thrust into Mr. La Mottée's arms.

A sensation rose up inside Grace, higher and higher, filling every cell and particle of her body, until it reached her throat, whisking her breath away before it surged over the crown of her head. The bubble burst.

"Bea!" she cried, furiously waving her hand above her head. "Over here!"

And then Grace was not so polite as she pushed her way down the gangplank, stumbling dizzily, blindly toward Bea, before cannonballing into her arms with a solid thump.

They clung to one another, a powerful rush of love swamping them both.

"Oh my God, Grace. I thought you were dead. We all thought you were dead. We heard about the camps, the bombing of your prison…" Her body trembled as she held her so tight. Grace felt like she'd swallowed the sun as she drew back and Bea clutched her face. She was sick. Dizzy. Overwhelmed. Her thoughts were racing and not quite connecting. In the height of her fever, she'd had so many dreams of this moment.

"I…it is you, isn't it?" Grace sobbed. "Please tell me this is happening and I'm not imagining. It's really you, isn't it?"

"Yes, yes, my darling Gracie, it is. You're home. I can't believe you're really home."

The tears streamed down her face as she gripped harder, incandescent with joy and relief.

"I promised you I would come home, didn't I?" Grace wept. "I sent Red Cross messages, so many."

"We never got them. We've been cut off from the whole world."

She tore off her wool jacket. "Let me get this awful scratchy thing off so I can hug you properly."

But she never got the chance. Mary flung herself at Grace with a deep, primal moan.

Mary La Mottée clung to her daughter, so incapable of speech that a medic was fetched to help. Taken aback at the fragility of her mother, Grace held her tenderly.

"It's all right, Mum. There'll be plenty of time to talk when we get home."

In that moment, Bea's face fell and guilt clouded her expression.

"Oh, Grace." She turned to Nancy. "I can't go. I'm sorry."

Grace had already worked out what was happening.

"I was planning on going to Whitechapel with Nancy to stay with my auntie, you know—a fresh start for baby Jimmy," she gibbered. "But I shan't go now." She turned to Nancy once again. "I'm sorry. Nance, I can't do it. Not now. You understand, don't you?"

"Of course," she soothed. "I'll explain everything to Auntie."

"No, Bea. You can and you will," Grace said, recovering her composure. "I didn't risk everything in order that you could stay with my beautiful nephew, only to see you chuck it all away again now."

She placed her hands gently on Bea's shoulders and looked her square in the eye.

"I'm home now. The war is over. We have all the time in the world."

Bea started to shake her head.

"No…no…no. This is too soon. I can't find you only to leave again!" she protested. "You've made too many sacrifices for me already."

"And this isn't another one," Grace insisted. "This is the satisfaction of seeing you travel to a place where you're free to be a mother to my beautiful nephew."

She touched his apricot-soft cheek, all rosy under a white bonnet, and felt her heart ache with the pang of love and loss.

"But I just can't believe I've got to say goodbye," Bea cried. "Please, let's just see if they can delay the boat."

"No, my love." Grace caught the tear sliding down her friend's face with her thumb.

"It is bitter, but the sweet is around the corner. I'll be over in a matter of weeks."

Bea looked from Grace to her mother to the boat.

"I mean it, Bea," Grace persisted. "You and I, we are united by something stronger than friendship, something deeper. It's always been that way. I would die for you."

She picked up Bea's case and kissed baby Jimmy softly on the top of his head.

"I'll be over to see you soon, count on it. Now go on. Go and be somewhere that isn't tainted by the past."

She glanced at the mast that rose at the end of the quay. The swastika had been replaced with a Union Jack.

"Go in search of *your* freedom."

The whistle sounded as the ship's engines rumbled into life.

"All aboard," yelled a steward. The ship shuddered as its mooring lines were cast off.

Bea smiled through her tears and hugged her again fiercely, as if trying to absorb the very essence of her, before reluctantly letting go. "I love you so much, Grace La Mottée."

She glanced over at the boxes being loaded onto the back of a lorry, all marked with the stamp *Channel Islands Book Committee.*

"Should have known you'd wash back in on a tide of books."

Grace smiled. "Oh, one more thing. My—"

"Library is waiting for you," Bea interrupted with a grin. "I've been helping to look after it, just as I promised."

Then she turned and stepped toward the future.

*   *   *

"Will you look at these books?" Grace marveled, pushing aside the tissue paper to reveal a gleaming stack of brand-new books. She pulled out the top copy, *The First 49 Stories* by Ernest Hemingway, and breathed in the rich alkaline smell of new paper.

"Nothing else in the world like it, is there?" Ash grinned.

It had taken weeks and weeks before Grace had felt able to leave the sanctuary of the farmhouse. The guilt that had consumed her on hearing of Louisa's death had floored her. Not even visits from her family and the local priest could assuage the savage sense of grief and shame that had burrowed deep in her bones. All the hopes she had clung to had been nothing but cruel lies. What was the last thing Louisa had said to her in the prison yard?

I'll be a little bit behind you.

But she hadn't been. Instead, she had been transported further east into the dark heart of the German Reich. Louisa had died the ugliest death, in one of the foulest spots on earth. Questions haunted Grace. *Why didn't I try harder to get her to escape? Why hadn't I physically dragged her from that prison?* And the most harrowing: *What had Louisa experienced in her last hours?*

There were no answers to these torments and there probably never would be. In the end it was Ash who had talked her out of her home and back into the library.

"You might as well be miserable in the library," he reasoned.

And so, as summer had gradually folded into the first autumn in peacetime, Grace had found her way back to her library. It had been like slipping into a warm bath. Just being back in her sanctuary hadn't dimmed her grief, but it was blunting the sharp edge of it. Ash had a theory that being around books released a happy hormone in the brain, that it was almost impossible to feel sad surrounded by a forest of books. Grace wasn't sure about that, but there were transient moments of joy where for the length of time it took to serve a patron, she forgot! And sometimes, simply forgetting for five minutes was enough.

"You were good to wait for me to return before unpacking these lot," she said, slipping Ernest Hemingway into a natty little dust jacket. "You must've been sitting on your hands."

He laughed, his little half-moon spectacles slipping down his nose.

"I won't lie. I did have a peek, but seeing as we have you to thank for all these books, I could hardly take this moment from you."

They locked eyes with one another as they did so frequently these days, almost as if neither could believe that they were back together in the library.

"However did you do it?" he marveled as he unpacked book after book. "It's *l'embarras des richesses*. Eight hundred brand-new books!"

"I got in touch with the Channel Islands Refugee Committee after I arrived in London in January. I was interviewed by British Intelligence about my experiences and it was a secretary there actually who told me about them. I offered them my services and they suggested I drum up donations for books to replenish our stock."

She stroked the spine of a rather beautiful new hardback on bird portraiture. "I visited all the London publishing houses and set out my case."

"You begged, you mean," Ash chuckled.

"Something like that," she grinned. "Editors and librarians were fascinated to hear of the censorship we endured in the library, the destruction of our books and also of how library loans soared under Occupation. A similar thing happened in England too, you know," she continued. "People flocked to libraries."

"Desperate for the diversion only a really good story can bring, I guess," Ash said.

"Precisely. Bad times are good for books."

" 'Twas ever thus," Ash agreed.

"During the Blitz, libraries popped up in the most unusual of places. Do you know, Ash, I even visited one that was built over the tracks of an underground Tube tunnel in Bethnal Green, East London, after their central library was bombed!"

She smiled at the memory of the most unique little library she'd ever been in. "It was run by a dynamic duo, Clara and Ruby."

"Never," Ash gasped. "Well, I'll be blowed, a library in a Tube tunnel! Makes the little library I formed in our internment camp seem quite pedestrian."

"There is nothing pedestrian about you, Ash," she laughed.

"But visiting bombed libraries in England was a comfort to me actually. We had felt so isolated here, and then to realize we were part of a bigger network of librarians working so hard to get books to people when people couldn't get to books was *inspiring*, I suppose.

"Shall I tell you what else was inspiring!" she exclaimed, suddenly remembering. "Meeting your favorite author."

Ash's eyes widened. "You never did. Please, tell me you met my literary heroine!"

Grace couldn't help but laugh. "Oh, Ash, your face. You look like a little owl! Yes, I went to Agatha Christie's publishers and when they heard about the popularity of *Cards on the Table* during the Occupation and my story, they invited me to meet her."

"Please tell me she's planning a new book!"

"Of course. She's prolific. She told me how she spent the war working at a pharmacy at University College Hospital.

Apparently her knowledge of poisons fed her homicidal imagination sufficiently to write a new book."

"I can die happy." He sighed.

"She was quite remarkable."

"*You're* remarkable, Grace," Ash insisted.

"Bah! That's piffle and you know it," she said quicky. "But I have learned a lot. Some days I feel closer to fifty than twenty-seven."

The fragments of her life, her youth, had been dashed away like tears in the rain. She touched her blonde hair, now gently graying at the temple, pulled up under a dusty turban. These weren't the only changes war had wrought upon her. The deep groove between her eyes, the waist-bands her mother had had to take in. In certain lights she looked more like a specter than a living thing.

"You've a beautiful soul, Grace," Ash said, sensing her insecurity.

A silence draped the library and Grace tried her best to plaster on a socially acceptable smile.

"On the way in I booked my passage to London to visit Bea and Jimmy. I'm planning on a week in November. Is that all right?"

"You don't even need to ask, Grace. That's terrific news. I'm thrilled for you."

"Yes. I suppose I ought to start looking forward, that's what we're encouraged to do after all. Stiff upper lip and all that…" The words crumbled away as she gripped the hardback book.

"There's no shame in looking back and remembering," Ash said softly. "We must never be resigned to the losses of war."

Maybe it was his gentle presence, or being back here in her own library, but she felt a locked box open inside her. The blurred figure she had buried at the back of her mind gradually took on a face with curious green eyes and red hair.

"I met an escaped American pilot before my trial," she blurted. "He was as potty about libraries as me." She smiled suddenly, remembering Red's passion, his energy.

"We talked of visiting all his favorite places together, the London Library, the traveling library. The whispering gallery at St. Paul's Cathedral. Silly really."

"Not silly at all. He sounds as if he's rather special," Ash said shrewdly.

"He was."

"Why don't you write to the American Red Cross? See if he made it?"

"Maybe."

But the truth of it was, she couldn't bear to know. Grace had read about the casualty levels of American forces in the final push through occupied Europe—that's if he'd even made it across the Channel in his rowing boat. She preferred to imagine Red alive, pushing open the door to his home in Boston, his mom and brothers falling on him like a returning hero. Maybe even settling down into middle age with a lovely wife and a large brood. She hoped he'd hold a little piece of her and this island at war in his secret heart. Maybe get the memory out from time to time in private moments.

She glanced at the space by the office window where he'd kissed her and the terrible ache of their final parting rippled through her again. That look on his face when she'd walked away from the prison fence. She didn't deserve him and maybe, if she was being truly honest, that's why she hadn't searched for him.

In London, she'd seen a bomb-battered building that was still standing but lurched toward the pavement, as if it might collapse at any moment. It seemed an appropriate metaphor for her heart.

"The truth might just surprise you," Ash remarked. "He could be alive and trying to find you."

"I very much doubt it." She picked at a flap of skin by her nail and felt the shame clog her throat. "I broke his heart, Ash, and I'm not proud of that. Anyway, please let's change the subject."

"Very well. I know this chap's off limits, but do you feel able to talk about what happened to you in France?"

She stared down at the hardback in her hands, of the delicate drawing of a hummingbird on the front cover, trying frantically to drink in the image of its beauty, but the other memories muscled in. *A hard boot in a soft belly. Louisa's face lit up by the flash of a bomb. Human intestines dripping from trees.* Grace dared herself to delve deeper into the abyss, to picture Louisa's face as their fingers parted, but there was nothing but impenetrable darkness.

Tears slipped down her ravaged face. The shame and grief consumed her like a living thing. "Sorry, I can't. I can talk about the book club, life here in the library, but I have to seal everything else away, the other memories of Red and Louisa. Maybe one day." She shuddered.

Ash put his hand gently over hers and Grace was grateful for the restrained gesture. A hug might well have demolished her.

"I understand. Catalog them like a book, then file them in a bookshelf in your mind. You can get them out anytime you like. Or simply put them away. That's the beauty of having a book of memories: you can open and close them at will."

Grace nodded. "That's a really good way of putting it."

"I've simply couched it in a term that a bibliophile understands."

She kissed the Chief Librarian on the forehead, so very grateful for his gentle presence.

"Oi! No kissing in the library," called out a shrill voice from the doorway.

"Molly," she exclaimed, as the garrulous redhead pressed an enormous bunch of blousy pink peonies on her.

"It's so good to see you back." She dabbed her eye. "I— Oh bleedin' hell, I'm lost for words."

"That'd be a first," laughed Mrs. Noble who bustled in behind her. Grace found herself pressed to Mrs. Noble's chest. "I never really said thank you, Grace, not properly, for warning me. You might well have saved my life... now we know about what could've happened."

Grace was welcome for the interruption when Dr. McKinstry and Peter Topsy walked in, all smiles and kisses, except for Peter, who didn't really do kisses, or smiles for that matter.

Instead he blushed when Grace couldn't help but hug him.

"Have I ever missed you!"

"What about Red?" he asked in his customary direct fashion. "Do you miss him?" Just the mention of his name derailed Grace and she had to fight very hard to stop herself from wanting to curl into a ball.

"Yes, I do," she admitted quietly. "Very much indeed."

"Mr. Bedane," she exclaimed as the affable physiotherapist walked through the door.

"Come now, I think, after all we've been through, we can use Christian names."

"Albert then," she smiled, holding out both her hands. After they had embraced, she realized there was a woman standing behind him.

"This is Mary Richardson."

No further explanation was required.

"I've waited a long time to give you this," said the lady, rustling around in a string bag.

"I crocheted it when I was in hiding. It helped me, along with books, of course, to keep my mind occupied."

She pulled out the most beautiful soft blanket with all the colors of the rainbow running through it.

"I had to make do with whatever offcuts of wool Albert could find for me, so I'm afraid it's a bit of a hotch-potch."

"I could not love it more," said Grace, instinctively drawing it around herself. It cradled her emaciated shoulders like a soft hug. "I'll treasure it."

Grace plucked one of the soft pink peonies from the bunch Molly had given her and handed it to her.

The two women locked eyes and a current of understanding ran through them. Like Mary, she too had been forced into hiding. Grace didn't need to ask to know how she was feeling.

The softness of the wool, the devotion and love that had gone into its creation, snaked a warmth around Grace's shoulders she had not felt in a good long while. Ever since prison, try as hard as she could, she simply could never feel warm.

When all the remaining members of the book club were sitting, Ash clapped his hands.

"How wonderful to have everyone back!" He reached over and clasped Grace's hand.

"Our dear, dear Grace is back in the fold."

A spontaneous round of applause went up in the library and Grace felt such a rush of love for their book club. She looked around with a full heart at the proud and resilient group of men and women who gathered here weekly to read, all mourning, all living alongside the enemy but never allowing them to control their thoughts or actions.

"We are of course not all back," she ventured. "Might I propose we hold a minute's silence for Louisa and Queenie?"

"Good idea," said Dr. McKinstry.

As they dipped their heads and fell into reflection, Grace gripped her kneecaps, almost as hard as she had gripped Louisa's hand that day when she had begged her to run. She pictured the warmth of her smile, her sincerity and goodness. A woman who had lived a simple, ordinary existence, running a little country shop. She tried hard to picture her weighing out food behind her wooden counter. Not as she had last glimpsed her, too terrified and broken to run from a Nazi prison. And big, bustling Queenie Gold, killed not in a concentration camp, but whose death was inextricably bound to Nazi brutality.

When the deep silence broke, Dr. McKinstry spoke first. "They were both ordinary woman who displayed extraordinary courage. May they never be forgotten."

"Well said," Ash murmured. "Now before we start our book of the week, might I pick your collective brains? Grace and Miss P did an outstanding job keeping this library open under trying circumstances."

"That's something of an understatement," Miss Piquet exclaimed. "It's not every day you have a Nazi breathing down your neck at work."

"Quite," Ash agreed. "So it's even more astonishing when you consider how many people came to the library to escape the grim reality."

He held up the Library Report Grace had written before her arrest. "There were 101,703 books issued in 1944. Book loans doubled during the Occupation. On one day you issued over 1,000 books. Astonishing stuff."

"We did read our way through the war," Grace said.

"But those numbers have come down somewhat," he admitted ruefully.

"Hardly surprising, is it," Molly said. "Now people are free to go on the beaches, dance, socialize and what not, they're hardly likely to come here, are they?"

"Don't forget all the banned clubs that have reopened," Winnie pointed out. "Did you know even my grandson's tiddlywinks club was banned."

"Ironic that Hitler should be scared of a tiddlywink," Mrs. Moisan quipped.

The group roared with laughter.

"All the above might be true," Ash sighed. "But we need to find a way to encourage patrons back into the library, make this a place that once again serves a need in their life."

"I've an idea," said Grace. "During the Occupation, the exchange and mart system of swapping goods was terrifically popular. How about once a week we hold a Library of Things in the Reading Room? People can come and donate and borrow an item for free, be it a football or a pair of shoes."

"A Library of Things," said Ash leaping to his feet in excitement. "Bravo, what a superb idea. We must broaden our scope beyond books."

"What about a memory box?" ventured Mary. "A sealed box to place our memories?"

"A repository of regrets, you mean?" Molly laughed.

"Not just the bad things, but anything we choose to remember our Occupation by. The painful memories yes, but also the pinpricks of light in the darkness." She glanced at Albert.

"That's a wonderful idea," said Grace, remembering the dark afternoon a French book lover had opened her door and safety had swallowed her. The bright new possibilities the library now presented broke through the deadening of her feelings and planted a small green shoot.

"We can leave it here for future library users to read," Ash said.

"What about a shelf dedicated to books banned by the Nazis, to remind people why we fought for freedom of speech?" Dr. McKinstry suggested. He looked at Grace and, she swore, winked.

"Like Jack London's *The Call of the Wild.*"

"Speechless at the ingenuity, sir," enthused Ash, hopping with excitement.

"Sit down, Ash," Grace laughed, tugging at his tweed jacket. "You'll do yourself an injury."

"What about a Record Library and a gramophone?" suggested Molly, leaping to her feet and taking Ash's hands. "Then some dashing young man might finally sweep me off my feet. What say you, Ash? Will you be the Rhett to my Scarlett?"

"Charmed, madam, I'm sure."

He plucked a peony from the bunch and dramatically dropped to one knee, holding the flower aloft. "Permit me this dance, fair lady?"

A kind of heady euphoria gripped the group as Ash waltzed Molly the florist round the library, narrowly colliding with historical fiction, to whoops and cheers from all.

"Say, this looks like fun. May I join?" a voice called from the door.

Grace had her back to the door, but something about the timbre of the voice startled her. Then she realized. Absolutely everyone in the library had frozen and was staring at her.

"Who is it?" she asked.

"It's Red," said Peter, a slow smile spreading over his usually serious face.

Grace could not bring herself to turn, or blink, or even move, because then the illusion would be shattered. Red was gone. There was absolutely no way in the world he could be standing here in her library.

"Grace? Angel Grace, baby, would you look at me?"

The book club stared expectantly and filled with disbelief, as Grace slowly turned.

A man was standing in the entrance, caught in the shadows of a bookcase.

In the gloom, she recognized the unmistakable silhouette. Long muscled legs, solid, broad shoulders.

Then he stepped out into the light and Grace's heart dissolved.

There he was. Gone was the shabby prisoner-of-war uniform and in its place, an immaculate United States Air Force uniform, complete with golden wings insignia at the top of his sleeve.

It was as if a Hollywood idol had walked in, judging by the slackness of Molly's jaw.

He was taller than Grace remembered. Thinner certainly. His face was grooved and weather-beaten, his cheekbones sharp and exposed.

But the wide, warm smile as it spread over his face, the faint dimple on his chin, was everything she remembered and more.

"You're here. You're really here." The words rushed out in a shudder. She was trembling so much Mary's blanket slipped from her shoulders.

"But how? It's simply not possible."

"Sometimes the impossible is possible." He took off his cap and ran his hand through a shock of thick red hair, blinking back tears. "Especially when you have a whole bunch of good friends behind you."

Grace turned slowly to face the book club, gobsmacked. Each and every one of them wore daft grins.

"Are you behind this?" she gasped.

"Guilty as charged," Ash said, flushed as the pink peony he was still holding.

"After you returned to the island I wrote to Bea in London," Molly gushed, finding her voice. "And I asked if there was anything we could do to cheer you up and she spilled the beans about Red."

"But how did you know how to find him?"

Dr. McKinstry cleared his throat. "A few phone calls and I was able to establish that his unit was still stationed in France."

"Then I suggested to my friend on the Victory Committee that wouldn't it be wonderful to invite one of the American escapees over for a Victory parade," said Albert.

"And I'm putting him up—again," said Mrs. Noble with a proud flush on her cheeks. "Though admittedly not in my soot house this time."

"I just can't believe it," Grace stammered. She clutched her chest, a queer cry echoing through the library. This was not real. It was her mind playing cruel tricks on her.

And yet…

"We just wanted to see you smile again, dearest Grace," Ash said.

"Because we love you," Peter said shyly.

"You've made that many sacrifices for others, it's high time you put your own happiness first for a change," added Mrs. Moisan.

"And in truth, it was only a matter of time," Red said. "You didn't honestly think I'd go back to America without coming to find you first, did you, Grace? What we had, what we shared, was so precious to me. I wasn't going to give that up without a fight. *You* are what kept me alive after I made my escape to France."

"Was it terrible?" Molly asked.

He shook his head. "You could say that, ma'am. Waves like roller coasters and sixty-mile-an-hour winds."

"However did you survive, lad?"

He shrugged. "To this day, I don't know. It was no human agency that saved me, that I know. I can only conclude the Lord was sitting on my shoulder."

He gently touched a small cross at his neck.

"That and the thought of you, Grace. I have *never* given up the hope of us."

He walked toward her and pulled her to her feet, his eyes shining with agony and love. "My feelings haven't changed, Grace. Not one iota. I love you with my whole heart."

"But the last time I saw you—"

"I know. That sure took the wind out of me, but when I heard about your confession, the trial and all, I knew why you'd done it. I knew you were lying to protect me."

Grace shook her head, bewildered. He had seen right through her. But he didn't know the new Grace. How, *how* could she tell him she was no longer the woman she used to be? She remembered that day in the prisoner-of-war camp, when they had talked of the menagerie they would have, of a home bursting with books, dogs, cats and of course children.

She said under her breath, so quietly only he could hear, "I am broken."

A silence hung between them in the shape of a question mark. Something unbuttoned inside her. Goddamn it but she was done with living with lies. Hadn't this island nearly sunk under the festering weight of secrets? No one saying what they truly meant for fear of recrimination.

The age of silence and restraint was past. It was time to live with an honest, open heart and if that cost her Red's love, well...her gaze flicked over the stacks and settled on the breathless book group. She'd always have friends and something good to read.

"I'll never be able to bear you a child. That privilege was stolen from me by a Nazi boot," she said quietly. "I'll understand if you choose to leave and I'd never judge you for it."

He stared at her for what felt like the longest time, those green eyes of his scrutinizing hers intensely until she could bear it no longer. The joy at their reunion had soured into something darker. She saw it flash in his eyes. Frustration. Anger. And though she knew he would never admit it, disappointment.

Her gaze slipped to the small patch of brown skin at his neck and she longed to nestle her head there, to fold into the warmth of his strong, familiar body one last time. The pain rushing over her was exquisite. To come so close to the perfect love, to touch the edges of it, only to have it wrenched from you was more than her aching heart could bear.

"I'm sorry," she said under her breath and went to turn, but all at once his arms were reaching for her, his mouth moving next to her ear.

"I don't care what you can or can't offer. *You are enough.* You always were, from the moment I first set eyes on you!"

Emotion thickened his voice.

"I can't lie, Grace. I would have liked to start a family, but if this war has taught me anything, it's that a family can be unrelated." He glanced at the book club. "These days, we get to choose who our family are. And besides, Grace, this smashed-up world is full of grieving children. Maybe we could offer a home to a child who really needs it?"

She nodded slowly, his words landing in her heart.

"Beautiful Grace, you are the only woman I have ever loved and the only expectation I have is to be loved in return."

"But why me? Why not go back to Boston and find a woman who isn't saddled to the past?"

He shrugged. "When there was no bread, you fed me cake."

Grace cast her mind back, to those uncertain times when gunshots rang out over the fields and she'd smuggled cake to a hero in hiding.

"We can never recover our innocence, Grace, but we must rebuild, make another life. We owe this to our dead. Yours and mine."

The image of Louisa's face finally came to her then, as if floating up from the murky depths, whispering a promise. *I'll be a little bit behind you, that's all.*

A tear broke free as she remembered their fingers sliding apart.

The whole library was staring at her now, waiting for her response. For a woman who dealt with words, she couldn't dredge up a single one.

"You never gave up on your friends and the library. Please don't give up on us," Red said softly.

Grace remained rooted to the spot, her mind in freefall.

"In forty-eight hours my furlough is up and I have to sail back to France and rejoin my unit."

"When will you be demobbed, sir?" asked Ash.

"Well now, that kind of depends on whether I get permission to marry." He turned back to face Grace. "Whaddya say, Grace? Will you be mine?"

The quiet in the library was deafening.

"Nod if you want to marry him, Grace," Peter urged. The book club stared motionless, Molly still gripping Ash's arm.

Slowly, Grace nodded and a sob escaped her lips.

"Yes ... yes, I do. I mean, I will. I will marry you."

"Thank God," he sighed.

He slid his hands along her jaw bone, tracing his fingers over the hollow shadows of her cheek before touching her turban, a spark of mischief returning to his eyes.

"You don't need to hide behind this."

He was right. She was covering her graying hair in the way she had veiled her heart. Hesitantly, Grace unknotted the turban, letting her hair slide free around her shoulders.

"You are so beautiful, Grace," he murmured. "And boy, do I want to kiss you!" He faltered. "Can I, kiss you that is?"

Grace nodded and felt her battered heart expand with love.

And there, surrounded by the bibliophiles and books of Britain's oldest library, he did.

The kiss was slow, deep and searching. It was a kiss hungry to make up for lost time, yet determined to savor the years that now lay ahead. A lifetime dizzyingly opened up with a man Grace knew would always cherish her. The relief was immense and when at last his lips left hers, Grace let out a breath she'd been holding since the war began.

Later it was said that the rapturous cheers and applause from the library could be heard on the other side of the island. Indeed, rumors about "that kiss" did more to boost flagging library membership than any number of Ash's new initiatives.

No one cared about the whys or the wherefores, for in the old library, a new and uncensored love story was beginning.

Grace
1995

Grace's finger throbbed as she worked the needle through the fabric. Arthritis was an unforgiving beast, but as she slid in the final stitch, an explosion of applause burst through the community hall.

"I think we can say that was close to the wire," she chuckled, taking off her spectacles and rubbing her aching eyes with the back of her hand.

"Did we really do that?" she asked the assembled group of women.

"We really did, Grace," said the Chair of the Embroiderer's Guild, taking a photograph of her.

When the idea to commemorate the fiftieth anniversary of the Liberation by stitching a tapestry was first floated, Grace had fallen in love with it immediately. The idea of community involvement, which allowed each of the island's twelve parishes to have their own panel to work on, appealed to her librarian's egalitarian spirit.

And so they had gathered weekly over many years, loving hands from all over the parish, to recreate in haunting intimacy something that reflected a shared experience. They'd even held open days, where schoolchildren could come and place a stitch in the panel and hear from the "old timers" as Grace liked to call herself.

Tomorrow their panel was due to be sent to the Textile Conservation Centre at Hampton Court Palace no less, where it would be stretched and mounted in order to preserve it. There it would be stitched together with the other panels so that it would be ready to unveil in front of Prince Charles at the anniversary.

What a long way they'd come, she reflected, looking down at the worn blanket on her lap. Its bright rainbow colors had long since faded to watery pastels, but its history was still rich and resonant after all these years.

"What are you thinking about, Mrs. O'Sullivan?" asked one of Louisa Gould's great-nieces.

"Old friends long gone." She stumbled, her throat growing dry. "Would you be a dear and fetch me a cup of tea, please?"

It wasn't as easy to express one's feelings through words as it was through stitches. Grace had poured all her memories into the cloth and at times, it had all felt like yesterday she sailed back to the island, not fifty years ago.

She wasn't a patch on some of the more experienced women of the Embroiderer's Guild, but as she had weaved in a medic's bag, to remind her of Dr. Noel McKinstry, the good Ulster man who had saved untold lives during the Occupation, including Bea's, she had felt the past come rushing back.

Turned out he had been a key figure in the island's resistance, taking escaped prisoners and forced laborers to safehouses and providing them with ration books and identity cards, as well as offering aid to island escapees. He was one of the most quietly courageous men she had ever come across.

It had been Grace's idea too to stitch a stack of books with a symbolic key left on a bookshelf, to represent the secret cupboard where she had hidden her *verboten* books.

Dear Ash would have liked that. She smiled at the memory of him. He'd been right too about her bookshelf of memories. Over time, he'd coaxed her to take the book out. He was the reason she had never said no to anything in life, and that included taking the opportunity to talk about what had happened when the Germans had made her a political prisoner. Once she'd been interviewed for a BBC documentary, journalists had beaten a path to her door with questions.

Grace was proud of the life she had made for herself. It had been a rich and rewarding life. Her only motto had been to say yes to everything. Her life was good and precious, all the more so for having nearly lost it. She'd never had much in the way of money, but so what? A much wiser person than she had once told her, "Books will get you through times with no money, but money will not get you through times with no books." Fifty years at St. Helier Public Library had taught her the truth of those words.

After she retired from the library she went into schools and helped children with their reading and volunteered so much at the library she was in danger of being re-employed, but as she was fond of telling people, "I'm only seventy-seven! I might have snow on the roof, but I'm not old. I've got stories to tell."

"Nan, there you are. Look at this! The modern-day equivalent of the Bayeux Tapestry." A lightness and energy filled the room.

The smell of Clinique Happy summed up Grace's granddaughter Poppy perfectly. She raced around the island in her little yellow Fiat 500, hair a mass of blonde unruly curls, her back seat stuffed with rescue dogs.

"Do you want me to take you to see Grandad now?" she asked, planting a big kiss on Grace's cheek. "Oh and I've finished changing the sheets in your spare room for Bea. Is it this evening she's arriving?"

"Yes, that's right. You're an angel. Now you're quite sure you have time to drive me?"

"Course. My assistant's covering for me."

"You've an assistant now?" Grace asked and Poppy nodded. "Full-time too. She started last week."

"I'm so thrilled for you."

People had cautioned Grace against gifting her granddaughter the money to rent a small premises in St. Helier, but 18 months on, the Grace & Gould independent bookshop was holding its head high.

"Islanders just love their books," Poppy remarked and Grace nodded. She'd never been in any doubt about that.

"Some things never change. Now let me just slurp back this tea and then we'll get going."

"Course, Nan. Take your time. This is so beautiful," Poppy marveled, looking over the completed panel. "The bookshelf and key are my favorite bits."

"You would say that, my little bookworm."

"And who made me that way?" she laughed.

Poppy had always been intrigued by the idea of her grandmother hiding books from the Nazis in a secret cupboard, so much so she'd had one installed in her own bookshop as a way of opening conversations with customers about censorship.

"Was it like the back of the wardrobe in Narnia?" She never tired of asking that question.

"Much smaller, but I suppose in a way, it did represent a gateway to other worlds."

Grace finished her tea.

"Come on then," she said, getting up with a groan. "Let's go and see your Grandad."

Ten minutes later they were hurtling along the twisty country lanes, in the direction of St. Helier.

Grace closed her eyes until they arrived, screeching to a shuddering halt.

She took a moment to compose herself. Why did young people insist on driving so fast?

"Give me a minute to put my teeth back in," she joked. Poppy laughed and then they both fell silent.

"You go on, Nan. I just need to make a quick call," Poppy said tactfully.

Grace took her time, weaving her way through the graveyard until she found his gravestone.

Captain Daniel Patrick "Red" O'Sullivan, 1919–1990. When there was no bread, islanders fed him cake. Devoted husband to Grace and father to Peter.

It had been typical of Red to request to be buried here in the Allied War Cemetery at Howard Davis Park, in what had been the American section of the cemetery. True to his word, he had campaigned hard to have the bodies of his fellow U.S. servicemen repatriated, and in June 1946, he fulfilled his word when their bodies were exhumed and re-interred in an American cemetery in Normandy.

He had been as self-effacing about that as he had been when a representative of General Eisenhower had pinned the American Medal of Freedom on his chest on the first anniversary of Liberation, in recognition of his service and escape.

"I had nothing to do with that," he'd often insisted about the latter. "The Lord was sitting on my shoulder." That was before Alzheimer's had stripped away his speech at just 71. Far, far too young.

To this day, it was a mystery to Grace how he'd survived such a treacherous crossing, but it had been the start of a deep and abiding faith and a lifelong journey of discovery for them both.

They'd married. Of course they had. Grace slowly raised her blanket to her cheek and smiled. Saying no to Red O'Sullivan was like trying to stop the sun from rising. They had become unofficial parents to Peter Topsy and he had moved in with them. Red's assertion that family didn't necessarily need to be of the same blood had shown itself in the love and care he lavished on the misunderstood boy. "Found family" Grace believed it was called these days. She rather liked that phrase.

As for Peter, living most of his life with undiagnosed autism had made life difficult for him, but being around Grace and Red had helped him to nurture his gift for drawing.

"He is not strange. It's the world around him that is strange," Red had always insisted. When he'd hit his forties, Peter had explained that he never felt like he was part of life, always floating above or below it, but never truly part of the human race.

But his extraordinary creative talent had drawn him together with a wonderful lady called Eleanor who had moved to the island from France to paint. They'd rented a studio together, and at long last Peter found acceptance and love. Thank goodness autism was so much better understood these days than it had been during the early twentieth century. His talent was now recognized around the world; even now he was showcasing a new exhibition in a London gallery, Grace thought, blistering with pride. Not bad for a boy the Nazis had dubbed *Untermensch*.

Nearby, tourists wandered through the graveyard, taking photos, and Grace sighed.

She wished she could impress on these visitors who came to the island each spring and summer, clogging up the roads, ticking off fortifications like a bucket list, that their Occupation was also fought in the home, it was a war of words and censorship. You'll find more revealing stories about the Germans' time in Jersey in the library and archives than in a graveyard or a musty old bunker, she wanted to tell them.

Grace caught a flash of blonde at the gates to the cemetery. Fat loafy clouds drifted overhead and the sun muscled out. A warm, wide smile spread over her cheeks. The arrival of Peter and Eleanor's daughter Poppy had been the most joyous occasion in all their lives. Grace and Red could not have been prouder. Having Peter in their lives and sharing his joys and accomplishments had helped to soften the blow of never having their own children.

Not that it had mattered much. Beside Peter, there was a small army of nieces and nephews. Red had persuaded not only his mom, but three of his brothers to move from Boston to Jersey after the war. A little like the flood of GI brides crossing the Atlantic, but in reverse!

The flame-headed O'Sullivan brothers had become something of a local landmark, running one of the most successful motor repair garages on the island, presided over by their mom, Grace's mother-in-law Mavis, the matriarch. She remembered the huge family beach picnics on St. Brelade's Bay, presided over by Mavis O'Sullivan each Thanksgiving. Games of cricket and baseball and huge steaming bowls of clam chowder and bean crock had kept the chill out. Halcyon days.

A soft ocean breeze combed through Grace's silver hair and for a moment she felt 21 again, bowling down the island lanes on her bicycle with a basket stuffed full of books.

"We didn't do too badly, did we my love," she whispered.

Slowly Grace bent down and laid a faded rainbow-colored crochet blanket down on his grave, taking care to tuck it gently around the sides.

"Sleep tight. Until we meet again."

She felt Poppy's hand rest softly on her shoulder.

"I've been thinking, Nan. You should write a book about your and Grandad's travels."

"And title it *The Call of the Wild*?" she replied and Poppy laughed.

"Why not? I never understood why he bought so many. Surely one copy is enough for any bookshelf?"

Grace smiled. The original, which Red's Nazi captors had found after his escape, was now housed at a museum on the island. As soon as Peter left home, Grace retired from the library, Red sold the business and they were off. The call of the wild had sounded and they had heeded it.

"How many libraries did you visit in your retirement?" Poppy asked.

"Oh goodness, let me think. There was the London Library, then we took the Orient Express, stopping off at Paris to visit the American Library, the Austrian National Library in Hofburg Palace, the Biblioteca Marciana in Venice, the Black Diamond, Royal Danish Library in Copenhagen...too many to mention."

A kaleidoscope of images slid through her mind at the rich treasures she and Red had uncovered on their travels. In each city, he had made sure to stop at a bookshop and purchase a fresh copy of *The Call of the Wild* in whatever translation was available, a reminder always of the power of freedom and reading. And of the vow she had made to herself during the darkest days of the Occupation.

"I'd like to visit all those places someday," Poppy said.

"*Someday* is a disease that will take your dreams to the grave with you, Poppy. Do your living today, sweet girl."

She ran her fingers over Red's gravestone. "Your grandfather taught me that."

A brisk ocean wind swept over them, ruffling the edges of Mary Richardson's blanket.

"However did you both survive it?" Poppy ventured and Grace shrugged.

"Those who have never suffered an enemy invasion in their own land can never understand what war truly is, to live with a jackboot on your neck. But your grandfather… he gave me something beautiful to cling to. Love."

Poppy nodded. "I think I understand. Are you ready to go and meet Bea now?"

Bea
May 2015, seventieth anniversary of the Liberation

Bea walked stiffly through the arrivals hall of Jersey airport, scanning the crowds. Her son Jimmy and two granddaughters walked behind her, hauling what felt like an excessively large amount of luggage for a few days.

"Would madam like a wheelchair?" asked a young man in a high vis jacket.

"No, madam would not. She's got two perfectly good legs she intends to keep using," she snapped.

"Mum," said Jimmy, "that was a bit uncalled for."

But Bea didn't reply. She was nervous. She always was when she returned to Jersey, as she did each year on Liberation Day. She and Grace had made a pact to celebrate

Liberation Day together every year since 1946, on the basis that they hadn't shared the first one. It had become an annual event that was set in stone, with the exception of the ones missed when Grace and Red went off on their travels.

Each year Bea had joked it would be her last, and yet here she was in 2015—96 years old! How had that happened?

"Bea," called a voice. Time slowed. A face emerged from the crowd and Bea felt emotion choke her.

"Grace." The two women fell into each other's arms as their families looked on, smiling indulgently.

"How do you do it, Bea?" Grace marveled, drawing back. "You look so good. Will your hair never go gray?"

"Not as long as I've hair dye in my cupboard and breath in my lungs," Bea remarked, tucking her arm through Grace's. "Come on now. We heading back to yours? My stomach think's my throat's been cut. And we need to crack this open." She showed Grace the expensive bottle of champagne she'd picked up at Gatwick Airport.

Every year they toasted their survival with champagne, because why not?

"We're not so bad for a couple of old biddies, are we?" Bea joked.

"I certainly never thought I'd make such old bones," Grace agreed.

"Neither of us did," Bea mused, remembering the explosive crack of a gun, blood seeping over the stones. In the ensuing 72 years, not a single day had passed when Bea had not thought of that moment.

They reached the carpark, where the island bus was waiting.

"Not many 96-year-olds who can say they've done prison time," Bea said, lowering her voice, as she slowly boarded the bus.

"Bea," began Grace in a tone Bea knew all too well.

"Please, Grace, not now."

Three hours later, Grace's granddaughter Poppy had driven them to an idyllic picnic spot on the west coast of the island. Poppy, Jimmy and Bea's granddaughters headed down a narrow cliff path to the beach for a swim before lunch, leaving the old friends alone, perched on picnic chairs with rugs and flutes of champagne.

A beautiful butterfly, its vivid orange wings scattered with white, like droplets of water on a mirror, settled on a patch of purple heather nearby.

"That's very rare, you know," Grace remarked. "It's called a Large Checkered Skipper. Not seen since the Occupation, would you believe. It's made a return."

"How strange," Bea said.

"A sign of hope and renewal? Or that the past is always there, nudging us?"

Bea could feel Grace's green eyes boring into her.

"Look at this, Grace," she tutted, pointing to the picnic spread. Scotch eggs sweating in little plastic coats, sliced carrots in yet more plastic, something orange and fizzy in individual bottles.

"So much waste. Why don't they just wrap stuff up in paper like in our day? I can't bear to see food go to waste.

Do you know, the other day I fished a perfectly good sandwich out of the bin, that one of my old biddy helpers threw out!"

"I see what you're doing, Bea, and it won't wash," Grace said shrewdly.

She took a sip of her champagne, her eyes twinkling.

"And I see what you're doing," Bea replied.

Grace laughed and reached her glass out, softly clinking it against Bea's.

"Do you know how much I love you, how much I treasure our time together at Liberation?"

"Of course I do. It's the same for me too."

"But the seventieth anniversary, it's got me thinking. It's later than you think."

A silence, in which they could hear the boom of the ocean battering the black rock below, the distant squeal of children's laughter. Every so often groups drifted past them down to the beach, clutching dripping ice creams, kites and buckets.

"This year, they're focusing less on the fortifications and more on the human stories," Grace persisted. "Examining how the need to share is overcoming the desire to forget."

"Oh, Grace, I know what you're getting at, but I'm not like you. Apart from with you, I never talk about the Occupation. It's ancient history."

Grace reached over and held Bea's hand.

"I spent so long forging a new identity in London that I buried the old me. I needed to, just to survive."

It was true. Once she and Nancy had arrived in England, her persona had changed. She became a war widow, left alone to care for her young son. No one stopped to question. She was utterly unremarkable. Just the way she wanted it. They'd all moved into a little bomb-shattered street in Whitechapel where everyone was so busy looking forward that no one stopped to examine the past. She had the right props to make her story believable. The wedding ring, the haunted look.

Bea had got a job in the postal service, with her auntie caring for Jimmy by day. That's where she'd met a postman called Eric Muckle. He was a kind and unassuming man. Older than her by some years. He'd been a civil defense worker in the war and had seen enough to ask no questions about the Occupation. He'd taken baby Jimmy on as his own, loving him without reservation. Jimmy had been joined by twin brothers two years later. Eric had died over ten years ago now. At his funeral, Jimmy wept bitter tears for the only father he'd ever known.

"Tell him, Bea. He deserves to know the truth."

As far as Jimmy was concerned, Bea had evacuated before the Occupation and lived out the war in London. They only returned each year on Liberation for the sake of childhood nostalgia and to keep her old friend company. Tragically, neither of Grace's parents had made old bones, dying not long after war ended. Personally, Bea felt the Occupation and their grief over the murder of their son had contributed to that. It did mean that Jimmy had no memory of their visits to the old farmhouse in St. Ouen's, so after meeting Eric, the lie over his real father had been easy to perpetuate.

They gazed at Jimmy, who had walked back from the beach alone. He had paused at a viewing platform and was gazing moodily out to sea, shoulders hunched.

"He's a troubled soul, Grace. He's enough of his own problems."

"Have you heard about the notion of inheritance of memories?" Grace replied. "That you will have communicated your pain and trauma over the Occupation to him. From his very first existence in the womb, when we all lived on adrenaline and terror, all that will have passed down to him."

Bea pulled her hand away. "What rot. I've never talked about it."

"Exactly."

Bea felt tears gather and she pushed them back angrily.

"Go and tell that lovely man who his real father is," Grace urged. "After all, if he doesn't know his roots, how is he to stand straight in the wind?"

Now Bea's tears began to fall freely and she felt a great knot of pain and fear dislodge somewhere deep inside. The premature death of Jimmy, that sadness which had never ever left her, sat inside her chest like a little caged bird. Time had healed, but memories clung to her like a muddy blanket.

"Open yourself up. Speak your truth."

Bea laughed through her tears. "Now you're sounding like one of those ghastly reality TV programs. This isn't who we are. All that stuff, it's self-indulgent." She dashed her tears away and took a large swig of champagne.

"Come on now," Grace chided. "You dared to be different

once. Where's fearless wartime Bea, cycling down the hill, forcing Germans off the road? Remember our three adjectives game? *Fierce. Flamboyant. Frank.*"

"Yeah, well now I'm more *crotchety, cranky and creaky.*"

Grace gently poked her. "Chump."

"Besides," Bea added, "you sure this isn't you wanting to claim auntie status?"

Grace laughed.

"Maybe a little, but more than anything, that lovely son of yours must know his real identity. Then he can make of it what he will."

In that moment the wind dipped and a blanket of silence seemed to drape the cliff top. Bea could picture Jimmy's face so vividly. The beautiful young man who'd never got to know his son. The butterfly took flight.

"The past is a place we must visit frequently, in order to make sense of our future," Grace continued. "You need to do it my love, before..."

"I pop my clogs?"

They fell into silence as Jimmy wandered back up the path toward them, hands thrust in his pockets, his city white face buffeted by the island breeze.

"Apparently there's a German bunker near here," he called out. "I'd love to see it."

"What's with the fascination for bunkers and fortifications?" Grace said. "You know, Jimmy, there is much more to the Occupation than concrete and machine-gun posts. Bricks and mortars tell stories of course, but human-lived experience, now that's different."

Bea could feel the weight of her gaze. She slipped a battered tin ring out of her pocket.

"Jimmy," she said as casually as she could, "I need to leave this ring at Devil's Hole. Would you drive us? It's rather an important place to me, you see. Well, to us both actually."

"Course, Mum," he said, anxiety flitting over his face. "What's Devil's Hole?"

Grace looked at her, gave her a reassuring nod.

"Don't look so smug," she said, causing Grace's face to split open in a huge smile.

"I'll explain all, but first I need you to take me back to St. Helier. I'm going to need your help in returning something. A long time ago, I took something that didn't belong to me."

Bending down, she reached for her tote bag and pulled out a bundle of old, thin parchment letters. Thank goodness she'd had the good sense not to burn these. The smell hit them all first, dust and mildew. Then the awful swastika symbol punched on the front of the envelope.

Grace's smile slipped.

"Bea, are those what I think they are?"

"*Engelbert Bergmann, Feldpost, Kanalinseln,*" Jimmy read out loud from the envelope on the top.

She nodded. "They're history, I suppose."

"Mum, why do you have German letters?"

"Beatrice Gold!" Grace exclaimed. "You wily old fox. I always suspected you—"

Bea shrugged. "I'm not proud of taking these. They've been hidden in my sewing kit at home all these years, but maybe you're right, Grace. I have a confession to make and I think it's finally time to come clean, in the spirit of reconciliation. I need to see if they'll help me return them to their rightful owners. It's probably too late, but you don't know until you try."

She turned to her son. "Then we'll talk, my love. There is so much to say."

She drained her champagne and then heaved herself up out of the picnic chair.

"Where are you going?" Grace puzzled.

"Why, the library of course. Are you coming?"

Author's Note:
The True Story of the
Mysterious Stolen Letters

In June 2022, I visited Jersey, on my last research trip to the island, and uncovered a story I shan't forget.

I had the privilege of visiting a charming elderly man, who shall have to remain anonymous, who told me a story that shows that some secrets simply can't be lived with.

"I was doing my homework one evening in 1941, eighteen months after the invasion, when in came my two older brothers," he told me. "They started to open the zips on their jackets and out fell letters, which they had stolen from the German Post Office on Beresford Street. It didn't surprise me. The pair of them worked as bank clerks and, together with a gang of young teenagers, were always up to tricks, mainly as a way to frustrate and antagonize the Germans."

That adolescent energy found its release in many outlets, including burning down a German warehouse and flouting curfew. The letter theft was an audacious way to demoralize German troops and could have resulted in deportation or even death.

"They were lucky not to have been caught. They swore me to secrecy and hid them in the bottom of the family piano."

The teenagers vowed never to speak of the theft again.

And there the stolen letters remained, gathering dust year on year, decade after decade. Until 2007, 66 years later, one of the brothers, no longer an impulsive teenager, but a much older and wiser man, decided to hand them back. He walked into Jersey Archive and handed them over after confessing to his brother. "They might be history."

Jersey Heritage Archive swung into action and took the 86 cards and letters to Jersey Post, who in turn teamed up with Deutsche Post. Handwriting experts, the German military and the German Red Cross were all consulted by Jersey Post and Deutsche Post during their research.

After months of painstaking research on the greetings, dated 16 and 17 December 1941, 10 of the letters were finally handed to their intended recipients.

One from Lance-Corporal Lothar Wilhelm to his fiancée, Kaete Schwartz, read:

> Christmas won't be so happy for me this year, because I'm only happy when I'm with you. God grant that we can spend next year's Christmas together again. Best wishes and a thousand kisses. Your bridegroom Lothar.

They were delivered to her grandchildren, who surely must have been astonished to hear from their deceased grandmother's wartime sweetheart.

But alas not all letters could be delivered and many remain at Jersey Archive. I went to view them and found myself lost in a world of forgotten letters. The sentiments and longing expressed by these young German men, a long way from home, reveal the frustration, loneliness and boredom of many fighting a war they did not want to be in.

Some of the stolen letters and photos,
yellowed with time, kept at Jersey Archive.
Images courtesy of Jersey Archive.

One soldier wrote with desperation:

> In your last letter you didn't write "your Maria" any more. I
> felt offended. I want to spend my life with you. We must be
> frank with one another. Do I have to be worried? You can
> be sure of my love.

Did his and Maria's love stand the test of war? Alas, we
shall never know. Some, it seemed, used the German postal
service as a kind of long-distance dating club. Writing to
Liesel, Josef says:

With this letter I am sending a picture of me that you can see what kind of man I am. On 6 July, it's my 26th birthday; size 174cm; my nose is in the middle of my face. I like water sports like you. Can you send me a picture of you in your next letter?

And another man wrote, with doomed irony:

Do my letters arrive in time? The war will pass. I'll be home soon. Your faithful husband.

The war didn't pass for another three years and you can't help but wonder if he did make it home.

It felt a bit voyeuristic handling the stolen letters, reading the innermost thoughts and desires of these men as they poured their hearts out onto the page, knowing in some cases, they might never get a reply. But as a piece of social history they are gold dust and, as you can see, inspired Bea's story.

Author's Note

I fell in love with Jersey on a trip to the Jersey Festival of Words in September 2019. I defy anyone who visits not to. Its color and charm are spellbinding. Warm pink-granite farmhouses. Glittering blue seas. Lush green meadows. The wild flowers that smother the countryside fill the air with their fragrance. But there is something else in the air in Jersey, a tangible sense of history, a connection to its cataclysmic past.

You see reminders of it in the glimpses of bunkers and other German fortifications buried beneath the wild brambles and hedgerows. But for me, history isn't about guns, fortifications and bunkers, it's about oral history. People. The most powerful reminders of the Occupation come from the people themselves.

I was privileged to interview many islanders about their memories of this time in my five visits to the island between 2019 and 2022. Some came in the form of pre-arranged interviews, others came when I pitched up at Age Concern coffee mornings and sat and listened spellbound to the back-and-forth memories, the unfiltered gush of social history that brings the past alive. Some islanders were suspicious about "what sort" of book I was writing, fearful it would oversimplify or focus on the clumsy and tired collaboration narrative. But I was always treated with warmth and hospitality.

I took only one major creative license, I hope. By the time of World War II, Jersey was largely rural and agricultural and there was little movement between the parishes. I have some characters moving freely between town and countryside. This was necessary for the plot development. I did speak to people who cycled daily between rural regions and town, but it was a tremendous schlep, especially on a bike with hosepipe wheels.

As I write this in 2023, it marks 78 years since the end of the Occupation and for some, these stories have rolled from islanders' lips many a time. But for others, they were telling it for the first time. "I don't know where that came from"; "I shouldn't really be saying this"; "I haven't thought of that for years" were common refrains in interviews. After so many years, the need to share overcomes the desire to forget, for this truly is an island simmering with stories.

I *love* interviewing our wartime generation. The more I listen, the more I hear. It can start off about the day-to-day stuff, tea dresses and Spam, Victory waves and vermilion, but then it graduates to the guts of wartime life, the pain and the loss, the hopes and the dreams. When I start a conversation without knowing where it will lead, the past is no longer dusty and sealed off behind a door, but bright, fantastic and vividly real.

Some of the most tantalizing memories were the ones I didn't get. I met a lovely lady at an Age Concern group. On hearing me ask a question about Silvertide, the notorious headquarters of the German Secret Field Police, she handed me her address. "Come and see me tomorrow. I have a true story for you, something that happened to me and my family."

I duly went along to the address.

"I'm sorry," she said, opening the door only a crack. "I've changed my mind. I can't speak with you. You can go away and forget what I told you, but I will have to live with it all over again, going round and round my head. I'm sorry." The door closed in my face and I walked away, deeply saddened at her turmoil.

If I have learned one thing from writing historical fiction and nonfiction, it's that the past never fades, only festers. Unshared stories tend to build up and then burst like a dam. We all have a story to tell, we none of us have lived in a vacuum so there must be millions of untold stories still to tell, especially from the war years.

I am enormously grateful to all those people who took the time to answer my questions and walk me into the past and I hope you find something in this book that speaks to your experiences.

I have nothing but respect for the people who survived five long years of Occupation and faced devastating moral choices, privation, starvation, fear and boredom.

The Channel Islands' Occupation in books tends to be framed by the narrative of collaboration vs. resistance, which remains contentious to this day.

On one of my trips, a tour guide told me how an elderly woman went into a care home recently and was roundly ignored by all the other women in the communal lounge. Her crime? She was a Jerrybag. Memories are long in the Channel Islands, as they are in *all* countries which have withstood war. As I write this, I am listening to a report on the BBC news about pro-Russian collaborators being targeted in the Ukraine. Occupations inject poison into the areas which have lived through it.

And yet not every woman who fraternized with a German was a collaborator. Sure there were some who slept or socialized with Germans, especially officers, for the gifts they bestowed on them, inspired by greed, malice or, in rare circumstances, ideological sympathy. But there were also a large number who simply fell in love. Fewer than 90 illegitimate babies were born as a result of these liaisons, despite press reports citing far higher numbers. And sometimes it gets more complicated.

A popular story recalls the girls who worked in a laundry, who were having relationships with Germans and therefore branded Jerrybags, but who refused to wash German uniforms and were even sent to jail for it.

Resistance such as that seen in occupied France simply wasn't possible. The geography of the islands meant that there were no vast forests or mountains to hide out in. The Channel Islands were simply too small and the scale of the German presence too vast. In France there was one German for every hundred civilians. In Jersey there was one German to every three civilians. (Though some sources say one German to every four civilians. Either way, there were a heck of a lot of Germans on a small island!)

My overriding sense is that we will never know the true extent of resistance. It might have been largely unorganized and organic, but there was a tribe of spirited men and women operating in a clandestine and subversive way to do their bit to strike back against a totalitarian regime. And the really wonderful thing about many of these stories is that they are only now, decades on, coming to light.

After appearing in the *Jersey Evening Post* with an appeal for stories, Jenni Illien got in touch to tell me about her sister-in-law Doris Illien (née Waters):

Doris's husband Ray was serving with the British Army during the Occupation so, as far as we know, she had lived a lonely, uneventful Occupation.

But then one day, in 1995, my husband Bernie and I were at Doris's house having tea. The doorbell rang and she asked me to go. A handsome man in a smart gray suit asked me, "Is this still the house of Doris?" He was obviously French. I said it was the right house, could I help him? He said I had perhaps tell Doris to sit down and tell her it was Roger.

Tears and hugs followed. To our amazement Roger told us that aged 16 he had been picked off the street in St. Malo by German soldiers and brought to Jersey as forced labor. He was taken to Elizabeth Castle where he was forced to break rocks.

After many weeks he saw a man shot for stealing a loaf off the back of a lorry. Before he confessed to the theft, the Germans had shot three men and Roger was next in line.

That night, he decided to try to escape as he had nothing to lose.

The tide was low and he somehow got to the shore undetected. The first Doris knew of him was when she found him in her garden. She brought him in, cleaned him up and fed him. She then kept the escaped prisoner in the house for the remainder of the war and told us that toward the end, with victory in sight, she was worried sick as he kept going into town! She was well aware that she could have been arrested and deported for harboring him. After the war, she never breathed a word.

The purpose of his visit was to invite Doris to be guest of honor at his daughter's wedding later that year, for as he said, "No Doris, no me, no family." We were bursting with pride and asked her why she had never told anyone. She said after the war no one would be interested and she didn't want to boast.

Doris would probably have carried that secret to the grave had the Frenchman not turned up on her doorstep all those years later. This is the epitome of quiet heroism. This comment left on an active Channel Islands Facebook page sums it up for me:

Although there were collaborators and informers here, there were also incredible feats of selflessness, compassion and bravery. My grandma stayed during the war and it was a nightmare which still resounds in some quarters of the islands. In extreme conditions, there will always be people that will collaborate or help the enemy. I would say, until you are the one in that position, you don't really know which side of your personal morality you'd come down on. Without the amazing effort of ALL the Allied forces, who came together from all around the world to fight tyranny, we'd all be in a much different position.

Reading Group Guide

Every book should have its own Book Club Kit to enable its readers to get the most out of it, but that's doubly true of a novel about a book club! So it's my great pleasure to share this with you and your book club. I hope you find something useful in it. Kate x

Book Club Questions

1. *The Wartime Book Club* is set during the Occupation of Jersey in World War II. They might not have had to contend with the Blitz, but they were forced to live alongside the enemy for five years. How do you think you would have coped living under the Occupation and can you see yourself landing in hot water with the German authorities?

2. Book censorship is one of the themes of the novel and I chose to start each chapter with details of a book banned by the Nazis. What is the effect of this and why do you think book censorship is on the rise once more?

3. The Occupation was a quagmire, presenting islanders with impossible moral dilemmas. The staff at Jersey Post Office found themselves in a position that would have been unthinkable before the war, steaming open letters instead of delivering them. Discuss the rights and wrongs of this. What would you have done in their situation?

4. I try to highlight "hidden histories" of women whose stories are rarely discussed. Why do you think working-class women's social histories get overlooked?

5. Grace and Bea are close friends despite being very different from one another. Discuss their different attitudes toward risk and the ways in which they are similar.

6. I set the Epilogue during the anniversary of Liberation Day and we see an elderly Bea finally reveal her stash of stolen German letters. Discuss why you think she waited all those years. How do you interpret the following phrase: *The need to share overcomes the desire to forget?*

7. *Reading was the only true form of joy and solace, the only intellectual freedom they still possessed.* Discuss the importance of books to the war-weary book club.

8. If your book club was banned like Grace's, do you think you would continue and how would you find ways to carry on sharing your love of reading?

Reading List

From my bookcase to yours…These are some of the books featured in *The Wartime Book Club*, or those I read as research and adored.

The Guernsey Literary and Potato Peel Pie Society by Mary Ann Shaffer and Annie Barrows

This charming book was turned into a film of the same name, which, in my opinion, is as good as the book. The novel was never supposed to be Annie Barrows's. The story was actually the brainchild of her aunt, Mary Ann Shaffer, an aspiring author, who dreamt up the story while stuck at Guernsey airport in thick fog back in 1976.

According to Annie, her aunt then spent the next 20 years researching the Occupation of the Channel Islands during World War II, before writing her manuscript and getting herself a book deal. Tragically she died before the book came out, leaving her niece to finish the story. I urge you to read it and defy you not to fall in love with its characters.

The Book Lovers' Anthology: A Compendium of Writing about Books, Readers and Libraries

I stumbled upon this compendium. It's basically a collection of writers' musings on books and it's great to dip in and out of. It's full of little nuggets like this: "Much reading is like much eating, wholly useless without digestion" (R. South). People who love books about books will love this.

The Call of the Wild by Jack London

Buck, a sturdy crossbreed, is a dog born to luxury and raised in a sheltered Californian home. But then he is kidnapped and sold to be a sled dog in the harsh and frozen Yukon Territory. Passed from master to master, Buck embarks on an extraordinary journey, proving his unbreakable spirit. First published in 1903, *The Call of the Wild* is regarded as Jack London's masterpiece. I read this survival story with my 12-year-old son and he loved it, I suspect, in the same way I loved *Black Beauty* at his age. Anthropomorphism of animals is intriguing to kids. I also felt this was a book that Red would hold close to his heart in his own quest for survival.

My Family and Other Animals by Gerald Durrell

Irrepressible and flamboyant author, naturalist and founder of Jersey Zoo, Gerald Durrell shot to fame in the 1950s. His autobiographical account of his idyllic Corfu childhood, *My Family and Other Animals*, was a best-seller. As an animal lover I devoured his books and loved the stories of his gloriously dysfunctional and eccentric family. Visiting Jersey reminded me of one of my favorite childhood books. I hope you enjoy it too if you decide to read it.

Rebecca by Daphne du Maurier
This classic book offered pure escapism to the Wartime Book Club and I was equally spellbound when I first read it. It's one of the few books I reread from time to time.

84, Charing Cross Road by Helene Hanff
This book is the simple story of the love affair between Miss Helene Hanff of New York and Messrs. Marks and Co., sellers of rare and secondhand books, at 84 Charing Cross Road, London. Like *The Guernsey Literary and Potato Peel Pie Society*, it's told entirely through letters. It's funny, beguiling and a must read for anyone who can't resist when walking past a dusty secondhand bookshop. I read it during research to remind me of why we need bookish friends in our lives. It's the perfect read for a book club.

The Lost Art of Letter-Writing

The Wartime Book Club is stuffed with letters and it made me reflect on how few letters I receive these days. Letter-writing is a dying art, but fortunately, there are some wonderfully creative souls around resurrecting old letters and breathing life into them. One of them is my friend Liz Maguire, originally from Washington DC and now living in Dublin, Ireland.

From her first acquisition as a teenager of a set of vintage love letters from a flea market, Liz now holds a collection of over 1,600 letters.

"In today's technological world the art and craft of letter-writing is disappearing," Liz explains. She goes on:

That's why I believe vintage letters can tell us so much about our history and our future. I've archived over 300 vintage letters, that have taken us to both world wars, through the roaring 1920s, the Great Depression and even Queen Elizabeth's coronation.

Letters capture the essence of what it is to be living through history. In attics, and drawers and shoe boxes under beds there are hundreds of stories waiting to be told.

Of all Liz's letters, my favorite are the correspondence between Sandy Silverman, a young British woman, and her American soldier sweetheart, Harry.

They met in London midway through the war, married and had two daughters, Ailene and Cheryl. Liz told me:

I really like Sandy for her sassiness... In a letter from January 1946, after filling Harry in on the everyday of home including a flu that's knocked her mother sideways

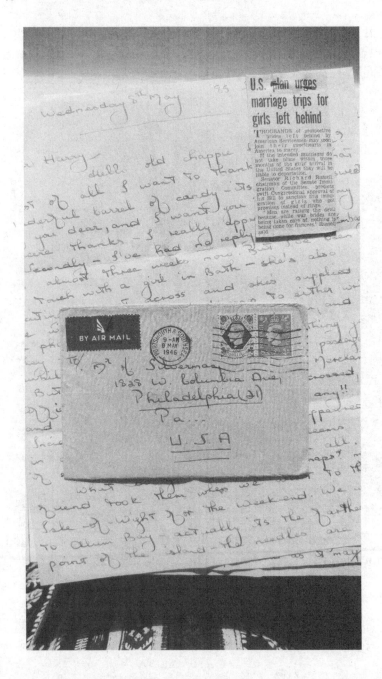

and a farewell party for a fellow war bride, Sandy reminds Harry to post her a snapshot. "*P.S. Hate to harp on it but how about that picture you promised me??? You rogue!! I'm still waiting.*"

Sandy was one of 70,000 British women who became GI brides during World War II. When the war was over, the U.S. Army's priority was getting its men home, not reuniting them with their brides. Sandy was clearly growing restless, and worried: "You don't sound as though you miss us as much as you did—getting used to being a bachelor again?" she wrote tersely to Harry.

The Queen's Coronation in June 1953 provided a good distraction.

I took Ailene to the pictures this afternoon to see the Coronation, and it was really lovely—we enjoyed it immensely—Ailene's eyes almost popped out when the golden coach appeared and she said, "How about Daddy selling his car and buying one of those for us to ride around." So how about it, Rockefeller? She (the Queen) really looked beautiful. Her figure is quite streamlined now, & she looked exquisite. What do you think about the British conquering Mount Everest—leave it to them, ducks—that was quite a nice Coronation present for the Queen.

Finally, Congress passed the War Brides Act, giving GI brides non-quota immigration status, and transportation at the army's expense. A fleet of ships was assigned to Operation War Bride. Sandy was on her way.

"The Queen Mary is scheduled to dock at New York on the 6th of July at approx. 2:15 p.m.," she wrote, concluding, "Well ducks, take good care of yourself for us—remember you've got 5 weeks to get good and fit for me."

Sandy's expectations of a bright new beginning in America were high.

I went to a meeting of the Brides Mothers' Club with Mum and a group of the women had just got back from a trip to the States to see their daughters and you should have heard them raving about it—I was very happy. They can't get over how much more advanced they are in the U.S. and how hygienic everything is and how bright the homes are. They were jawing for 3 hours about it.

Well dearest it'll be a week today that we'll be with each other again—like you I can hardly wait. So until then take good care of yourself for me—we love you madly—see you on the 6th with bells on—Love hugs and kisses until the 6th—

All our love,
Ailene—Cheryl—Sandy
XXXXXX
P. S. Pray for calm sea!!

Did Sandy and Harry find their happy ending after her boat docked at New York? "The bittersweet crux of this whole story is that we will never know the end," says Liz. "But as a reader, I feel privileged to have shared in part of it."

You can find out more here https://www.fleamarket loveletters.com and if you're game, why not join the

Handwritten Letter Appreciation Society? https://thehand
writtenletterappreciationsociety.org.

Or, try this wonderful site, From Me to You, inspiring
people to write letters to those living with cancer. https://
www.frommetoyouletters.co.uk.

Eat like an Islander

Researching a book can sometimes be a lonely affair. I was saved from an evening on my own in my hotel room when a wonderful local lady, Ann Dunne from St. Helier, whom I met on a Jersey Facebook page, took pity on an English author and invited her into her home.

Ann's warmth and hospitality blew me away. She served up a delicious Jersey bean crock stew and while the rain and wind battered the windows, she shared with me the delightful story of how her parents met.

Her mother, Edna Loftus Channing, was one of the thousands of people who welcomed the British Liberation Army, Force 135, as they landed in St. Helier to liberate the island after the long years of Occupation. And a few days after the liberation Edna met one of the soldiers, Silas Martin, and found lifelong love.

After the British soldiers' job was done, Silas did not go home like his comrades. Instead, he stayed, married Edna and had two children: William, born in 1947, and Ann in 1949. Ann told me:

My mother had come through all those harsh years of German rule. She walked past my father at his sentry post, he smiled and said hello. The spark must have been strong, because he never went home. He came to liberate and found love.

They loved each other desperately and were together for 32 years. I am a product of the Liberation, so today I remember it with enormous pride.

After an evening with Ann I left with my heart and belly full.

Bean crock is a Jersey staple. It's a traditional casserole of dried beans with meat, either pork or beef, cooked in a large clay casserole dish. This is how Ann makes hers if you want to give it a go yourself.

"There are many variations of the Jersey bean crock, I only use my Mum's recipe," says Ann. "There's not many ingredients as money was scarce in the 1950s. She did use a clay bean crock pot, but a large saucepan will do."

Bean Crock

Ingredients:

- A good handful of belly pork, cut into chunks
- Mixed beans, haricots or dried butter beans. My mum would soak them in a saucepan of water overnight and rinse them the next day. (You can of course use a tin of beans if you want to avoid soaking overnight)
- Two chopped onions
- A bouillon cube

Method:

If Mum had a few bob, she'd buy a small piece of shin of beef to add to the mix. Put it all into the crock, season with salt and pepper, cover with water, put it in the oven and cook for hours and hours on a slow heat, checking every few hours to see how it's thickening. The longer it cooks, the tastier it becomes, and better the next day. Bean crock was originally a breakfast and people would take their crocks to the baker's to put in the big ovens overnight.

Inspirational Islanders

These humble, hardworking women and men who lived—and tragically in one case died—during the Occupation aren't widely known outside Jersey, but they deserve to be.

The Shopkeeper

Louisa Gould's registration card. Image courtesy of Jersey Archive

Louisa Gould from the book club is based on a remarkable Jersey woman. In July 1941, Louisa received a message that her son Edward had been killed in action in the Mediterranean. Three months later, in October 1941, a Soviet plane, piloted by a young man named Feodor Buryi, was shot down in Germany. He was caught and sent to a prisoner-of-war camp, before being transported to Jersey to work.

Feodor was one of many captured Russian soldiers termed *Untermenschen* (sub-humans) by the Nazi regime and used as slave labor. Many of these soldiers were sent to the Channel Islands and used to build a concentration camp on the island of Alderney—the only one on British territory during World War II. The prisoners were treated with sadistic brutality. Many of the people I interviewed witnessed their beatings and pitiful state.

Feodor was sent to a notoriously brutal work camp called Lager Immelmann at the foot of Jubilee Hill, St. Peter, Jersey. (Most of the camps for workers in Jersey were named after successful German U-boat commanders.) He escaped but was recaptured and as punishment was made to strip naked and push a wheelbarrow loaded with stones until he collapsed. He was then made to stand outside in a freezing water butt all night and beaten. On the basis he was going to die anyway, he attempted another escape.

This time he was given shelter for three months in a hay loft belonging to René Le Mottée until someone from the local community informed their occupiers. Feodor then approached Louisa for help, and with her dead son in mind, she bravely agreed to help him, saying, "I had to do something for another mother's son." She treated him with love and respect, bathed his wounds and altered her son's clothing to fit him. "Bill," as he became known, stayed with Louisa for 20 months until she was denounced and arrested, along with other members of her family, including her brother, sister and two friends.

Louisa was taken to Ravensbrück concentration camp; her brother Harold Le Druillenec, who had simply listened to Louisa's wireless, was sent to Bergen-Belsen concentration camp. Harold was the only British man to survive the camp. He returned to Jersey after the war, testified at the Nuremberg Trials and became headmaster of St. John's Primary School before dying in 1985, aged 73.

Louisa never came home to Jersey.

She and her friend Berthe Pitolet, who had been arrested along with her, were taken to Jacques-Cartier Prison in Rennes. When the Allied forces bombed the prison, Berthe saw her opportunity to escape. For whatever reason, Louisa did not follow her friend. And so it was that she was loaded onto a convoy heading east. Ravensbrück was her final destination.

Worn out by forced labor in the camp, she was no longer of any use to her captors and in the last winter of war, was murdered in the gas chamber at Ravensbrück. She acted with unimaginable courage, giving English lessons to other inmates and helping to care for the sick.

I don't suppose it occurred to Louisa for one moment that she would end up in such a place for her misdemeanor. Why would it? Sheltered from the knowledge of the camps and with all their news censored, she could never have dreamt that such a place of apocalyptic horror awaited her. I don't suppose any of the islanders who perished in camps did either. Please do read the article further down about the Channel Islanders who died in some of Germany's most notorious death camps and prisons.

Louisa's appearance at the Wartime Book Club is fictional, as is my interpretation of why she didn't escape from the prison when she had the chance. But more than anything, I hope the courage and humanity I have my Louisa displaying in this novel stays close to the spirit of this extraordinary woman.

Louisa's story is beautifully brought to life in the film *Another Mother's Son*, released in 2017.

To the best of my knowledge, Louisa's informers, or indeed any informers, black marketeers, fraternizers or collaborators based in the Channel Islands during the Occupation, faced no justice after the war. Indeed, many who had been interviewed by British Intelligence were sent to the UK for their own protection.

Not a single Nazi, or member of the SS stationed in Alderney during the war, was arrested or faced a war crime trial.

Jersey's Plucky Posties

Jersey Post Sorting Office, where informers' letters were intercepted. Photo reproduced courtesy of Dave Vautier.

Bea's activities in wartime are based on another true story. For the first time in Jersey's history, the wartime postal workers were hell-bent on *not* delivering the mail! When it came to delivering hateful informers' letters like the one below, for many it was a step too far, especially when they knew that those who had been denounced faced arrest and a potential death sentence in a Nazi prison. The posties of His Majesty's Government embodied the kind of quiet determination and personal bravery that undoubtedly saved countless lives.

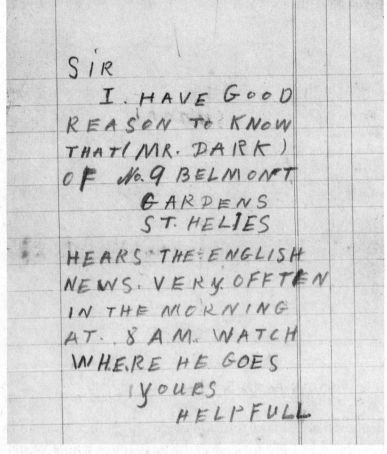

*A "poison-pen" letter written during the
Occupation. Photo: CIOS Jersey.*

Dave Vautier, former postman and author of *The History
and Stories of the Jersey Post Office,* told me:

The Post Office consisted of men who fought in the
First World War, one gaining the Victoria Cross, and

men and women who had faced ordeals of five years of Occupation by a ruthless enemy, and none had fallen by the wayside.

Men who had helped in the Dunkirk retreat, members who had been prisoners of war, three members who had suffered deportation to a prisoner-of-war camp, and several who had faced the wrath of the Secret Field Police by destroying information necessary to carry out their vile practices.

Certain postmen either chucked these informers' letters straight in the boiler, or they would steam them open. Letters which weren't destroyed would be held back for three days before they were date-stamped and then delivered. In the meantime, the postman on his rounds would have warned the recipient that a search was imminent, and the radio or other forbidden item would be hastily removed.

The British Post Office paid tribute to them at the end of the war, but many of these unassuming and heroic postal workers—like Eric Hassell, Billy Matson, Harold "Peddler" Palmer and Philip Warder—were never properly recognized.

Jack Thomas Counter (who I've based the character of Arthur on) was awarded the Victoria Cross in 1918. He came to live in Jersey in 1929 and worked as a postman until his retirement in 1959. He died in 1970 and his ashes are buried in St. Saviour's churchyard.

Philip Warder shouldn't even have been there. He was due to follow his wife to England, but stayed behind to disconnect all the GPO telephone equipment at the last possible moment before the Germans arrived and got stuck there for five years, separated from his wife Trix and their three children. Instead he turned his hand to intercepting poison-pen letters at the Post Office.

"He felt it was his duty to intercept these letters," his historian grandson Mark Lamerton told me.

My grandfather also worked with Dr. McKinstry to smuggle a transmitter into Les Vaux Sanitorium in order to secretly transmit intelligence to the English. They chose this location because the Germans were terrified of tuberculosis and so were unlikely to visit the sanitorium.

He had planned to escape from Jersey with some other men in September 1944, but was under an obligation to the bailiff and could not go with the others who successfully escaped from the island.

With food strictly rationed, he came up with an ingenious method of transporting fresh meat around the island without it being confiscated by the Germans. He would collect the meat, such as pork, from the farm in a hearse. Luckily for him the German guards at the checkpoints never asked to look inside the coffin.

But of all Philip Warder's many acts of ingenuity and bravery during the Occupation, it was the interception of informers' letters, which left the most profound mark.

My grandfather kept these letters for years after the Occupation. He would show them to anyone who showed an interest, as he couldn't believe this despicable behavior between islanders. He was baffled by people's spite. Eventually he parted with them and gave them to a local museum.

Post Office worker Philip Warder, whose courage saved lives. Copyright Mark Lamerton

To me this is one of the greatest untold resistance stories. There is something so intriguing about postmen destroying letters instead of delivering them. I loved studying the photo above of the sorting office, to see what sleight of hand might be occurring, what letters were slipped in pockets in order that lives might be saved.

Heroic Americans*

These two aren't strictly speaking islanders, but as the story of these two daring young men is not only true, but also inspired the character of Red, I felt it would be remiss not to include it here.

It sounds like the plot of blockbuster film *The Great Escape*. Captain Ed Clark from the Lower Rio Grande Valley in Texas (Assistant Division Engineer of the 25th Armored Engineers) and Yale-educated First Lt. George C. Haas from New York (Aerial Observer with the 6th Armored Division) were captured in Brittany, in August 1944, and brought to Jersey to avoid falling back into Allied hands.

They were imprisoned in a prisoner-of-war camp at South Hill, St. Helier.

Plans were made to try to escape by digging a tunnel from the toilets, but the plan was scuppered when a guard noticed that George took a considerable time when going to the loo. The guard investigated and signs of tunneling were discovered. As punishment, George was sent to Newgate Prison for 10 days' solitary confinement only to discover it was easy to chat to other inmates, all locals in for resistance activities. His stay proved useful as he was able to find out detailed plans of the island and a list of loyal islanders to stay with.

* Source: Margaret Ginns, "British and American POWs in Jersey," in *Channel Islands Occupation Review*, 1983, and written recollections by George Haas, kept at Jersey Archive.

"It is amazing how much more generous people become when they are undergoing troubles together," George later wrote. He returned to the prison camp with a rough map etched on toilet paper tucked under the inner sole of his shoe and a plan forming in his mind.

Just before dawn on 8 January 1945, Ed and George escaped over the 12-foot-high wall and barbed wire using a crutch and a bent iron poker as a ladder. It wasn't until 10 a.m. that their German captors discovered two dummy body shapes in their beds. The Americans were treated like old friends at two homes on the island before managing to escape on a rowing boat with donated food, water and warm clothing.

Dodging German patrols, the plucky pair battled 60-mile-an-hour winds, waves "like rollercoasters and freezing snowstorms," before arriving in Countances on the French coast after 15 grueling hours. "The Lord was sitting on both our shoulders," George later recollected.

Their travels ended in Paris with a return to duty and an eventual return to the United States. George went home, got a job with Pepsi-Cola, married and had three daughters. Ed stayed in the U.S. Army, retiring after 25 years of service. On the fiftieth anniversary of their great escape, George and Ed returned to Jersey to witness the unveiling of a monument in their honor.

NOTICE

On January 8th, 1945, the American prisoners - of - war Captain Clark and Lieutenant Haas escaped from the German prisoner - of - war camp. They will attempt to obtain shelter and help from the English civilian population.

It is expressly announced that anyone who takes in or extends help in any way to Captain Clark or Lieutenant Haas will be punished by death according to paragraph **9** of the Order for the Protection of the Occupying Forces.

DESCRIPTION.

Captain Clark. About 29 to 31 years old. Fair, curly hair, brushed back. Slim athletic build, about 5 ft. 8 ins. to 5 ft. 9 ins., small face, looks ill, grey eyes. Probably wearing American uniform (khaki) and fatigue dress.

Lieutenant Haas. About 22 to 24 years old. Dark hair, sticks up somewhat, small, pale, boyish face lower jaw somewhat prominent, dark eyes. Face long and full. Tall, slim build about 5ft. 9 ins. to 5 ft. 11 ins. Limps somewhat due to a wound in the leg. Probably wearing American uniform (khaki) shirt or fatigue dress.

Der Kommandant Festung Jersey

gez. HEINE

Oberst.

Jersey, 8/1/45.

Islanders were warned against helping the escaped Americans. Despite the death penalty, two brave families came to their aid. Poster reproduced courtesy of Jersey Archive.

*Ed (left) and George (right) returned to the island
50 years after their great escape to witness the
unveiling of a plaque in their honor. Courtesy
of the JEP Collection at Jersey Archive.*

The Single Mum

Henriette Marie Louise Sidané le Chavalier.

There is a curious irony to the story of Henriette Marie Louise Sidané le Chavalier. She was freed from a bad marriage *because* of the German invasion. As her daughter, 87-year-old Maggie Moisan, admits:

> My mum suffered a great deal at my father's hands. He was a truly horrible man, who ran up debts, drank too much and used my mother as a punchbag.
>
> He would get paid on the Friday and have drunk it all away by Monday, leaving my mother with no housekeeping to raise four daughters. The weekends were just horrible.

I shan't list all the violent episodes Maggie witnessed growing up, suffice to say the admiration she feels toward her mother is entirely understandable.

> It was my job to pick out Dad's army issue false teeth from the toilet, where he'd cough them out drunk, and clean them for him. Sometimes I used to have horrible thoughts toward him. I loved my mother so much and I hated him for what he did to her.

Henriette's liberation from her controlling husband came when he joined the army, leaving her to care for Maggie and her sisters Lily and Doreen (her other sister Phyllis had joined the ATS). This hardworking, resilient woman then found herself living under German Occupation, but after the violence she'd already endured, it was perhaps the lesser of two evils.

"My mother blossomed under the Occupation, out from under her husband's domineering shadow," Maggie says.

She was no stranger to hard work. Mum had returned to work in the fields growing tomatoes when I was just a couple of days old, simply parking me in a pram nearby, breastfeeding me when I needed it. She had to, she had 30,000 tomato plants to tend to and no work, no pay. After Dad left she got a job at a farm and worked her way through the Occupation. Mum was a typical country woman, always in wooden clogs, called sabots. She smoked cigs and spoke Jèrriais. We lived a rustic, rural way of life, Mum would draw water from an outside well.

Like many women of her generation, Henriette was resourceful.

I never knew her to have a day off. When she wasn't working the farms, she was haggling, bartering and scouring the countryside, just to put clothes on our backs and food in our tummies.

Despite this, there was never enough food. When I was hungry, I went to the farm where Mum was working and she would squirt milk from the cow's udder straight into my mouth. Once we were given a piece of soap as a gift at Christmas from school. Me and my friend tried to eat it we were that hungry.

Maggie's mother also worked as a herbalist, concocting remedies for every ailment from herbs and plants, just as well as there was precious little medicine. "Somehow she managed to cure me of boils, impetigo and whooping cough. She also used to help local women deliver their babies. She had so much feminine knowledge," Maggie says. "Mind you, that generation never knew anything about the menopause."

As the Occupation wore on and food became even more scarce, Maggie was devastated when her pet dog Beauty went missing: "The Germans had stolen Beauty and eaten her!"

As if having your pet dog eaten wasn't enough, Maggie also witnessed the death of one of the Russian slaves.

I was out picking rabbit food for Mum, when I saw this slave worker in rags leaning on this spade. He slumped onto the floor. I saw the OT worker kick him to see if he was dead. Then they just picked him up and slung him on top of the rubbish and drove off. I was only nine. It left a big impression.

On Liberation Day, after completing her jobs, Maggie and her mum walked to St. Helier to soak up the atmosphere.

"Everyone was euphoric, but I saw a huge crowd round a naked woman, chanting 'Jerrybag' over and over. I was very frightened to see that."

Tempering Henriette's relief that the war was over was the sobering knowledge of her husband's return.

Mum had managed to pay off all Dad's debts while he was away. Then, a few months after the Liberation, Dad turned up looking like a spiv in his demob suit and polished shoes and my Mum was still in her rags. "I'm a changed man," he said. Sadly he was. He was even worse.

Maggie's beloved mother died in 1967, aged 76, leaving an enormous hole in her daughter's life. "I always say the mothers were the heroines back then, with what they had to put up with," she ruminates.

Maggie was a delight to spend time with. Bright, energetic and wise, with a mischievous twinkle in her eye. After an absorbing two hours, I reluctantly took my leave and stepped outside. "Oh it's raining," I complained. "That's not rain, my love," she laughed. "It's liquid sunshine."

The Angry Young Man

There's something about the cut of this young man's jib that tells you he is crackling with patriotism. Look at the

Don Dolbel during the Occupation. Photograph reproduced courtesy of Don Dolbel.

hint of mischief in that smile, the forbidden Union Jack handkerchief poking out of his breast pocket.

Don Dolbel was 15 when the Occupation began and 19 when it ended. His biggest regret was being too young to join the Royal Navy and fight. He was just two months off being fifteen—back then the legal age to join up—when the Germans invaded and put paid to his ambitions. Instead he got a job working as a baker's apprentice, and in his spare time boxed to channel his anger. "I boxed professionally all round Jersey," says Don.

> Back then I was light on my feet, King of the Ring. I was young and fizzing over with energy.
>
> The day war broke out I buried a gun and a Union Jack flag beneath the apple tree in our garden. I was what you might call "a bit of a lad" and often got myself into scrapes.

Those scrapes including breaking curfew, throwing tar over the home of a farmer who used to give all his potatoes to the Germans, cycling past a German sentry with a dead pig covered in a white sheet on the back of his trailer and shinning up the flagpole outside German Naval High Command to rip down their swastika, as well as distributing RAF leaflets. Any one of these breaches of German rule would have been enough to get him jailed or deported. You get the sense he was almost goading them into arresting him.

"I remember once walking round with a knife in my pocket determined that I would stab a German if I saw one. I never did. What was I thinking?" he reflects.

For Don, the greatest loss was the theft of his youth, and all the possibility of adventure that promised. On 1 July

1940, his world disintegrated and for a high-spirited man this was too much to accept. At moments in our conversation, that frustration was still palpable and Jimmy's character came to me as we were talking. Don was 96 years old when I interviewed him and sharp as a tack. The memories were still vivid in his mind.

> We saw the slaves, dressed in rags. It was a pitiful sight. One time we saw them shuffling past and my father said, "I'm not very hungry tonight," and left his plate out for them by the hedge. It was only potatoes and veg but they fell on it. Tomorrow it would be my mother's turn not to be hungry, and so it went on. We tried to do what we could to help.
>
> Toward the end of the war—the siege—people were starving, I had to sit up all night at the bakehouse I worked in with a hockey stick, in case of someone breaking in. Theft was rife; slaves, foreign workers, Germans, everyone was pinching, we were starving.
>
> To keep up morale we'd listen to Churchill's voice and the chimes of Big Ben on our secret wireless in the attic. I knew we'd win eventually.

"What got you through it?" I asked.

"Wickedness," he replied with a wink.

Today, he's less inclined to get into scrapes, and as well as volunteering, plays his accordion at events, including, to his credit, at the German town of Bad Wurzach, which is twinned with St. Helier. He celebrated his 91st birthday with a tandem parachute jump, so perhaps the maverick's not left him yet.

Don's a charming man: dapper, garrulous and full of life, a walking history book some might say.

The Savior

Albert Bedane, top, sheltered Mary Richardson,
bottom, for over two years in the cellar of his
St. Helier home. Images courtesy of Jersey Archive.

During the Occupation, Albert Bedane was a physiotherapist with a secret. Behind the doors of his imposing townhouse in Roseville Street, St. Helier, he was hiding a Jewish Dutch woman called Mary Richardson in his three-room cellar. Given the close proximity of his home to that of the German Secret Field Police, this was a courageous act. If he had been caught, he would have been deported and probably died in a concentration camp.

As the Germans were preparing to deport Mrs. Richardson she managed to escape and hide with Albert for more than two years until the end of the war.

After the war, Albert rarely talked about what he'd done. Today, he is an island hero.

In 2000, Albert Bedane was posthumously recognized as "Righteous Among the Nations" and awarded a medal by Israel's Yad Vashem for saving Mary's life.

Jersey Archive has a really excellent Resistance Trail, which tells you about people like Albert and Louisa, as well as many other islanders and places intimately involved in the story of Jersey's resistance. You can view it online or perhaps try it yourself if you visit Jersey. https://www.jersey heritage.org/media/Resistance%20Trail/Leaflet.pdf.

Postscript

"Wolf of the Gestapo" sounds like a pantomime villain, but he too is real. He may not have threatened to burn down the library (as I included in the plot), but he definitely *was* part of the machinery which sent Louisa and others to their deaths. I don't wish to dwell on the life of Heinz Carl Wölfle, deputy head of the Geheime Feldpolizei, the German Secret Field Police in Jersey, not when there are so many other people who are more deserving of space in this book. Suffice to say he was responsible for countless arrests in Jersey during the Occupation. On liberation he was rounded up by British Military Police and interviewed by British Intelligence officers. Wölfle was apprehended in the prison he sent many civilians to. His name cropped up in so many interviews with the islanders that after the war he was held back long after his colleagues were sent to prisoner-of-war camps in England. Unable to prove anything against him despite finding him a "thoroughly nasty piece of work" he was eventually, in October 1945, sent to a prisoner-of-war camp in Colchester, Essex. He was repatriated to Germany in 1947.

The Price of Bravery

Throughout this book I have woven in the names and stories of real islanders who paid a heavy price for daring to stand up a totalitarian regime. Warning, some of these details make for harrowing reading.

Let's remember:

June Sinclair

Born 1920, London, United Kingdom.
Arrested for slapping a German officer after he made rude
 remarks about her and tried to kiss her. Half-Jewish
 orphan June was deported from Jersey.
Died Ravensbrück concentration camp, 1943. Age 23.

Maurice Gould

Born 31 May 1924, Leicester, United Kingdom.
Arrested for an unsuccessful escape attempt from Jersey,
 along with his friend Dennis Audrain and Peter
 Hassall. Dennis drowned. Peter and Maurice were
 deported.

Died Wittlich Prison, Germany. October 1943. Aged 19.
Cause of death: Beatings. Starvation. Tuberculosis.

François "Frank" Le Villio

Born 13 September 1925, St. Saviour, Jersey.
Arrested aged 19 for stealing a bike and deported.
After surviving the Neuengamme and Sandbostel concentration camps, he died weakened from his experiences of tuberculosis in Nottingham, in 1946. He was buried in a pauper's grave aged 21. In September 2018, his body was brought home and laid to rest in Jersey.

Canon Clifford Cohu, Rector of St. Saviour Church and Chaplain of the General Hospital

Born 1 January 1883, Guernsey.
Arrested in Jersey for disseminating anti-German news, by sharing BBC news bulletins in the hospital on his rounds and while riding his bike through the streets.
Died at Zöschen Forced Labor Re-Education Camp, 20 September 1944, aged 61.
Cause of death: Beaten to death by guards clutching his only possession, a small Bible.

Charles Nicholas Machon

Born September 1893, St. Peter Port, Guernsey.
During the Occupation, Charles worked as a linotype operator at the *Guernsey Star and Gazette* newspaper.

Arrested February 1944, along with colleagues, for writing and distributing an underground newspaper, called *GUNS* (*Guernsey Underground News Service*). Providing accurate and trustworthy news was vital after radios were confiscated by the occupying forces.

Died on 26 October 1944 in Hamelin prison, Germany, aged 51. Today remembered as an island hero.

Father and Son, Clarence and Peter Painter

Clarence born 2 November 1893, Abingdon, Berkshire, United Kingdom; Peter born 11 April, 1924, St. Helier, Jersey.

Clarence was arrested for illegal possession of a wireless and spreading news; Peter arrested for taking photos of German planes and assembling maps of German fortifications.

Peter died 27 November 1944 of pneumonia in his father's arms at Gross-Rosen Concentration Camp, aged 20.

Clarence died 16 February 1945 after three days' travel in an open goods wagon without food or proper clothing, fleeing the Russian advance when the camp was evacuated. He was 52.

Marie Ozanne

Born September 1905, Guernsey.

Marie was a member of the Salvation Army. She is remembered for fearlessly and openly challenging the German commandant for Nazi persecution and treatment of slaves and forced laborers. Marie was banned from wearing her Salvation Army uniform and preaching from the Bible—orders she ignored.

Arrested September 1942.

Died of peritonitis in February 1943, aged 37. She wrote in her diary before her death, "Guernsey is beautiful, so why so much war, darkness and hatred?"

James Houillebecq

Born 24 February 1927, St. Saviour, Jersey.

Arrested for theft of ammunition (in the hope of giving assistance to an Allied invasion force).

Died at Neuengamme Concentration Camp on 20 January 1945, aged 18.

Official cause of death: "blood poisoning."

George James Fox

Born 22 May 1896, St. Helier, Jersey.

Arrested for stealing food from German barracks to feed his seven children.

Died 11 March 1945, Naumburg Prison, aged 49.

Cause of death: sepsis

Joseph James Tierney, a Sexton at St. Saviour Parish Church

Born 23 October 1912, St. Helier, Jersey.

Arrested for listening to a forbidden wireless and disseminating the BBC news.

Died 4 May 1945, aged 33, Kaschitz in Germany.

Cause of death: Imprisoned in various camps, including Zöschen Forced Labor camp, before being transported in a "death march" cattle truck fleeing Allied advance. Inhumane conditions in the trucks were too much for Joe. It's believed that he died in a fellow prisoner's arms.

For a complete list of all the Channel Islanders who were deported to continental prisons and camps, visit this incredibly informative site: https://www.frankfallaarchive.org.

Places to Visit:
Eat, Drink, and Dive into the Past

If you are lucky enough to go to Jersey, these are some of the places I visited as research for this book. But you don't need to be researching a book, or particularly be a history buff, to visit and fall in love with these places.

The Occupation Tapestry

I loved this place so much I visited twice. As I described in the Epilogue, loving hands from Jersey's parishes came together to stitch a stunning tapestry to show life under the Occupation. Apparently it took seven years from inception to conception and 30,000 hours of work by 227 embroiderers, but wow, was it ever worth it! What's really incredible is the detail; you can spend hours absorbed in it. It tells the story of Jersey's war in a completely unique and vivid way. I also love the idea of Jersey's older generation getting together to embroider and share stories of the Occupation with the younger generation. What a brilliant way to pass down history. I'd have loved to have listened to some of those conversations.

It's at Jersey's Maritime Museum.

Read about it in *Threads of History: The Jersey Occupation Tapestry* by Tessa Coleman.

https://www.jerseyheritage.org/visit/places-to-visit
/maritime-museum-occupation-tapestry/.

The Lighthouse Memorial

Standing immediately outside the Maritime Museum, on
the New North Quay of St. Helier Harbour, is the Lighthouse Memorial. The lighthouse stood at St. Catherine's
Pier for over 100 years, before it was decommissioned in
1996. It was then installed there as a memorial to the Jersey
21—the men and women who died in Nazi prisons and
camps, having been tried and deported for breaking
German Occupation regulations. Their names can be read
on the plinth around its base, where wreaths are laid each
year on 27 January to mark Holocaust Memorial Day. I
found this information on the excellent Frank Falla Archive,
(https://www.frankfallaarchive.org/search-people/), which
is a wealth of information on the Jersey 21 and Guernsey
8, who did not return from Nazi-occupied territories.

Jersey War Tunnels

An absolute must visit if you're interested in the Occupation.
This vast network of underground tunnels was designed to
allow the German occupying infantry to withstand Allied
air raids and bombardment in the event of an invasion. In
1943, it was converted into an emergency hospital. Today
it's a really immersive museum.
https://www.jerseywartunnels.com.

The Channel Islands Military Museum

Housed in a former German bunker, this is an evocative way to get close to the past.

Weapons, uniforms, motorcycles, photographs, radios, Red Cross messages and a plethora of other items transport you back to the Occupation. La Grande Route des Mielles, Jersey, JE3 2FN, located at St. Ouen's Bay. https://www.facebook.com/profile.php?id=100063753360746.

Jersey Public Library

Grace's library is no longer based in the Royal Square, St. Helier, but in a bright modern building in nearby Halkett Place. It's a stunning building with welcoming staff, late opening and, of course, acres of books. It's well worth a visit. When I was over there I lost myself in many of their Occupation books. The library really was a godsend for so many islanders during those dark and dangerous years and islanders donated thousands of books to the library. What an indignity for the Chief Librarian, Arscott Sabine Harvey Dickinson, to watch his library plundered by the German censors for any authors "uncongenial" to the regime.

Jersey Heritage History Archive

A hive of stories, photos, books, pictures, oral and written archives relating to Jersey's rich history. https://catalogue.jerseyheritage.org. You can also search and access the records online.

Havre des Pas

No. 2 Silvertide, Havre des Pas. The German Secret Field Police, run in part by the odious Heinz Carl Wölfle. It struck me as sinister that the organization many civilians referred to as the "Gestapo" should choose to run their interrogations from a typically English seaside villa.

The Bathing Pool, Havre des Pas

This beautiful, horseshoe-shaped saltwater pool nestled in a white sandy beach is a stunning place to swim and it's

Kate by Havre des Pas bathing pool.
Copyright Kate Thompson.

free! Apparently the Germans loved to swim there during the Occupation, according to local resident Leo Harris, who told me how he once found one of their guns on the bottom of the pool. Walking with bare feet on the warm wooden planks of the bridge as you cross over to the pool and plunge into the bracing saltwater is one of the great joys of life. Sadly I didn't find any World War II ephemera during my swim.

Tours

I took two tours in Jersey: one by day with the incredibly knowledgeable military guide Marc Yates (www.history alive.je); and one touring the bunkers by night, with Jersey War Tours, which was thrillingly evocative and creepy, as you'd expect (www.jerseybunkertours.com).

Both are well worth doing for a really good insight into the Occupation and stories galore.

Fish and Chips in a German Bunker

Faulkner Fisheries runs a quirky and excellent fish restaurant in a converted German Bunker in L'Étacq at the northern tip of St. Ouen's Bay. The famous summer BBQ is a unique experience. Step inside the bunker and choose from fresh fish and shellfish and eat al fresco overlooking a stunning beach, with local Jersey Royal Potatoes and homemade Jersey garlic butter, washed down with a glass of local wine. https://www.faulknerfisheries.com.

Kate enjoying an al fresco glass of wine at L'Étacq. Copyright Kate Thompson.

Or eat mussels straight from the bowl like Kate's son Stanley. Copyright Kate Thompson.

Bouley Bay

On the rugged north coast, Bouley Bay is my favorite beach. Swim through crystal-clear waters to a small pontoon where you can gaze up at the rugged cliffs, before striking back to land for a fresh crab sandwich at Mad Mary's Café on the beach. Mary has almost legendary status with locals and is fighting hard against the massive development of a former hotel in the bay.

Idyllic Bouley Bay. Copyright Kate Thompson.

Jersey Zoo

Growing up, one of my favorite books was Gerald Durrell's *My Family and Other Animals,* so it was a real thrill to visit the beautiful zoo and the Durrell Wildlife Conservation Trust he founded in his adopted homeland of Jersey. This is a must visit. https://www.durrell.org/visit-jersey-zoo/about-jersey-zoo/.

All information correct at the time of writing.

Bibliography

There is no shortage of reading material about the Occupation. Here are some of the sources I found helpful as research.

Protest, Defiance and Resistance in the Channel Islands by Gilly Carr, Paul Sanders and Louise Willmot (Bloomsbury, 2015).
This book offers a corrective to the accepted histories of the Channel Islands, which often overlook the issue of resistance and tend instead to focus on the overblown histories of collaboration. It's a fascinating read that makes you realize how integral women were to the resistance movement.

In tandem with this is the Frank Falla Archive. Frank Falla was a Guernsey journalist who produced an underground news sheet called *GUNS* (*Guernsey Underground News Service*), which was a vital link for islanders to discover what was really happening in the war. He and other men in his movement were denounced and deported to Nazi prisons. Frank survived but dedicated his life to acting as a spokesman for other islanders who had suffered or died as a result of their imprisonment in prisons and camps. In the mid-1960s, he also helped many survivors claim success-fully for compensation for their persecution. This impres-sive archive contains much more detail. This is investigative and campaigning journalism at its finest. https://www.frank fallaarchive.org/people/frank-falla/.

His book *The Silent War* (Blue Ormer, 2018) is a riveting insight into the life of a journalist living under censorship. I would recommend all journalists, or anyone interested in censorship, read it.

The German Occupation of Jersey: A Complete Diary of Events from June 1940 to June 1945 by L. P. Sinel (Villette, 1995)
Fascinating insight into day-to-day life during the Occupation, from how much a jar of Marmite cost to what the ordinary man and woman on the street saw.

Hitler's British Isles: The Real Story of the Occupied Channel Islands by Duncan Barrett (Simon & Schuster, 2018)
One of my favorite books on the subject. Duncan under-took exhaustive interviewing to get a lively, poignant and at times heartbreaking account of those five years, seen through islanders' eyes.

The Model Occupation: The Channel Islands Under German Rule, 1940–1945 by Madeleine Bunting (Vintage)
One of the more controversial of Occupation histories, it whipped up fury in the Channel Islands on its release because of criticism of the States of Jersey and accusations

of acquiescent behavior toward the Germans. Bunting does raise some interesting points though, especially over the authorities' handling of the Jewish population.

A Doctor's Occupation **by Dr. John Lewis (Transworld, 1982)**
Who better than the local doctor to reveal the most fascinating nuggets of Occupation history?

The German Occupation of the Channel Islands:The Official History of the Occupation Years **by Charles Cruickshank (Oxford University Press, London and The Guernsey Press, Channel Islands, 1975)**
Heavy on facts, this reveals how much has changed in the exploration of the Channel Islands Occupation over the past four decades, as the focus shifts from fortifications and tin hats to people and social histories.

The Shadow War: Resistance in Europe 1939–45 **by Henri Michel (André Deutsch, 1972)**

Jersey Occupied: The German Armed Forces in Jersey 1940–1945 **by Michael Ginns, MBE (Channel Island Publishing, 2009)**

A Peculiar Occupation: New Perspectives on Hitler's Channel Islands **by Peter Tabb (Ian Allan Publishing, 2005)**
A remarkable testament to the triumph of the human spirit over evil and the survival of a quintessentially British way of life under the Nazi jackboot.

The Channel Islands Occupation Review Journal by The Channel Islands Occupation Society
Read back copies of this journal and also attended one of their open days and talks. They also have interviews with islanders recalling their Occupation experiences—"Occupation Conversations"—that are well worth a watch.

Liberated by Force 135 by Mark Lamerton
Twenty-six years of research has gone into this bible to the Liberation and its planning. To order a copy email: liberationlamerton@gmail.com (email correct at the time of writing).

The History and Stories of the Jersey Post Office by Dave Vautier (2007). Available at Jersey Heritage Archives
Wonderfully written book that really summons the spirit and camaraderie of Jersey's postal workers through the centuries.

Out of the Frying Pan and into Der Führer: The Story of the Channel Islands' Kitchen Front of World War Two by Bryan Chalker (Redcliffe Press, 1989)
Fantastic for details on food and domesticity.

Memoirs:

Night and Fog Prisoners by Peter Hassall (1997)
One of the most moving Occupation memoirs I read is by a man named Peter Hassall. Peter was a patriotic young

man from Jersey, who despised what he described as "the rape of the islands by the Occupation." Together with two friends, Dennis Audrain and Maurice Gould, he attempted to escape from the island. In the attempt, Dennis drowned and Peter and Maurice were both arrested by the German forces. They were deported and entered the hell of Hitler's "Night and Fog," NN decree. Peter and Maurice were sent to a German concentration camp, where they suffered unimaginable horrors. Maurice succumbed to tuberculosis. Peter survived and managed eventually, in 1997, to get his friend's body repatriated from Germany and "brought home." This is a blistering insight into Hitler's Night and Fog Decree.

You can view the manuscript at Jersey Heritage Archive (https://catalogue.jerseyheritage.org).

A Boy Remembers by Leo Harris (Apache Guides, 2000)

This utterly charming man, whom I had the privilege of interviewing twice, writes with such passion and soul about a time that transformed his young life. This is more than a memoir about a young boy recollecting life under the Occupation. At times it reads like a thriller as he recalls his older brother's arrest at the hands of the German Secret Field Police and how time and again his canny Scots father outwitted the Germans. A lovely man, sadly now passed away.

Occupation Memories: Personal Reminiscences of Childhood during the Occupation of Jersey 1940 to 1945 by Therese Tabb (2020)

This fascinating book collates a host of personal reminiscences of childhood during the Occupation. A must read for a good insight into how it really was.

Jersey Occupation Diary: Her Story of the German Occupation, 1940–45 by Nan Le Ruez (Seaflower Books, 2003)

Banned Books by Anne Lyon Haight (R. R. Bowker, 1970)

This was a brilliant find. Really interesting look at books banned throughout history and why. Some titles in there you might find surprising.

Acknowledgments

With sincere thanks to:

Mark Lamerton and his forensic Occupation eye and kindly agreeing to be an early reader. And as if that weren't enough, sharing stories and photographs of his grandfather, whose wartime interception of informers' letters at the post office formed the central thread of this book. I am indebted to you.

Eric Blakeley, MBE, broadcaster, journalist, Occupation expert and adventurer. Thanks for showing me the wall with the painted-over swastika, sharing your wealth of stories and a really good bowl of risotto.

Jenni Illien, I really enjoyed talking about the Occupation and hearing the wonderful story of your sister-in-law.

Huge thanks go to Therese Tabb and her husband Peter for the enlightening conversation over lunch and the wonderful work you do in documenting the social histories of Occupation islanders.

Leo Harris. I wish I'd had the chance to meet you again, but I'll treasure my conversations with you.

Maggie Moisan, you're a treasure. Thanks for speaking so candidly and eloquently about your heroic mother.

Don Dolbel, what a raconteur and irrepressible spirit you are. Thank you.

Enormous thanks go to Eric Falle, for helping me to see the Occupation through a child's eyes.

My sincere appreciation goes to Dermott Curry, just 12 when the Germans invaded and his mother died. My conversation with you helped shape my understanding of the legacy of the Occupation years, including a hatred of waste. Keep sharing your mini-marmalade pots.

Audrey Falle, thank you for sharing your fascinating memoir with me and allowing me to interview you. I so enjoyed my time with you.

Norman Syvret, thanks for your colorful wartime memories.

Bob Le Sueur. Something of a legend and an Occupation hero in Jersey. This remarkable 102-year-old man told me in exceptional detail about how he helped escaped Russian prisoners in Jersey, including the escapee whom Louisa Gould harbored. He was awarded an MBE for his bravery in 2013. It was thrilling to talk to someone who was actually alive at that time and knew the people whose lives and personalities I was trying to uncover. Bob died in November 2022. He will be sorely missed by the people of Jersey.

Michael Dubras, a lovely gentleman, who shared some fascinating stories with me about growing up as a child during the Occupation, and thanks to his charming son Tony for arranging the interviews. Michael passed away in August 2023. My sincere condolences to his family and friends.

All the wonderful and incredibly helpful staff at Jersey Heritage Archive and Collections (https://catalogue .jerseyheritage.org) and Jersey Public Library (https://

jerseylibrary.gov.je), who helped me navigate their collections and were always generous with their time and expertise, on the phone, email, Zoom and face to face. Libraries and archives at their very best. Special thanks to Ed Jewell, Chief Librarian, for being so enthusiastic about this book, Stuart Nicolle from Jersey Archives for answering all my questions so patiently, and to Geraint Jennings, Jèrriais Promotion Officer, who helped me with translations. Any mistakes are my own.

I also visited the archives of the Postal Museum in London (https://www.postalmuseum.org), who hold information about the postal service in the Channel Islands.

Thanks to the Wiener Library, for sending me their online exhibition, *On British Soil,* about victims of Nazi persecution in the Channel Islands.

Howard Butlin Baker, extremely knowledgeable local historian who was very generous with his time and expertise, kindly introducing me to plenty of people to interview and acting as a fantastic sounding board, as well as being an early reader. Enormous thanks.

St. Helier resident and loyal Jersey lady, Ann Dunne, who told me the fabulous story of how her mother fell in love with and married a liberating Tommy soldier, over a bowl of homemade bean crock. Your warmth and hospitality made for a memorable trip.

Paul Simmonds, local director of Age Concern, who allowed me very kindly to come along and talk to their regulars.

All at The Channel Islands Occupation Society, especially Damien Horn, who showed me round his fascinating military museum housed in a former bunker in St. Ouen's.

Two distinct and amazing tours with: Marc Yates (marc@historyalive.je); and Phil at Jersey War Tours (https://www.jerseybunkertours.com).

Fabulous Jersey writers and residents, Gwyn Garfield-Bennett and Deborah Carr (https://deborahcarr.org). Deborah's Occupation novel, *An Island at War* (One More Chapter, 2021), is an absorbing read, as are Gwyn's gripping thrillers (https://www.gwyngb.com/about/).

My grateful thanks go to Jenny Lecoat. Jenny is the great-niece of Louisa Gould and writer of the film *Another Mother's Son* (2017), as well as an Occupation novel, *The Girl from the Channel Islands* (Polygon, 2022). Thanks, Jenny, for the coffee and reminding me that when it comes to the Occupation there are "a hundred different truths."

Huge thanks to Dave Vautier, author of *The History and Stories of the Jersey Post Office,* for sharing your book and memories of some of Jersey Post's heroic and colorful wartime characters. It was an enormous help in the research of this book.

My thanks to a lady I never met, but wish I had. While at the archives, I spotted a brilliant and funny poem written during the Occupation by a lady called Eileen, which I featured in Chapter Twelve. I wasn't able to locate the identity of this lady, but if by some chance you recognize the poem and know the author, or her family, please let me know.

Enormous thanks to Charmaine Bourton, the Queen of Anachronism-Spotting and all-round good egg.

And finally, my wonderful agent Kate Burke and all the team at Blake Friedmann, including Julian Friedmann, James Pusey and Hana Murrell. My warm, wise and wonderful editors, Kimberley Atkins and Amy Batley in the UK, and Alex Logan in the U.S. (and her incredible team at Forever Publishing, including Nicole Andress, Estelle Hallick, Alli Rosenthal and Carolina Martin). Without their collective efforts and talent this book would not be in your hands. I am forever grateful.

Any mistakes are entirely my own.

If you enjoyed this book then you might also like my previous novel, *The Little Wartime Library,* which is available to buy now. The library built in a Tube station, which Grace tells Ash about on her return from London, is a true story. *The Little Wartime Library* is based on this forgotten little library.

Get in Touch

I'd love to hear your thoughts. You can contact me using the below:

katharinethompson82@gmail.com

www.katethompsonmedia.co.uk

www.facebook.com/KateThompsonAuthor/

Instagram KateThompsonAuthor

Twitter—@katethompson380

TikTok @user5702621797306

Want to hear more stories? I have a podcast called *From the Library with Love*, where I interview authors, librarians and our wartime generation. Ordinary people sharing extraordinary stories. Available at Apple, Spotify, or from wherever you get your podcasts.

About the Author

Kate Thompson is an award-winning journalist, ghost-writer, and novelist, who has spent the last two decades in the UK mass market and book publishing industry. Over the past nine years Kate has written twelve fiction and nonfiction titles, three of which have made the *Sunday Times* top-ten bestseller list. *The Wartime Book Club* is her thirteenth book.